PRAISE FOR

TUNNEL WAR

"SOLID, FACT-INSPIRED ADVENTURE MELODRAMA . . . Derring-do plus high-toned nostalgia and authentic engineering detail—a satisfying blend for fans of historically colored suspense-action."

The Kirkus Reviews

"A WELL-WRITTEN THRILLER WITH ENOUGH ACTION TO SATISFY AND A NASTY SURPRISE ENDING."

Columbus Dispatch

"NOTHING SHORT OF WONDERFUL! From the death of a gull on the first page to Churchill's musings on the last, there is a grand yarn laid out that strengthens its suspenseful hold on the reader with each paragraph."

Savannah News Press

Books by Joe Poyer

TUNNEL WAR (1979)
THE CONTRACT (1978)
THE DAY OF RECKONING (1976)
THE SHOOTING OF THE GREEN (1973)
THE CHINESE AGENDA (1972)
THE BALKAN ASSIGNMENT (1971)
NORTH CAPE (1969)
OPERATION MALACCA (1968)

TUNNEL WAR

JOE POYER

FAWCETT CREST • NEW YORK

A Fawcett Crest Book
Published by Ballantine Books
Copyright © 1979 by Joe Poyer

Library of Congress Catalog Card Number: 70-63628

ISBN 0-449-20295-X

This edition published by arrangement with Atheneum

Manufactured in the United States of America

First Ballantine Books Edition: July 1983

> **History is a record of exploded ideas**
> SIR JOHN FISHER to WINSTON S. CHURCHILL
> **27 April 1907**

Author's Preface

In one of those rare strokes of good fortune, I happened to attend an auction at Christie's in London one icy day in February 1974, where I purchased a lot from the estate of Lady Violet Bonham-Carter, Baroness Asquith of Yarnsbury and the daughter of Sir Herbert Henry Asquith, prime minister of Great Britain from 1908 to 1916.

In the collection was a handsome chest containing a slim, handwritten manuscript marked on the cover with a government cipher which I later discovered belonged to MI.5.* There was also a rubber-stamped paragraph pasted into the front, mostly illegible, headlined Official Secrets Act. The manuscript described the observations of Lady Bonham Carter—a close friend and biographer of Sir Winston Churchill—on events in the years preceding World War I. Among them were notes on and a startling revelation concerning the English Channel Tunnel and World War I counterintelligence.

When I first began to look into her allegations, I probably knew as much about the Channel Tunnel as anyone—that is to say, next to nothing. There have been numerous companies, it turns out, organized to construct such a tunnel since it was first proposed by Albert Mathieu in 1802, and at least three serious attempts to excavate—the last in 1973. Probably the most successful from the standpoint of work accomplished was that begun in 1909 by the Anglo-French Submarine Railway at Hope Point, north along the coast from Dover. It is with this tunnel that Lady Bonham-Carter concerned herself.

---

* Military Intelligence, Office 5, organized in 1908 to provide Great Britain with a counterintelligence arm. Also called the Security Service.

Although the manuscript was originally intended for publication in 1938, Winston Churchill seems to have persuaded her to withhold it until the European situation was clarified. Lady Bonham-Carter agreed and, in 1940, went so far as to surrender the manuscript voluntarily to MI.5, where it was immediately classified. During World War II, British counter-intelligence carefully orchestrated a ring of "turned" German agents to send false information to Berlin. So successful was this activity that it is credited with convincing Hitler and his staff in the spring of 1944 that the real invasion of Europe would come ashore at Calais, and thus German panzer forces were restrained from the Normandy beachhead for a vital six weeks.* In her manuscript, Lady Bonham-Carter describes a similar operation conducted during World War I and credits Churchill with its design. The secret was kept so successfully between the wars that the operation was repeated in 1939-45. Finally, she asserts that it was the construction of the English Channel Tunnel and the events surrounding it that led to the discovery of a ring of deep-plant German agents as early as 1911.

I have taken the liberty of supplementing the manuscript with material derived from archives in London, Bonn, and Berlin. Old MI.5 files, those that have been declassified, were made available to me, as were the records of the now-defunct Anglo-French Submarine Railway Company, currently housed in the British Museum. In the basement of a shiny new federal office building in Bonn, I ran across two scorched cardboard boxes containing files from the old *Gefährden Intelligenz Zustellung* (Imperial Intelligence Service), some of the very few records of the Imperial regime to survive the destruction of Berlin in 1945. They provided independent confirmation of certain information contained in the manuscript. They also supplied part of an official dossier on one enigmatic Colonel von Dorn and a detailed description of the role played in Germany's designs on Great Britain by the Irish revolutionary group known as the Fenians in the pre-World War I period.

In the company records I found a personal diary kept for

*For a complete discussion, see J. C. Masterman's *The Double-Cross System in the War, 1939-45*, Yale University Press, 1972.

the year 1911 by James Bannerman, engineering director of the Tunnel project, and this provided tremendous insight into one side of the struggle. Other information came from the files of Special Branch, Scotland Yard, for the year 1911 and the early part of 1912.

To place the manuscript and its revelations into proper perspective, it is necessary to have some understanding of the political situation that existed in Europe as that second fateful decade of the century began. It is clear, given the makeup of governments, the thinking that prevailed at the time, and the distribution of land and resources among the nations of Europe, that war was inevitable. The question even at the time was not if, but when.

And the when was the subject of tortuous strategic and tactical considerations dictated by complicated existing alliances: Germany and Austria on the one hand, Russia, France, and Great Britain on the other. The German army was considered the best equipped and trained in the world. France's was a close second. Russia had an army larger than both, but it was archaic and still had not recovered from its resounding defeat at the hands of tiny Japan in 1905. Great Britain's army was weak and in the throes of reorganization, but its navy was the strongest in the world. "Britannia rules the waves" was far more than a line in a light opera; it was an international fact.

German planning for war was based on the work of Count Alfred von Schlieffen, which demanded a strong right thrust through neutral Belgium to the English Channel, a pivot south across the French frontier and a fast march to the valley of the Oise to outflank the French army, and then a fast march to Paris. Once France was finished—thirty days after mobilization—the bulk of the German divisions were to be rushed east by train to meet the slower-mobilizing Russians. The war was expected to be over within three months, leaving Germany the victor on both fronts, the preeminent nation of the world and the possessor of the rich *lebensraum* of the Ukraine. The stakes were heady.

But there was a problem. Great Britain had guaranteed the neutrality of Belgium since 1839. If Germany marched on Antwerp, which Germany intended to do, Britain would surely come in on the side of France and Russia. And if that happened, the British army, small as it was, in league with viii

the Belgian army, could very well tip the balance against Germany.

The Imperial *Generalstab* planners, across the Königplatz from the Reichstag, determined that the British would need fifteen to twenty-one days (the British said thirteen) to cross the Channel and reach their positions in Flanders—far too late to be of any help. The last obstacle seemed to have been removed.

Then, in 1911, two events occurred that shook the *Generalstab* to its foundations. Completion of the Channel Tunnel was announced for early 1913. Those British divisions so contemptuously dismissed the year before were again a mortal threat to German expansionism. It was estimated that the entire six-division British Expeditionary Force could be entrained, moved *beneath* the Channel and on to their front-line positions by railroad, all well within eight days. Once more it appeared as if Germany were destined to remain a third-class power, and this was confirmed that very same summer when Great Britain joined France and Russia to force Germany to back down at Agadir in Morocco. The Kaiser and his staff, humiliated before the world, vowed that it would never happen again.

The stage was set. As Germany saw it, her survival was in the balance.

JOE POYER
California, 1979

For
GILES GORDON
**in appreciation of all his support,
encouragement and perseverance all these years.**

Anglo-French
Submarine Railway Tunnel
Beneath The English Channel

Prepared for
His Majesty, George V

1. Iron Plate
2. Grout
3. Brick Surface
4. Safety Shelter
5. Conduits
6. Service Mains
7. Ventilator Shaft
8. Navigation Beacon
9. Metal Rails

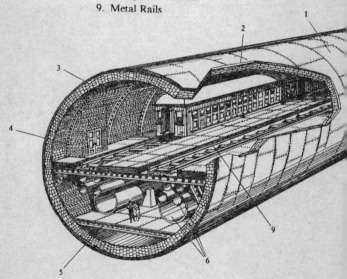

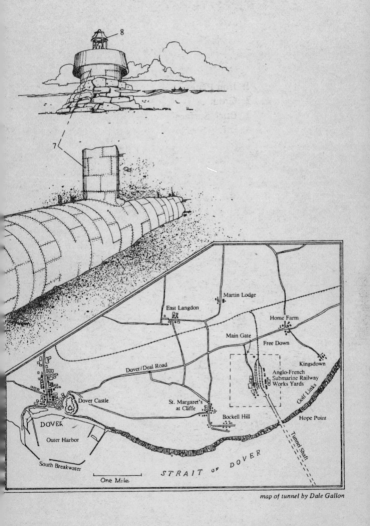

8

7

Martin Lodge

East Langdon

Home Farm

Main Gate

Free Down

Kingsdown

Dover / Deal Road

Anglo-French
Submarine Railway
Works Yards

Dover Castle

St. Margaret's
at Cliffe

Golf Links

DOVER

Bockell Hill

Hope Point

Outer Harbor

South Breakwater

Tunnel Shaft

One Mile

STRAIT OF DOVER

map of tunnel by Dale Gallon

chapter ———— 1

The *herring gull had ranged the English Channel for* hours, riding the fierce wind currents generated by the succession of anticyclonic highs that had gripped the British Isles ever since the end of the hot, fine days of that idyllic summer. All during the autumn, gale after gale had swirled down from the Arctic wastes, lashing the country with a vengeance, as if to exact retribution for one of the finest seasons in human memory; better even, it was said, than the Jubilee Summer of '94.

The gull drifted inland, beating once to clear the crest of Bockell Hill and catch the updrafts created as the wind swept over the barrier formed by the Dover cliffs. In the gathering dusk, the lights were bright across St. Margaret's Down and he circled the area as though seeking a place to rest until finally he spilled air and dropped, flaring graceful wings at the last moment. A few exploratory steps, a quick flutter of feathers, and he found a warm position beneath a pipe from which issued a wisp of steam.

It was a most unfortunate choice; the moment the gull had settled comfortably, the pipe issued a blast that would have reduced the life expectancy of even the most imperturbable animal. The gull was gone in an instant as the shrieking whistle woke echoes across the downs as far south as Dover, five miles distant. Even the ceaseless clatter of steam engines went unnoticed in the mindless milliseconds before the urgent shrieks pulsed again and again and echoes came flooding back in agonizing jumbles of sound. Arc lights blazed across the waste of cinders, mud, and industrial debris that littered the once green farmland.

It was six o'clock, the end of an exhausting, cold afternoon. Yet tired men were galvanized by the piercing whistle. Each lived in constant dread of its peculiar rhythmic cycle, many of

1

them—the tunnel men—in outright fear that could and did produce screaming nightmares. Not one, not even the dullest of the uninitiated, could have mistaken the urgency and horror which that whistle generated. Tools were dropped and men surged across the yard toward the Tunnel entrance, slowly at first, then quickening as the initial shock was absorbed and replaced by fear.

Near the center of the immense works yard stood a cluster of single-story buildings constructed of corrugated tin. Electric lights flooded the area between the buildings and glimmered in the deep puddles that had gathered around the duckboard walkways. The door of the central building opened and a man, coatless and in shirt sleeves, hesitated, looking toward the immense concrete Tunnel mouth a hundred yards distant, then vaulted down the steps and began to run. He ignored the puddles as he raced across the yard, careless of the mud that splattered expensive shoes and well-tailored trousers.

Even in their anxiety, the workmen recognized the tall figure of James Bannerman, the project's engineering director, and stepped aside hastily at his grim expression. He reached the line of rails, jumped the switch points, and thrust through the crowd gathering around a shunting engine. A work gang was pushing steel hopper wagons up to be coupled to the engine and loaded with bundles of tools and gear.

A small tin building, like the others in the works yard, was set beside the rails. Through a rain-streaked window Bannerman could see two men, one bent forward to listen intently at a telephone, the other scribbling quickly on a scrap of paper.

The shunting engine whistled and its wheels began to churn, slipping on the wet metal. Bannerman stumbled alongside, cursing the wet ballast and glancing impatiently over his shoulder at the shack. A switchman struggled with the points, then waved a lantern, and the engine slid neatly onto the Tunnel line. The man at the telephone burst from the door and raced after them. Ahead were the great steel doors that had rolled smoothly shut to seal the mouth of the Tunnel at the first whistle. The engine stopped twenty yards away, its electric motor humming quietly.

"Here, for God's sake," the man's heavy Irish voice, blurred by years of whiskey and tobacco, shouted as he threw a bundle. Bannerman caught the yellow mackintosh and struggled into it as he listened.

"That was Callahan on the wire . . . said it's fire!"

The single word slashed across the uproar stilling the men instantly. *Fire*. The tunnel man's worst nightmare. Fire was worse than cave-in or sudden flooding, its choking smoke robbing strained lungs already partially filled with dangerous gases. Suffocation, the worst way to die—slow, lung-searing strangulation.

"Where?" Bannerman demanded.

"Venilator Shaft, Mile Six. Two dead. Maybe more."

Both men were climbing into the first wagon, eager hands helping them over the coaming as they talked. A swift glance to assure himself that respirators were aboard and Bannerman shouted to the lock keeper to open up. The shunting engine ground forward, picking up speed as the three-story-high doors rolled open, then clanged shut again behind them. Ahead, the brick-lined Tunnel, thirty feet in diameter, curved upward in optical illusion, the dimly lit way seeming a road to hell.

The engine's top speed was twenty-five miles per hour, but rarely ever was that speed reached inside the Tunnel. Tonight it would be. Even so, it would take fifteen minutes to reach the site of Ventilator Shaft Six. Bannerman peered ahead into the depths of the Tunnel as if willing himself to see through the miles of concrete, iron, and chalk as he calculated the probable cause and the amount of fuel available to the fire.

Five minutes passed and they saw the headlight of another shunting engine in the distance. Bannerman signaled his own driver to halt and stood up, waving an electric torch. The approaching train ground to a stop beside them in a babble of terror-stricken voices.

McDougal, the massive Irish engineer with the whiskey voice, roared for silence and pointed a gnarled finger at the shift supervisor. "Callahan! For Christ's sake, man, what's happened?"

The fear was plain in Callahan's voice as he struggled for words, and Bannerman felt a surge of despair. Callahan, next to McDougal, was their most experienced tunnel man. If he was this panicked . . .

"Ah, Holy Mother . . . fire, the likes of which . . . two men dead, four trapped. They—they must be dead now . . ."

"Where, you bloody bastard, where?" McDougal demanded. He vaulted from the car and shook Callahan, roaring at him in an effort to bull through the panic.

Callahan drew a breath, half sob, half gasp. "Inside the ventilator housing. We was workin' in there to check the lining and the fan housin' when I smelled burning flex. Afore I could say or do anythin' there was a flash of fire." Callahan's eyes began to roll, but McDougal shook him again.

"Ye've seen fire afore, man, get on with it!"

"A—a flash and a sheet of flame that struck down two boys—ye remember Marston and Reilly?"

"Get on with it!" he roared.

"Crisped them it did! God in heaven, to see them rollin' on the plate, all afire . . . !" Callahan was screaming, his eyes rolling wildly in his blackened face, the whites gleaming like those of a maddened horse.

"God damn you!" McDougal slapped him with one huge paw, a blow that might have killed a lesser man. Callahan stumbled backward across the wagon, knocking aside two other workers, and McDougal swarmed in after him.

"We've got no time for your panty-waist mewlings!" he bellowed, grabbing the huge foreman by the lapels of his canvas jacket and yanking him upright. "Is the fire still going?"

Bannerman started to intervene but thought better of it. He knew that McDougal, even in his rage, would obtain better results.

Callahan's head wobbled, but the panic was gone from his eyes. "The fire—still burning. Tunnel flooded with smoke—too thick to breathe. There may be others down there, in the safety shelters." He gasped for breath as if inhaling the smoke himself. "The inside of the shaft's a furnace! We almost didn' get out." He moaned and his body was wracked with shudders. McDougal thrust him away in disgust.

But Bannerman's mind was racing ahead, ignoring the panic that was beginning to communicate itself to his own crew. If the fire was in the fan motors, then it was already limited. The flash would have been caused by a short circuit—those two men had died most probably because they had defied safety rules requiring rubber shoes rather than their traditional leather half-boots. They would have been electrocuted instantly as they stood on the iron floor plates of the massive motor mounts. The dense smoke would be coming from the burning electrical insulation. He had seen and dealt with this kind of fire before.

Already Bannerman's apprehension was easing and, in a confident voice, he issued his orders.

Callahan's engine driver was to bring back an augmented fire-fighting crew, checking each safety shelter below Mile Four as they approached Ventilator Shaft Six. The others were to report to the medical officer for treatment, and Callahan was to organize the relief effort as quickly as possible. This last braced the man quickly; the change was visible as the fear disappeared from his face and his bearing came erect again.

At Mile Four they encountered the first sign of smoke and donned the heavy respirators. A few hundred yards farther on they saw four workers struggling up the long incline. Respirators were thrown to them and encouragement shouted as the shunting engine sped on. Bannerman was thankful that the fire had broken out near the end of the day shift when the number of workers in the Tunnel was at its lowest.

The lights, already dimming, had begun to flicker as they approached Mile Five—each half-mile of Tunnel carried its own separate electrical circuitry—and the smoke had become a dense mass in parts of the Tunnel. They crossed into the last half-mile section before Ventilator Six and the shunting engine ground to a stop. The engine driver indicated the ampmeter and only then did Bannerman realize that the battery-powered emergency lighting was in operation.

"Out," Bannerman rasped and the fifteen-man gang scrambled from the wagons, knowing what was expected of them. The two wagons were uncoupled and backed to the previous section, one at a time. The engine itself weighed nearly a ton, and the track ran uphill at a deceptively gentle two-degree slope. With repeated curses, they got it moving back, foot by foot, Bannerman agonizing over the lost time. It took ten minutes to move the engine and wagons the seventy feet back to where the electric motor hummed to life again. Ten precious minutes gone, but Bannerman knew it could have been disastrous to leave a dead engine on the rails if they were suddenly forced to abandon the Tunnel.

They still had half a mile to go, and as they trotted along the cement roadbed the smoke thickened, forcing them to a walk with hands pressed against the brickwork of the Tunnel wall for guidance. Even electric torches were useless, the beams unable to penetrate more than a few feet.

"The fans are stopped," McDougal growled. "We'll need more than these few to put this fire out."

Bannerman realized that McDougal was correct in his assessment. The ventilator shaft should have been acting as a huge chimney, drawing the smoke from the Tunnel, even if the three massive fans were not in operation. Each shaft had been driven up from the Tunnel proper, through the seabed and the Channel waters to create an artificial island some fifty feet above the waves. Swivel-mounted storm shutters, each twenty feet on a side, were counterpoised over each shaft to protect it from the fierce Channel storms. Judging by the amount of smoke accumulating in the Tunnel, the storm doors must have been sucked closed as the fire drew massive drafts of air into the ventilator shaft.

They reached the first safety shelter in the final half-mile section and Bannerman manipulated the latch. Quickly, the men slipped inside, throwing back their respirators to gulp the semi-fresh air greedily. While McDougal cranked the telephone, Bannerman told him what must have happened to the storm doors. Swearing, McDougal spun the handle again but the line remained dead. He sent one of the men hurrying back to the next section to find a working telephone, with orders to phone through for a service boat to check Ventilator Six and open the storm shutters manually.

A few minutes rest and they went on. The feeble battery-powered electric lights, the dense smoke, and the reddish glow of the fire ahead had turned the Tunnel into a Dantean vision of hell. As they approached the shaft, a wind quickened about them as the fire sucked the air of the Tunnel to itself, and Bannerman knew, even without the low muttering from the men, that their situation was becoming very dangerous.

A Tunnel fire, unvented, unable to draw upon air from the outside, would eventually destroy itself by consuming the oxygen in the Tunnel. But before this happened, a raging windstorm would be created as more and more air was sucked into the flames. The curving, cylindrical shape of the Tunnel would serve as a venturi, compressing the air and causing it to move faster until gale-force drafts swept the Tunnel's length. With the huge steel doors at the mouth of the Tunnel shut, the storm shutters of the other ventilator shafts, each spaced one mile apart, would also be drawn closed. The fire, already in the Tunnel, would feed upon itself, exhausting the remaining air within an hour. And in doing so, it would kill everyone inside by suffocation. Hence the panic infecting the work gang; each and every man was only too aware of what such a fire could mean.

The Tunnel shaft was thirty feet in diameter, the Tunnel floor a cement platform resting on iron bracings some five feet above the lowest point of the curve. Below the floor ran a conduit for the electrical, exhaust, gas, and water systems. Every two thousand yards a massive concrete reservoir had been excavated to hold a million and a half cubic feet of water. Water seeped into each reservoir from the surrounding chalk substrata through which the Tunnel had been driven. A complicated system of vent shafts to the surface furnished two hundred pounds of pressure per square inch to power the heavy-duty fire hoses installed beside each safety shelter. Those hoses could very well be their only chance. Bannerman was beginning to realize the extent of his miscalculation. It was far more than a smoldering electrical fire.

The crew swung into action as they reached the last shelter before the great ventilator shaft, long practice serving to overcome—for the moment—their fear. Already the heat was well over 100° F. Farther along, they could hear the fire's roar. At this point, the Tunnel was six hundred feet below the Channel waters, and the scaffolding of pine and fir filled four hundred and ten of those feet. Flaming debris rained from the shaft, but the smoke was thinner here as the fire drew the air up greedily in huge swirling drafts.

Bannerman stood rigidly in the center of the Tunnel, feet straddling the useless rails, fighting for control as he studied the furnacelike interior of the shaft. The situation was worse than he had imagined. The fire had spread from the motor housings and damned quickly. How in God's name were they to control this raging inferno with a few fire hoses? But the alternative was to run for the entrance while there was still time and flood the Tunnel from Ventilator Shaft Five.

He weighed the possibilities, struggling to ignore the mindless imps that shrieked at him to run, to save his own life. If he flooded the Tunnel, he would doom any workers trapped between here and the end of the Tunnel beyond Mile Eight, where they would surely have taken refuge in the airlock. The immense airlock's own supply of compressed air might enable them to survive for two to three days, but three miles of flooded Tunnel would require two weeks to pump out. There could be as many as twenty men beyond . . . twenty lives, a month lost, millions in damage. It would take the service boats an hour yet to reach and board Ventilator Six in the heavy weather gusting through the Channel. Christ, how he had misjudged!

As he struggled to suppress his own panic, Bannerman thought he saw another way. If the sea cock controls installed in the ventilator's control booth could be reached, the ventilator shaft could be flooded to douse the fire. But the control booth was fifty feet up, *inside* the shaft. Was it far enough below the fire? Could the hail of debris be avoided?

He made his decision and turned to shout for McDougal only to find him at his side, waiting for orders.

"Do we evacuate the Tunnel, then?" McDougal bellowed above the fire's roar.

Bannerman shook his head and explained while McDougal nodded ponderously. "Aye, it might work. And how will we do it then?"

The sea cock controls were located inside a control booth on the lower balcony level of the ventilator shaft. An access ladder led up the curving side of the Tunnel, into the shaft proper to the balcony, well below the burning scaffolding. The heat was growing as air was sucked into the maelstrom above. There wasn't much time left and both men knew it.

"It only needs one man, Sean. The balcony overhang should give enough protection. You stay here to direct the hoses. Now give me your gloves."

McDougal hesitated. "Man, this is insane. Ye—" He stopped abruptly, recognizing the uselessness of the argument and handed the heavy gauntlets to Bannerman. "I'll watch them," he growled and stepped to the firepoint, where the fat rolls of canvas hose had already been attached. He shone his torch along the length of hose and, satisfied there were no kinks, shouted for water. The man at the nozzle braced himself. Air spit from the end with a crack like a rifle shot and the canvas tautened with a jerk, causing the man to scramble for a foothold before others jumped to help. A solid stream of water leapt down the Tunnel. McDougal directed the stream across the floor, blasting a path through the pile of burning debris below the shaft. Clouds of hissing steam exploded upward. McDougal moved forward beside the men struggling with the writhing hose, directing with hand signals a sweep up the Tunnel walls and into the shaft opening. More steam spewed before it was swirled into oblivion by the draft. When the water had cooled the lower region of the shaft, the nozzle lever was opened to produce a fan-shaped spray which would cool the air and brickwork.

It took five minutes to work forward to the shaft opening, and even then the brick and metal remained uncomfortably hot. Bannerman had forgotten that he was wearing only thin-soled dress shoes, but there was no time to do anything about them now.

He pulled on the leather gauntlets, took a short-handled ax from the equipment pile, and thrust it into his belt. Buttoning the mackintosh to his chin, he pulled the rubber hat down to shield his face and started forward. The shock of cold water was unexpected after the heat, and the abrupt temperature change of more than seventy degrees left him shivering violently. McDougal ordered the spray narrowed to a cone thirty degrees across and kept it full on his back as he ran across the Tunnel to the access ladder.

The spray had missed the lowest rungs and they were hot enough to raise steam from the gauntlets and burn his feet as he swarmed up the ladder. The Tunnel wall curved inward and for the last few rungs, his feet swung free. Bannerman ducked instinctively as a baulk of timber plunged past, a splinter ripping open the mackintosh and nearly tearing him from the ladder. He hung on grimly, knowing that to fall into the pile of smoldering debris below would cripple him at the least.

The air was hot, even with icy water drenching him. He risked a glance downward but the emergency lights were not strong enough to compete with the mixture of smoke and steam and the misted eyepieces of his respirator. The draft threatened to peel him from the ladder; it had become a strong, unvarying flow at, he judged, fifty miles an hour or better.

Of a sudden, he was aware that water was filling the respirator. He ripped it away and sucked the hot air into his tortured lungs. Immediately, he was blind, smoke fumes and spray making it impossible to see or even to open his eyes.

Bannerman continued to climb, one hand feeling above the other, struggling to find the rungs, cursing the pain each time his weight came down on his burned feet, doggedly struggling upward, knowing that he had committed himself to an insane, impossible course of action. The fire was much worse than he had judged, and he castigated himself for his stupidity; he had misjudged everything—the extent of the fire, the danger to the Tunnel, their very chances of survival. The fire was a raging inferno above; he could feel the heat, even through the cooling spray, cooking him slowly, making it difficult to think, to react, to keep on. It was scorching the top of his head and his hair was beginning to crackle.

How many more rungs, how many more damned rungs, he repeated over and over, long after he had lost count. He raged at himself, unable to think coherently; he knew every rivet, every brick in the Tunnel, every water point and conduit. He had designed and redesigned, studied and restudied until he could walk the twenty-four-mile finished length of the Tunnel blindfolded, identifying every protrusion, every fixture, every rail along the way, and now he could not remember how many rungs to that damned balcony ladder.

Flaming debris showered past, and he pressed against the hot brick, sobbing for breath, knowing that he had not the strength to go on. The failing hose spray afforded the only relief from the intense heat, but he was exhausted and half suffocated, and his lungs burned unbearably with every breath. The stream of water disappeared and the heat pressed in. His grip on the rung began to slip and there was nothing he could do about it. Desperately, he leaned into the brick, feeling its heat scorching through the coated fabric of the mackintosh with the stink of hot rubber. In spite of his exertion, his fingers came free and he felt himself falling away from the wall. He opened his mouth in a final curse and something solid struck his back, driving the air from his lungs, slamming him against the wall. The man at the hose, seeing that he was slipping, had narrowed the spray to a stream and was using that to plaster him against the wall. He sought wildly for the rung above and his hand smashed against a railing. It was hot, burning his hand even through the gauntlet, and he screamed with agony and tried to pull away, but the hose forced him up. Steam hissed from the wet leather where his glove clutched the rail and Bannerman, mouth open in a soundless scream of agony, scrabbled up until, without knowing how, he was standing on the balcony where a single emergency light gleamed through the glass window. He hobbled across the steam-shrouded iron plate, wrenched the latch down, and plunged through the door.

The heat was all but unbearable inside the glass cage. Bannerman groped his way to the control panel, found and threw the switches to open the underwater floodgates, and turned, expecting to see a deluge of cascading water. But nothing happened. Smoke still swirled upward in the fierce glare, and burning debris shot past. Swearing with frustration, he tore at a small door enclosing the manual controls on the wall above. It was locked; locked contrary to all standing instructions. His anger burst at that point and he became a raging maniac. Some fool had locked a panel that should never have been locked and it was going to kill him, along with the fifteen men waiting below with McDougal and who knew how many others trapped in the Tunnel. He slammed his fist against the panel and, forgetting the ax in his belt, struck again and again until it splintered.

He flung the pieces aside, grabbed the red-painted stirrup handle, and pulled, oblivious to the pain from his burned hands. Slowly, steadily, the handle moved toward him and stopped. He braced himself and pulled again, cursing and at the same time praying that the intricate mechanism of compound levers stretching six hundred feet above was not jammed or warped by the heat. Only a few inches, only a very few inches, would be needed and the sea would pour in, endless, swirling gallons scouring the fire from the shaft.

The steel lever snapped loose from the shackle, catapulting him across the floor and his head slammed against the wall. Pain exploded and a roaring grew and grew until it became unbearable. Only then did Bannerman realize that it was the sound of water flooding the shaft. The balcony rocked and glass splintered and he was swept across the floor by the flood.

The balcony was disintegrating as the seawater, spun into a giant swirl by its six-hundred-foot plunge, swept the shaft clean of burning scaffolding. Bannerman struggled to his feet and groped forward until he found the panel. His torch had disappeared in the flood and he struggled in almost total darkness to find the lever. His right hand brushed it where it dangled below the box. The swivel pin in the knee joint had snapped and there was now no way to exert the leverage needed to draw the vents closed.

He slumped against the wall, exhausted, knowing that he was going to die now, in spite of everything. The balcony would give way under the seawater's pounding and plummet the fifty feet to the Tunnel floor. The electrical switches were burned through or shorted out. There was no way now to stop the flooding from here. It would have to be done from the top of the shaft, a totally impossible six hundred vertical feet away. Even without the swirling flood pouring down the shaft, in his condition it would have been an impossible climb.

For a moment more, his mind refused to work and he shuddered as something slammed against the balcony.Then he remembered the tool chest and pawed below the control console. Bannerman found the screwdriver he needed and waded through the swirling water that was quickly filling the control booth. He worked the knee joint into position and, with difficulty, fitted the screwdriver through the holes so that the shank would serve as the swivel pin.

Bannerman set his feet and began to pull up on the stirrup handle. The ill-fitting screwdriver was causing the knee joint to wobble, increasing the difficulty of the work the compound lever system was being called upon to do. Praying desperately for the hardened shank to hold, he threw his back into it and the handle snapped up, his own wrist striking his chin a stunning blow.

The roar of cascading water was driving all else from his mind, and he buried his head in his arms as he went to his knees, shivering with cold and exhaustion, numbed by pain. A moment later the roar diminished, then stopped. An eerie silence filled the vast chamber of the ventilator shaft, and it was a moment before Bannerman could comprehend that the flow of water had been shut off.

He never knew how much time passed before he tried to get to his feet. Someone was supporting, lifting, guiding him out onto the heavily damaged balcony.

"Easy, man," he heard McDougal's whiskey voice rasp. "You have done enough for one day, now. Lean on me."

His chest heaving, how much time passed before he tried to
rise to his feet. Someone was supporting under whatever him,
with against the heavily damaged balcony.

"Easy, man." The hand held a white's white's voice. Two
... ... now Dornson ...

chapter ____ 2

In spite of the brilliant afternoon sun, the air in Berlin was
crisp enough for puddles remaining from recent rains to be
covered by skins of ice. Linden trees, stark and lifeless,
dotted the Alsen Platz as *Oberstleutnant* Eric von Dorn strode
along the footpath, expression grim, back rigid, boot heels
clicking on the hard-packed gravel. Two junior officers passed,
but in his preoccupation von Dorn did not see them and so
missed their salutes.

He was sandy-haired, in his late thirties, with the erect yet
relaxed carriage of a military officer. Broad shoulders and
narrow hips emphasized the tight-fitting uniform of the 3d
Fusilier Guards. His forehead was high, nose long yet matched
by a strong, jutting chin which effectively concealed the
overbite that would have resulted in protruding teeth if the
chin had been weaker. He was tall, a bit over six feet, and
gave the impression of a modest if strong-willed individual.
The latter was correct, the former achieved only after long
practice. Von Dorn was anything but modest, but he had
learned early on that his superiors preferred the pretense of
modesty, if not its practice.

The lieutenant colonel's objective was a singularly unim-
pressive Kaiser yellow, rococo-style building at the end of the
Platz, backed against the River Spree. He stamped up the
steps and the porter, spotting his uniform and insignia, hurried to hold the door. Von Dorn barely acknowledged the
courtesy. An aide-de-camp was waiting for him and, sensing
his mood, greeted him respectfully and led the way without
further word.

Von Dorn was kept waiting in an outer office for twenty
minutes, studiously ignored by a noncommissioned officer
whose only duty seemed to be to ignore visitors. The aide

14

finally appeared again with a murmured apology and ushered him inside. General Otto Helmuth Langenscheidt was standing behind a massive desk. Von Dorn came to attention and saluted and the general returned the salute impassively. For a long, uncomfortable moment they stared at one another.

"Sit down, Colonel," the general said finally, indicating a chair set squarely before the desk and nodding to the aide, who went out, closing the door behind him. The general regarded von Dorn for another long minute before pointing to a green folder bound with red ribbon, the only item on the bare expanse of polished mahogany.

"It would appear from your latest report that you have been quite busy, Colonel. I would like an explanation."

"An explanation, sir?" Von Dorn's face remained impassive, but inwardly he was seething.

"Yes, Colonel. An explanation of exactly how you managed to interpret your instructions to include sabotage against a friendly power." The words were spoken quietly.

"My *orders*, sir, were to monitor progress being made in the construction of the English Channel Tunnel and to do whatever possible to hinder that work." He paused, then held the general's eye as he repeated, "to do *whatever possible to hinder that work*."

The general smiled a bit and tapped the report. "Yes, I saw the copy of those orders, which you so thoughtfully included. My question, however, remains."

Von Dorn looked stubborn. "The orders were open to broad interpretation, sir. They were so phrased."

"I am not referring to *those* orders, Colonel, which came from another department. I am referring to *my* orders, sir, which state very succinctly that you were to *monitor* progress of the Tunnel only. But by far the most important paragraph of my orders referred to your main task, which is to establish a network of native sympathizers able and willing to assist our agents in time of war. Do I remember correctly, Colonel?" he asked gently.

Von Dorn nodded, not trusting himself to speak.

"Then how in the name of God," Langenscheidt roared—and in spite of himself, von Dorn jumped—"could you possibly have interpreted those orders to mean sabotage?" He slammed a meaty hand on the desk with a crash and shoved himself up. "Your instructions and orders come from this office, sir. From me and from me alone! What the General Staff requires of you will be passed through this office. Intelligence matters are my business. You are an intelligence officer. You will follow my orders. Do you understand that, sir?''

Von Dorn had risen to his feet and stood at rigid attention, eyes fixed over the general's shoulder on the bare oak tree outside the window, unable to believe what he was being forced to endure. No one, high-ranking officer or not, had ever spoken to him in this manner, not even as a military cadet. Yet now he was being dressed down like a common private, shouted at for the entire building to hear.

The general sat down abruptly, face purple, his breath coming in hoarse gasps, and for a moment von Dorn thought— hoped, rather—that the man was having an attack. But the spell passed and the blood drained from the general's face. He shifted his vast bulk and waved irritably at von Dorn to resume his seat.

"I realize," he muttered, voice under control again, "that you have been under great pressure from certain members of the General Staff to take the course of action which you did, but that is no excuse. Discipline must be maintained *along* lines of authority. I have already spoken to several people on the General Staff and it will not happen again." He glared at von Dorn. "It will not happen again! The embassy in London is a choice posting for one so young. There are positions in the African colonies which are not so desirable but which do wonders for instilling respect for discipline. Do I make myself clear?" The general's voice had risen steadily until, nearing the end, he was shouting once more.

"Very clear, sir." The words nearly choked him, but von Dorn managed to get them out.

"This nonsense about a tunnel between England and France—" The general waved a pudgy hand. "It is foolishness. A waste of time and money. If it can even be built." The general was having a difficult time regaining his breath, but he was determined. "It will be an economic disaster. Even though the estimates have never been revealed, it is known that every month the cost rises by one or two percent. And it is the same in France. Meanwhile, sentiment grows in England to abandon it as a potential military disaster. That is what you should be concentrating on, sir. Encouraging such opinion. Your actions, sir, if they should become known, could very well contribute to the government's determination to see the Tunnel completed. It was foolish, sir. Foolish. And what did you accomplish except a possible rupture of Anglo-German relations? Come, sir, what did you accomplish?''

Von Dorn fidgeted in the chair, cursing himself for doing so. The general always made him feel like a schoolboy caught in some nasty act.

''Work has stopped and might remain so for another week. Damages have been estimated at £400,000, sir. It is judged a major disaster in London. The Tories are using the incident as an excuse to mount another attack upon the project. There is talk of a new parliamentary inquiry. Several questions have been raised in the House of Commons as well, by members of both sides. Only the Labour Party members remain unanimous in their unqualified support, but their numbers are too low to have any effect.''

''Ach, and you call that significant?'' The general's sarcasm was scathing. ''The Tunnel project is under constant attack by the Tories and inquiries are made in Parliament every week. They always come to nothing. The government is firmly in control, and as long as the Liberals remain in power, the project will go forward. And there are no signs that they will fail in the near future, are there, sir?'' He paused to wait for von Dorn's agreement and when it came, he snorted to himself and picked up the folder. ''The remainder of your duties have been conducted with the efficiency and dispatch expected of you. In that I am well pleased. However, we need more details concerning the proposed new budget, particularly as it relates to naval construction. Have you made any headway in that regard?''

For the moment the grilling was over, an it was with relief that von Dorn turned to the discussion of more mundane matters. Yet the relief was only temporary, for the general returned again and again to harp on the folly of the Imperial General Staff's attempts to sabotage the Anglo-French Submarine Railway. The general was clearly of the opinion that they were fools and charlatans and once or twice went so far as to make disparaging remarks about the Kaiser himself, who fully supported the General Staff.

''The Kaiser feels he has lost respect after the nonsensical way in which the Moroccan crisis was handled this past summer. How the General Staff ever felt they could challenge Britain and France over a matter such as that is beyond my comprehension. But there, they did it and gave Germany a black eye in the process. And the Kaiser, poor misdirected man, instead of firing those responsible, makes heroes of them and listens avidly to every further bit of stupidity they utter.''

He looked up as von Dorn coughed. "You disagree, *Obersleutnant?*'' he asked in mock surprise. "Perhaps you also feel that this Tunnel is indeed a threat to Germany?''

"If I may be permitted a personal opinion . . .'' He hesitated but Langenscheidt waved a hand to indicate that he should continue.

"I am of the opinion that the Tunnel, if completed, could be a definite economic and military threat to Germany.''

The general inclined his head in a courteous gesture of interest, but von Dorn did not miss the tightening around his porcine eyes. The general did not like having his opinions contradicted.

"Germany has achieved great acceptance on the European continent for her manufactured goods due to their quality and low cost. That low cost is made possible by our excellent network of railways. On the other hand, England's manufactured goods are popular in the Americas and throughout her Commonwealth, also because of quality and low cost. Again, that low cost is made possible by efficient transport—in this instance ocean shipping. England cannot compete successfully with Germany on the Continent as cross-Channel shipping costs must be added to railway freight charges. Therefore, she finds herself priced out of the continental markets. However, if railway goods wagons could be loaded in England, then brought by rail through a tunnel *under* the Channel and on to their destinations, still in the same wagons, the price of those goods could be lowered. Raw materials would also be more easily available, and therefore cheaper, to England, and Germany might then face a reversed situation in markets she has heretofore dominated.

"From a military standpoint, I also feel the advantages to England and her allies on the Continent are extremely great if the Tunnel is completed, and, obviously, France does as well. An English expeditionary force could be transported through the Tunnel to France in a matter of days rather than weeks.

Troop trains made up at English camps and barracks, with equipment and logistical supplies included, could be sent directly to debarkation points in France or Belgium. The entire plan for a European land war would be altered to the vast detriment of Germany."

The general stared at him for a moment, then leaned back in his chair and shook his head. "Colonel von Dorn, what you have said is causing me to reassess my opinion of you."

Von Dorn stiffened but remained silent.

"Each and every one of your arguments is easily demonstrated false. First, Germany need never fear economic competition of the kind you describe, as the quality of German manufactured goods is well known, and quality is always demanded over price. And even if this were not an economic fact, the difference in gauge between English and European railroads is such that the goods wagons are not interchangeable. Upon reaching France, they would need to be reloaded into European gauge wagons. This applies equally to the transportation of soldiers and military supplies. This argument has been made in England itself, and a blind man can recognize its validity. In addition, in the event of war, a small commando force could take and occupy the Tunnel entrance on the French coast early in the game. The commandos could be moved into position in goods wagons in advance of the actual attack and at the appropriate moment could occupy the French end of the Tunnel. It might even be possible to send commandos through the Tunnel itself to capture the English side. Has such a thought occurred to you or to those geniuses on the General Staff, Colonel?"

"Permit me, General—"

Langenscheidt stood up abruptly. "No, Colonel!" he snapped. "I will not. I know exactly which arguments you will make. That goods wagons with wheels adjustable to differing gauges can be developed, that both sides of the Tunnel can just as effectively be held by an Anglo-French force, and that a commando attempting to occupy the Tunnel would easily be destroyed. No, Colonel, such an argument would continue endlessly and serve no purpose. I have no need to remind you that I am your superior officer and that you are under my orders. You will in future inform me immediately of any and all communications to you from any member of the General Staff. You will further submit any reports requested by the General Staff through this office. I will, in turn, undertake to transmit them to the War Office. You are the military attaché, but you are an intelligence officer as well and under my command. Remember that, sir.''

Langenscheidt moderated his voice and sat down. ''There is a great deal more to be gained in providing our agents with proper identities and safe refuge in England when the war comes. Your organization of the Fenians to this end is most admirable. However, political reports from London suggest most strongly that the Home Rule Bill for Ireland will pass during the coming session, now that the House of Lords can no longer use the veto as before. If that does happen, Ireland will be independent in three years and it will become that much more difficult to recruit among the Irish. In the meantime, I suggest that you will have little time for other activities. Do I make myself clear?''

''Yes, sir.'' Von Dorn managed to keep his voice from cracking.

The general picked up the report and dropped it into a desk drawer. ''You will find instructions awaiting you with my aide, including reservations on the train returning to the coast tonight. You are dismissed, sir.''

Von Dorn, near to choking with anger, saluted, spun rigidly on his heel, and strode from the room. The aide met him in the anteroom and, without a word, handed him a thin manila envelope and retired. Von Dorn stamped across the lobby and through the door, again catching the dismayed porter napping.

The bright sun had disappeared in the time he had been inside, and the heavy cloud that had moved across the sky created an atmosphere as dismal as his mood. In his anger, he crossed the Alsen Platz without being aware of it and now found himself standing on the curb of the Zelten Allee. A continual stream of vehicles, horse drawn, electric, and gasoline-powered, swarmed along the broad, cobbled boulevard. A stiff gust of wind swirled past, and he discovered that he was still carrying his greatcoat. Abruptly his sense of humor reasserted itself and he grinned as he put it on. Von Dorn turned back onto the footpath and began to walk toward the Brandenburger Thor, uncertain as to whether he should laugh at what had happened or be concerned by the threat that Langenscheidt posed to his career.

But was he a threat? The general was correct in one

respect: von Dorn was not subject to the authority of the General Staff but to that of the Intelligence Service, which was a separate function reporting directly to the Kaiser through Langenscheidt. Intelligence functions were divided into military and political categories. The General Staff conducted all military intelligence, while the *Gefährden Intelligenz Zustellung*, the Imperial Intelligence Service, conducted all political intelligence outside Germany. The post of military attaché in German embassies or consulates aboard was most often used for this purpose, and army and naval officers without connections to military intelligence were employed and specially trained for that duty. This peculiar organization of military and diplomatic intelligence services was a vestige of the Bismarckian administration which had been set up in the 1880s and had resisted change ever since. Von Dorn, along with many of his colleagues who smarted under Langenscheidt's dictatorial and arrogant rule, was convinced that it was essential to combine the two intelligence systems into one centralized organization under the control of the General Staff if Germany was to retain her position as the most powerful military and economic force in Central and Western Europe.

He was so engrossed in these thoughts as he passed through the Brandenburger Thor to the Unter den Linden that he was unaware of the motor car that had pulled to the curb and was keeping pace with him. They went on like this for some way until the rear door was thrown open and an exasperated major of Dragoons stepped down and shouted, "Eric! My God, man, are you blind?"

Von Dorn turned in surprise, and his expression changed to a sheepish grin as he realized what had happened. He stepped forward to clasp his friend's hand.

"Hans, I'm so sorry. I was not paying attention."

Hans von Rittenbaugh laughed and steered him toward the motor car. "Think nothing of it, Eric. After all, the General Staff has all day." He grinned and looked sly. "General von Epping is waiting for you, but I'm sure he won't mind another hour or two."

Von Dorn stopped abruptly. "Von Epping. My God, Hans, after the dressing down I've just had it would be suicide to go anywhere near the Tempelhof, let alone to an appointment with the Old Man."

Hans smiled, expression full of sympathy. "The old bastard chewed you out, did he? Well, I wouldn't worry about that. Von Epping seems quite pleased with what you accomplished . . ." He left the sentence unfinished. "Still and all, I agree that you should be circumspect. That is why I came for you myself, and in my own motor rather than a staff vehicle. I'm sure that old Langenscheidt has his spies about, but what can he say to two old classmates meeting by accident and then driving off to lunch? Hey?"

"He has his spies on the General Staff as well, and don't ever forget it," von Dorn growled. "That man knows what the Kaiser drinks, when he defecated last, and with whom he slept last night. And in two more minutes, he could provide the same information for any other member of the court, military, civil service, or diplomatic corps. For anyone who matters, in fact."

"Then perhaps the man is too dangerous to the state to continue in office," von Rittenbaugh suggested, and von Dorn had to look closely to see whether or not he was joking. He was not, von Dorn decided, and the realization made him bolder. Perhaps something was in the wind after all.

"In any event, I am certain that von Epping has a staff of spies equal to your General Langenscheidt's." Rittenbaugh laughed. "And, my friend"—he leaned closer and lowered his voice—"I have the feeling that perhaps von Epping is testing you. It would not do to fail now, would it?"

That suggestion persuaded von Dorn. Rittenbaugh gave his chauffeur instructions and the automobile dove into the stream of traffic.

Three hours later, von Dorn emerged from von Epping's headquarters in the right wing of the Garde Dragoon Barracks in the Tempelhof quarters and strode across the cobbled courtyard. It was raining slightly but at least the temperature had risen. Darkness had fallen and the clusters of gas lamps were surrounded by misty yellow haloes. He stepped into a waiting taxicab and gave the chauffeur the address of his rooms, 44 Treptnow Am Park, and settled back, wondering if he had made the correct move. He lit a cheroot and inhaled the luxurious smoke, but it did nothing to relieve his anxiety. Von Rittenbaugh at least had been correct in his assessment; it had been a test. A double test in fact. The first test had been to see if he would carry out orders that did not exactly *conflict* with his instructions but did require, as von Epping had put it, "individual and intelligent initiative suggestive of an understanding of the underlying political situation." The second test was of his willingness to place the greater good of the Fatherland before his own personal advancement . . . or safety. Apparently, he had passed both. Von Epping's double role as commandant of the Kaiser's Dragoons and head of the General Staff Intelligence Corps made him a rather powerful individual, but not, von Dorn was certain, as powerful as Langenscheidt, who was from an old Junker family and who could count without qualification upon all of the family and class support that such membership entailed. Even the Kaiser stepped softly around the Junkers.

Von Epping's proposal had been short and to the point: he was to continue, as military attaché, to carry out Langenscheidt's instructions, while at the same time making himself available to the General Staff for occasional assignments. Von Epping had wrapped the entire unsavory proposition in high-flown talk regarding the needs of the Fatherland and the trust the Kaiser reposed in him. But neither had been fooled. Whereas von Dorn had so far done the bidding of the General Staff insofar as he had interpreted the request to be within his instructions, von Epping had not previously asked him to betray his own commanding officer.

The entire affair had little to do with Germany's needs, he knew, but much to do with power struggles between opposing factions. Choosing von Epping's side might very well lead to certain rewards, as von Epping had hinted. *Might* very well. But von Dorn had been in the army much too long to place any trust in a superior officer's vague promises, especially those going beyond the bounds of good military discipline. He was just as likely to be abandoned, his career ruined, and all for the good of the service, if von Epping should deem it necessary. And if Langenscheidt should discover his dual role, which he surely would in time, the threatened posting to Africa would seem a paradise compared to what he would receive.

Darkness had fallen by the time the taxi drew up before the three-story tan brick building facing Treptnow Park in which von Dorn maintained his rooms. His aide rushed out with an umbrella. Von Dorn took it, and, holding it above his head to spare his uniform, hurried up the walk, leaving the aide to pay off the taxi.

He brooded over von Epping's proposition for the rest of the evening, snapping and snarling at the inoffensive little aide's every move until he had driven the poor man nearly to distraction. The traveling trunk had to be packed and re-packed twice before von Dorn was satisfied.

He had just shouted for his aide to find a taxi when a knock sounded. A tall Dragoon officer wearing the aiguillettes and magnificent dress helmet with the sculptured standing eagle of the Garde du Corps, the Kaiser's personal bodyguard, was framed in the doorway.

"Herr Oberstleutnant Eric von Dorn?"

"Yes, Lieutenant, what is it?" he snapped.

"I am commanded by Herr General von Epping to bring you immediately to the Royal Opera."

In spite of himself, von Dorn gaped at the resplendent figure. Von Epping had the power to send an officer of the Kaiser's own guard as a messenger boy? He glanced at the clock above the mantel. It was already 10:30 P.M. The young officer interpreted his glance. "I am to give you General von Epping's personal assurance that you will board your train before it leaves Berlin. Will you come with me? I have a motor waiting."

Von Dorn's own aide arrived at that moment, and there was just time enough to instruct him to take the trunks to the Hauptbannhof Am Friedrichstrasse and wait for him there. Then von Dorn was seated in the staff vehicle as it wove its way through the evening traffic to the Royal Opera.

It was eleven o'clock when von Dorn was ushered from the stage entrance to a small anteroom off the main lobby. He felt awkward in his plain traveling uniform. He was not even wearing white gloves but a casual pair of gray doeskin he had purchased in London. He decidedly was not dressed for the opera. And why would von Epping bring him to the Royal Opera . . . except that Langenscheidt had been known to have incurred the Kaiser's displeasure several years before by refusing to attend. General Langenscheidt detested opera, which he characterized as one of the maladies infecting the Germany military. His other hatred was the homosexualism reported to be rife among the upper echelons of the officer corps. Langenscheidt had been one of the men behind the scenes who had conducted the investigations leading to the arrest, conviction, and dismissal of a number of the Kaiser's closest advisers, chief among them Prince Philipp Eulenberg.

That the general could survive such incidents involving those closest to the Kaiser had led von Dorn and others to the conclusion that Langenscheidt was a singularly powerful man, much too powerful to betray. Now faced with the necessity, von Dorn assumed, of giving von Epping a definite decision before leaving Germany, he decided to refuse and report the incident immediately on reaching London. Whatever vengeance von Epping might attempt would be nothing compared to what Langenscheidt could arrange.

The anteroom was fashionably decorated, he noted, trying to find something to distract his mind. Watered silk, dyed pale red, lined the walls. The wainscoting was carved black walnut, heavily gilded at the corners to match the intricate Austrian furniture with its contrasting silk cushions. He was staring at a badly done portrait of Strauss's *Elektra* when he heard the door open behind him. Turning, he was surprised to see not von Epping, but a smallish man in a smart uniform, head down and left arm held behind his back. Only when the man raised his head did von Dorn recognize Kaiser Wilhelm II. Automatically, his heels clicked together and he bowed deeply. The Kaiser hastened across the room to clap him on the back. Astonished, von Dorn nearly lost his balance and the Kaiser steadied him with his good right arm.

"Enough bowing and scraping." The Kaiser laughed. "There is no time. We understand that your train leaves at midnight and we certainly would not like you to miss it. General von Epping tells me that you have agreed to his proposals this afternoon. Fine, fine!" The Kaiser bobbed his head several times, staring at von Dorn with bright eyes.

Von Dorn could only mumble agreement. The last person in the world he had expected to see was the Kaiser, and he was still befuddled. As the Kaiser talked, however, he began to recover, and with the recovery came relief that here might be the answer to his qualms, if only he could play it out properly.

He listened politely as the emperor enthused over the operation that von Dorn had undertaken in England the week before, and von Dorn gladly supplied him with further details. When he was satisfied that he had the entire story, the Kaiser stepped back and regarded von Dorn with a close look.

"General von Epping feels you may have one or two reservations yet concerning our proposals."

Von Dorn gasped. *Our* proposals, the Kaiser had said. *Our*. Then this was a *high* echelon struggle for power.

Wilhelm must have interpreted von Dorn's thoughts correctly as he chuckled and bounced on his toes. "Young man, you should be aware that General von Epping was acting under the strictest orders when he spoke to you this afternoon." His voice hardened abruptly. "My orders, sir. My orders. What you are being asked to do is of the utmost importance to Germany."

Von Dorn nodded, managing to mold his features into the proper attitude of respect, agreement, and yet doubt at the same time. Again the Kaiser was quick to note his expression.

"Well, Colonel? Do you doubt that the Channel Tunnel is a threat to Germany's destiny, to her rightful place in Europe and the world? Can we afford the threat of continental invasion and war? With Germany caught between the French and Russian war machines, both allied with England, can there be any doubt of our fate unless all are neutralized?" He turned and began to pace about the room. "Colonel, the imperial designs of France and Russia are facts of life. The French hate us for 1871, and the Russians fear us for our vitality. Both would crush us in an instant, but without England, they dare not attempt it." He stopped and turned to face von Dorn, tapping his chest. "I proved that this past summer in Morocco. Agadir was for me a test of English intentions."

Von Dorn was quick to note that the Kaiser had dropped the use of the royal collective pronoun.

"Neither France nor Russia was willing to act against me until the English strengthened their backbones. So, the course of action is clear. England must be brought into alliance with Germany or diminished as a military power. Attempts since 1903 to arrange an alliance have failed and she is more confident than ever now of her power. With the English Channel Tunnel completed, she will be insufferable. So, now, I must make certain it is never completed. We will destroy it completely. If I cannot have England with us, then England must be neutralized. I have so little time to secure our position. Four years. It must be accomplished within four years or Germany will remain forever a second-class nation.''

"Your Majesty, I find myself in complete agreement on every point!'' von Dorn exclaimed. "And that is the reason I was concerned to see that General von Epping's request was carried out. However, I fear that I am not in a position to carry the burden of trust he wishes to impose upon me. The circumstances of my appointment—'' He broke off as the emperor held up his good right hand and the smile broke forth again.

"Colonel, we understand your problem completely. We had assumed it was something of the kind. And your loyalties do you credit. Much credit. Your superior is General Langenscheidt, and it certainly is no secret that the general does not regard the English Channel Tunnel as a threat to Germany. We respect the general's beliefs. His years of service to the Reich have earned him a trusted place in our counsels where his analyses are always given our utmost attention. But, in this instance, it is our opinion that the general is incorrect when he maintains that the Tunnel is of no economic or military threat to Germany. And only after giving General von Epping's proposal much thought did we permit him to approach you.''

The Kaiser drew himself up and his expression became stern again. "Lieutenant Colonel Eric von Dorn, it is your emperor's express wish that you assist General von Epping in his endeavors. You will earn our undying gratitude and respect as you undertake your task. At the same time, General Langenscheidt's plans for operations in Ireland must also be carried through as they are also vital to our interests.''

The orders given, the Kaiser smiled. "Now, we must return, much as we would rather remain to discuss your mission further. If we are gone long, it will be remarked and rumors will fly again.'' He grinned like a small boy about to involve himself in mischief, and von Dorn could not restrain his own grin. The rumors the Kaiser referred to had reached even London. Madame Flaubert, the French soprano so much in vogue that season, was rumored to be the Kaiser's latest favorite. It was noted that the Kaiser attended many of her performances and was always absent during the second act when she was offstage. Von Dorn doubted the worth of the rumors. He had calculated as an idle exercise that Madame was absent from the stage for exactly eleven minutes. Although it may have seemed long to the audience, it was in fact a short time for anything very exciting to have happened. After all, it would have taken her at least half that time to divest herself of the gown and numerous petticoats the role called for, and he was doubtful if she could even have dressed, with the help of a maid, in that time. Von Dorn was an expert in that area.

But he played along with the Kaiser for his sake; the man seemed to derive such enjoyment from the harmless deception. It was not until later that it occurred to von Dorn that perhaps the Kaiser himself was encouraging the rumors to counter those spread by his enemies that Wilhelm had the same predilection for young junior officers that so many of his closest advisers had shown.

The Kaiser turned when halfway to the door. "Colonel"— his voice was sly, that of a comrade imparting a bit of gossip—"due to the delicacy of this mission and our interest in it, we would be appreciative if you would provide us with holographic copies of any reports sent to General von Epping. This request, of course, will remain between us."

Von Dorn did not miss the Kaiser's final use of the collective pronoun. "Of course, your Majesty. As you wish."

He bowed as the Kaiser strode from the room, then sighed and took a cheroot from his pocket. As he drew on the fragrant smoke, it dawned on him that he had been ordered to disobey a superior officer by no less than the Kaiser himself. He thought about that for a while, remembering the Kaiser's veiled hints that Langenscheidt had at last fallen from favor.

The door opened again and the Garde officer beckoned to him. With a start he realized that it must be late. He snapped open the cover of his watch: 11:35.

"This way, if you please, sir. We have just sufficient time. A cab waits outside."

The young officer led him through the lobby, down a narrow corridor, and pushed open a small door that led out onto an alleyway. A horse-drawn cab was waiting for him.

"The chauffeur has instructions to take you direct to the railway station. If you do not reach it in time, he will drive you on to Potsdam. The train will be held for you there. Naturally, the general would prefer that you board the train at Bahnhof Friedrichstrasse, as less attention will be attracted. Good luck, sir."

With that he was gone and the blue-coated cabby hissed at him, "Inside and quickly, sir."

The rain was just short of torrential as the cab dashed through the empty streets. On the seat was an envelope. He picked it up, angling it to see the inscription in the feeble carriage light shining through the isinglass window. It was addressed to him in what he recognized as von Epping's careless handwriting.

The train was well past Brandenburg when von Dorn finished reading three typewritten sheets describing his mission in England. Too weary to think about it any longer, he undressed by himself and got into the narrow bunk. With a sigh, he got up again and dug through the suitcase on the rack opposite for his silver flask. He poured a generous measure of brandy into his traveling cup and sat back on the bunk. Shortly he turned out the light and sat in the darkness, sipping the brandy and watching the lights slip past as the Berlin-Aachen express ran on through the night. The steady rain had turned to snow and he sat hypnotized by the flickering grayness beyond the glass.

In spite of his resolution, the day had given him much to think about and it was only now, in the quiet of the sleeping compartment, relaxing with the brandy and a cheroot, that his busy mind could begin to sort out the threads of the vast political tangle. The Kaiser did not trust either von Epping or Langenscheidt; that much he understood. By requesting copies of all reports sent to von Epping, he was in effect spying upon his own general. Turn and turn about, he thought. *Who shall keep watch upon the watchers.* It was, at the very least, a valuable insight into the workings of the topmost level of the military and made plain the validity of rumors he had heard in the past. Von Dorn could not help but feel disappointed that it was no different at the top than on lower levels: the same jockeying for power, the same blatant back-stabbing, the same mistrust, all the way to the emperor.

As the hours wore on to dawn and sleep continued to elude him, the brandy sank lower in the flask and the air in the compartment grew thick with smoke until at last, an hour or so before dawn, von Dorn slept, having worried his problem past the point of solution. Only one thing was crystal clear to him. All instructions were verbal and there were no witnesses.

He could be abandoned to the tender mercies of General Langenscheidt at any moment. And he would have no defense. If it became politically expedient, he would be discarded, and he knew perfectly well that even the Kaiser would not come to his defense. The Kaiser's request for duplicate copies of reports in his own handwriting made that perfectly clear. If he succeeded, he would be rewarded. If he failed . . . it was better not to think of the consequences.

His aide, Schram, knocked timidly on the compartment door shortly before eight and, receiving no answer, opened it quietly. Von Dorn was in his nightgown, stretched on top of the rumpled blankets. The empty flask had fallen to the floor, and the small ashtray on the wall of the compartment was filled to overflowing. The aide collected the flask for refilling, lowered the window a bit to allow the interior to air, and went out, long familiarity with his master's whims prompting him to let von Dorn sleep as long as possible.

Von Dorn was an unpredictable man given to great swings of temperament, roaring with laughter one minute, sunk in the depths of depression the next. In the former, he was kind and thoughtful, aware of the feelings of those around him, and generous. In the latter, he was morose, impatient, and angry.

Sergeant Karl Schram was, through long practice, acutely sensitive to von Dorn's moods and, in spite of them, totally dedicated to von Dorn in every respect. For hadn't the *Oberstleutnant* saved his life, shot down the charging Moroccan rebel an instant before his sword slashed at Schram's head. Even now Schram could hear the thin whistle the sword made, see the bristling mustache glinting in the African sun. Lieutenant von Dorn, as he was then, had shot the man from the saddle with his Mauser pistol, grinned at Schram, and run on. Since that moment, Schram, who hated the life of an infantryman, had attached himself securely to von Dorn's side. Even in the worst of his moods, when he ranted and found fault continuously for days on end, it was better than constant drilling and marching, and if the fatigue was similar, at least the bed was soft and, best of all, clean.

They changed trains at Aachen at ten in the morning. The frigid air braced von Dorn, easing away the last traces of the headache with which he had awakened. The snow that had fallen during the night lay thin in the rail yard, and the air had a cutting effect to it. Van Dorn stamped up and down the platform, breathing deeply, while Schram huddled between the traveling trunk and the wall of the stationmaster's cabin in a vain effort to keep warm.

"Come on, Schram," von Dorn bellowed. "Walk with me. The air will do you good. Get rid of that sallow complexion, heh? Can't have an unhealthy-looking subject of the Reich about in England, can we? Enough of those damned Englishmen looking that way. Come on, man. Walk."

A very reluctant Schram left the meager shelter and together, fifty paces along the platform, fifty paces back, they marched, the handsome blond officer and the wizened little sergeant, up and down the platform bawling regimental songs to the astonishment of a staid burgher and his family who had puffed up the steep stairs to the platform. The burgher took one look and fled below again, hustling his plump but not unattractive daughter before him.

The Belgian saloon train was comfortable enough, but von Dorn's good humor evaporated as soon as two young Englishmen crowded into the compartment after him. He met their good-humored attempts to converse in atrocious but understandable German with frosty silence, pretending that he did not understand, and they soon left him alone. One began to read and the other fell asleep, mouth open and grunting from time to time as the train swayed.

Von Dorn sat stiffly in the upholstered seat, watching the snow-covered mountain forests of the Ardennes give way to farm land while the train whistled its way through the Belgian countryside. The unfamiliar mood of indecision was on him again as it had been since the interview in von Epping's office. Was he getting so old, he wondered, that security now meant that much to him?

Von Dorn had very little concept of patriotism. To him, Germany and the army were a means for garnering position and privilege. Forced by his family's impoverished circumstances into a technical school and then a pioneer regiment instead of the 2d Guard Cuirassiers as he had wished, advancement and preference had eluded him for years until a posting to Morocco in 1905 had led to an incident, his single combat experience, that had brought him the Iron Cross and the attention of both the General Staff and the Imperial Intelligence Service. How much simpler it had been in those days, he mused, although one never thought so at the time. His engineering company had been sent from the railroad town of Youssoufia to construct a series of fortifications in the expectation of a French-encouraged Moroccan advance, merely another of the endless moves and countermoves in the quest for empire. And so they had marched from Youssoufia at dawn behind a straggling column of ragged rebels armed with single-shot .43-caliber Remington rifles. He had been grateful, he remembered, as the rebels mustered, that the nearest contingent of the sultan's troops was encamped near Magazov, a good hundred kilometers north along the coast.

Von Dorn could still recall with the utmost clarity the piercing scream that split the night as a howitzer shell exploded in the midst of the rebel camp. The staccato sound of rifle fire and the war cries of the Moroccan regulars had thrown the rebels into panic. The German troops had camped some distance away to avoid the stench and disorder that seemed to spring up instantly wherever the rebel troops stopped, and so their casualties had been relatively light. The infantry captain in overall command had been killed, and von Dorn had managed to withdraw the two companies of German troops to a low hill while the rebels were massacred to a man.

They had suffered through an endless hot day, repulsing two half-hearted attacks and knowing that the Moroccan commander, advised by a French officer, would wait for darkness before mounting an all-out charge to overwhelm them.

The French officer had disposed the Moroccan troops well. He had created a thin circle around the base of the hill, well out of rifle range, and supported the infantry troops with three howitzers spaced at roughly 120° intervals. A squadron of cavalry was clearly visible as well.

All the long broiling day on the treeless hill, von Dorn had studied the positions below, searching until he had found the single point of weakness that might be exploited—a howitzer sited too near a shallow wadi. He knew that the position of his troops was desperate; the Moroccans would never allow them to surrender. Sharp notes might be exchanged afterward, but that would do him no good at all.

That night, von Dorn had led a small force along the wadi and attacked and taken the howitzer position, turning back a cavalry charge with rifle and machine-gun fire from their only

Maxim. Hauling the cannon to the crest of the hill, his men opened a rapid and disciplined fire on the enemy camp. It had been an act of desperation but it had paid off. The chances of success and failure had been calculated to a nicety, and unexpected events had been turned to his advantage—a lesson that von Dorn was never to forget.

At dawn, they found the Moroccan camp deserted. Fortunately, he had had the presence of mind to search it thoroughly before starting the long return march to Youssoufia. Beneath the body of the French officer, whose throat had been slit, they found documents that indicated the Moroccan commander had turned aside to deal with this small body of rebels during a march to the coast where he was to link up with a government force marching north from Agadir. The combined armies were then to invest and reduce the rebel-held port city of Safi, with the assistance of French marines to be landed from two cruisers which would also provide a sea bombardment. Capture of Safi would cut the rebel forces in two, sorry as they were, and place the sultan under further obligation to France—not to mention placing French marines in the city. France would have single-handedly managed a fait accompli and cut the ground from beneath Theodore Roosevelt's proposed international conference to settle the fate of Morocco. The Moroccan commander's anticipation of a cheap victory had become a disaster when von Dorn had scattered his forces to the winds.

It was von Dorn's analysis of the documents even more than his military exploit that had served to attract Berlin's attention, and within a month he had found himself standing for the first time before General Otto Helmuth Langenscheidt. His first intelligence posting had been to St. Petersburg, a choice post for even a career intelligence agent. Promotions had followed quickly during the next five years—captain, then major, and then, a year ago, lieutenant colonel, and he was named to the most sensitive post in the Imperial Intelligence Service, London.

The guard rapped on the sliding door, interrupting von Dorn's reminiscences, shoved it open, and rumbled at them in the atrocious Flemish language. His watch showed thirty more minutes before they would arrive at Ostende. Low, scudding clouds had swept across the sky as the train sped through the amazingly flat Belgian farmlands so drenched by winter rains.

The canals brimmed with runoff, and geometric lakes appeared in what were once farm fields.

The incident in Morocco which had proved so pivotal to von Dorn's career was just another of the many obscure skirmishes in the undeclared wars among the European powers as they struggled for control of the African continent. German troops had fought that summer of 1905, they had fought during the past summer, and they would fight again the following summer and the summer after that and as long as England continued in the role of power broker. The Kaiser had told him that he was determined to break the impasse, to destroy any chance of the English army swarming across the Channel to reinforce the French, to prevent England from dominating the European continent as it dominated the world's seas. The Channel Tunnel was the key. With it, England decided Germany's fate. Without it, England would hardly dare support France in the event of a major war, faced with a powerful German Navy. It was a gamble the Kaiser was taking, and the Kaiser had asked von Dorn to gamble with him.

Von Dorn drew a long breath and reached for a cheroot. Would this gamble pay off? He thought of the Kaiser's remark concerning Langenscheidt's service. Had he really detected a note of sarcasm or was it imagined? Was the general to be dismissed into retirement? The Kaiser's words suggested as much. And he saw Langenscheidt's retirement, forced or otherwise, as the pivot on which his decision would revolve. Not until that was settled could he commit himself fully.

Schram rapped on the door and stepped in with a cup of tea. He sipped idly as the train began to slow and the two Englanders began a desultory conversation. The train rounded a long bend and outlined against the drab cloud was the city of Ostende—its church towers stabbing skyward—where the sleeve of the German soldier on the right flank would brush the waters of the Channel, as von Schlieffen had once remarked.

The train was losing speed now and entering the yards. Tracks ran alongside, crossing and recrossing in an optical illusion resembling writing snakes. Air brakes hissed and the train shuddered. A line of packets and fishing smacks in the Channel opposite slipped into view and the train eased to a stop. Von Dorn drew a last time on the cheroot and stubbed it out, eyes narrowing as he stared at the coast guard vessel moored across the Channel. It was flying the colors of Belgium. A sailor worked lackadaisically beside the outdated deck gun. It seemed prophetic somehow.

While Schram went off to superintend the loading of their baggage aboard the Channel packet, von Dorn stepped into the terminal building, conscious of the guards staring at his army uniform. Three trains, one of them the Moscow Express, were making up. The signboard was freshly chalked with its major stops—Berlin, Warsaw, and Moscow. The cobbled piers were covered with dirty snow, and a train guard huddled against the cold wind sweeping in from the Channel. An attractive matron leading two small children and a servant hurried toward the terminal and a guard sprang to hold the door for her. American, he judged, from the cut of her clothes and the friendly smile she gave the guard. No European woman of her station would have deigned to spare the guard a glance.

Behind, a whistle sounded, and von Dorn turned to see a fresh chalkboard rising to announce that the Ostende-Dover packet was available for boarding. He walked into the small post office, bought two stamps, and placed them on envelopes which he addressed to himself at Durrant's Hotel in Manchester Square, London, then dropped them into the postal slot. That taken care of, he went into the lavatory and stepped into a cubicle. Von Dorn took two belladonna pills from an envelope and swallowed them with a mouthful of brandy from the flask. He had always been ashamed of the fact that he became seasick so readily, and a glimpse of the Channel had suggested that it would be a rough crossing. Resigning himself, he left the lavatory and crossed to the departure hall.

chapter———3

James Bannerman *struggled down the steepest part of the* ascent and trotted stiffly onto the beach. He stopped at the high-water mark, taking a deep breath of salt air, and shoved his hands deep into the pockets of his duffel coat as he turned from left to right to scan the Channel. The seas were light today, and the waves breaking on the shingle lacked the ferocity he had grown used to during the autumn.

Bannerman was an imposing man, well over six feet and with powerful shoulder and chest muscles that suggested he had learned the practical side of his profession from the end of a pick and shovel. As the wind caught at his watery brown hair and laced the seamed, permanently sunburned skin of his face, with an involuntary grin he turned his back to it and trudged along the beach between cliffs and waterline, enjoying the rare outing. His feet were still tender but healing fast, and the medical officer had promised to remove the last bandages from his left hand before the meeting with the Board tomorrow. The cold seemed to have kept most Sunday strollers indoors, and he had the beach to himself.

A coasting vessel was standing well out to clear the South Foreland, and far beyond he could see a Channel packet making for Dover. He climbed onto a groin and walked down toward the water until he was past the beach. The tide was at its lowest ebb and some twenty feet of groin was exposed, every inch thick with gray-green sea growth. After a while he tired of the waves and turned back up the steeply sloping beach. The cliffs towered above him, surfaces cloven into great planes and facets where slabs of chalk had broken away. Scraggly growth showed here and there against the weathered gray, and the cliff tops were lined with brambles and other plants hardly enough to survive the constant battering of the Channel winds.

He had come across the downs through St. Margaret's-at-Cliffe, a tiny village older than the Norman Conquest, now deserted, isolated and bypassed by the road leading from Dover to the works and on to Deal, six miles northeast. Its houses and shops were empty and already beginning to decay. The entire village was scheduled for removal in the spring to make way for access roads and rails to the Tunnel.

The Tunnel. The sole purpose of his life these past two years. It had become his mistress and his enemy, exerting a hold he found impossible to break. Bannerman was not an introspective man and knew it, and so the difficulty in understanding his ambiguous feelings. Yet there was something beyond the fact that it would rank as the greatest engineering work of the twentieth century, far surpassing even the Panama Canal, that drew him, that kept him there in spite of the killing frustrations.

A gull squawked and lifted a wing to catch an updraft, wheeling away as he approached. The sound shook him from the mood and he chuckled at himself. This surely was the place for depressing thoughts. The lowering sky full of scudding cloud, the methodical wash of surf on the shingle, the absence of any living things but the gray gulls—ghosts of drowned sailors, according to the ancient legend. He found the spot in the cliffs where the path began and, curiously thankful, started the climb.

Halfway up he stopped and turned to stare out across the Channel. The packet had passed the South Goodwin Lightship on its way to the Dover breakwater and the coasting vessel had disappeared into a low bank of fog lying a few miles off shore. A scattering of gulls wheeled over the waves, rising now and again to search for prey. Barely visible against the encroaching fog, the winking light of the South Goodwin Lightship made him feel better and he climbed on to the top, where he paused to rest after the steep ascent. When his breathing had eased, he took a cigarette from his gold case and, cupping a hand around a safety match, lit it. He inhaled deeply and walked on, leaning back against the wind. His leg muscles were stiff from hospital confinement and beginning to ache. He paused on the hill's crest, with his back to the Channel and facing away from Bockell Hill. From here he could see out across the sprawl of the works, filling the shallow valley below and spilling out over the crest of East Hill to Old Bottom Down beyond. St. Margaret's-at-Cliffe was on his left, dark and shadowed in the failing light. Beyond the deserted village he had a glimpse of the battlements of Dover Castle as the watery sun broke through for an instant, flooding the landscape with diffuse, opalescent light.

From this vantage point, the sheer immensity of the works was borne in on him again. Spreading north nearly to Kingsdown two miles distant sprawled sheds and yards crammed with rusting steel rails, reinforcing rods, wooden forms, stacks of timber for shoring, piles of coal and petrol storage tanks. A smaller enclosure was just visible two miles inland at Martin Mill, where huge chimneys belched smoke and steam into the damp air from the coal-fired power station that surmounted Hollands Hill and furnished electricity to the Tunnel works. It would continue to power the Tunnel facilities and its electric engines after completion.

Only an occasional dwarfed figure could be seen striding between buildings in the central yards this Sunday evening. As Bannerman continued along, the great three-story-high Tunnel doors came into view. Only the repair and maintenance crews would be at work in the Tunnel now. Greatly augmented crews, he thought bitterly, due to the fire at Ventilator Shaft Six. Resolutely, he turned his mind away from the fire. He had come up here to relax.

He went on north following the line of cliffs, pausing only when he was directly over the great iron and brick shaft of the Tunnel as it emerged the cliff at Hope Point and plunged into the Channel waves, finally submerging completely two hundred yards out. A wind was scattering the fog bank and he could follow the line of the Tunnel nearly to the horizon, the way marked by the great ventilator shafts thrusting through the waters on their man-made islands, each topped by a rotating beacon to warn shipping clear.

A fine rain began and he hurried on, reaching the old golf links a few moments later. Its once carefully tended lawn had reverted to wild pasturage, and he found the contrast between its winter green and the industrial grays and browns of the yards striking. He turned his back on the Tunnel and stared across the waving sea of grass to the feeble lights of Kingsdown. A memory nagged and it was a few minutes before it came to him. He had stood like this before, gazing across a sea of grass, only then it was near Bloemfontein, in 1900, where he had watched an attack driven back in the fading light. Again, there had been a cluster of lights in the distance—those of Bloemfontein—and again the grass had been thick and green in the rain of a dying autumn afternoon.

He had been a young lieutenant then, commanding a company in the Royal Engineers. For three weeks they had endured the boredom, the flies, the rain, and the dysentery of winter camp on the outskirts of the town, a vital stop on the long road to Pretoria. Except for the occasional excursion up-country by armored train, or a railroad track to be mended, they had done little more than wait for the town to be taken.

He remembered very clearly—always would—the specific night of the raid. The burghers had come out of the black night—a part of DeWet's commando, it was discovered later, who had avoided the British patrols with the ease of long practice. The first attack had come soundlessly, sentries ridden down on the edge of the camp and the burghers racing among the neat rows of canvas, shooting down soldiers as they stumbled half asleep from their bedrolls. Behind each Boer rifleman rode a man swinging a torch. Then they were gone as fast as they had come, hidden by the glare and smoke of burning tents, before an effective resistance could be organized.

The second wave struck while the British were still milling about in shock. Bannerman had stumbled unscathed from his tent, revolver in hand, as the first wave rode past and he was still holding his Webley when the second commando group burst upon them. Standing beside his tent he was trying to see through the flames ahead when he heard the horses and the high-pitched Boer battle cry, and he had swung around to see a rider, a young man with a shock of blond hair, bending low over his horse, working the bolt of his rifle. The Mauser's sharp crack and the splat of the bullet striking the tent post beside his head had come simultaneously. Bannerman brought his revolver up in reflex, and the heavy .455-caliber slug lifted the Boer from the saddle as the horse thundered past. Bannerman shook himself slightly, pushing the memory away as he did every time it came to him. The boy could not have been more than sixteen years old.

Bannerman's father had been a London merchant banker, powerful, rich, and bitterly disappointed when his only son had chosen engineering rather than finance. For as long as he could recall, Bannerman has been interested in building— anything so long as he could design and see it assembled. As a boy on their country estate in Suffolk, he had often pressed the gardener, the half-wit hostlery boy, and whomever else he could persuade to help bridge the small streams that crisscrossed the estate. The break with his father had been almost total when he had entered Victoria University to study engineering rather than the classics at Oxford. From there he had gone to Sandhurst and, in 1892, had entered the army as an engineering officer. Since then, he had never had the inclination to do anything else.

After resigning his commission in 1902, Bannerman returned briefly to England and, with his father's grudging help, obtained a post with the great Charles M. Jacobs, who was then completing the Hudson River Tunnel, started in 1874, between New York and New Jersey.

The Hudson Tunnel was a nightmare of silt, mud, and sagging clay walls which had ruined three successive companies. It was also one of the earliest to employ compressed air to hold back the mud and water beyond the unstable clay walls until the permanent lining could be installed.

Charles Jacobs' company was well capitalized, and he managed to keep going until the very ground itself seemed about to defeat him. It was Bannerman's suggestion that made it possible to finish the tunnel—a modification of the technique he had seen used in the South African gold fields. Five huge kerosene burners were played onto the wet soil of the tunnel face, drying it to a fine, firm clay that could withstand the shocks of blasting. The northbound tunnel was completed in 1904 and the southbound in 1905. In that year Bannerman returned to South Africa and the gold fields before accepting a teaching post at the Colorado School of Mines two years later.

The Anglo-French Submarine Railway Company had been formed in 1906 to explore the idea of constructing a tunnel beneath the English Channel. The project had first been proposed by Albert Mathieu in 1802; had been reconsidered several times since, and was actually started by the Submarine Continental Railway Company in 1880. A seventy-five-foot shaft was sunk from the top of Abbotts Cliff a few miles south of where he now stood. Two seven-foot pilot shafts were begun from both sides of the Channel. The tunneling machines advanced at the rate of one hundred yards a week, and the Tunnel was to have been completed in six to seven years. Each bore was then to have been enlarged to fourteen feet. The excavation actually got more than a mile beneath the Channel, drawing in its wake severe opposition from the insular-minded British public—Bannerman preferred to think of them as provincial—who saw immense danger in a physical link to the Continent. The army, a guiding force behind the campaign to scuttle the Tunnel, harped on the specter of invasion until fear and emotion overruled logic and scientific rationale, and the Board of Trade, in 1882, ruled that the Tunnel, a private venture, passed through Crown lands—the foreshore and the seabed—to the three-mile limit and was therefore trespassing. The project was abandoned in that year.

But the new company was serious and the Liberal government which had just come to power was anxious to demonstrate that it could and would help solve the unemployment problem as it had promised. The cabinet saw in the Tunnel a chance not only to employ thousands of workingmen but to increase Britain's share of the European market as well. No insurmountable obstacles were placed in the company's way and engineering studies completed in 1909, with construction of the approaches beginning late that same year.

Bannerman had written an article for an American engineering journal suggesting that the Tunnel engineers make use of compressed air in the Tunnel heading to relieve the need for immediate shoring in the relatively stable chalk and so speed the entire operation. The article came to the attention of Charles Jacobs, his old boss and then chief consultant to the Anglo-French Submarine Railway. Wishing to retire, he put Bannerman's name forward as his replacement. Bannerman had at first declined; he was at that time engaged in a project at the Colorado School of Mines to develop new tunneling techniques that could be applied to mineral mining.

The Board of Directors, at first annoyed that Bannerman had turned them down, finally offered him the post of engineering director, confident that he could not resist the most important engineering position in Europe, and he had accepted. Now, after more than a year of excavation, the Tunnel was nearing the end of the eighth mile. The French team pushing out from Calais had advanced to more than seven miles as of Saturday night's shift. That meant twelve more months would see the Tunnel completed, thank God.

Bannerman went on down the gentle slope to a small outcropping several hundred feet above East Bottom Road. From here he could look southwest across the works, dominated by the great humped entrance to the Tunnel. There was still sufficient daylight left for him to pick out the massive steel doors designed to close off the Tunnel mouth, a safety precaution against enemy attack.

His feet were beginning to stiffen with the cold and Bannerman decided on a short cut down the slope to the works, worrying over his problems in spite of his resolution not to do so. From the first there had been trouble with the Badger, the great tunneling machine which drilled through the chalk strata at the rate of 142 feet per day. It had not lived up to its optimistic nickname. The developers had been accused of attempting too great a technical stride. No tunneling machine yet invented had managed to achieve the rate of one hundred feet a day, let alone the 180 for which the Badger had been designed. At first bearings burned out weekly, requiring a full day to replace. Once the bearing problem had been solved, the thirty-foot cast iron revolving arms began to fractured. The designers had at last been persuaded to replace cast iron with nickel steel, and the new arms now withstood the huge shear forces generated nearly seven times as long.

And finally, the hydraulic jacking system that drove the Badger forward had prove insufficient as the excavation moved deeper. The chalk, compressed by pressures approaching 1.6 million pounds per square foot was, in places, almost as hard as granite. The strain generated on the entire machine as the cutters sliced paper-thin sheets from the chalk with every pass had proven too much for the jacks which, anchored to the tunnel floor, drove the huge machine forward by hydraulic pressure. The braces had held but a cylinder wall burst, spewing hot oil throughout the Tunnel heading and scalding two workmen. The damage to the Badger had taken two weeks to repair, only to have it fail again a month later, this time killing a worker.

An improved system substituting twin compression chambers had been fabricated in the yard's machine works to

Bannerman's own design and installed following the second incident, with the further loss of two working weeks. Since the early summer then, they had experienced minor but constant mechanical failures that only added to his frustration and ate away his narrow safety margin.

But in Badger, when it performed properly, was a source of unalloyed pleasure. He enjoyed standing behind the operator in the wire mesh cab as the thirty-foot cutting arms revolved and the chalk face peeled away in strips, was crushed, mixed with water, and flushed through the long drain pipe that led back through the airlock and up-Tunnel to the surface. The immense machine shook and roared as if all the demons of hell were in residence and, magically, the chalk face receded before the mechanical assault. Behind the Badger, workmen maneuvered new sections of iron ring supports through the airlock and bolted them into position. They were followed by the grouting crews, who pumped the slurry of cement and pea gravel into the wooden forms erected between the new ring supports.

And it was the grouting that was steadily pulling the work further behind schedule, eighty feet behind as of the end of shift yesterday—in Bannerman's estimation, a critical distance. The ring supports were in place but offered only meager support for the chalk walls as the compressed air-supported heading moved farther ahead of the airlock every day.

The cement used for grouting was the problem. The mixture had proven so viscous that it could not be pumped more than fifty feet, even with the most powerful pumps he could find. And so it had to be mixed beyond the airlock, carried through the lock and up to the work site in cars. Sufficient grouting mix could not be delivered fast enough. The frames were composed of three ringlike segments, each of which required 2,000 cubic feet of grouting to fill it completely, but each hopper car could carry only 112 cubic feet, and it was impossible to bring more than six hopper cars into the airlock and the heading at any one time. A complicated lineup process had been initiated that assured sufficient grout for one segment at a time, but as the Tunnel heading lengthened, the process became ever more unwieldy and grouting fell further behind.

He had ordered new pumps that would be capable of

moving the grouting mixture a minimum of three hundred feet, but until they were redesigned and installed, the pace of Tunnel construction would shortly have to be reduced to that of the grouting crew, which was now about fifty feet a day. And if that happened, the project would overrun both budget and contractual dates and would be in serious trouble.

The sun, blacklighting a bank of dense cloud, had created one of those spectacular Constable sunsets in which rose pinks and reds mingle with sulfurous yellows above an indigo horizon. For an instant a shaft of light broke through, a javelin cast at the Channel, then it was gone and the colors faded rapidly as the sun disappeared.

Bannerman was facing heavy pressure from the Board to allow the Badger to continue to excavate well ahead of the grouted sections, depending instead on the compressed air to support the walls. The result of a morning spent calculating safety margins was hardly reassuring, and he knew he faced a stiff argument.

If a significant blowout occurred it was conceivable that water rushing in would compress the air in the shaft and explode it down the Tunnel like a tremendous piston or hammer until friction with the walls overcame it. But by then, at least a mile of Tunnel would have been destroyed by the water's force and several more flooded. The Board of Directors would think it a safe enough gamble. The Tunnel heading was pressurized to 22 pounds per square inch to support the chalk walls until the lining could be completed. The airlock was itself a significant barrier, constructed as it was of the same dreadnought armor plate as the doors and capable of being pressurized to one hundred pounds per square inch if necessary. He knew that his insistence on following safety regulations to the letter would in this case seem unnecessarily conservative, but he was too good an engineer to discount such an accident merely because it was remote. The Board, however, was composed of hard-headed businessmen only two of whom were engineers, and Bannerman knew that they would press him to push on. If Jacobs were still alive, he would not be facing this problem. But Jacobs had died of heart failure during the summer and Bannerman had to depend now upon his own resources.

It was nearly dark as he topped the final rise. The works below were still bright, wrapped as they were in a tracing of artificial lighting. A steam locomotive pulling a string of goods wagons was being switched from the main track. As he watched, it gathered white puffs of steam for the climb.

Standing in the gloom, looking down over the acres of construction equipment and the webbing of railroads, he knew that he had only one choice; the Tunnel was too important to be jeopardized by selfish financial interests. Bannerman was not privy to the series of secret economic forecasts that had been prepared by several government ministries over the past ten years and submitted to both Conservative and Liberal governments. But he, as well as many others in England, was well aware that the place of Great Britain as the world's greatest trading nation was doomed unless the Tunnel was completed. Britain could not continue to maintain a negative balance of payments with increasing losses every year. For too long England had ignored the Continent, preferring instead the protected markets of her colonies and the Dominions that constituted her new Commonwealth as it was called. But those days were ending as other nations began to offer cheaper goods. The Tunnel could reverse that decline and put England in a commanding position once more.

And, on a more personal level, there was his own career to think about. He had recently received a private solicitation from a syndicate in San Francisco. They were proposing to bridge the Golden Gate and were anxious to have him as a managing director. Not just engineering director, but *managing director*.

He stood on the top of the cut and watched the locomotive rush past below with its string of goods wagons. Smoke swirled for a moment; a sudden premonition gripped him and with it the urge to finish his letter exploring the offer from California. Yet as he wavered, the lure of the Tunnel caught at him and, with a rare moment of insight, he knew that patriotism would enter not at all into his decision. The Tunnel, if completed, would cap his career. If it failed, it would destroy him.

chapter ━━━ 4

Bannerman *strode into the room without knocking and* tossed his hat to the servant. He took his seat at one end of the oval table and glanced with some distaste at the nine men waiting for him. Through the windows at the end of the room he could see fresh cumulus clouds moving across Dover Harbor against an intense blue sky.

The chairman of the Board of Directors, Sir Henry Keithley, stiff in morning coat and high collar, rapped for attention. His voice was a parody of his youth when, as Master of the Oxford Hunt, he could make himself heard above the clamor of dogs, wind, and hunting horns. Now, however, whiskey, cigars, and good living had combined to reduce it to a whining rasp. Bannerman fumbled for a cigarette and lit it, ignoring the snort of disgust from Lord Grennan across the table. Grennan was a nonentity, he knew, elected to the Board for his social rank only, and could safely be ignored. No matter what the issue, he could be depended on to vote with the majority.

"Gentlemen, I wish to thank you all for traveling to Dover." Keithley paused a moment to make certain that the clerk was busy with the stenographer's pad. "We thought it best to meet here so as not to interfere with Mr. Bannerman's efforts by making him endure a time-wasting journey to London. You all know, I am sure, that the Tunnel excavation must not meet with further loss of time." He gave Bannerman a thin smile. "Perhaps Mr. Bannerman would like to begin his explanation."

Ah, Bannerman thought and stood up. Condemned before I start.

"Mr. Chairman," he snapped, deciding to take the offensive, "we know why we are here and I suggest that in the interest of time we stop any further verbal fencing and go

46

directly to the matter. We all know," he went on relentlessly, ignoring the chairman's stricken expression at his bad form, "that the Tunnel is behind schedule. And if any of you have bothered to read the reports which I send each week, you will know why. It comes down to this. We can return to schedule within one month, providing we are willing to gamble with our employees' lives and perhaps with the Tunnel itself. To date, we have not been able to find a way to enable the grouting gangs to keep pace with the rate of excavation. You may recall that I warned you when you voted to purchase the Collier pumping system that it was insufficient for our needs. You chose to ignore my warning then, I assume you will do so again today."

He glanced at their faces. Only one or two were noncommittal, the rest openly hostile. Keithley, angry that Bannerman had usurped control of the meeting, was ready with a sorching reply, but Bannerman was having none of it and pushed on without hesitation.

"Gentlemen, while the chances of a catastrophic blowout are remote, it was, I believe, Brunel who formulated the first of what have come to be known as Murphy's Laws . . . if anything can go wrong it will. We are tempting fate, playing with the lives of our loyal workmen and entertaining the destruction of the entire Tunnel and the loss of your investment. And finally, there are the lawsuits that can and will be filed by the survivors, the widows and orphans of the deceased, the investors, and perhaps by the government as well."

It was clear that while many had already made up their minds, Bannerman's forceful presentation succeeded in sobering them for the moment. It was Keithley who recovered first.

"Mr. Bannerman," he snapped, "we have been very patient with you. You have wasted our time with arguments which we have heard before and you threaten us with lawsuits. I for one will not tolerate such behavior. You were summoned here today, not to lecture us, but to hear our decision. We met yesterday in London to hear the results of a survey conducted by an independent engineering firm of the highest repute. Their findings are much the same as those you reported, with one important exception. They state that grouting can fall behind the excavation to a total distance of two hundred feet before the situation becomes, in their term, at risk. We therefore, acting on their recommendations, are meeting today to instruct you to proceed with the excavation, and we are authorizing you to do so up to two hundred feet in advance of the grouted sections.''

He motioned, and the clerk hurried around the table to hand Bannerman a thick, bound report. "You will find a new set of safety specifications therein and instructions on timbering and shoring that will—''

Sir Henry Keithley broke off as the report thudded onto the oak table.

"What is the name of this consulting firm?'' Bannerman asked in a quiet but intense voice that barely concealed his outrage.

"Why, it is right there on the cover,'' Sir Henry spluttered. "I don't . . .''

Bannerman stared at him. "Masterson? I recall no consulting firm of that name at the works since this problem arose.'' He stared around the table. Several of the members avoided his eyes, although there were one or two hostile stares.

"I—I—'' Sir Henry sputtered, astonished at having to defend himself and his methods to an employee.

"One moment.'' Archibald Armstrong-Flood shoved back his chair and struggled to his feet. His massive bulk dominated the room and he stared disdainfully along the table at the man who had replaced him as engineering director of the Anglo-French Submarine Railway. It was an open secret that the Board, fed up with his indecision and demands, had acted in the face of a cabinet threat to halt government support unless the project was moved forward and quickly. Armstrong-Flood was much too well known and respected to be dismissed, so he had been elected to the Board—"kicked upstairs'' was the phrase Bannerman had heard once in Colorado—and Bannerman hired to replace him. But Bannerman guessed that, since the death of his friend Jacobs, Armstrong-Flood had patiently been gathering support. Bannerman had not worried about it, knowing that the reason for the man's promotion to the Board was all too fresh in his colleagues' minds. As a member of the Board of Directors, he was no threat to any person or faction. Or so Bannerman had thought.

Armstrong-Flood surely had been one of England's greatest engineers—in the 1870s and '80s. Several of the most difficult railway tunnels had been built under his direction. However, with age had come an increasing conservatism which manifested itself in an outright refusal to take any decision without absolute assurance of one hundred percent success. Yet now he was urging that the Tunnel be moved forward under circumstances that were clearly hazardous, and it was not until that moment that Bannerman realized how bitterly the man had resented being replaced by someone young enough to have been his son. He suspected that Armstrong-Flood had also offered to resume the position of engineering director, relying upon the fears of his fellow Board members that the Tunnel would fall even further behind schedule if Bannerman's argument for safety over progress won out. The penalties if Armstrong-Flood's proposal failed were clear enough but quite remote. They were much more clear-cut and immediate if excavation was slowed to the pace of the grouting work. Financial penalties alone could bankrupt the company if guarantor bonds had to be forfeited.

"There was no need for the Masterson people to visit the Tunnel," Armstrong-Flood rumbled at him. "There is a sufficiency of engineering reports and geological estimates already available for that purpose. Their reputation is of the finest and their recommendation is to proceed. You can be too damned careful, young man. Too damned careful!"

Bannerman had a great deal of trouble to keep from laughing at that. He stood also and indicated the report. "For those of you who are not engineers," he said quietly, "this discussion may at times be difficult to follow. However, one thing should be made clear to all.

"If you insist upon adopting the recommendations contained in this report as Sir Henry and Mr. Armstrong-Flood propose, then you do so without me. I am tendering my resignation, effective immediately. Good day, gentlemen."

He started for the door as the elderly porter fluttered toward him.

"Just a moment, Mr. Bannerman, if you please." He paused and turned. Halfway along the table on the left, a stout, gray-haired gentleman was motioning to him.

"Please close the door, sir. I have a question or two if you will indulge me."

Bannerman hesitated, then complied and returned to the table. He remained standing, however.

The speaker was Benedict Vincent Benet, whom Bannerman knew only slightly and who represented French interests on the Board. French interests in the Anglo-French Submarine Railway totaled some thirty-four percent of the stock, and it was rumored that Benet controlled at least seventy-five percent of that total.

"You have made your position quite clear regarding the danger to our workers and the Tunnel if the excavation should proceed without immediate grouting. Yet, when a report from a respected engineering firm is submitted, you dismiss it out of hand and insist upon resigning. May I ask why, sir?"

Bannerman nodded. "You must forgive my bad manners, gentlemen. I suppose I do owe you an explanation. It is quite simple. First, the structure through which the Tunnel is being excavated is chalk. Chalk is nearly the tunneler's ideal medium. But it has two major drawbacks. Under pressure, it has a tendency to fracture, especially along lines of stratification. Historically as the Channel bed sank and was inundated by the Atlantic and the German Sea, the chalk absorbed water and some has flowed into the fracture lines and filled natural cracks and reservoirs. The Channel bed in places along the Tunnel route rests under more than 160 feet of seawater, exerting a pressure of 70.4 pounds per square inch—that is 10,138 pounds per square foot, gentlemen. Imagine, if you will, the effect of this force on a crevice in the Channel bed containing several hundred million gallons of water.

"At the moment we are approaching those deep areas of the Channel where, because of the angle of the Tunnel itself, the thickness of the seabed above is least. We estimate that if we should break through into a water-filled fissure or cavern, we can expect an inundation of water under as much as ten thousand pounds per square foot of pressure. Imagine, if you will, a fire brigade hose playing against a chalk cliff. How long to weaken a section sufficiently for it to break down and collapse? Imagine then what would happen if, instead of the two-hundred-odd pounds in a fireman's hose, that stream of water was at ten thousand pounds!

"If we should strike such a fissure during excavation, it is most liable to erupt into the pilot bore. At the end of that pilot bore is the exacavating machine, the Badger, braced now to the Tunnel floor rather than the walls as called for in the specifications. The Badger was designed so that sufficient grouting could be injected through the hollow stem of the pilot drill into the bore to seal off the water flow in minutes. But there is no grouting available. It is all going to the grouting crews as fast as it can be mixed and brought into the heading. This being the situation, I say that there is no way in which a disaster can be prevented. If a blowout occurs, every man in the heading will be killed. If the water pressure is sufficiently high, the airlock may collapse. If that happens, the water will act like a piston, compressing the air in the Tunnel into what I choose to call an air hammer, killing everyone in the Tunnel by concussion except those near the entrance and destroying at least one mile of Tunnel.''

Bannerman stared at each man, as if challenging them to dispute his words. ''The facts and the figures are quite clear. Only by sacrificing safety margins can you proceed. And that, Mr. Benet, is why I dismiss the consulting engineer's report out of hand and tender my resignation. I will not be a party to any solution that jeopardizes lives or the Tunnel project itself.''

''Does this mean that you will go to the press with your opinion?'' Benet asked.

The coldbloodedness of the approach caught Bannerman flat-footed and it was a moment before he could reply. ''In all honesty, I hadn't thought about it . . . but, yes, I certainly will. I have too much respect for the men to see their lives played about in such a manner.''

''I see.'' Benet glanced about the table, his expression wry. ''I would suggest, gentlemen, that Mr. Bannerman has put forward a powerful argument.'' Then, more seriously, he continued. ''One thing does disturb me about the consulting engineer's report in any event. I was not aware until Mr. Bannerman mentioned it that the consultants had not visited the Tunnel works. I do not see how they could have arrived at a correct conclusion without seeing the project at first hand. Would any of you gentlemen consider investing a large sum of money in a factory without first visiting its site?'' He turned to Sir Henry and Armstrong-Flood at the head of the table.

The old engineer snorted. ''In my opinion, Benet, it wasn't necessary and I told them so. Plenty of information available. All they had to do was read it. Couldn't come to any other conclusion.''

"Perhaps they might have if they had taken the trouble to see the Tunnel and inspect the situation for themselves. But then"—and his voice became silky—"that would have alerted Mr. Bannerman that his competency and judgment were under attack, would it not?"

Both men jumped to their own defense and the argument raged for another hour, with Bannerman taking no further part. Once or twice, he touched his jacket pocket, feeling the crisp outline of the letter from the San Francisco combine. Nothing like burning your bridges, he thought, so long as there is another on the horizon.

It was Benet who suggested the compromise. He questioned Bannerman closely about the possibility of developing a technique to pump the grout into the heading. Bannerman hesitated. It was strictly a question of technology, he answered, and one that sooner or later would be solved.

"But you feel certain that the problem will be solved?"

"Of course. It is only a matter of time. Within the next month or two, perhaps."

"Then," Benet answered, straightening the single sheet of paper before him, "I would propose the following: that excavation be allowed to continue for a limited period of time— say, thirty days more—during which time it shall be allowed to precede the grouting work by up to two hundred feet. I think you will agree, Mr. Bannerman, that such a risk for so short a time will be acceptable and will allow your engineers additional time to solve their problem. At the same instance, it will allow the Board to report that the Tunnel is being pushed ahead as rapidly as possible. Such a response will disarm even our most severe critics." Benet studied Bannerman for a moment and then shifted his eyes quickly to Armstrong-Flood at the head of the table. Bannerman got the message and, with a show of reluctance, he accepted.

A sharp breeze laden with the smell of coal, oil, and salt was blowing in from the harbor when Bannerman left the hotel an hour later. Far out across the harbor he could see waves crashing in fans of spray against South Breakwater. The waves, generated by the succession of storms, were still strong, and the Dover-Calais packet steaming into Outer Harbour past the signal station was pitching violently.

His driver was waiting at the curb with Bannerman's new

Armstrong & Wentworth motor car. They drove along the Marine Parade turning into the town at Woolcombs Road and then on from Laureston Place to the Deal Road, which led up the long, tortuous climb past the Castle perched on the cliffs in commanding position above harbor and town.

At the top of the hill they turned northward onto the downs. The newly metaled road stretched ahead and Bannerman settled back to enjoy the run as he always did in fine weather. The sun blazed down from an absolutely cloudless sky and the grass was heavy and green as far as he could see. Once past Edinburgh Hill, the grass ended abruptly as the cliffs began and the sea, made pale by the sunlight, glinted and ran into the misty distance. They went on by a weatherbeaten milestone on which the mileage was hardly visible—Deal 7, Dover 2—and passed a group of cadets of the Duke of York's Royal Military School marching along the roadway. The road began a gentle slope and the downs spread before them.

Perhaps it was the weather and the sunlight that gave a lift to his spirits which had flagged so badly during the past few weeks. The Board meeting had produced a solution he had not anticipated, but he had at least not been forced into a resignation he did not want. Thirty days was a gamble, but the odds in his favor were astronomical. And in a way, he was grateful for not having won. If he had done so, the outcome would have been inevitable—bankruptcy. The company could not bear further losses.

Once past the road leading off to the village of St. Margaret's, the works yards became visible. The contrast between industrial waste and green downland was startling—much as Manchester or Leeds must have contrasted with the countryside in the early days of industrialization. Row after row of unpainted, two-story, semidetached houses, all with brave if muddy front gardens filled with bundled children, had been thrown up for the Tunnel workers at nominal rents. Medical care and schooling were provided free, but the shops belonged to the company and of course charged exorbitant prices—in spite of angry questions raised in Parliament every so often. The average employee of the Anglo-French Submarine Railway received a wage slightly above that of a coal miner—perhaps the best-paid industrial workers in England—yet as the conditions of the men and their families showed, it was still far from sufficient.

The driver turned at the main gate and the elderly gate-keeper waved to them as they drove through. The motor car threaded its way among the deeper puddles filling the unpaved roads that wound between the works buildings, warehouses, and sheds and stopped before a single-story corrugated-iron building placed so as to provide an uninterrupted view of the Tunnel entrance.

Bannerman strode through the outer office jammed with clerks. Several nodded respectfully to him and he motioned his secretary to follow him into his office. He hung up his coat, stretched, and sat down behind the massive walnut rolltop desk as Margaret Doyle silently took her seat in the cramped room.

The white lace trim on her dark, ankle-length dress was the only concession to her femininity. Her reddish hair was pulled back in a tight bun and the sunlight streaming through the windows emphasized the myriad freckles scattered across her face. She was a not unattractive woman, but it seemed, Bannerman thought idly, as she flipped through her pad to an empty page, that she went out of her way to make herself so. Rather tall and spare, she did have a good figure but concealed it well beneath heavy dresses several years out of fashion. She dressed more like a grandmother than a young woman of thirty. But she was efficient and quick, and that was why Bannerman had hired her. During the past year she had come to be more an assistant than secretary, screening the less important correspondence and often preparing answers to routine letters for his signature. She also ruled the outer office with a strict hand, an accomplishment he never managed to understand. The rest of the clerks were male, many in their forties, and as conservative as the most distinguished occupant of a seat in the Lords.

"Anything new on the grouting problem?"

"No, sir." Her voice was soft and rather melodious in spite of her crisp way of speaking that tried to hide a Dublin accent.

"There is an engineering meeting in progress. But Mr. McDougal said not to bother." She waited, assuming that he would tell her how the Board meeting had gone, and he found her assumption slightly annoying. But then it was better than having to answer persistent question after question, he supposed.

"The Board has given us another thirty days to find a

solution. In the meantime we are to continue with the excavation. I'll discuss it with McDougal as soon as he's through."

She nodded and made a note on her pad.

"I'm going to spend the rest of the day going over the new estimates, so if you will bring in the files, I'll get to it. Have the mess send over sandwiches and coffee at two o'clock, and I've asked my driver to call for me at six. I'll stay in town tonight."

"Yes, sir." She opened her notebook to the back and removed a handful of empty envelopes. "These appear interesting, Mr. Bannerman. They are from this week's mail. There is a Russian postal stamp among them," she said as Bannerman quickly sorted them by country.

"Thank you, Margaret. One or two of these I do not have. And I believe that the French issue is new."

Bannerman slipped the envelopes into his pocket. "I'll work on them this weekend. By the way, will you be going up to London?"

Her face colored instantly, and he grinned.

"Yes, sir. I'll return on the early train Monday, if you approve, sir."

"Of course. But don't take the early train, take the nine o'clock from Holborn Viaduct. Another hour or so won't make a difference."

"Oh, I couldn't do that, sir. But thank you anyway," she said simply, dismissing all further discussion, and Bannerman smiled again as she went to collect the files.

chapter _____ 5

Eric von Dorn dismissed the hansom cab at the intersection at Oxford and Holles Streets. He stood on the curb a moment as if deciding which direction to take, then strode east toward Oxford Circus. The temperature had dipped into the thirties and the combination of wind and cold seemed to have kept all but the hardiest Sunday afternoon strollers indoors. During the night, low clouds had swept in across the city, ending the brief spell of fine weather.

Reaching Oxford Circus, he crossed and, without hesitating, crossed twice more so that he reached the southwest side just as a few pedestrians came up from Regent Street. Turning slowly to scan the area, he was satisfied that he had confused anyone who might have been following. It was unlikely, but one never knew. The tall German in mufti went down Regent Street, stopping occasionally to peer into shop windows as if he were merely another Sunday stroller. His dark gray suit, cut in Bond Street, topped with a camel coat and a pearl gray fedora made him look, he thought, more English than the English.

Reaching Conduit Street, he went along to New Bond Street, where there were more strollers, crossed and walked up as far as Blenheim Street. He paused there, pretending to stare into a shop window while he checked again to see that he was not being followed. Blenheim Street was narrow, dark, lined with flats, and situated so as to collect wind-blown rubbish. A small boy sat on some steps. He was shivering in a worn coat as he hung onto a string the other end of which was tied to the collar of a very small dog which looked nearly as woebegone as the master.

Von Dorn stopped and they regarded each other for a moment and then the boy nodded and said politely, "Good afternoon, sir. I am takin' me dog for a bit of a walk. 'Is name's Charlie."

Von Dorn smiled. "Isn't it rather a cold afternoon for a stroll?"

This statement was agreed to with due solemnity and the dog yawned and rested its chin on the boy's knee.

"We're about to go home. Ma said she'd warm some milk for Charlie."

Von Dorn nodded. "I think that is a very good idea. Do you live far?"

"Oh, no, sir. Just in Meard Street."

Von Dorn thought a moment before placing the street, in Soho, a ten-minute walk—twenty for a small boy. "You've come a long way," he observed. "Do you know what I saw?"

"No, sir."

"A hot chestnut vendor. In Regent Street." He took a tuppence from his pocket and flipped it to the boy. "Hot chestnuts would make the walk shorter, I should think. Good day, sir."

The boy stared at the coin in his hand, then wiped his nose with the other. "Thank you, sir. Thank you very much," he called out and von Dorn waved as he turned the corner into Sedley Place. A silly thing to do, he thought, and dangerous. If the boy should remember . . . but for God's sake, who would question a little boy who lived half a mile away or better.

Sedley Place was even darker and narrower, but there was less rubbish strewn about. Von Dorn paused beside number 4, stubbed out his cigarette, then pushed the door open and went up the narrow flight of stairs to the first floor. He knocked on the door of the second of the three flats.

"Who is it?"

"Eric Schneider."

He heard a chain latch drop and the door flew open. Margaret Doyle smiled and pulled him inside.

"It's been such a long time, darling. I thought you would never come today," she murmured as she came into his arms.

He nuzzled her hair, then tipped her face back and kissed her. "I was with some business associates, dearest. Couldn't get away until a short while ago. But we have the rest of the afternoon."

He disengaged himself, went across the room to the bookcase, and found the bottle of cognac. Margaret brought two glasses from the cupboard, and he broke the seal and poured generous measures into the glasses. Silently they toasted one another, and Margaret led the way through to the bedroom.

Von Dorn watched the cigarette smoke curl toward the ceiling. The window opposite opened onto a brick wall, but from the gathering shadows he could tell that the afternoon was slipping away. Carefully, so as not to wake her, he propped himself on one elbow and regarded the woman by his side.

Margaret was only partly covered by the blanket trailing across her left side and one thigh. Her hair, almost titian in this light, was spread around her like a fan. Half turned as she was, her posture emphasized the curve of her breast and hip and he thought again of the surprising passion contained in that thin body.

She had first been pointed out to him in the new Selfridge's department store, only a few blocks away, by a carefully cultivated contact, one Thomas Finnigan, who had known her as a child. It had been easy enough to effect an introduction as Eric Schneider, a German businessman living in London. This was the cover story he had given Finnigan. At first he had remained in the background as she and Finnigan renewed their acquaintance. They had all gone to a small tea room in Portland Street where Finnigan and Margaret had reminisced about their childhood in Ireland. At three o'clock Finnigan left, pleading a previous appointment, but only after insisting that Eric Schneider accompany Margaret home. They had gone first to a bookseller's in Charing Cross Road; with the excuse that he needed a new English dictionary, he had persuaded her to help him select one. That evening she had shyly consented to go with him to the Palace Theatre in Cambridge Circus, where they saw Dan Leno and a bioscope. Von Dorn called upon her twice more before her employment took her to Dover; each time there had been the baffling reserve that he never managed to break through.

But three weeks later, when he met her train at Victoria, that reserve had vanished. He was inclined to attribute it to the fact that they had not seen one another for some time, but later that evening she casually mentioned a letter she had had from Finnigan in which he mentioned that Eric Schneider could be depended upon to support the Cause. Which Cause needed no further definition, and he knew he had been accepted.

That weekend had been a surprising time for both of them. He was keeping rooms then in Berkeley Square, and Margaret was staying in London with friends, two very modern working girls as she described them. That first evening they had gone to a new musical at the Palladium and to a late supper at which they had both drunk quite a bit of champagne. She had evidently gone to great pains for him. Her clothing was inexpensive but stylish enough—so long as he himself kept to plain suits and avoided formal evening dress. In the taxi returning her to her friend's flat, she had whispered a proposition that had left him speechless for a moment, so out of keeping with her character was it.

She had taken his momentary silence for a rejection, and he felt her body stiffen before she moved away from him. In the dim light of the interior, he could see her furious expression and he knew that to say anything to her at that moment would be disastrous. He rapped on the window and told the chauffeur to take them instead to number 14 Berkeley Square.

His rooms had a private entrance and, in any event, the landlord did not live on the premises. He led the way in and turned on a single electric lamp, glad that he had given Schram the evening off. Margaret turned slowly in the middle of the living room, noting the heavy masculine furnishings.

"It is very nice, Eric." It was her first remark since he had changed their destination. She removed her coat, draped it across the couch, and walked into the bed-sitter. Bemused, he followed this thin, crisp girl to find her unbuttoning her dress. She might have been thin and rather plain, but there was an essence of sexuality about her now that came as a considerable surprise. No coy posturing to make the most of her attributes as he was used to with other women, and he caught his breath when she unpinned her magnificent hair and let it cascade down her back in one rippling mass. She turned as if it were the most natural thing in the world for her to undress for him and removed his clothing. She had taken the initiative, and in his bemused condition he picked her up and placed her on the bed. Leaning over her, he moved a hand from shoulder to thigh, lingering a moment in the mass of reddish curls, but she grabbed his arm and pulled him down on top of her.

"I am not a virgin," she whispered fiercely. "Make love to me now." It was a command and not a request.

Margaret Doyle continued to astonish him that night. She was an accomplished lover and, taken off guard as he was, he went so far as to question her obliquely as to how she had gained such experience, but she gently turned aside the questions. It wasn't until some weeks later that Finnigan told him she was a widow. Her husband, a member of an Irish literary association in Belfast, had been lynched by a pack of drunken Protestant Unionists one night. Many things had become clear to him then; her sexual hunger, her deep and abiding hatred of the English, and her disgust at moderates such as the Irish Nationalist Party and their parliamentary stooges—as she termed them.

Finnigan's assessment of her character and capabilities had been more than correct. Before the month was out she had proven her worth with a diversified sampling of confidential reports made by her employer, the engineering director, to the Board of Directors which confirmed in his own mind the very shaky economic and engineering foundations upon which the Tunnel was being constructed. The information provided greater insight into the project than had any produced by his regular Dover agent. And beyond her utility as an espionage agent was the abandoned sexuality that had enthralled him in the beginning. After that first night, he had carried through with a plan long under consideration and rented the flat in Sedley Place in her name, both to maintain his cover as a German businessman and for the privacy it afforded on their occasional weekends together in London. But von Dorn soon discovered that her aggressive affection began to cloy until making love to her had become a chore that *must* be performed if he was to maintain his hold over her.

During that first surprising weekend together, von Dorn had also found out that he had met his match when it came to extracting intelligence. Every item of information was given on a quid-pro-quo basis, and he once joked that she had managed to obtain more rifles and ammunition than any other Irishman in the history of the clandestine Gaelic/German alliance.

She had not thought it funny at all and had delivered a

lecture, accompanied with appropriate histrionics, an oppression in Ireland until he had grown impatient and tried to take her in his arms. She had pushed him away, taken her coat, and left. From that incident he had learned that she neither liked to be made the butt of jokes nor considered the Fenian cause as anything but a deadly serious matter.

Von Dorn sat up abruptly and stubbed the cigarette out in the dish that served as an ashtray. He glanced around the dingy bedroom with distaste. The cheap saucer for an ashtray— it was symptomatic of the tastelessness of the flat, the woman, and, by inference, that part of the job he was required to do. His need to associate with the fringe elements of Irish politics, the fools, informers, murderers, the trash of Irish society, was more than he could bear at times. There was no denying that they could be useful, but the contrast between the arrogant, derby-hatted Fenians and the disciplined troops he had once commanded could be measured in the light-years that astronomers talked about lately.

Time was growing short. He swung his feet to the floor and took a robe from the cupboard. From past experience, he knew that she would sleep for several hours yet. He put the kettle on the ring to boil, opened the large envelope that lay on the table, and glanced quickly through the documents, each marked "Most Secret." When the water boiled, von Dorn made a strong cup of tea and settled down to read with the intense concentration that had been drummed into him as a cadet.

The first report was a final assessment of the damage caused two weeks before by the fire in Ventilator Shaft Six. The second and third were revised budget and engineering estimates and the fourth report contained minutes of the latest Board of Directors' meeting.

Von Dorn stopped only once in his reading, to switch on the electric lamp. When he finished, he lit a cigarette and stared thoughtfully at the documents spread before him.

On Tuesday he had received a coded message from General von Epping in Berlin urging another incident. He would have found an excuse to put von Epping off if it hadn't been for the inclusion of the Kaiser's personal cipher at the end of the message. The fire in the ventilator shaft had neither done as much damage nor caused as great a delay as he had hoped. It was clear that something on a much larger scale was needed.

The second document interested him, and he picked it up and flipped idly through the pages. He had had no clear idea before this just how much money was involved in the Tunnel project, although the sums he had guessed were immense. The latest estimates contained in the document called for excavation to be completed during the winter of 1912, and all supporting construction work to be finished in early 1913. The first trains were tentatively scheduled to cross beneath the Channel that summer, if everything went according to the engineering manager's revised schedule. With the facts now before him, the cost *was* staggering—an estimated expenditure of £300,475,675 remained between now and mid-1913, bringing the total expenditure to £575,435,235. He whistled softly as he estimated that the same money would purchase 115 new dreadnoughts, enough to equip every navy that mattered in the world. Astounding, that one country—no, two, he corrected himself, even though it was clear enough that France was the junior partner in every respect—could supply such capital reserves and from private sources as well.

An expenditure of £1,200 for the fabrication of steel cases caught his eye as he skimmed through the financial breakdown once more. The sum was for the procurement and installation of explosive mines. He checked the reference number and turned to that section. Yes, there it was. A brief discussion of where the explosive mines would be placed to seal the Tunnel if an invasion should threaten. It was common knowledge that such steps were being taken, but the details were carefully guarded. Reading through the section once more, von Dorn noted that someone had penciled in the number sixty-four. No other reference was given. On a hunch, he opened the engineering estimates document to page 64. There was a map showing a cross-section of the Tunnel between Miles Two and Four. Broad arrows—the army proof mark—pointed to a section between Miles 3.2 and 3.7. These were, he guessed, the locations of the explosive charges or mines referred to in the budget estimates. But why so far into the Tunnel proper? It did not make sense, he thought. The intent was to collapse the Tunnel to block an invading force's progress. But that would also flood the Tunnel. . . . He snapped his fingers and turned back to the map of the English Channel area fastened to the cover. Of course! At that point, the Tunnel was six fathoms beneath the English Channel. The

Tunnel sloped downward at a gentle two-degree incline which made it—he performed the calculations rapidly in his head— at least 105 feet below the Channel seabed. That was it then. The Tunnel roof could be collapsed to block passage, but there would be more than sufficient chalk strata above to prevent flooding. Ingenious! The shaft could easily be cleared after the danger had passed, but a half-mile of collapsed Tunnel would be an impenetrable barrier to the kind of raiding force required to capture the English entrance.

Turning back, he reread the passage in the engineering report dealing with the mines. The charges were placed in specially prepared shafts, five at each of the four locations drilled into the chalk walls to a depth of fifteen feet. A total of four thousand pounds of explosive in specially prepared steel cases, all wired for electrical ignition, were to be used. Probably blasting gelatin, he thought. Although the type of explosive was not specifically mentioned, no other would make sense.

Three sets of explosives had already been placed; the fourth set was due on November 21, the day after tomorrow. The engineering estimates only briefly discussed the effect of the explosives, but it was sufficient for von Dorn. Estimates of time, manpower, and money to clear the rubble were also given; four days, twelve-man crews round the clock, and £175,000 for a single set of charges; for the blockage produced by the ignition of all four sites together, six months, twelve-man crews round the clock, and £675,000. The government had undertaken to reimburse the company for the cost of any clearance operations and the rebuilding of the damaged sections. Ah, they had made certain of that, he thought. Such patriotism.

Von Dorn lit another cigarette and tossed the report aside. As he stared through the curling smoke, he began to see how he might satisfy von Epping while protecting himself from Langenscheidt's wrath. The immediate problem lay in the fact that he would be required to make use of the Fenian network he was building to support the German agents infiltrating into Great Britain. He was not yet certain that the Fenians could be trusted to carry out orders, but as he pondered the idea it seemed simple enough. If it did fail, he would lose only a few minor cogs.

Von Dorn had spent hours analyzing past intelligence operations and had isolated as a major cause of failure agents who betrayed the network through carelessness or stupidity. He had, he was confident, eliminated these two factors by making certain that his agents operated in isolation, thus forcing them to report to him through a dummy—in this case, the nonexistent Eric Schneider.

Tom Finnigan served as his liaison with the Fenian high command in Dublin and Liverpool and with the highly placed agent in Dover. He himself had met the agent once before, unavoidably, and much preferred to have Finnigan handle him, even though he was certain that the two of them were in direct communication at times, in defiance of his strict orders. While not yet a serious breach of security, it could quickly become so, and, in addition, it did provide them with an opportunity to second guess him, and that he could not tolerate.

But by using Margaret as an additional dummy to deal with the Dover agent, he had isolated them once more and improved his security. Neither the Dover agent nor Margaret was aware of the specific identity of the other as all communication between them was by blind letter drop, a technique that Finnigan could not have used as he had recruited the agent and therefore knew his identity. Von Dorn could, however, serve notice on the Dover agent by the simple expedient of having Margaret deliver his new set of instructions as well as the list of Fenians approved for use by Berlin. Both he and Finnigan would quickly see that he was aware of their disobedience. Von Dorn stubbed out the cigarette. As far as he could see, the risks were minimal and the benefits manifold.

The next hour was spent in working through the series of equations estimating the amount of blasting gelatin required to achieve the desired effect, after which he double-checked to make certain that they were correct. Von Dorn then copied the results and instructions in block capitals. They took up twelve sheets of paper to which he added a thirteenth, listing the approved Fenians.

Margaret's flat had been selected because it contained, in addition to a sitting room and bedroom, a large lavatory with its own geyser, water closet, and bath, and a large series of cupboards. It had taken him long hours to do so, but he had installed in the lavatory a complete photographic darkroom that could be hidden when not in use.

He went into the lavatory now, bolted the door, and draped

heavy curtains over the single window. Within five minutes he had converted it to a darkroom by removing the cupboard doors and laying them across the bath, installing the safelight bulbs, and bolting the large copy camera to the wall. He filled trays with photographic solutions and, working swiftly, placed the first sheet of paper beneath the camera lens. He stepped onto a small ladder and pulled the slide from the ground-glass viewing plate. He racked the lens up until the block lettering was in sharp focus and inserted a film holder. Next, he arranged two powerful gooseneck lamps to illuminate the paper and exposed one piece of film, flipped the holder over, and exposed the second. It took him twenty minutes to develop, fix, and dry the negative sufficiently to press it between two pieces of glass, working the remaining water bubbles out toward the edges, and insert it beneath the lens of the camera. The reversed image thrown onto a blank sheet of paper was satisfactory, and he proceeded to photograph each of the remaining twelve sheets in the same manner. During the next two hours, he repeated the process four more times until the final set of negatives were each less than a millimeter wide.

The film he used was an especially fine-grain silver halide, gelatin-base negative developed in Germany by Agfa. Due to its fine grain, the film required long exposures at small f stops, the last being five minutes at $f.64$. He changed the lamp globes, and when the final negatives were washed he carefully cut each away from the surrounding waste and, with a bulb syringe, dried them thoroughly. Placing each under a microscope, he angled the reflecting mirror to obtain an even field of light and focused the lens. The images were blurry but readable.

Satisfied, he emptied the chemicals, cleaned and stored everything away. The intermediate negatives would be burned in the grate. He unlocked the lavatory door and went into the other room, carrying the microscope slides and a pair of tweezers.

Margaret had already awakened and prepared a meal. She brought a hot plate to the table. "I had two very nice chops from the butcher yesterday morning."

He felt a twinge of annoyance at her domesticity, but suppressed it and sat down to attack the overdone meat swimming in thick, greasy gravy. What little cooking skills Margaret possessed she had from her mother and, like all cooking that emanated from these benighted Isles, he thought, the results were always fried or grilled meats cooked to unpalatable lumps, surrounded by vegetables boiled into an unrecognizable mess.

She poured ale into a glass, sat down as he helped himself to the potatoes and the broiled tomato, and watched him eat, occasionally taking small sips of his ale. While he ate, he questioned her about other matters relating to the Tunnel and the report to the directors regarding the damage caused by the fire. Margaret's remarks, based on what she had overheard plus what she was able to infer from her employer's comments, had often shed unexpected light on obscure details.

She answered each of his questions, chin cupped in one hand. Her robe had fallen open and for a moment he felt a curious sense of distaste for her . . . or for himself?

As he finished both the food and his questions, she took one of his cigarettes, lit it, blew a thin stream of smoke toward the ceiling, and said with disconcerting directness, "Eric, we must talk. Can you come again next Sunday if I travel up from Dover?"

Fortunately, she caught him with a last mouthful of food, and chewing and swallowing allowed him time to think. He knew that tone of voice and all that it implied, for this was not the first time the subject had been broached by a woman.

"Of course, darling. If it is possible to get away from the office . . ."

Margaret stood up, gathering the robe about her spare body, and stubbed out the cigarette with quick, nervous gestures. "Eric, please don't evade."

Von Dorn wiped his mouth with the napkin and reached for her, drawing her down on his lap. Separating the robe, he buried his face against her breasts, tickling with his tongue. She giggled and pushed his head back. "Don't . . ." she whispered.

He pulled the robe down, pinning her arms at her sides, and teased with his tongue until she strained against him, gasping for breath. "Please . . ." she sobbed, breath coming in gasps, "now . . ."

It was shortly after midnight when von Dorn laid the last tiny square of negative over a period mark and fastened it down with water glass on the typewritten note he had prepared beforehand on the letterhead of a genuine Belgian company, headquartered in Liège. He had misjudged the length of the message, however, and the final negative containing the names of the approved Fenians had to be placed in the alternate position beneath the stamp. Muttering over his carelessness, but knowing there was no time to wait while the note was retyped, he added the appropriate code mark to the envelope to alert the Dover agent and studied the letter a final time until he was satisfied that only the most careful search with a strong glass would reveal the tiny pieces of negative.

He folded the sheet and slipped it into the envelope with its canceled stamp—one that he had mailed to himself from Ostende—then got his coat and went into the bedroom. He turned up the lamp and shook Margaret awake. She muttered in her sleep and half turned. Her eyes were puffy and rimmed as if bruised. He evaded her arms gently and shook her again to make certain that she was awake.

"I will leave the envelope on the sideboard. Do not forget to take it with you. Schedule it through the office mail but leave it at the drop point as you have done before. Do you understand?"

She tried to take his arm but he pulled away. "Not again, darling," he apologized. "I must be at the office early. I have much to do tomorrow."

Margaret nodded and sat up in bed, drawing the covers to her chin. She regarded him for a long moment. "We *must* talk, Eric. We must talk and soon. When?"

He shrugged. "Margaret, I have already told you. If it is possible for me to leave the office on Sunday . . ."

"Next weekend, Eric," she said, her voice flat and hard. "I must come up to London to make arrangements for a meeting Mr. Bannerman is attending."

Her voice and the stubborn set of her face warned him, and he nodded soberly. "Of course, darling. Of course. Now lie back and sleep. You have an early train in the morning." He tucked the covers around her. *"Du schläfst, liebchen,"* he said quietly, knowing that she hated to be spoken to in German, and shut off the light.

Von Dorn turned onto Oxford Street. His hotel was Durrant's in Manchester Square and, finding no taxis or hansoms, he was forced to walk. As he strode along the deserted streets, he tried to ease his anger at Margaret's annoying behavior. You could never, he thought with irritation, maintain an intimate physical relationship for long with a woman without awakening her emotional and domestic instincts. Yet he could not even consider ridding himself of her just when it appeared that her usefulness to him was about to become invaluable. Somehow he would have to find a way through this conflicting maze of loyalties and dangers that she was creating, in addition to those already emanating from Berlin. And that meant that he would have to guard his temper most carefully. That report to the Board of Directors had been a stroke of luck, more than he had ever expected to obtain from her. The woman had proved her worth in that single instance alone, no matter what other nonsense and annoyance he must endure. The operation he had developed that afternoon would add sufficient damage to what he had already accomplished to cause dangerous delay to the entire project. Not a two- or three-week delay but one of at least three months this time. The delays and costs would mount and soon—he smiled—the project might be abandoned altogether as untenable. And for now, he could hold both von Epping and Langenscheidt at bay. The results, with a little luck, would be attributed to an accident caused by the project's own explosives.

Soon he was whistling in spite of the rain that had begun again.

chapter———6

NOVEMBER 23, 1911. THURSDAY

Heavy pounding woke Bannerman and he sat up, disori-
ented. It had not been a dream after all. He fumbled to light
the bedside lamp, then stumbled from the bedroom to the
door and threw it open. The landlord was in the act of
inserting a passkey and, behind him, Bannerman recognized a
chauffeur from the works, wrapped in a wet greatcoat.

"Mr. Bannerman!" The landlord was startled. "We were
not able to rouse you. I thought it best to use the passkey. . . ." He fluttered his hands and Bannerman tried to
calm him.

"All right, Mr. Olden, no harm. I was sleeping soundly.
What's the trouble?"

The chauffeur shouldered past the landlord and nodded
toward the open door. "Best we speak of this in private,
sor."

Because he was still befuddled with sleep, it took a moment for the man's words to sink in. "Ah . . . yes, come in,
by all means." He motioned the driver inside. "Thank you,
Mr. Olden, for your trouble. Sorry to have had you disturbed," he finished, shutting the door on the puzzled little
man.

"Now, what is it?" he demanded. "In fact, what the hell
time is it?" Bannerman went into the bedroom for a robe.

"I don't know the time, sor, don't own a timepiece. You
have to come right away, sor. Trouble at the Tunnel."

Bannerman reappeared, half into his robe. "Trouble? What
kind of trouble, man! Out with it! Why didn't they telephone?"

"I don't rightly know, sor," the chauffeur answered, his
voice as stolid as his manner. "Was only told to fetch you
and be quick about it as the telephone wires are down. Have a
motor waiting in the street, sor."

Bannerman ducked back into the bedroom and began to

69

dress. "Certainly you heard something . . . ah . . . ah . . . I'm sorry, I don't remember your name."

"Be surprised if ye did, guvnor. Name's Meakin. Jack Meakin. Only talk I heard was 'bout explosion. Nothing more. Only told to fetch you as soon as I could."

Bannerman dragged on his boots and rummaged in the cupboard for his mackintosh. Explosion, for God's sake? He clamped down firmly on his imagination. No sense in becoming excited until he knew if there was a reason for doing so—but why would they send a motor?

He found the coat. "Let's go," he snapped and headed for the door.

The long drive to the works was a nightmare of gale force winds and rain. The motor car was thrown violently about on the slick, metal-railed road, and rain found its way in at every crack in the curtains. The spell of fine weather had ended the previous Sunday, and since then the winter gales had come in earnest. The rain reduced their progress to a crawl; the long hill past the Castle was nearly impassable and twice Bannerman was certain that they would be forced to turn back. But Meakin's skillful handling got them to the top at last and they settled onto the Deal Road. Here on the cliffs tops the wind, sweeping round in a great anticyclonic arc, drove at them with the bone-chilling cold it had brought down from the Arctic. Rain lashed them in solid sheets and the headlamps were all but useless. When finally they topped the last rise, the lights of the works yard were a welcome sight after the howling black desert of rain and wind.

Meakin negotiated the flooded sections, but a hundred yards short of the gate the roadbed had given way under the rain's violent onslaught and subsided into a jagged crater. The heavy Benz motor car sank to the tops of its wheels. Cursing, both men clambered out and Bannerman, leaving Meakin behind to see to the vehicle, trudged on toward the gate. A stand of trees that had escaped the road improvements of the previous year were thrashing about like damned souls. Violent gusts slashed across the high wall of the valley and, even at this distance, Bannerman could hear the harsh booming of the surf on the shingle beach. With the wind behind, he was pushed along, dancing in an effort to keep his feet on the ground. He caught hold of the wire fence and felt his way along to the gate, where he had to pound for several minutes before he was heard above the storm.

The gatekeeper helped him inside where he stood streaming water beside the coal stove while he tried to phone through for another motor car. The connection had just been made when the line went dead. Cursing at the top of his lungs, Bannerman went back out into the rain and struggled on through the flooded yard toward the engineering office. It took him fifteen minutes to negotiate the half-mile, and he was soaked through to the skin by the time he pushed the door open and stumbled inside.

A group of mackintosh-clad men clustered around the table looked up in surprise. McDougal hurried forward and literally dragged Bannerman to the fire, shouting for someone to find dry clothes.

"I'll be damned," he roared as he pulled the dripping coat off. "It's glad I am to see you. We thought the gale put paid to your traveling up tonight."

While Bannerman stripped off the rest of his sodden clothing and dried himself with the rough towel, McDougal described what little they knew so far.

"At four this morning a report came through from the airlock. Some kind of trouble, but the line went dead before the details could be gotten. Arden, the duty engineer, sent a man to find the break. He rang through from Mile Two safety station to report an engine driver had brought his shunting engine out after hearing a loud bang inside the airlock. He also picked up a maintenance crew from Ventilator Shaft Six. The telephone to the airlock was not working and all other phones was dead for four miles. The maintenance crew reported having heard a rumble ten minutes before, the same time as the engine driver heard the explosion.

"Arden's man . . . his name is Brian Donnelson . . . sent the maintenance gang on and took the shunting engine all the way back to the airlock. There was no answer from inside, even when he beat on the door with a pipe. So then he went and came back up to the first working phones at Mile Three." McDougal paused dramatically and Bannerman swore at him.

"Damnit, Sean, what the hell did he find?"

"The bulkhead . . . it was chilled, James." McDougal laid a rough hand on his shoulder. "The metal was sweating."

Bannerman closed his eyes. The chilled and sweating metal

could only mean seawater flooding into the lock, water at 36° F cooling the airlock and causing moisture to condense on the outside walls.

"How high up did he feel the cold . . .?"

"Just above his head, not more than six and a half feet above the floor."

Good Christ! he thought. Where in hell was that much water coming from? The pressure must be immense.

The airlock served to pass men and equipment into and out of the Tunnel heading, where the air pressure was maintained at a steady 22 pounds per square inch to act as a barrier against water seepage that could weaken the walls. But water bursting in through a breech would be under thousands of pounds of pressure and as the water level in the heading mounted, if the inner airlock door was blocked open, it would squeeze the air inside the lock until it blew out joints and seams. To prevent this, air vents had been installed to release trapped air as the pressure neared the critical point.

"He could hear the vents operating," McDougal answered Bannerman's unasked question.

"And there was no answer at all from inside the lock?"

McDougal shook his head.

"Where is Donnelson now?" he demanded.

"Still in the Tunnel with the engine driver, James. I sent them back down to check on the airlock again. They took an emergency telephone set with them and mounted a roll of wire on one of the wagons."

Bannerman was hardly listening now, running over again in his mind the latest geological findings. The afternoon pilot-bore report had found no faults or seepage. Accordingly, he had authorized the excavation to continue. He thought of the compromise he had been a party to at the Board meeting ten days ago. He had, of course, no way of knowing yet that a blowout really had occurred, but every sign pointed to it. Of a sudden, the lethargy induced by the fire and the dry clothes fell away and he grabbed up a dry mackintosh.

"I want a crew of volunteers ready to go in ten minutes," he snapped. "I want two divers as well. Get a second shunting engine made up and bring the divers down in that." His voice was brisk and the orders came without hesitation, a clerk noting them down as fast as he spoke.

Ten minutes later, the steel doors were rolled aside to allow the train into the Tunnel. McDougal had started to climb into a wagon and when Bannerman began to object, the big Irishman whispered fiercely, "Just try and keep me out. I'll no have you doing something foolish to get yourself killed."

Bannerman grabbed him by the arm. "Sean, I appreciate your concern. But I need you here. You're a better engineer than most of these university graduates. I'm giving you a direct order. Stay here!"

He hurried to the second wagon and swung aboard, shouting to the driver to start. He looked back and managed a wan grin as McDougal, silhouetted against the harsh arc-lit glare of the Tunnel mouth, shook his fist after him.

Bannerman made his way through the wagon crammed with workmen and supplies.

"Damnit, Jackson," he bellowed, "what do you have here, your old woman's cupboard, for God's sake?" Jackson, a solidly built young man and one of the most reliable gangers on the work force, gave him a ribald answer that lightened the tension for a moment. But only for a moment. Bannerman could feel it beginning to mount in his stomach as the train penetrated deeper into the Tunnel and he was absurdly grateful to Jackson for the joke that had distracted the men, if only for a moment. So that they would not see the fear in his own face, he climbed into the next wagon and squeezed past the packs of accumulators two electricians were wiring in series.

"What's this?" he demanded.

"Mr. McDougal's idea, sir," one of the electricians said, not looking up. "In case the power is shut off. We can hook these to the electric motor. Should have enough to take us a mile or more."

I should have thought of that, Bannerman railed at himself, aware once again of that nagging feeling of inadequacy which was affecting him more and more of late. He slid over the coaming and down into the engine driver's compartment. The man nodded to him without taking his eyes from the track ahead.

The engine's speed was reduced to fifteen miles per hour with the heavy load, and Bannerman calculated that it would require thirty minutes to reach the airlock. He took a deep breath to ease his nervousness, causing the engine driver to look around.

"Didn't get much sleep last night," he said and at once regretted it. The driver nodded sympathetically.

Bannerman breathed deeply but slowly so as not to attract any more attention as he tried to submerge the mounting fear of what he would find at the heading. It seemed to help, and he felt the knot loosen in his stomach.

They met the ascending train twenty minutes into the shaft. The two weary men leaned on the cab coaming and described conditions ahead.

"It's getting cold and damp down there, Mr. Bannerman," Donnelson said, exhaustion affecting his voice. "We banged on the airlock door with a pipe again. We thought we should come up to report. I think . . . ." He left the sentence unfinished. There had been thirty-one men inside the Tunnel heading on the first of their two-hour work sections: the six men of the excavating crew, a foreman, and the twenty-four men on the grouting gang.

"The bulkhead is a bit colder, sir, and another half foot higher," Donnelson's driver added quietly, knowing that he was pronouncing the deaths of those thirty-one men.

Bannerman nodded angrily. "Anything else?"

The two men looked at one another and both shook their heads. "No, sir," the engine driver muttered. "It's like Mr. Donnelson said. There was nothing from the other side when we banged on the bulkhead."

"All right. You two go back to the entrance and tell Mr. McDougal what you told me. Tell him also that we are continuing down to the airlock."

They watched the shunting engine move away. "Shall I start ahead, sir?" the engine driver asked after a moment.

"What? Oh yes. Go ahead. Make the best speed you can."

Donnelson had been correct. It was growing colder the closer they got to the airlock. And the air was full of dust. What could have caused this much dust? Bannerman wondered and shone a powerful torch along the walls. The lighting was normally dimmed to conserve power in the sections of the Tunnel where no active work was going on and the torch beam slipped across the brick work as if it were a spotlight. The facing was dry enough, yet the air was considerably damper and colder than it should have been.

Bannerman glanced at his pocket watch. Five minutes to go. Still the beam where he flicked it along the walls showed nothing, but the dust was much thicker now. Of a sudden, he grabbed the engine driver's arm. "Stop!" he commanded. "Reverse slowly."

The driver complied and the train inched back up the Tunnel. And there it was. Bannerman climbed out, several of the men following him, and he heard one swear softly under his breath. A long crack had appeared in the wall, spreading across nearly a dozen bricks. A stream of water trickled along the line of the break. He shook his head as if not quite believing what he saw.

The brick work was four tiers thick and laid against a foot of grouting—iron-reinforced cement. Yet here was a crack!

"Back into the wagons," Bannerman ordered abruptly. The train jerked forward and he stood on the foot plate cursing their snaillike progress. He was off the train and running as soon as the emergency telephone Donnelson had installed came in sight. Bannerman spun the crank and the line crackled. He could hear the burring of the bell on the other end before McDougal's voice came on.

"Sean," he shouted, "we've found a crack in the wall, Mile Seven point three-two-twenty. Start a grouting crew along with a high pressure pump. If there's one crack, there will be others."

McDougal sputtered for a moment. "How in the name of all that's holy . . . are ye certain?"

"No doubt but that it's a crack and through to the chalk as well. We can see water. Don't waste any time, start that crew moving."

The train drove on, the men watching the walls closely now. Bannerman drummed impatiently on the cowling. How in the name of God, he wondered, could that crack have happened? He recalled the equations simulating the force necessary to crack the Tunnel walls; a series of shocks, similar to those seen in severe earthquakes were needed to set up sufficient sheer force. But earthquakes just did not occur in Great Britain and, therefore, the Tunnel's circular cross-section had been wholly designed to resist compression rather than sheer forces.

"There, sir," the engine driver nudged him as the engine's headlamp picked out the gray mass of the airlock ahead. Its bulkhead filled the entire space of the Tunnel shaft. A spidery set of steps led up to the man lock fifteen feet above the larger material lock which was flush with the roadbed. The engine stopped well back and Bannerman climbed down. The emergency gang assembled behind him, the murmur of their voices eerie in the stillness.

"Four more cracks sir," the gang foreman, O'Conner, reported.

Bannerman nodded, still staring at the airlock, his attention caught by the circular area illuminated by the engine's headlamp where moisture glistened. "Report to Mr. McDougal," he muttered and went forward without waiting for an answer.

He forced himself up the steps to the catwalk, he put out a hand, and touched the tomb of thirty-one men. The metal surface was cold, a bone-penetrating cold that could come only from the seawater inside. The noise of the second shunting engine and its string of wagons coming to a stop behind the first drew his attention. As with his own crew, the men got out to stand beside the tracks, staring at the airlock, expressions apprehensive, suspicious, angry, or fearful, depending upon the individual.

Hating the need to do so, Bannerman picked up the sledge hammer left there by Donnelson. He set his feet and swung with all his might. The hammer rebounded, producing a deep, harsh clang. Bannerman closed his eyes for a moment. It would have rung like a bell if empty. Needing to do something, he threw the sledge hammer down and stepped to the rail. "Rig the emergency airlock," he shouted down to the bemused group. "We will use the man lock. Get moving."

An hour passed before the emergency lock was bolted together, sealed in place over the man lock, and tested. The Tunnel airlocks were essentially tubular chambers with doors at either end. The door on the far side opened into the heading, higher pressure serving to hold it securely closed.

Two carts containing bottles of compressed air had been dragged up to the emergency airlock and the hoses coupled. The gang foreman gave it a thorough check before nodding to Bannerman.

"Start it up," Bannerman ordered and the foreman began calling out the pressure readings from the gauge mounted in the steel door. Behind them the two divers were putting on their heavy, rubberized diving suits. A ganger struggled across the metal rails with two pairs of lead shoes and placed them directly before the airlock door.

Both divers were young, stockily built, and experienced ex-naval personnel. Neither was likely to panic or to make foolish mistakes, and so Bannerman kept his instructions to a minimum.

"Don't try and reach the Badger," he warned. "I want you back inside in fifteen minutes. Concentrate your efforts there. I want to know why water is leaking in. If the airlock door is jammed open, try to clear it. If you cannot, come back out. We've plenty of time now. I'll settle for an assessment of damage rather than have to send another diving party in after your bodies."

"Ready, Mr. Bannerman," the foreman called as the hiss of venting air died away. The red electric light above the door was out, indicating that the door would open into the airlock. Helpers lifted the heavy brass helmets onto the divers' shoulder plates and bolted them into place. A petrol engine racketed to life and the compressor spun up. One at a time the divers inserted canvas boots into the lead shoes which were then strapped up by the ganger. The door was opened for them and they shuffled inside. Air hoses were attached at one end to fittings on the bulkhead while the divers plugged the other end of the heavy rubber coils to matching fittings inside and safety lines to studs near the door. They closed their face plates and swung the steel door shut. A red light began to flash, signaling that the divers had opened the cocks to fill the emergency airlock. Bannerman found himself pacing back and forth before the airlock, waiting for the green light indicating that the divers had opened their inner door and were into the flooded main airlock.

"They're inside the Tunnel now, Mr. Bannerman." The foreman handed the telephone headset to Bannerman.

". . . cavern filled with water." The voice was tinny and distant, but understandable. "We are moving in, following the metals . . . sediment's very thick. Can't see much . . . like a black wall. The lights aren't much help . . . what . . . wait . . . there, we can see the brickyard. It's been scattered all along the Tunnel floor . . . the bricks are hard to walk on . . . they're all in piles and we are going to have to climb over . . . Watch it, man," one called sharply to the other, "they slide easily."

The disembodied voice continued its running commentary as Bannerman watched the pressure gauge until it stabilized at

36.9 pounds per square inch. My God, he thought as he worked the pressure calculation in his head. Better than fourteen pounds—no fifteen pounds—*higher* than the pressure maintained in the heading. They were at fourteen fathoms depth at this point in the relatively shallow waters south of the Goodwin Banks. Fourteen fathoms or eighty-four feet, multiplied by the approximate density of sea water—36, no 37 pounds per square inch, exactly the same pressure as the Channel bottom. Better than 5,000 pounds of pressure per square foot. Christ, he thought, the knowledge chilling him to the bone. The Tunnel had been breached. A massive blowout, the very thing he had feared all along. The one-in-a-million chance had happened.

He handed the earphones to the diving master and walked back to the shunting engine, where the emergency gang waited with the telephone. Of a sudden, he was unutterably weary and he stared at the headset for a long minute before he cranked the handle. When a voice answered on the other end, he asked for McDougal and gave him instructions to put a boat out with divers to locate the breech as soon as the storm abated. There was only a single grunt from the other end, and they both replaced the handsets simultaneously without a further word.

The diving master waved to him. "The men are back inside, sir."

The steady hum of the pumps began and the pressure gauge jerked downward, but it would be thirty minutes before the pressure reached normal. Thirty minutes was the minimum decompression time the diving master would allow at 37 pounds per square inch.

Time dragged and Bannerman paced, impatient for the decompression process to be completed and the second team to be sent in. He spoke once more with McDougal, who confirmed that a third gang had been sent down-Tunnel to survey the damage to the cracked walls. He also questioned the two divers still in the airlock, but they could add little more to their previous observations—they had worked halfway down the heading, stringing the hand line as they went, but the sediment was so thick that little could be seen, even in the strong beam from their electric torches.

* * *

The second team had reached the limit of the hand line at 8:30 A.M. They reported the sediment beginning to settle, an indication that the pressure had equalized inside the heading and seawater was no longer swirling in. Visibility was now some ten feet, the water temperature was 36° F, and even though they wore canvas suits over woolen underwear, wool sweaters, and pants, Bannerman could still hear their teeth chattering. The combination of brass helmets and pressure lent a peculiar high-pitched tone to their voices, and it was difficult to understand what the divers were saying. And as they tired, the men tended to speak less distinctly, words slurring together. The diving master patiently encouraged them to speak up and repeat when they could not be understood.

One of the divers reported that he could make out a dark shape ahead. A moment later, the other diver spoke, but his voice broke so badly that even he was aware of it, and he repeated the words.

"Wait now . . . there, I'm leaving the rails . . . piles of timbers and iron . . . watch out, Jack, the iron rods . . . ends are jagged . . . My God!" For a moment there was only the sound of static along the line. In the Tunnel, men began to gather around, sensing something about to happen as the diving master repeated word for word what he was hearing through the headphones.

"There, along the wall where it begins to curve to the roof . . . see it, Jack, that black . . ."

"Merciful Jesus," the other diver muttered, half to himself. "We've found the rupture."

Bannerman pressed a hand to his temple. My God! he thought.

"It's eight feet long and two to four feet wide . . . a hole in the wall. I'm shining the light in . . . it seems . . . same width as far as . . . goes."

Bannerman leaned against the cold metal of the lock bulkhead. That was it then; what he had feared the most. A rupture in the ungrouted, unreinforced wall. And it was behind the Badger, so that ruled out a fissure in the chalk cut into by the pilot drill. Good Christ, he had killed thirty-one men, murdered them because he had not been strong enough to stand his ground against the Board of Directors. The Board had overruled his decision and then called his bluff. That made him personally responsible.

". . . still a slight inflow but . . . no more than an eddy."

"Tell them to mark the spot," he rasped at the diving master. "Then get them out."

At six o'clock that evening, Bannerman was at his desk, having slept for several hours. Pumps had drained the main airlock and divers were already rigging hoses to pump grouting into the fissure in the Tunnel wall. McDougal sat across the desk from him, and they were both drinking whiskey in morose silence. McDougal tipped the last of the whiskey from the bottle, dividing it evenly between the two glasses.

"Well, James," he muttered, "it seems we have the devil to pay now."

Bannerman nodded and closed his eyes. "Right enough." He was silent a moment, then opened his eyes and stared at McDougal. "I want to see that fissure for myself. Tomorrow."

" 'Tis a daft notion, James!" McDougal stared back at him for a moment, then looked away, muttering in Gaelic to himself.

"I want to see it for myself, Sean," Bannerman repeated stubbornly. "I'd go right now, but I'm so tired I don't think I could walk across the yard."

He picked up the telephone and asked Margaret to call up his driver. "I need a good uninterrupted night's sleep," he said, replacing the phone.

Margaret came in, a sheaf of papers in her hand. "If I could have your signature on these letters before you go, Mr. Bannerman, everything else has been taken care of." Her voice was strangely cold, as if she were holding herself under tight control.

He nodded and hunched forward to thumb through the neatly typed letters, answers to various requests, many of them for speaking engagements which he routinely declined. Margaret had evolved a set of standard answers and he no longer bothered to look at them. He scribbled his signature on each one and leaned back in his chair.

"Will you be going up to London this weekend?"

"Yes, I will." Margaret's voice was sharper than usual and he glanced at her in surprise.

"Trouble with your aunt?"

"Oh, no, sir. Nothing like that at all."

Bannerman winked at McDougal. He sometimes made a game of trying to find out what Margaret did during her infrequent weekends in London, pretending not to believe she went to visit an aunt. Often Margaret played along with him, but today she appeared quite agitated. Bannerman attributed it to the excitement of the Tunnel blowout.

"Don't I have that meeting with the Board subcommittee on Monday and the parliamentary inquiry on Thursday?" Margaret nodded and he continued. "I may go up Sunday evening and stay through to the end of the week then. Sean can handle matters here. And," he said thoughtfully, "I need a few days to myself to settle certain matters. Look here," he said, sitting up abruptly. "Why not stay in London on Monday. You can accompany me to the Board meeting and take notes. I'd like to have my own record for once, just to compare with theirs."

He had often before been uncertain about the Board's official minutes, half convinced at times that someone was editing them to reflect favorably upon the directors. This was his chance to obtain an independent record or bring matters to a head if someone objected. And with the past night's disaster, it had become a matter of vital concern to him. He was all too familiar with the biblical scapegoat.

"Stay over the weekend and I'll see you at Townshend House at one o'clock, Monday afternoon. I'll arrange to have a taxi pick you up."

Margaret looked as if she were trying to decide whether or not he was having a joke at her expense. But his expression was so intense that she dismissed the notion. Standing to leave, she thought of something and turned back.

"I found this in the mail on Tuesday, Mr. Bannerman." She held out an envelope. "I thought you might like it for your collection."

Bannerman took the envelope, noting the company's postal code, and glanced at the stamp. A rather colorful but common Belgian commemorative. "Thank you, Margaret. That was very thoughtful of you."

Margaret gathered up her letters and left without another word.

"Now what the devil has gotten up to her," McDougal growled. "She's jumpy as a cat."

"Nerves," Bannerman replied absently. "Too much happening in one day."

McDougal growled a response and opened the door. "Sleep, boyo. That's what you need. A good night's sleep," and went out.

Bannerman swiveled the chair toward the window and turned off the desk lamp. He sat quietly in the darkness finishing his whiskey and watching the wind-tossed lights outside. At least the rain had stopped. Thirty-one deaths this morning, he thought. Men had died in accidents before; it was expected. But never in such wholesale lots. He had managed to establish the best safety record for any tunnel construction project of a similar magnitude—less than one man killed per five miles of tunnel, where the recent average was one man sacrificed for each mile. Now, of course, the project was showing the worst record, perhaps the worst in the history of modern tunneling.

Several points had raised themselves during the long night and day waiting outside the airlock and at least one of those questions he hoped to answer tomorrow. He saw the envelope on the desk, slipped it into his wallet, and left the office.

Bannerman wriggled his arms into the canvas sleeves, hunched his back, and shrugged the suit onto his shoulders. The brass shoulder piece was surprisingly heavy and he was content to lean back and let the line tender fasten the suit together. He could see the airlock door past the bobbing heads and as he watched, the red light went off. The door opened and a thin stream of water ran out as two divers emerged, stooped and shuffling like old men.

Bannerman was helped to his feet and the line tender reached for the brass helmet. He was to be accompanied by one of the two divers who had gone in first the night before. As they approached the airlock, his diving partner stopped him and bent his helmet close so that he could speak directly into Bannerman's open face plate.

"Mr. Bannerman, I've something to say." He swallowed and his face worked in embarrassment.

"Out with it."

"You are my boss. I've no doubt o' that. But once inside that airlock, you aren't no more." He paused, trying to find the right words. "You must do as I say, when I say. In there, I'm boss, do you . . .?"

Bannerman nodded. "Aye," he said, unconsciously dropping into the man's Welsh vernacular. "You've no need ta fear. I understand."

The man nodded, his face scarlet, and turned away, motioning impatiently for the ganger.

The sleep Bannerman needed so badly had eluded him most of the night and he felt nearly as exhausted now as when he'd left the yard the evening before. It was hot and close inside the heavy suit and even without the lead-weighted belt and shoes, the stiff folds of rubberized canvas made it difficult to move. The suit chaffed between his legs and under his armpits, and he grew impatient at the delay. The ganger made a few adjustments to the hose connections at the back of the helmet and the unexpected pressure caused his knees to buckle. The ganger felt the movement. "Are ye all right, sir?" he asked anxiously.

Bannerman waved a hand, not trusting himself to speak. His breath was coming damp and hollow inside the helmet and his eyes roved its interior, seeing without seeing the brass fittings, the vents for the airhoses, the small box of the telephone mouthpiece, the scratches and dents of years of use. The odor was rubber and metallic brass and sweat and something else—almost intangible, but nevertheless present—*fear*. The smell of fear was as much a part of the suit as the odor of mud and decay and salt. Bannerman was afraid, more afraid than he had ever been in his life, and though his eyes were bright and his head nodded as the diving master spoke to him, he heard nothing the man said, so preoccupied was he with his own fear. He felt the vomit rising and fought it down by sheer willpower. The world had receded to the tiny space inside the helmet and the jolt as the face piece swung shut and was latched into place staggered him but did not break through the blanket of fear that was smothering his minuscule world. He knew that the fear was as much for what he might find as for the physical danger that waited beyond the airlock door.

". . . ready, Mr. Bannerman?" The patience in the diving master's voice told him that the question must have been repeated at least once.

"Yes," he croaked and arms helped him to the airlock, guiding his feet in the lead shoes, then across the threshold into the interior of the emergency airlock. He turned to see McDougal give him the "thumbs-up" sign as the door was swung shut with a hollow boom that echoed inside his helmet. A moment later, water gushed across the floor. He stared, fascinated at the way it eddied and crested as it rose past the tops of the lead shoes, working its way up the canvas legs. The sound of air hissing into the helmet increased in pitch, and he felt the heavy, cold canvas folds begin to move with a life of their own and shuddered.

He had been down in diving suits before—no expert, but certainly not a novice either. In Panama, he had gone down to the footings of the Gatun locks; in South Africa, into a flooded mine; in New Jersey, to the river bottom; and in the Channel, to see for himself the nature of the sea floor. Then why was he so frightened now? But he knew the answer to his own question: because of the bodies of thirty-one men beyond that door. It was not a question of superstition, he knew—the men were dead and could do nothing to harm him. He had seen to that. His cowardly acquiescence to the Board in something he had clearly known was wrong was about to be verified. Just in time he stopped himself from ordering them both out. The urge to run was strong, to run and run and never stop running, to leave the Tunnel behind, the dead men and his own cowardice.

"Mr. Bannerman!" The diver's voice . . . what was his name . . . Thompson . . . yes, that was it . . . a Cardiff man. With a conscious effort Bannerman dragged his mind back, grasping at anything that offered a hold. He had to get himself under control.

"Mr. Bannerman, can you hear me?" The brogue was thick in his ears and he became aware that the water had risen to his waist and the pressure against his eardrums was intensifying. He swallowed and shook his head, trying to relieve the pain.

"Yes . . . I can hear you."

"Are you all right?" Thompson moved closer to stare at the air pressure dial on Bannerman's chest. He tapped the gauge with a gloved finger and appeared satisfied.

"Yes. My ears were plugged a bit. They're clearing now."

The cold was fierce, much worse than he had expected. His feet and legs, his body from the chest down, were tingling in spite of the heavy woolen clothes he had pulled on over his own. The level of water slipped past the face plate and he started, then controlled himself, fearful that he might have shouted, but all he could hear was the sound of his own breathing.

"The chamber is full," came the disembodied voice of the diving master. "You may open the inner door."

Thompson acknowledged the information and, leaning forward against the water's resistance, slipped the catch and shoved the door open. Bannerman felt the gorge rising in his throat again as Thompson disappeared. He swore at himself then and tightened his diaphragm muscles to control the gag reflex. After a moment, he was able to force the fear down, realizing that it was better to move than to stand rooted on the spot, allowing the terror to play havoc with him.

Thompson led as they half-shuffled, half-floated through the entrance into the main airlock and on into the black confines of the Tunnel. The dragging weight of the suit and lead belt had disappeared, but even so, within a few steps, he was breathing hard, fighting for every move against the water's resistance. The light beams, harsh and glaring where they sprang from the electric torches, were quickly absorbed by the sediment-filled water. But instead of the pitch blackness that Bannerman had expected, they faced a gray wall that was almost but not quite black. The effect was eerie beyond belief; total darkness would have been easier to face. At times the grayness was opalescent, and it was a moment before Bannerman understood. The sediment was composed of chalk dust reflecting in the torch light so that each particle moved in a faint halo, almost beyond the limits of the eye to discern.

He groped for and found the safety line with his right hand and felt ahead with his left for Thompson's suit. His arm seemed to drift with a will of its own and his gloved fingers brushed the brass shoulder piece on the other man's suit.

"I'm starting forward, Mr. Bannerman. Keep me in sight. Keep yer hand on me shoulder if it makes it easier."

And Bannerman did, realizing that Thompson was feeling some of his own fear as they moved into the not-quite-blackness, feet shuffling across the wooden ballasts, kicking occasionally against the metal rails.

The thought of the bodies returned to him abruptly. Where were they? Two had been brought out yesterday, found in the airlock where they had drowned when the door to the heading was blocked by rubble. There were twenty-nine more bodies somewhere inside, but where. He started to turn his light upward and thought better of it, afraid that he might see a body jammed against the Tunnel's ceiling, buoyed by the gases within the corpse.

The mutter of voices over his headset was a grateful interruption and he tried to concentrate on the conversation between Thompson and the diving master as Thompson continued the safety practice of describing every move they made. Every step, every pile of rubble, every obstruction, every feature was noted as they made their slow way into the heading. If anything happened to them, the divers who followed would know what to avoid . . . and where to find their bodies.

It took six minutes to reach the limit of the hand line where it had been tied off to a protruding reinforcing rod. Thompson flashed his torch against the wall and Bannerman added his own to it.

And there it was: a black hole at the one o'clock position, angling upward toward the surface of the seabed. Bannerman moved forward, fears forgotten as he studied the regular shape of the hole, feeling a slight eddy. The rim of the hole fascinated him. The edges were smooth, more so than he would have expected. He probed into the interior with his torch but the darkness stifled it within a few feet. He shone his light down to the base of the wall. There were no piles of jagged brick and concrete, only a slurry of chalky mud covering the Tunnel floor, half hiding the metal rails. But the opposite wall was another matter. Huge gouts of brick and concrete had been torn away, exposing the tangled remains of the network of iron reinforcing rods—testimony to the immense power of the water blasting into the heading. The chalk beyond the rods had been carved into an immense disk twenty feet in diameter and five feet deep as near as he could judge in the feeble light.

Bannerman backed away and stood pondering a moment. "Thompson," he said slowly, "I want to examine the blowout hole."

The diving master broke in before Thompson could answer. "You have ten minutes left, Mr. Bannerman. Time to start back."

"Mr. Thompson is in charge here," Bannerman snapped. "He'll make the decision."

"Mr. Bannerman, there—"

"Look at the hole, Thompson." Bannerman overrode the diving master's voice and swung his light back to the wall. "Notice how regular it is, almost as if a plug were blown out."

Obediently, Thompson turned his light to match Bannerman's. "Yes . . . but . . . ."

"I've never seen a blowout carve such a neat hole, Thompson. Have you? And where is the rubble that should be covering the Tunnel floor? All we have is a fine slurry."

A new voice broke in. "James! This is Sean. You're to do what the diving master says. You have only time enough now to get back to the lock."

Bannerman ignored McDougal. "Well, Thompson?" he demanded. He swung his torch further into the heading as if searching for the Badger. But it was nearly a hundred feet farther on, far beyond the reach of their life lines. And Bannerman was profoundly grateful that it was. The blowout would have cut the men off from the airlock. Water blasting into the Tunnel had probably formed an impenetrable barrier. He shivered again and this time he knew it was not due to the cold. They would have sought refuge in the upper levels of the huge excavator as the water inexorably rose to fill the heading, compressing the air trapped above the water level to unbelievable density. The bodies would not be very pretty when found.

"Five minutes, then, no more," Thompson muttered, not quite understanding what Bannerman wanted, yet realizing he would not have asked if it was not important. Thompson unclipped the safety line from his belt, fastened the shackle to an iron rod, and shuffled toward the wall, leaning against the water's resistance until he was almost horizontal. Bannerman followed, kicking through the muck which rose in an opaque fog about them. Sweat ran down his face and neck in spite of the cold. He longed to brush a hand across his forehead, to wipe it away from his eyes where it was burning, causing them to tear and making it even more difficult to see. And, ridiculously enough, he wanted a cigarette badly. The earphones crackled with static, indicating an open line. Thompson, sensing the intensity of Bannerman's concentration, had forgotten to provide a running commentary until a sharp command from the diving master snapped him back to reality.

His voice broke as he began and he coughed and cleared his throat and began again. "We've left the mess of reinforcing rod behind . . . no more bricks . . . the sediment is thick here . . . move slowly or you kick up a dense cloud . . . seems to have settled . . . can't see the Badger . . . wall directly before us." Thompson watched Bannerman as he moved past and leaned back to study the black hole some fifteen feet above. Grunting, Bannerman closed the exhaust valve on his suit and fumbled with the clasp of his weight belt until it came loose. He handed it to Thompson, who had moved up behind to steady him as the buoyancy of his suit increased and he was lifted upward. Bannerman placed a hand against the wall and Thompson let his own gloved hands slide over the smooth canvas suit until he was hanging onto Bannerman's legs. Bannerman reached for a handhold near the hole but the lip had been worn smooth by the pressure of inrushing water. He had to reach up and brace his hands against the top of the break to stop his progress.

The pressure on his eardrums was becoming painful and he swallowed several times, then ducked his head down inside the helmet to peer at the hole. The slight inflow of water, combined with his instability, caused him to drift back and he caught only a brief glimpse. But it was enough.

It was becoming difficult to bend his elbows; a few minutes more and his suit would be rigid. The diving master was demanding to know what was happening. Struggling against the inflated canvas, he managed to open the relief valve and air bubbles flashed around him as the pressure decreased.

A gabble of voices, magnified by the pressure on his eardrums, roared at him from the headset as Thompson explained what was happening. He felt the silt-covered floor under his lead shoes and waved his arms for balance. Thompson draped the weight belt around his waist and he was stable again. As soon as he had buckled it on, Thompson pointed back down the Tunnel, his arm extending into the torch beam like some gaunt tree branch.

"Yes," Bannerman muttered, and at the sound of his voice they fell silent on the other end.

"James, what the hell is going on . . ."

"Sean, I'll tell you when we return to the office!"

McDougal spluttered a moment, then, understanding the tautness in Bannerman's voice, fell silent.

A pile of rubble forced them to go carefully, lights probing the way, and suddenly Bannerman was weary beyond belief. The cold, the exertion, the tension, and his fear were combining to take a fearful toll. He staggered once and almost lost his footing. They were almost at the entrance to the airlock and Bannerman found that it was more effort than he could manage just to cover the remaining distance.

"Only a few more feet, Mr. Bannerman," he heard Thompson say. Ahead was a twisted mass of iron reinforcing rod and jumbled brick. Part of a cast-iron ring support was balanced precariously atop the pile and Bannerman saw it happen as if in slow motion. Thompson, half turning to steady him, stumbled and brushed against an end of the ring support, knocking loose the rubble beneath, and before Bannerman could move, the pile was tumbling onto him. Thompson, off balance already, was pushed from his feet and fell against the open airlock door. The rubble swept down so quickly that Bannerman had time to do no more than twist his airhoses aside before his feet were swept from beneath him and he was pinned face down against the Tunnel floor. His head banged hard against the microphone, dislodging it from its mounting. Dazed, he felt the rubble pressing down on him, a sensation not unlike the weight of heavy blankets. The inflated suit had acted to cushion some of the impact, but blood was running from his forehead into his eyes and he could not see.

He lay still for a moment, knowing he was trapped. The steady wheeze told him that his air lines were clear but there was no counterpoint of static from the headset, meaning that he had smashed it when he fell. Below his waist he could feel only intense cold; his right hand was held securely by a sharp edge. His left arm was free but blocked, so that he could only move it through a limited arc.

A minute passed while he fought the panic. It had happened at last; the irrational fear that had stalked him had triumphed. He was trapped in the Tunnel with the bodies of the men he had killed. The sound of a whimper came to him and it was a moment before he realized that it was his. When he did, anger burst forth and he began to curse steadily. A thud broke through the sound of his own shouting and he stopped, puzzled. It came again, and he realized that his helmet was pressed against the Tunnel floor, possibly in contact with one of the metal tracks.

He felt a movement against his leg, then a sharp jolt as if something had dropped onto it. His leg was forced down but the heavy lead shoe was caught. The pressure became unbearable and he gasped, certain that the bone would snap. Abruptly, the pressure eased and his leg was free. A moment later something clanged against his helmet. He heard Thompson's distant voice shouting to him as he pressed their helmets together.

"Are . . . all right?"

Bannerman waved his left hand, shouted, "Yes. I'm all right."

". . . trapped. Girder across you. Can't lift it. Need help . . . worry."

Then he was gone and Bannerman could hear the sounds of rubble being moved, with an occasional painful bang as objects struck the rail against which his helmet was pressed. After a while, he lost track of the time. The iron cold was robbing him of his will to resist and he began to float in and out of consciousness. In moments of awareness, he knew he was freezing to death, but even that no longer worried him.

Bannerman came awake suddenly; the suit seemed to have collapsed around him and he found he could not breathe. Silence filled the Tunnel, a silence complete even to the absence of air hissing through the helmet's intake valve. He moved his left arm and felt it respond, then his leg where Thompson had cleared some of the rubble away. He was so cold that it was a moment before he realized that his lungs hurt.

A red blur was replacing the darkness and he welcomed it. His mind was fading into the softness that precedes sleep. He was exhausted and he wanted to be done with it. He knew then that in a few moments it would be over. The Tunnel was collecting its due. There would be thirty-two sacrifices now to his stupidity, his cowardice, and it no longer seemed to matter. At peace now, he closed his eyes.

Light approached with dizzying speed and blood pounded in his head. Sound that was little more than a painful jumble of noise crashed in his ears, and Bannerman knew he was alive. For a moment he was irrationally angry; he wanted to scream and curse at those who had brought him back to life. A shadow moved across his closed eyes, and the smell of nicotine-laden breath was against his face. An eyelid was forced open and the glare exploded like a bomb inside his head.

"Jesus!" he heard clearly. "He's still alive."

Mouthing incoherent obscenities, he struggled to push away the fingers that held his eyelid open to the painful arc light.

"Lie back, laddie," McDougal's voice rumbled. "You've nearly died."

Hands tucked a blanket around him and McDougal held a hand to shield his eyes, but afterimages lingered and he could not see.

"You'll be all right now, James. The air pump had a breakdown. You've nearly suffocated . . . Christ in heaven I was that worried."

McDougal moved aside as someone stooped over him and he felt himself being lifted.

"Sean," he tried to whisper and found that his throat was so raw he could do little more than croak. "Sean . . .?"

"Wheesh, boyo, wheesh. I'm here . . ."

"Sean . . . the Tunnel . . . the Tunnel . . ."

"Aye, the Tunnel. I'll see to the clearing of it. You're not to worry . . ."

"No, damnit, Sean," he forced out in a harsh gasp. "Listen to me. The wall . . . explosives . . . it was blown out . . ."

McDougal patted his arm. "There, now, you're to rest. Don't talk. They'll have you in dispensary before you know . . ." The stretcher bumped and McDougal's voice began to recede.

"Sean, listen to me, man," he tried to shout while tears of frustration streamed down his cheeks. "The Tunnel was sabotaged!" But the shunting engine was already moving away up-Tunnel.

chapter ___7

An icy fog, iridescent in the winter sunlight, drifted through the trees in St. James's Park. A single carriage moved along the Mall. Across and along the road, he could see the Georgian facade of the Admiralty Building and, leaning against the glass, could just make out the right side of the Admiralty Arch. Only the tops of the buildings showed as the lower stories were shrouded by the fog. As dreary as the day was, at least, he thought with some satisfaction, he was not forced to endure the incessant clatter of motor lawnmowers as he had all summer past.

Eric von Dorn sipped his tea and watched a groom lead a horse from the stables below and a figure, he could not see who from this angle, walked rapidly down the Waterloo Steps and mounted as he himself had done earlier. He finished his tea and had just seated himself at the desk when his aide knocked and put his head into the room.

"Yes, what is it?"

Sergeant Schram was very happy to see that his master was in a good mood this morning. A brisk ride in the park always had a soothing effect, and he suspected that von Dorn was going to need all the composure he could muster today.

"Telephone for you, sir. The private wire for Eric Schneider." He emphasized the name. "A lady, I believe."

"Jesus Christ! What in the name of God . . ." He had never given that number to any woman but Margaret, to use in case of an emergency. Ostensibly the number belonged to the *Präzision Maschine Gesellschaft* of Hamburg, the business he used as cover for his intelligence activities.

"She sounded quite agitated, sir."

"Agitated?"

"Angry, sir."

Von Dorn frowned and picked up the telephone as Schram left the room.

"Eric? I must see you immediately," she broke into his greeting.

Von Dorn was so surprised at the hysteria in her voice that he stared at the telephone for a moment. "Margaret?"

"Do you hear me? I must see you now."

Anger overrode his concern then and he hissed, "You are never to telephone me. You know that."

"I don't give a damn. You must come now."

"I cannot and I will not. Perhaps later, if I am free." He emphasized the last word. "Do not call again." With that he slammed the receiver down. What in the name of God, he wondered, had possessed her to telephone him here. Von Dorn leaned back in the chair, trying to calm himself, to think it through. But he was too angry, and he got up and paced the room for a moment before bawling for Schram. The little orderly popped into the room as if on a string.

"Yes, Herr von—"

"Accept no further calls from that woman. Do you understand?"

"Yes, sir. Of course."

Von Dorn stopped at the window and stared without seeing; what was she up to? He recalled that he had promised to go to her that weekend, but the pressure of work had caused him to forget. There had been two sets of reports to draft and transmit to Berlin: one to Langenscheidt describing his progress in recruiting more Fenians, the other to von Epping —with a private copy to the Kaiser—detailing the damage done to the Tunnel. Suddenly he recalled the intense look on her face when he left the flat the previous Sunday evening.

Good God, he thought, surely that could not be what had driven her to such anger. She was unstable, of course, anyone that intense had to be. But he was certain that she had been well aware of the nature of the dangerous game in which they were engaged. She had to see that their work came before personal considerations.

He paced for twenty minutes before he felt calm enough to resume his seat behind the desk and continue scanning the routine reports that had come in overnight. He had almost managed to forget the entire incident when Schram knocked again and came in.

"Please, sir. She has telephoned three more times. She is now threatening to go to the police."

Von Dorn left the embassy shortly after three o'clock and walked down Waterloo Place to the Pall Mall, where he flagged a hansom and directed the driver to Berkeley Square. He did not neglect precautions yet fumed at the delay as he hurried across New Bond Street and up Conduit to Regent. He made a wide circuit that brought him back through Hanover Square, crossing New Bond again before he turned into Blenheim Street and found the flat in Sedley Place.

He hurried up the stairs and knocked. The door was flung open, and Margaret's anger was so obvious that for a moment his own was forgotten and he hesitated on the threshold.

"Come in," she snarled and flung herself across the room to the sideboard where a newspaper lay. As he closed the door and started to remove his coat, Margaret threw the paper at him and burst into tears.

"What in the name of God?" He picked the paper up and stared at the headline over the right-hand column.

CHANNEL TUNNEL DISASTER
THIRTY-ONE DEAD

Margaret knocked the paper from his hands and struck him sharply across the face. The unexpected blow caused him to lurch against the door and she was on him like a fury, hands striking at his face and chest. He swore and, without thinking, lashed a hand across her cheek. She stumbled and fell across the tea table, and he reached her in two strides, yanked her up, and slapped her hard again.

Margaret twisted away and backed against the wall, spitting and swearing as von Dorn rubbed the side of his face where her first full-handed slap had caught him. "What the hell is the matter with you?" he demanded.

"You bastard," Margaret hissed. "You murdering bastard. Thirty-one men were killed. Twenty-eight of them were Irish workingmen. You killed them. You murdered them just—" She broke off, at a loss for words.

Von Dorn stared at her. "What are you talking about?"

Margaret pushed herself from the wall and stood facing him, breasts heaving with the intensity of her breathing, hands clenched rigidly at her sides. "You made me an accomplice to murder, the murder of my own people. You murdered them. You had those men blown up and killed."

"Margaret!" The reason for her apparently insane anger was clear to him now and he swore at himself for not having thought of it before. "I never meant those men to die. Something went wrong. The explosives should have gone at a time when the heading was empty."

"No!" she screamed at him. "Don't lie to me. There are always men in the heading. You know that. You said you would help us, but instead you are helping to kill us! My God!"—she threw her hands to her face—"it isn't bad enough that the English kill us, now the Germans do it as well."

Tears streamed down her face, running into her mouth; her hair, shaken loose, was plastered across her cheeks. Her dress was ripped at the shoulder, and she tried to push past him, shouting, "I'll see you burn in hell for this, you rotten bastard!"

Von Dorn caught her shoulder. "Margaret, darling, please, believe me. I didn't know that there would be men in the Tunnel. The explosion was—"

"Take your hands from me," she snarled and struck at his face in fury. He narrowly avoided the slashing nails and she came at him again, screaming obscenities. The frustration and rage engendered by all that had happened that day overpowered him, and he struck her hard with a closed fist. Margaret stumbled and he hit her again. She fell to the floor, scrabbling away, trying to get to her feet. But her abrupt change from anger to fear only acted as a catalyst, and von Dorn kicked at her as she scrambled on all fours around the table and jumped to her feet. She threw the teapot, but he fended it off and it crashed against the wall. Von Dorn lunged, catching the collar of her dress, and when she pulled back the material parted down the front. The sight of her body caught him up in a violent sexual frenzy, and he slapped her again and again as adrenaline coursed through him, increasing his excitement. He ripped her camisole away and forced her down, pinning both arms beneath her back and straddling her naked body. He raped and then beat her nearly senseless.

"You bitch," he gasped finally, lapsing into German as he

struggled to regain his breath. "Go to the police? No, you won't do that, will you." He took her chin and shook it roughly. "You will keep your mouth shut and do as you are told. Do you hear what I say?"

Margaret opened her eyes and the depths of the hatred he saw there sobered him for a moment. But only a moment. Margaret gathered herself and spat at him and he lost all control. He became aware that his hands were clamped about her neck and, shocked at what he was doing, released his hold and started to get up, his mind a confused jumble of thoughts. Margaret whimpered and her body shuddered as she gasped for breath. Von Dorn stared at the great purplish bruises already forming around her neck and shoulders; he could not take his eyes away.

Then his mind was clear and he knew what he had to do. There was no other choice. She could no longer be trusted. He placed his fingers around her neck as if in a caress and rested his thumbs against her windpipe.

"There is no other way, Margaret," he whispered, soothing her. "You've done it to yourself." Her eyes were wide with terror as he pressed his thumbs down and waited until the feeble spasms of her body ceased.

Von Dorn stumbled into the lavatory and filled the sink with cold water. He splashed huge quantities on his face to relieve the pressure in his temples. Finally, he drained the water and, unable to look at himself in the mirror, found a towel and dried his face and hands. He went back into the sitting room where he sank into a chair and tried to think.

He avoided looking at the body across the room as he waited for his breathing to regain its even tenor and then began a methodical search. First, he piled all clothing that belonged to him on a chair by the door. Then he went through every cupboard and drawer looking for accessories, pictures, anything at all that could be traced to him. When he was satisfied that he had missed nothing, he sat down and lit a cigarette. He was thinking coherently again, as he had been trained to do. He realized that while it was only a matter of time before her body was discovered, this was Sunday afternoon and she would not be expected to return to Dover until sometime Monday morning. There was a cleaning woman who looked in once a week, but he could not remember the schedule Margaret had told him about in a moment of idle chatter. No, better not to leave anything to chance, he decided. It must be done tonight. In the bedroom there was a small traveling bag into which he stuffed his personal belongings. He found an empty box and, in the bathroom, he opened the cupboards and removed as much of the photographic equipment as would fit into it. The packs of the special Agfa microfilm went into his jacket pockets.

Back in the front room, he steeled himself for the next part. Margaret lay on her back, arms still caught beneath her. Her hair was in wild disarray and her face and neck were badly bruised. He had seen many dead before, even those he had killed himself. There had been men and women and children, some shot, some hacked to death by fanatical Moroccan soldiers, some still alive but so far beyond human help that a bullet had been the kindest treatment. But he had never known any of those dead bodies, never touched them in life, caressed them, made love to them. A wracking shudder took him. That he could ever have made love to her, he found difficult to believe. In death, she appeared wasted, skin grayish, and he turned away. It was a sight that he knew would haunt him for the rest of his life. He could not bring himself to touch her, and then he knew he was in no mental condition to finish. He needed help.

Outside, he walked rapidly to the end of Sedley Place, breathing the frosty air deeply to rid his lungs of the miasma of death. He paused for a moment, leaning against the wall until a spell of dizziness passed. Clouds had been forming during the late afternoon and together with an icy fog swept inland from the Thames had formed a pall of twilight. Lights were on in the streets and a motor passed with headlamps lit.

Von Dorn found Finnigan in a Mercer Street pub where the man's landlady had directed him. He pushed through a crowd smelling of sweat and damp and grabbed Finnigan by the shoulder. The Irishman's oath died away when he saw who it was, and he jumped from the stool and led von Dorn to the back. Pushing open a door to the storeroom, he urged von Dorn inside and closed it after them, then fumbled in his pocket for a match to light the kerosene lamp. The room smelled of dirt and the must of ages.

"Are you daft, Schneider? What are you doing here?" Finnigan demanded. "This is no place for a gent. And you're the one as told me—"

"Shut up and listen to me," von Dorn snapped. "Margaret Doyle is dead."

Finnigan's mouth fell and he stared at von Dorn, mouthing air for a moment until von Dorn grabbed his shoulder and shook him viciously.

"Listen to me, damn you. She is dead because I killed her."

Finnigan pushed his hand away and stumbled back against the wall. Von Dorn knew he was taking a chance telling Finnigan that he had killed the woman, but he had to make certain that he had his full cooperation. And to involve him was to obtain it.

"How . . . why . . . ?" Finnigan stuttered.

"She was convinced that the men who died in the Tunnel this past week were all Irishmen and that the Movement had done it deliberately."

"The Movement . . . ?"

"Yes. She said we were all guilty." That lie, he knew, would only strengthen his case. "She mentioned you specifically, Finnigan, and all those in Dover and Liverpool as well. She threatened to go to the police. I tried to stop her but she began to scream. Before I knew it, she had attacked me with a kitchen knife. I slapped her—God, it was horrible. I must have hit her harder . . ." He paused and drew a shaky breath. "But she was dead and I had to leave quickly. I must not be involved in this. You can see that. Think what it would mean if the police should discover my involvement with her."

Finnigan lit a cigarette with hands that were shaking badly and sat down on a wooden box. He inhaled deeply and von Dorn could see that he was trying to bring himself under control.

"I've removed everything that belonged to me," he said. "But there was not time to remove all of the photography equipment nor to dismantle the darkroom."

"Aye," Finnigan muttered. "Nor will there be. It would take a carpenter a full day to do so." He looked up at von Dorn. "The equipment must be taken away. Somehow we've to hide the darkroom . . ." He waved a hand as von Dorn started to speak. "No, let me think a bit."

Surprised, von Dorn did as he was told. It had been a long time since anyone but a superior officer had given him an order, and he looked with an increased respect at the little Irishman. The shock of red hair and the thin, almost weasellike face disguised a better brain and steadier nerve than he would have guessed. Finnigan was obviously frightened, but for all that, he was in control. Perhaps von Dorn's own feigned fear had helped to steady him.

Finnigan stubbed the cigarette out and stood up. "You, then, have to go on to wherever you would normally go of a Sunday evening. Let yourself be seen, establish an alibi. I'll take care of the rest."

"How? What do you intend to do?"

Finnigan glanced at him in annoyance. "I'll remove as much as I can and burn the flat. That way the coppers will have nothing but ashes. Now get away." The runty little Irishman glared at the German, then yanked the door open and motioned von Dorn out. Not knowing whether to be annoyed or amused, von Dorn left the pub and walked down to the Strand. There was a restaurant in Knightsbridge that he had been meaning to try. Perhaps now was the time to do so. Surprisingly, he found that he was hungry.

chapter ___8

NOVEMBER 26, 1911. SUNDAY EVENING

The London train was crowded for some inexplicable rea-
son this Sunday evening and Bannerman was forced to make
do with a second-class carriage. The windows were tightly
shut against the winter air and the interior, filled with clouds
of heavy Balkan tobacco and the smell of damp, close-packed
bodies, was close to suffocating. He was greatly relieved
when the rail yards of Battersea came into view. The gas
works frowned black and ugly over the sea of flats and
tenements south of the Thames and the train ran across the
bridge into the yards leading to Victoria Station. People were
already standing to gather belongings and children. Bannerman
folded his newspaper and stared through the window, waiting
patiently for the train to stop. The metal rails writhed across
one another like snakes and the sooty walls of the buildings
edging the yard frowned blindly on the activity below. A
guard in worn greatcoat and rubber boots watched from his
stand beside a switchpoint, curved pipe dangling from his
mouth, as the train slid into the dim twilight of the vast
building. There was a brief period of jostling and shoving as
people jammed forward, but Bannerman remained in his seat
until the crush had dissipated. He had never understood the
strange urge that pushed people into jostling crowds, fighting
for balance, as the conveyance—be it bus, tram, or train—
slowed to a halt.

He found his case and descended from the train into the
damp, noisome air and bustle of Victoria. The new electric
loudspeaker system boomed unintelligibly, announcing, he
supposed, scheduled departures and arrivals. People scurried
to and fro behind busy, distant porters with two-wheeled
carts, and he dodged several in the course of his journey to
the front entrance. There was a queue at the taxi rank and he

100

waited, trying to ignore the bite of the wind and the freezing fog.

He had not been up to London in two months, and the fact that the Channel Tunnel and all his cares and problems were ninety-seven miles behind was a load lifted from his shoulders. While he waited in the queue, he glanced around for a Chelsea pensioner to deliver a message to Margaret, telling her that the time of Monday's meeting had been moved up to ten o'clock. But to his chagrin, tonight he could not spot one of the high-hatted retired soldiers in their winter blue coats. He took out his watch. Only five thirty. Well, he thought, he would direct the cab around by her flat and tell her himself. He chuckled. It would be interesting to see exactly where she lived. The address was a perfectly acceptable one, but not what he would have expected of a widowed, working-class young woman who lived with an elderly aunt. A taxi drove up and he gave the chauffeur the address in Sedley Place.

They maneuvered through the congestion of taxis, private motor vehicles, and horse-drawn cabs on Buckingham Palace Road. Dusk was settling in, dragging the fog with it and Bannerman shivered in the cold confines of the compartment. He was hungry and tired, but the long trip across the city was preferable to his empty rooms in Chelsea.

Now approaching forty, Bannerman had long ago come to terms with loneliness. It was a rational decision based on recognition of the fact that he was more interested in his work than personal relationships. He had been married once, and his wife had tried, bravely, but construction camps in tropical countries were no place for a woman, and she had died at Cape Town of blackwater fever in 1906. Her death had left deep scars that preyed increasingly on his mind as the years went by. Once, in a rare bout of introspection, a practice in which he rarely indulged—perhaps being afraid of what he might find—he had come to the conclusion that it was not the hardships, heat, and diseases of foreign countries but his single-minded dedication to his work that had destroyed his wife. And so the decision to remain unattached had been a conscious one which, while regretting its necessity, he had found no reason to change.

Even so, he wondered why he was bothering to call around at Sedley Place. Margaret was an enigma, and he suspected that behind that prim, cold Victorian facade lay an extremely attractive and perhaps passionate woman.

Bannerman was no prude by any means, although a succession of tutors, the worst examples of the Victorian education—cum—Established Church, had done their level best to make him so by instilling their own warped prejudices and abnormalities into his young mind. But army service and exposure to other races and cultures in the years since had long erased any damage they might have done. In fact, definitely on his agenda for the week was a visit to a private gentlemen's club in Chelsea just off the Kings Road, where he was certain of a welcome at any time of the day or night. His sexual appetites were entirely normal, as several of the young ladies employed by the club could testify, and he grinned ruefully to himself as he wondered about Margaret in this connection. There was something about her that attracted him, although he could not say what. Yet the attraction was enough to create a sense of excitement as the taxi made its way through the London traffic.

Perhaps it was due to the isolation brought on by the Tunnel project, but she interested him lately as only one or two other women had. He had few interests outside the details of his work. One was stamp collecting, and it had become his passion. His grandfather had started him with a small collection as a child and it had grown to major proportions, filling fifteen volumes, each entry meticulously mounted and cataloged. He was considered an expert and on occasion even found time to write articles for philatelic journals. His work proved a ready source of modern stamps, and his excellent salary afforded the means to collect rare and antique issues. One of the few holidays he allowed himself was the annual three-day Royal Philatelic Association meeting in London every summer.

He stared as the taxi drove past Buckingham Palace, wondering if the new king would make it his residence as rumored, rather than Windsor. They rounded the Victoria Memorial and drove along the Mall, and the chauffeur paused for traffic, then ducked into Marlborough Road.

As they crossed Piccadilly to Old Bond Street he began to feel apprehensive. After all, Margaret might resent his intruding upon her private life. He was merely her employer and that, in spite of the prevailing opinion of the time, gave him no claim to her affairs outside working hours and again, he found he was grinning at himself. Perhaps the feminist claims of the Suffragists were having an effect after all, though paternalism was still the order of the day, especially toward female employees. The Empire was still the Empire in 1911 and, in Kipling's phrase, the "white man's burden" still meant England's assumed responsibility to civilize the world in spite of itself. And the emphasis was still on *man*.

Bannerman was jolted from his musings as the taxi chuffed to a halt.

The driver rapped on the window and Bannerman slid it back. "Far's I can go, chief. This yer's Blenheim Street. Sedley Place is just around there." He pointed to a street too narrow for the motor. "Does yer wants me to wait fer yer?"

Bannerman, very uncertain of his reception, agreed and climbed down. The wind had picked up and was whistling through the narrow road, blowing dust and scraps of paper at him. Wrapping his coat about him and clutching his hat, he hurried into Sedley Place. A single lamp high on the side of a building rocked in the wind, casting shadows in dizzying arcs. He found the proper number, hesitated, feeling foolish, then pulled the bell. He waited for several moments and when there was no answer, tried once more. Chagrined that he had made the trip for nothing, he tried the door and found it open. A dark stairwell, rather steep and ill-lit, climbed away into the dusk of the first floor. He went up, one hand on the wall. There were three flats at the top of the stairs and he peered at the cards on the doors. The ones to either side held old, faded pasteboards with names barely legible. The center door had no card at all and, recalling Margaret's penchant for privacy, he felt that it was in character. He knocked and to his surprise the door swung open. A single lamp gleamed from another room and he saw the shambles. With an oath he pushed inside and the odor of paraffin oil struck him just as he noticed a white form half-hidden by an overturned table. In two strides he was across the room, bending to kneel over the nude body of a woman lying on her back, both arms caught beneath her. Shocked, he recognized Margaret and as he reached to touch her face, a red flower burst across his vision.

A deep voice argued, the sound of it droning on for an interminable time. He was trapped in the Tunnel, could smell the fear pervading the rubber suit. After a while, a hand touched his head, then another hand felt inside his coat. He tried to strike the hand away, and the voice made soothing sounds. He wondered if they had gotten him out, and the memory of McDougal's face puzzled him. He could not see. Something cold went across his forehead and for a moment the ache in his head diminished. But only for a moment. He opened his eyes, wincing at the pain the flare of light caused. When it began to diminish, he could see a blue pillar that gradually took on the shape of an overcoated policeman.

"Are you all right, sir?" the policeman, the possessor of an extraordinarily deep voice, asked.

Bannerman raised a tentative hand, amazed at how weak he was. Even the slightest movement caused his head to throb with pain. "My head hurts like hell," he mumbled.

The policeman chuckled. "Shouldn't wonder, sir. You was hit quite hard."

Bannerman closed his eyes. As he did so, the vision of the body came back and he knew then that he was in London. He started to rise, but the policeman moved quickly to push him back down. "Best to stay there, sir, until the doctor comes look at yer."

"No, let me up," he struggled. "I saw—"

"Yes, sir." The policeman's hands were firm, and Bannerman lay back, head throbbing badly. "It were a woman, sir. She was murdered. Probably strangled. Now I want—"

"But I know her," Bannerman protested.

"Yes, sir. I was certain yer did. However, you must lie back or yer might faint away again. Then you'd be no good to us, now would yer?"

Bannerman took a deep breath, recognizing that the policeman was making sense. "What happened?"

The policeman straightened and clasped his hands behind his back, peering down at Bannerman's white face in speculation.

"Don't rightly know, sir. Can only guess at this point. From what she—just a moment, sir. You lie there and relax."

Bannerman saw him move across the room to the doorway where a middle-aged man in a gray Chesterfield and homburg had just entered and was motioning at a crowd of people peering in.

"Get them out of here and downstairs," he heard the man

say. "Then come back. Has the medical examiner been rung up?"

The policeman told him he had and stepped through the door, using his bulk to herd the onlookers back. Bannerman heard his deep voice patiently ordering them down to the ground floor.

The man in the Chesterfield glanced keenly about the room, then walked to the blanket-covered body. He knelt and turned a corner of the blanket back, bent closer and peered, then stood up again and regarded Bannerman.

"I believe it was you found the body, sir?"

The pain had receded to the point where it was bearable, and with an effort, Bannerman got himself to a sitting position. He rested his head against the back of the couch.

"Yes. But I am afraid I can't tell you much more than that." He closed his eyes and inhaled to contain the nausea.

The man waited patiently until Bannerman opened his eyes again. "Do you know who she is?"

"Of course. She is . . . *was*," he said after a moment, "my secretary and assistant."

"And you are, sir?"

Bannerman stared at him a moment. "Perhaps you might introduce yourself?"

The man gave him a tired smile. "I apologize. My name is David Powell, chief inspector, London Metropolitan Police. I am assigned to Special Branch." He removed his wallet and showed Bannerman his credentials.

"I see." Bannerman closed his eyes and waited for the nausea to ease away. "She was Margaret Doyle, my secretary and assistant. My name is James Bannerman."

For a moment the inspector continued to study him, then nodded. "The James Bannerman who is building the Channel Tunnel?"

"Yes."

"I see. And perhaps you could tell me why you had come to Miss Doyle's flat? I assume she was unmarried."

"Yes. A widow, rather." His annoyance at what the question implied was barely contained. "Her husband died several years ago."

There was a babble of argument from the stairwell, and Powell turned as a man pushed into the room. For a moment, Bannerman did not recognize the taxi chauffeur.

"Look, chief, I can't wait out there forever." He peered at Bannerman's face, into which the color was beginning to return.

"And you are?" Powell asked. The chauffeur turned to him, a flippant remark ready, but he must have recognized Powell for a police officer as he instantly assumed a respectful manner.

"Apologies, chief. That's me taximeter cab below. Found the two of them here, I did. He was unconscious on the floor. Out colder'n a mackerel. He had me wait while he came up. When he didn't come back right away, I came up to find him. Sunday night's a busy night and me company'll be mortal put out wiv me. . . ."

"Yes, I see. You saw them both. And did what?"

"Well, I knelt down to see if they was still alive. Both of them. Lady 'twasn't, but he was still breathing."

"Did you touch or move anything?"

The chauffeur gaped at him and his face grew red. "Oh, no, sir. Wouldn' do nuffin' like that. Ran out I did, sir. Right up to Marylebone Police Station I did, sir. Just up the ways, cross't Oxford—"

"And you didn't touch anything?"

"No, sir, like I says. And anyways I was too scared."

"Did you see anyone enter or leave this building?"

"Oh, no, sir. Could'n if I wanted to. I was waiting in me taxi in Blenheim Street. Road bends and I couldn't see nuffin'."

"All right. Give your name to the policeman downstairs. We may want to talk to you. How much was the fare?"

"Well, with the trip from Victoria and the wait—near enough twenty-five minutes now—" He turned his eyes up and then caught Powell staring at him with a skeptical look. "Ah, twenty pence, sir."

Powell gave him two shillings and dismissed him with a wave of the hand. The driver stared at the two coins, then shook his head and went out.

"Now then, where were we? Ah, yes. You had just mentioned that the deceased is a widow and was in your employ. I assume that means you keep an office in London?"

"No, we are both up to London for the weekend. Mrs. Doyle lives—lived here with an aunt." He glanced around. "Do you suppose . . ."

Powell studied him. "I'm afraid, sir, there's no one else living here. My men have had a good look round."

"But she told me she lived with an aunt. She even came up periodically to see to her."

"We'll look into that, sir. But you still haven't told me why you called here this evening."

Bannerman felt his pockets for a packet of cigarettes, found it, and offered one to Powell, who declined. He struck a match for Bannerman, however, and Bannerman drew the smoke deep into his lungs and leaned his head back against the couch. "No, I didn't, did I. She was expected to attend a meeting with me tomorrow. I came to tell her that the time had been changed. I tried . . ."

He was going to explain that he had looked for a pensioner at Victoria Station to deliver the message and, unable to find one, had come by himself, but a wave of nausea engulfed him.

"I see," he heard Powell say as if from a great distance. He felt the cigarette drop from his fingers and a great roaring swept over him.

"Now just you lie back, sir, and breathe normally. You'll feel better shortly." The face above him swam into focus. It was not that of either policeman, but a dark-haired, craggy-faced individual who regarded him with some concern.

"What . . ."

"You passed out, sir. Shock it is. That's all. Shock does funny things to the body, squeezes the blood vessels and drains blood from the brain. Purely defensive measures on the part of the organism. If you had suffered a great wound, it might save your life by helping to prevent loss of blood."

Bannerman realized that the doctor was talking to calm him and he closed his eyes, feeling the room swirling about. He heard the doctor speaking to someone else as if from a great distance. "He seems to have suffered a concussion. I want to have him in hospital, at least overnight. Please call for an ambulance, and I will need some blankets."

That was the last he remembered, that and a pair of clumsy hands tucking a blanket around him.

* * *

A freezing wind whipped rain along the deserted street as the taxi deposited him at his rooms in Draycott Place. The porter came scurrying out to help with his suitcase.

"Just lean on me, sir," the old man, twice Bannerman's age and less than half his size, ordered. Grinning, Bannerman allowed a little of his weight to fall across the man's shoulders and together they shuffled up the walk. Once inside, though, he made the porter sit down and carried his bag himself up to his rooms on the second floor.

He had awakened several hours before, disoriented and, surprisingly enough, ravenous. A sister had looked in, smiled, and gone off to find a doctor. At his insistence, they had released him immediately after breakfast. He had sent word to Townshend House that he would be unable to meet with the Board and requested a postponement to the following day. There was no reason to enlarge upon the request, as the murder and his part in it had been reported in the morning press.

The porter had already been up to light the fire and the flat was warm. Bannerman removed his overcoat and sat down, more tired than he had realized. He stared at the flames dancing above the grate, letting his mind run as the weariness spread through him like an uncontrolled flood. The doctor had warned him that he would feel this way for the next day or so and instructed him to sleep as much as possible and to drink plenty of liquids. It all sounded rather unscientific to Bannerman; very much like the instructions doctors always gave when they did not know what else to tell you.

His mind kept returning to the sight of Margaret's nude body crumpled on the floor and again he felt a wave of distaste for the casualness with which she had been murdered. He realized, with some chagrin, that at least part of his distaste was directed at himself for the half-formed intentions that had occasioned his spur-of-the-moment decision to go around by her flat.

He sighed without realizing that he did so and leaned his head against the back of the chair, careful to tilt it to one side and spare the bruised lump. He felt rather foolish and decided to confine the easing of his personal needs to the Chelsea clubs from then on.

He must have slept, for when he woke to the sound of someone knocking, the fire had burned low. He pulled himself from the chair, rubbing his face, and stood for a moment, not certain that what he had heard was more than a dream.

"Mr. Bannerman?" he heard the anxious voice call and recognized it as belonging to the porter's wife. He opened the door to see her standing in the hall with a large tray of tea things and Inspector David Powell smiling at him from behind her.

"Come in, both of you." He stood aside.

"This gentleman is from the police, Mr. Bannerman," she said, glancing behind her with apprehension as Bannerman took the tea tray from her.

"Yes, Mrs. Wickslaw, I know him. Good morning, Inspector."

"Morning, sir!" She gasped. "Afternoon, more like. It's gone past four, Mr. Bannerman."

He straightened from the table where he had placed the tray while Mrs. Wickslaw exclaimed at the cold and bustled to the hearth to add more coals to the fire.

"I must have slept most of the day." Bannerman's voice was rueful. "No wonder my back aches."

Mrs. Wickslaw quickly served the tea, instructed him severely to call for her or her husband if he needed anything, clucked once or twice, and bustled out. Both men laughed, and Bannerman shook his head.

"She really is a good soul. Never had any children of their own, so she adopts all the single gentlemen in the building."

Powell blew his nose with a rumpled handkerchief and watched while Bannerman devoured the biscuits and poured a second cup.

"I thought of coming round to the Yard tomorrow to speak to you," Bannerman said as he lifted the cup. "I was curious as to why Special Branch was involved. I thought you people were concerned only with major crimes and treason?"

Powell smiled at that. "I happened to be at the Marylebone station last evening on another matter. They asked me to look in on the way home. They're always short-handed of a Sunday evening."

"I see." Bannerman nodded.

"I suppose you're wondering what did happen last night," Powell said and, without waiting for agreement, continued. "It appears as if someone broke into Mrs. Doyle's flat, thinking she was not there.'' He paused and glanced at Bannerman as if to gauge the effects of his words.

"She must have been struck from behind initially, as the M.E. discovered a large bruise at the back of her head. Perhaps this did not render her unconscious and she began to scream. In any event, the burglar must have panicked and strangled her.''

"My God,'' Bannerman muttered and set the cup down with an unsteady hand. He leaned back in the chair, and Powell, alarmed at the way he had paled, leaned forward as if to support him. But Bannerman waved him away.

"I'll be all right. Just need a moment.''

Powell sat back and waited, mentally eliminating Bannerman from his suspect list. Beyond the fact that it would have been impossible to strike his own head from behind, that type of reaction could not be faked on cue. And, given his reaction, Powell was glad now that he had stuck by his decision to conceal the fact that the poor woman had been raped as well.

After a moment, he went on in an effort to distract Bannerman. "But, and this is where I am not certain of my analysis, the burglar must have returned just before you arrived. Then you entered the flat, surprised him, and he struck you down and escaped.''

"Why would he return?'' Bannerman asked.

Powell shrugged, relieved to see color returning to Bannerman's face. His eyes had also lost their glassy look. "Apparently, he wished to hide the results of his handiwork. The flat had been splashed with paraffin oil. He must have been ready to light the match when you entered. In fact, I would say you were quite fortunate he did not do so anyway.''

"Yes, I remember now. I did smell paraffin oil when I entered. I'd forgotten about that.''

Bannerman paused at the realization of how close to death he had come. "When—when do you think it happened,'' he asked after a moment.

"The medical examiner estimates that Mrs. Doyle died at least three hours before you arrived. Rigor mortis had begun. During the autopsy he established that the bruise at the back of the head was new and filled with blood, indicating that it occurred before death. Then there were the other bruises indicating that she had been quite severely beaten.''

Bannerman nodded, his expression distant. After a moment, he picked up the cup. Powell leaned forward to see him better.

"And her aunt?"

The police inspector gave him what could only be described as a penetrating stare. "I'm afraid we have not been able to locate any of Mrs. Doyle's relatives in London. The landlord was questioned last night and he knew nothing about another woman living there."

Bannerman nodded, suspecting that Margaret had created the fictitious aunt. A young woman living alone in London would raise eyebrows among her co-workers. As long as they thought she was being properly supervised, they would suspect no impropriety. But why would she want to live alone in such a city? he wondered. He could understand her feelings about not wanting to remarry. The memory of her husband was still fresh, in all likelihood. He said as much to Powell, adding that she had once told him her husband had died of cancer.

For a moment Powell was taken aback. Did the man really believe that, or was he just making excuses for the woman? But a glance at his face told him that Bannerman did not in the slightest believe anything else. That Margaret Doyle would make frequent trips to London to meet a man, had never occurred to him . . . at least not yet. Powell sighed inwardly. He certainly had no doubt that when the building's landlord was interviewed it would turn out that a man was paying the rates—but, he was certain now, it would not be Bannerman.

"She did tell me," Bannerman said after a pause, "that she had an older brother, in the army I believe, stationed somewhere in India."

Powell made a note of that and, after assuring himself that Bannerman would be all right by himself, took his leave, insisting that Bannerman remain where he was. The inspector hesitated, noticed that the big engineer was sitting hunched forward, staring into the fire. For a moment before the door closed, Bannerman looked to him like an old man, and Powell wondered if there was anything else occupying his mind beyond the murder of an employee.

chapter ———9

An icy wind swept off the Charles River and sought a way through the ranks of dingy warehouses. It was midmorning, and the sky was leaden as the young man in ragged jacket and cloth cap dodged among the horse-drawn wagons and trucks crowding the Boston waterfront. To cross the streets, he had to force his way over mounds of snow where the horse plows had scraped it aside. His face was almost as red as his hair from the wind, and his lips were pinched and bluish. His worn boots had gaping holes in the soles and his thin coat had been patched once too often. He had eaten no breakfast; the newspaper jammed into his pocket had taken his last nickel.

It took him twice as long as usual to reach the storefront at the end of Brookline Avenue. He tugged at the door, jerking it back and forth against the snow that had frozen in the jamb until it opened enough for him to squeeze through. The front was empty but for a pile of refuse in the middle of the floor, and it was nearly as cold inside as out. The boy stamped snow from his boots as he crossed the room and shoved open the ludicrously heavy oak door leading into the back, where he made straight for the iron stove.

The man sitting at a desk looked up. He was not good-looking in any sense of the word; at first glance, most people would have called him ugly. His face was long, with thin lips added as an afterthought between a short nose and hard chin. He retained the heavy mustache he had grown in his youth in spite of the fact that mustaches had gone out of style some years before. The eyes that stared out at the world with mistrust, and often with hatred, were flat gray. Heavy brownish-colored brows hooded them so that the second impression was one of intense anger. His hair was dark auburn, in the right light almost black. He had cropped it short in the fashion of the day and it did little to help the blunt shape of his skull.

His equally blunt hands were those of a laborer, and the overall effect when he stood and moved to the stove was of a strong, hard man capable of looking after himself and perhaps something more.

"Collin, me boyo, what are ye doing about on sich a cold day?"

Michael Connigham had long ago lost his rough Dublin Liberties brogue. It was much too identifiable in a country where the Irish were only now gaining a measure of respectability. His accent was the result of three years in the western United States, as a working cowboy, a miner, a drifter, and then as a *Clan Na Gael* organizer and, some said, a socialist. He had learned to hide his Irish birthright unless he was with his own kind. But it amused him, on occasion, to use the old way of speech.

"Ah, Michael . . . give me a chance to warm up. The snow and the cold are vicious, and I had not the carfare. I'm that frozen!"

Connigham grinned and slapped the boy on the shoulder before turning back to his desk. Sitting down, he pushed his books away and nodded to the side table. "There's coffee. Help yourself. It'll do more good inside than the stove will do outside."

Collin nodded his thanks, poured coffee into a dirty cup, and added three large tablespoons of sugar. Connigham watched as he drank it quickly in spite of its heat.

"Another cup?" he asked, guessing that his visitor had had nothing to eat yet. And when the boy nodded eagerly, he asked for one as well, but without the sugar.

The boy, Collin, brought Connigham his cup and set it down on the desk. He pulled up a chair and sat huddled in his ragged coat, not looking at the man across the table from him. The walls of the room had once been painted years before, but it would have been impossible now to determine the color of the paint used. A single decoration hung above the desk, an old Civil War rifled musket converted to the .58-caliber cartridge by the Needham system, a relic of the Fenians' failed raids on Canada in the late 1860s.

"You look like a man with a problem, Collin," Connigham observed.

"Aye." He fell silent again, rubbed his nose, and fidgeted. "Aw, hell!" He tugged the newspaper from his pocket and opened it to a page that had been folded as a place mark. He put it on the desk and shrank back, then jumped up and went over to the stove.

A story was marked in pencil, near the bottom of the page. Connigham picked it up and turned it to the meager light from the single window. He noted the date at the top, the twenty-eight of November.

WOMAN MURDERED IN LONDON FLAT

In smaller type below: *Secretary to Builder of Channel Tunnel Found Murdered in Flat*

For an instant the page darkened and he groaned.

A woman, identified by Scotland Yard as Mrs. Margaret Doyle, was found viciously murdered in her London flat this Sunday past, by her employer, the engineering director for the Tunnel being constructed beneath the English Channel. Police were summoned by a taxi driver and found the engineer, Mr. James Bannerman, unconscious beside the body. Police surmise that he surprised . . .

"My God," he breathed. Margaret Doyle was his sister.

. . . the burglar who killed Mrs. Doyle. A police spokesman said it was fortunate that Bannerman was not killed as well. Police have no leads at present, the spokesman said, but will bend every effort to apprehend the murderer. He noted that London's growing crime rate has become . . .

Connigham flung the paper on the desk and shoved himself back in the chair. "Jesus Christ," he said aloud. It had to be her. Her last letter six months ago had been full of news about her position in the project offices of the Channel Tunnel engineering staff.

"I'm sorry, Michael, I thought you would . . ."

Connigham waved a hand at him and continued to stare at the wall. Little Meggy . . . God damn it to hell, what a rotten life. Her husband lynched before her very eyes, her father a drunk, and her mother dead before the girl herself was ten. And two brothers who had deserted her.

"You did the right thing, Collin," he muttered.

After a moment, the boy asked, "Is there anything I can do, Michael?"

Connigham did not answer but picked up the paper and

shuffled it together. For a long time he sat staring at the page, face immobile. After a while, he turned the pages until he found the shipping register. He read through it carefully and, not finding what he was looking for, gave equal attention to the New York listing. He placed the paper on the desk when he had finished and looked at the boy sitting by the stove, struggling to stay awake.

"Collin," he said quietly, "I want you to go round to Lipshutz. Tell him I'll be there to see him tonight." Connigham fished in his pocket and brought out a silver dollar. "Bring me back a New York City newspaper. Use this for tram fare. And get something to eat as well."

Collin bit at his lip and reached for the silver dollar. "Michael, I don't want no—"

"Go on, damn you. It's for the tram fare."

The boy hesitated, then grabbed the dollar and ran from the room. Connigham heard the scrape of ice as he forced the door open and its slam as the boy went out. His expression was unchanged as he turned the pages back to the story of his sister's murder.

Connigham changed trains at Hartford. In the hour before the next one left for New York, he had time to complete his purchases in a surplus store off Portland Street. He left his good topcoat and suit jacket in trade for a seaman's pea coat, wool cap, and heavy sea boots. Then he walked swiftly back to the railroad station, arriving just in time to see the signboard announcing the departure of the 4:30 train for New York's Grand Central Station hoisted over the main gates. He showed his ticket to the gateman, walked down the platform to the second-class car, and swung aboard. The interior of the coach was hot and reeking with the odor of perspiration and tobacco. The stove at the end of the car was glowing dull red. He pushed his way through the crowd until he found a seat near the front on the aisle. His companion was a seedy individual whose dirty topcoat was open to expose an equally dirty and grease-stained suit. His legs were bent at sharp right angles over a heavy suitcase, and from that and the bottle projecting from his pocket, Connigham guessed him to be a drummer.

The uproar in the car began to subside, and he heard a door

slam in the rear. A whoosh of steam shot past the windows and the train jerked into motion, banging and rattling, car by car, until the whole assembly was moving.

The train picked up speed as it left the yard and Connigham watched the industrial landscape of cinders, rusting iron, stunted trees, and stunted people speed past. The train rattled and clicked its way past blocks of tenements and warehouses, then open fields, where schoolchildren returning home stopped to wave in the gathering darkness.

Connigham leaned back in the seat, ignoring the gurglings and snufflings of the snoring salesman. He had grown used to such traveling companions in the six years he had been in the States. Six years, he thought. But for all that they had been full of hard times, they were a paradise compared to Ireland. Six years he had been on the run. It was hard to credit that that much time had passed. It had been six years since he had last seen Margaret, and he recalled her as she was then, a young wife full of the love of living.

The bastards had killed that for her, as surely as they had killed her husband. And as senselessly. The bloody Prods. But he could think of them now without rancor; his hatred was far too encompassing to focus upon any one event, person, or group in his life. In fact, he admitted to himself, he had lost the emotional basis for his hatred so long ago that he had almost forgotten the series of incidents that had caused it. It had become hard, implacable, indescribable, something that resisted definition; but it was the sole reason for his existence. Connigham was a man who had come to terms with himself years ago. Now, untroubled by doubts, he made decisions instantly. Any humanity that he had possessed had long ago been burned away. He knew this, realized its implications, and was untroubled.

The train ran through the lush tobacco lands edging the Connecticut River, and the geometric forests of bare poles that supported cheesecloth mesh in the summer marched away from the fleeing train like regiments of giants. The drummer opened his eyes and stared as he fumbled for the bottle in his coat pocket, poking Connigham with his elbow. He shifted over without comment. The man pulled the cork and swallowed several times, then sighed with gusto, emitting a cloud of fetid breath that not even the alcohol could dissolve. He snugged the cork in the bottle, returned it to his pocket, and promptly went back to sleep.

Darkness was complete now, and the Connecticut farmlands lying along the river were dusted with snow. It had been a cold autumn so far and promised a colder winter. Perhaps it was better to be going back to England after all, even if two murder warrants were waiting for him there.

chapter ═══ 10

McDougal *had traveled up to London by the early train in* response to Bannerman's telegram. It was now eleven o'clock, and the stocky Irish engineer had finished his review of the week's events and was ensconced in the overstuffed Morris chair before the fire, large glass of whiskey in hand. He was watching Bannerman closely, had been ever since he arrived. Except for the stiff way in which he held his head, the young man—as he always thought of Bannerman—did not seem to have been unduly affected by Margaret Doyle's death; or if he had, he gave no sign. Even Bannerman's startling statement of a moment before, laying the blowout in the heading to sabotage, had a weird explanation that was concise and, on the face of it, irrefutable.

"Then there isn't any doubt, is there?" he rumbled.

"No, Sean," Bannerman answered. "There is not. At least in my mind."

Bannerman went to the sideboard and poured himself a whiskey, an action he had been prone to take of late, and earlier in the day as well. He sipped at it as he went across to the windows and stood looking down into the street where the Georgian facades lining the narrow road caught the cold sunlight in glass panes turning them to dark mirrors. On such a day, drink in hand, the room warm around him, it was hard to credit the idea. Dover, the Tunnel works, and this after-noon's parliamentary subcommittee hearing seemed to belong to another world. Yet he had nearly lost his life in the depth of the Tunnel, his secretary had been murdered, and in a few hours he must defend the greatest engineering work of the twentieth century against the foolish depredations of politi-cians and poltroons. He grinned. It was a good word, poltroon.

"What tack will you take then, James?" McDougal asked.

It never ceased to surprise Bannerman that two people so

dissimilar in manner as he and McDougal could have become friends. McDougal was at heart little more than an Irish navvy, a common laborer who had risen by dint of his own intelligence to become engineering manager of the Tunnel project. He had no formal schooling and possessed only the self-taught abilities to read and write. But he had an instinct for engineering that was far more valuable than anything he could possibly have been taught. He had gone from the Cork slums to Bristol at ten years of age to work on the laboring gangs digging the Severn Tunnel. He had been involved in tunneling ever since.

And he was a master at drawing the best from his labor gangs, perhaps recalling his own experiences as a laborer. Always ready, even at fifty-one, to back his orders with fists and feet and on more than one occasion in plain view of Bannerman's office window. And Bannerman gave him much of the credit for the fact that the Tunnel project had been singularly free of labor troubles during the past summer when Great Britain had been threatened with its first general strike. They hadn't lost a day or a man to the strike gangs that roamed the country.

He would never have imagined that he could have developed such a rapport with a man like McDougal. And yet, perhaps they complemented each other. Instinct could take you only so far; then an understanding of engineering principles was required. Sheer forces, pumping heads, distribution of loads, all these must be calculated to a nicety. He supplied that end of the partnership, for this was how he was coming to view their working relationship.

"I asked, James, what tack will you take this afternoon?"

McDougal's peevish voice woke him from his reverie. "I don't know yet," he admitted, turning. "I'm not certain I have the proof to tell them the truth."

"Aye," McDougal muttered. "And I suppose it would do you no good if you did. They are such liars themselves, no doubt they would not know the truth if sworn to."

"In any event," Bannerman pointed out, "I would be acting irresponsibly if I did not first inform the Board of Directors that the Tunnel had been subjected to sabotage. And I was not certain until last night."

McDougal nodded. "But who?" he demanded, pounding a

hand against the chair arm. "Who would want to destroy it to the extent of murdering innocent workmen?"

Bannerman shook his head. "I don't know, Sean. Unless it could be some of those fanatical empirists who are afraid a continental power will swarm through, the day the Tunnel is completed, to invade 'fair England.' "

"Aye, perhaps. But I would like to know how the explosives were taken into the Tunnel in the first place."

"They were already there," Bannerman said suddenly.

McDougal stared at him. "What do you mean, James?"

"They used the army's emergency demolition charges. Someone removed several charges that had already been installed and placed them in one of the drainage shafts cut into the heading wall." Bannerman unlocked a drawer and removed a folder as McDougal stood and came to the desk.

"I worked these calculations last night," he explained, pointing to a sheet of paper filled with equations. "I couldn't imagine why someone would try to rupture the Tunnel in such shallow waters. If they wished to destroy it, they would have been better off in the deeper waters beyond the Goodwin Sands. Look here, Sean. My calculations suggest that sixty pounds of cordite were used. Now, if it had been sixty pounds of blasting gelatin, the wall would have been severely damaged and perhaps a few of the excavating crew would have been injured. Certainly enough damage would have been done to shake the morale of the workmen and slow the work even more. But, instead of blasting gelatin, those containers held cordite, taken from the naval stores at Dover. Only the military engineers and I knew that. Whoever was responsible for placing the explosive containers would have assumed they held blasting gelatin."

"Ah, James, for God's sake. Cordite is a weaker explosive than gelatin."

Bannerman dropped into the desk chair and tapped the sheet of paper. "Cordite *is* a slow-burning explosive, unlike blasting gelatin, which is a high explosive. Blasting gelatin burns quickly, producing a great gout of pressure that literally punches a hole, whereas cordite is normally a slow-burning explosive used for propelling shells through a long gun barrel. By burning slowly, it develops increasing pressure as the warhead proceeds up the barrel. But a gunsmith knows that if a slow-burning propellant such as cordite is ignited in an oversized container, it does not burn; it can detonate, and the resulting pressure can burst the chamber. Several national armories and ammunition manufacturers have reported this phenomenon since smokeless powders began to replace black powder fifteen or so years ago. Much less smokeless powder is required than black powder. In a large-caliber cartridge such as the .38 Smith & Wesson Special or a .455 Ely, certain kinds of smokeless powder fill only a small portion of the space and can detonate rather than burn.

"That is exactly what happened in this instance. A certain number of cordite charges were packed into oversized steel containers."

McDougal's face suggested that he still did not understand. Bannerman hesitated, then decided to tell him. Someone else should know, just in case.

"Look, Sean, you knew that there were plans to prevent a sudden invasion of the Tunnel in the event of war. Well, they were to have worked this way. A section of Tunnel nearly half a mile long was to be collapsed. Cordite charges in steel containers were placed in shafts cut into the chalk beyond the Tunnel walls. One-third of the cordite charges were placed in steel containers of a size calculated to allow the cordite to detonate. The detonation would crack the chalk. The other cordite charges would burn normally, causing a rippling shock wave to loosen and crush the chalk, the grouting, and the brisk lining, and collapse the Tunnel roof.

"Whoever set the explosives in the heading was not aware that he had both kinds of charges; in fact, he probably took one of each container, as they look alike unless you are familiar with the coded labels."

McDougal retrieved his glass from the table. He paused at the sideboard to refill it before he turned back to Bannerman, his expression thoughtful. "Then the damn fools, you think, didn't know what they were about? You're saying the flooding was an accident then?"

Bannerman nodded, still studying the sheet of calculations. "Yes, I think so," he replied absently.

"But what was it made you suspect?"

Bannerman lit a cigarette before answering, seeing in his mind once more the black depths of the hole surrounded by the obscene white rim. "The cracks in the Tunnel wall. A rippling shock wave moving laterally would have been required to produce them. It would have been caused by the normally packed cordite. And, when I saw the hole that had been made in the heading wall, I could not account for the huge amounts of chalk dust suspended in the water until it occurred to me that the sharp explosions produced by the oversized containers would have shattered the walls, producing the dust. Those explosive charges are the only answer. When we open the shafts, we will find two containers missing.''

McDougal nodded slowly. ''No matter what, they did their damage well.''

''You are certain that the rupture in the seabed can be sealed and the heading pumped out within three weeks?''

McDougal nodded. ''Aye. It only wants a spell of calm weather for the divers. Three days.''

Bannerman nodded. ''Then it's worth the gamble,'' he said.

''Aye. The damage to the sea floor isn't as great as we expected. If the fill will hold long enough for the pumping, then we can seal the Tunnel from the inside afterward. Certain that it's a gamble. But you'll save the two months having to bypass. And you'd still have to pump out the abandoned heading.'' McDougal drew out his old-fashioned key-wind watch. ''You'll be late if you delay longer, James.''

Bannerman nodded and got up reluctantly. ''Will you be staying over?''

''I'd best get back to Dover. I don't trust them wet-eared youngsters to do anything without supervision.''

The joke about wet-eared youngsters drew a smile as McDougal knew it would. Most of the engineering staff, the pick of European and North American tunnel and mining engineers, were in their thirties and forties, and all possessed college degrees and experience on the great engineering and mining projects of the time, from the Rand mines to the Simplon Tunnel. But, still, McDougal did not trust a single one of them.

A taxi was waiting for him and the porter had already given the chauffeur his instructions. They drove off down Draycott Place, passed through Cadogan Gardens, and turned south into Sloane Street. All traces of the recent rains had vanished, and although it was cold, the city seemed springlike in the sunshine. The Botanic Garden glistened; it needed only budding trees to convince him that spring had come before winter. The bright uniforms of the guards pacing off their sentry goes at Chelsea Barracks glittered in the strong light.

The driver turned from Chelsea Bridge Road onto the Grosvenor Road and slowed considerably. Traffic was heavier here, Londoners out to enjoy a rare day of sunshine and warm air. Bannerman lowered the window and the illusion was destroyed as he caught the odor of mud flats and the ever present city stink of coal smoke which always startled him after the clean air of the Channel coast.

Traffic had come to an abrupt halt opposite Page Street. Taxis, horse cabs, trams, and buses blocked the road. Swearing under his breath, he glanced at his watch. It was already one thirty and he was due in the hearing chamber at two. He paid off the driver and started out on foot, wondering what was causing the disturbance. Ahead, several policemen were attempting to sort out the traffic jam. One was holding a frightened horse while another argued with an angry lorry driver. The remainder were waving to the cabs and taxis that could be made to move down a side street. Across the road, a solid mass of people pressed into the Victoria Tower Gardens. A huddle of blue uniforms along the fence tried to resist the heaving mass of onlookers.

Snatches of conversation came to him as he found a way through the crowd that had gathered to watch. "Bloody fools . . . looka the mess . . . I heard it were a woman . . . chained herself ta bloody fence."

The lady in question was small, well-dressed, if old-fashioned—she still wore a Dolly Varden. Bannerman was nearly knocked down by a phalanx of police who swept down on the crowd in flying wedge formation and finally broke through to the woman. She scrambled higher on the fence rails, kicking at the clutching hands and screaming obscenities at the bobbies. The crowd, mostly working men, were laughing and hooting at the woman, urging the police on. Bannerman escaped before they pulled her down but he could hear her high-pitched curses nearly to the Westminster Hall yard entrance.

The porter summoned a page who led him along stone corridors and through the vault of the Palace of Westminster's original Norman structure. As always, Bannerman felt the sense of history as they crossed the stone flags, their footsteps echoing beneath the arched roof that had seen so much of England's pageantry, the best and the worst. The page turned sharply down a corridor and led him into a dark, dank stone cloakroom and up a narrow stairway.

At the top, the sense of medieval England was lost in the warm woods and fine rugs and morning-coated gentlemen conversing. The page indicated a door and a uniformed porter swung it open for him. Bannerman took a deep breath and entered.

As Bannerman emerged from the committee room, a messenger with an envelope sought him out. Absently, he accepted it and continued along the hall to the porter's desk, where he retrieved his hat and coat and left, still thinking of his reception in the hearing room.

Fortunately, several of the Conservative members had been absent from the session and the Liberals and one Labour member present had managed to monopolize the agenda. Still, there had been hard questions concerning cost estimates and schedule delays that had put him at times at a disadvantage. Once again he had neatly sidestepped the issue of the Tunnel's being used to invade England. He had noticed reporters from the Tory press waiting in the corridor, but at least they would have nothing new to add to their almost daily accounts of projected invasion attempts. And at the moment he was inclined to think that security threats were much more immediate than anyone in the hearing room could have guessed.

There were sharp questions from both sides about the two recent disasters, but he had answered them fully and honestly, hedging only over the cause of the two accidents. On balance, Bannerman thought he had retained the committee's sympathies, or at least those of the Liberal majority.

He was always surprised at how cold and dank it was inside the drafty halls of Westminster, as if the moisture and cold of the centuries had been trapped by its ancient stones. Outside, in the wan afternoon light, Bannerman glanced at the envelope and was surprised to see that it was on ministerial stationery, marked with the cipher of the Admiralty. Curious, he opened and read the note and whistled in surprise.

My Dear Mr. Bannerman. I heard the testimony you so aptly supplied this afternoon. Was most impressed. If you

have no other plans, would appreciate it if you would take
supper with us tonight at 33 Eccleston St.

It was signed: Winston S. Churchill. How did he rate an
invitation to dine with *that* man, Bannerman wondered? He
stepped back inside, found an usher, and dispatched a message stating that he would be honored to dine with the First
Lord of the Admiralty. It would be an interesting evening he
reflected as he went back out to find a taxi.

A serving girl met him at the door. She took his hat and
overcoat and, with a warm smile, directed him to the drawing
room where several people were already engaged in lively
conversation. He paused awkwardly on the threshold until a
well-built, rather handsome man, inclined to plumpness, saw
him and with a broad grin came across the room. Bannerman
noted with surprise that Churchill came only to his shoulder,
and for a moment he did not notice the extremely attractive
young woman who appeared beside him.
"My dear sir. You must be James Bannerman. What an
honor, sir, what a pleasure. Please, let me introduce my wife.
Clementine, this is Mr. James Bannerman, whom I spoke to
you about this afternoon."
While Churchill pumped himself up and down on his toes,
his wife extended a hand and welcomed him warmly. She
was, he thought, a singularly attractive woman. Not beautiful, but striking in the extreme, with the kind of figure and
features that would turn heads anywhere. Her hair was done
in the crisp ringlets which were the latest style and her
blue-gray eyes smiled at him from beneath straight brows.
She had a long, patrician nose whose up-tilted end negated
any trace of hauteur, and a sensitive mouth. Her strong jaw
would have been unattractive on any other woman but only
seemed to emphasize Clementine Churchill's femininity.
Churchill took him by the arm and marched him across the
room where he was introduced first to Violet Asquith, an
attractive young woman and the daughter of the prime minister. A tall, rather sad-faced military officer, Sir Henry Wilson, director of Military Operations, and a tall, quite handsome
man in naval uniform, Rear Admiral David Beatty, completed
the party.
"Keep this a secret," Churchill stage-whispered with a

laugh, "but the admiral is about to become my Naval Secretary."

Beatty chuckled at that. "I was only accepted because the Admiralty may need financial assistance in carrying through all of the First Lord's plans for new dreadnoughts and an aeroplane fleet."

As they moved away, Churchill noticed Bannerman's puzzled expression. "David's wife is heir to the Marshall Field fortune," he explained. "At this rate, England will have married into every American millionaire's family before 1920." He steered Bannerman to the liquor cabinet while apologizing for his brother Jack and his wife. "We had expected them, but they were delayed in coming down from York.

"Having been in America so long, you must be familiar with my favorite drink, sir." He raised a half-empty bottle of Jack Daniel's bourbon.

"Most assuredly." Bannerman chuckled. "I was beginning to think that I would have to return to the States to taste it again." The man clearly knew something about him, Bannerman thought, and wondered briefly exactly how far his knowledge went.

Churchill filled two glasses with the amber liquid and added a few drops of water. "I am afraid this is not branch water. It comes from the metropolitan water supply, but I presume it isn't long out of the Thames. In an emergency, I suppose any river or creek"—he gave it the American Midwestern pronunciation, *crick*—"will do."

Bannerman raised his glass and Churchill responded. "I hope you do not mind being invited here tonight. I wished to speak to you in private before you returned to Dover. Today is my birthday, and Clemmy arranged a small party, otherwise we could have met in more formal surroundings."

"Indeed not, First Lord. In fact, I am quite honored . . ."

"Please, no titles. It has only been a few weeks since I've moved from the Home Office to the Admiralty. 'First Lord' sounds rather ridiculous and I must endure it all day. Winston, and if I may, I will call you James."

"Please do. And allow me to congratulate you on your birthday."

"Now, then, James." Churchill peered closely at him, all the while bobbing disconcertingly up and down on his toes. The man seemed an inexhaustible storehouse of energy. When he walked, he lunged. Even when walking slowly, he leaned forward from the waist so that he seemed to be charging. "I wish to hear more about the disaster at the Tunnel last week. My reports suggest that naval stores were implicated. Even though I have left the Home Office and no longer have any control over the Tunnel project, I am still quite interested."

He turned to look at Bannerman, who was staring at him in surprise. "How did . . . how did you know?" he began.

Churchill smiled. "Thought it was a secret, heh? Well, it is, only I'm in on it. When the damage reports came through to the Home Office, I asked for them to be sent across to the Admiralty. My new staff admirably calculated that the damage described could have been accomplished only with the cordite demolition charges placed in the Tunnel. Your reaction confirms their analysis."

Bannerman's expression hardened at that and he said stiffly, "I'm sorry, First Lord, but I resent being—"

"Of course. Of course. Anyone would. But the higher you rise in government, the more necessary it is at times to play tricks. I am certain that you often find yourself in the same position."

Bannerman could not help laughing at that. "Of course. And I apologize for my rudeness, even if I do not admit to the validity of your analysis."

"No need. No need." Churchill waved a hand, dismissing the subject. "In any event, I view the incident as a very serious matter. Is it a question of sabotage? And if my staff is correct in their analysis, it certainly is. The next question then—who is the guilty party? Is it someone with a grudge? Someone inside the country who is dead set against the Tunnel, or is it the result of foreign intervention?" He bit on the end of his cigar for a moment. "Whichever, we must find out and put a stop to it. I would be pleased to have your views."

Bannerman coughed and took another sip to hide his embarrassment. Churchill saw it and nodded. "Out with it now."

"Well, sir. If it is sabotage, isn't it a matter for the police? I don't understand why the Admiralty is interested."

Churchill nodded. "I suppose you are correct. It is properly a matter for the Home Office. But as an officer of the government and a member of the cabinet, it is my responsibility as well. Particularly so if naval stores are involved."

Bannerman took a sip of his drink to allow himself time to think. "To be perfectly honest, I do not know what the answer is. And in any event, I would be duty bound to discuss any such suspicions with my superiors first."

Churchill nodded, peering at him intently. "Quite right. However, I am really asking for a private assessment that would not go beyond these walls."

The maid entered just then to announce dinner, thus saving Bannerman the need to answer for the moment. But he suspected that his host would not let the matter drop so easily. Churchill turned and smiled as Clementine came up. He took her arm. "If you please, James, will you escort Miss Asquith in to dinner?"

Bannerman found Violet Asquith and offered his arm, most impressed with what he saw. She was of middle height, dark-haired, with a pleasant face and figure and the most engaging smile he had ever seen. Unlike most fashionable young ladies of the day, she was neither coy nor simpering, but direct and very much an individual.

Dinner proceeded pleasantly enough; the conversation ranged from the past summer's coronation and general strike to the latest stage offering in London, and Bannerman found himself relaxing. By the time they had finished the savory and coffee and cigars had been passed around, he was comfortably sated. The ladies did not retire as he supposed they would, but stayed to take an active part in the after-dinner conversation, and their laughter at some of the more outrageous sallies was in pleasant contrast to other dinners he had attended of late. It was the first time in a year, he realized, that he had relaxed quite so completely, and nothing seemed important enough to disturb his sense of well-being. For a moment he even toyed with the idea of retirement. The notion of a life with no pressures, no worries seemed momentarily attractive.

So easily had the conversation run from topic to topic that it was several minutes before he was aware that Sir Henry Wilson was expounding upon the current military and political position of Great Britain.

". . . so you see, it is vital that England be able to react swiftly to any challenge to world peace. She has only one means of doing so at the moment, the navy. But we English tend to underestimate the importance of a strong army. It was Marlborough"—he bowed toward Churchill with a grin—"a rather obscure ancestor of yours, I believe, who first made good use of a modern British army.''

Churchill chuckled but remained silent.

"Marlborough saw very clearly that the growing military power of France could be a direct threat to British commerce not only on the Continent but in the rest of the world as well. It was also clear to the allied European powers, who practically begged Marlborough to assume overall command, that any one power strong enough to control the Continent militarily spelt ruin for all. England's army tipped the balance against France. And one hundred years later, we again found ourselves in a similar position. It was the English army and navy—not the navy alone—that tipped the balance against Napoleon. Without us, the rest of Europe would have succumbed to French expansionist aims centuries ago. And the situation is unchanged today, only the villain is different.''

"I assume you are referring to Germany," Miss Asquith observed.

Wilson nodded. "Yes, I am. She has come late to the scene and therefore is insecure, ambitious, and rather a bit unscrupulous.''

"Colonel, are you saying that Germany *is* our enemy?"

"Ah, my dear Miss Asquith." Admiral Beatty smiled, taking up the debate, and Bannerman had the impression they had played this scene before. "Not necessarily an enemy in the classic sense, but a trade rival. And these days, the two are inseparable, as I am sure you have heard your father say before. Not only our enemy—rival, if you will—but that of all of Europe. Germany is certain to attempt to extend her hegemony to the rest of the Continent one day. And can you blame her for trying? There she is, smack in the middle of a landmass with only a tiny coastline on the North Sea, and that directly menaced by the British fleet at Rosyth. Her naval forces would barely clear their harbors before they met our dreadnoughts.''

"I would certainly hope so!" Churchill replied.

"As for the rest, she has France on one side and Russia on the other. Where can she expand to meet the needs of her growing population? Overseas territories? The best are taken. Yet, as you can see from the press reports, Germany scrambles hard in Africa, China, and the Pacific. Poor Germany.

She is made to feel like the poor relation of Europe—in the words of the Kaiser.''

Wilson nodded and when he spoke, his voice was somber. ''You'wait and see. One day a miscalculation will occur, and a general war will rage across Europe. And it will be different from any we have ever fought before. France and Russia will face the might of Germany and Austria and it will be a catastrophe.

''Until 1907, France's main concern was an alliance with Russia. Now that she has that and the promise of our assistance as well, she is searching for a way to speed up Russia's mobilization. The Russians themselves estimate four weeks but no one who understands the problem would accept even six weeks as the minimum figure. The Russians are constrained by distance. When they complete their railway network in 1915 their time for mobilization will be halved. That leaves, however, a four-year gap, during which time Germany can act with an excellent chance of beating France in the first month. Unless . . .''

''Unless . . . ?'' Bannerman was fascinated by Wilson's analysis. This was a side of the War Office he had not seen before. Wilson must be one of those young, vigorous men— the ''technicians,'' as they were disparagingly dubbed—whom Lloyd George and Churchill were so determined to move into the various government offices. God knew they were needed. His few contacts in the War Office to date had been with officers who had spent their lives fighting small engagements against spear-carrying natives.

''*Unless*, my dear Mr. Bannerman, the British army can be induced to land a large force in Flanders to help contain the German war machine until the Russians are able to come up in the east. Between us then, we might squeeze brother Fritz until he begs for an armistice. The secret of success for either side will lie in speed of mobilization.''

Bannerman inclined his head politely but his expression was skeptical. ''The French army is the most powerful in Europe and they have the Russians as allies. Between them, they should be able to deal with Germany without England's help.''

Wilson smiled. ''You, sir, are assuming that the Germans will attack headlong across Alsace and the Saar, driving through the fiercest of French defenses to Paris. And if they do so, of course the French and Russians will win. French planning, as our own, is based largely upon this expectation. And if we are correct, our expeditionary force will not require quick movement across the Channel. Two to three weeks will be sufficient. However, the Germans would be fools to attack right into the arms of the waiting French forts, wouldn't you say?''

Bannerman called up an image of the European map in his mind, envisioning the French border area with Germany. Between Switzerland and Belgium the border, as best he could recall, described a right-angle turn, each heavily fortified leg of which was approximately a hundred miles long.

''Assume now,'' Wilson went on, ''that Germany takes the offensive in the east as well, sending in double or even triple the number of divisions they are expected to throw against the Russians within *four weeks* of mobilization?''

''They would be attacking Russia before her armies were fully mobilized, of course,'' Bannerman responded carefully. ''Germany would probably win the war, at least in the east. But where will she get those extra divisions? The press reports all suggest she needs two-thirds of her divisions in France.''

''But she wouldn't if France were already defeated.''

''Impossible!''

''Not if Germany occupies Paris before Russia completes mobilization.''

Bannerman shifted in his chair. ''How?'' he challenged. ''The French will not repeat the mistakes of 1871. They will be ready for the Germans this time. The line of forts along the Franco-German border was built specifically to prevent another German breakthrough.''

Wilson nodded soberly, and exchanged glances with Beatty and Churchill. ''That is the exact objection I received at the War Office.'' He got up from the table and went to the bookcase for an atlas while everyone watched—not Wilson, but him, Bannerman, and he knew that he had been correct; they had all heard this before. But why were they putting on this act for him? he wondered. Wilson found his page and, dutifully, everyone joined him at the library table. Bannerman had the sense of a trap closing as Wilson opened the book to a map of Europe.

''The German armies,'' he began, ''will attack through Belgium—''

"That's preposterous!" Bannerman snorted. "I do not know much about political affairs, but I do know that Germany has guaranteed Belgium's neutrality. If nothing else would, such an attack would bring England into the war."

"They will drive," Wilson went on, ignoring Bannerman's objection, "into Belgium along a line extending from Liège to Brussels, wheel south, and take advantage of the level, open country of Flanders to march into France. The valley of the Oise will provide their highway to Paris, where, attacking up from the southwest, they will capture the city and destroy the bulk of French armies. The war in the west will be over."

He smiled at the engineer. "Please, Mr. Bannerman, do not be so surprised. If the Germans do not first violate Belgium, the French will. Clausewitz wrote almost a hundred years ago that 'the heart of France lies between Brussels and Paris.' How else to enter that heartland than through Belgium?"

Wilson tapped the map with his fingertip. "The German time schedule as laid down by von Schlieffen in 1906 calls for Paris to be occupied thirty-one days after the start of mobilization. We estimate that up to thirty-five German first-line divisions will then be withdrawn from the west and moved by railway to the eastern front. It is expected that this will require a further two weeks, using up to 250,000 railway wagons. There will be a total of one hundred and thirty divisions moving against Russia, ninety German and forty Austrian. Against them, the Russian Army will have been able to mobilize fully less than fifty of her one hundred and fourteen."

Churchill cleared his throat and Wilson stepped back a bit as if deferring to him. "In early 1913," he said quietly, "the Channel Tunnel will be completed and we will have the capability of moving six divisions to Flanders within five days. That, added to six Belgian divisions and the bulk of the French armies, will effectively halt the German advance in the west. Having failed to beat France, she will not dare continue in the east as a war on two fronts would mean certain defeat."

Churchill smiled at him. "So you see, Mr. Bannerman, Germany must enter and win the war before the end of 1912. To delay past that year will mean stalemate at best or defeat at worst. If you were responsible for the security of Germany as the Kaiser and his General Staff are, would you not be feeling most anxious?''

"But you are assuming that war is inevitable," Bannerman protested.

"We are," Churchill agreed, "because it is. The pressures are building up—the Balkans, Africa, the naval race, the Austro-German alliance, the Triple Entente. Those pressures will have to be relieved. Diplomacy will not do it but cannon fire will. So, examine it from the Kaiser's viewpoint. Within the short span of two years your country can be attacked and defeated by surrounding hostile powers. You have until the end of 1912 to prepare—which he is doing at all costs. But,'' Churchill added slyly, "consider this. If there were no railway tunnel beneath the English Channel, you, as the Kaiser, would have until 1915 when the Russian railway network is scheduled for completion. A lot can be done in two years.''

Bannerman stared at the map, conscious that he had been privy to very secret information and not caring for it at all. Churchill was clearly placing a great deal of responsibility on him.

"The key to your supposition," he said slowly, "would seem to be German readiness to go to war and to invade Belgium despite the fact that both Germany and France have guaranteed her neutrality.''

Wilson nodded. "So they have. Nations pay lip service to the concept of honor but abide by it only when it is in their interest to do so. Germany will excuse her perfidy by proclaiming an encirclement by hostile nations. Make no mistake about it, Mr. Bannerman. Germany will attack and through Belgium, and she will do so before 1913—as long as the Channel Tunnel is perceived as a threat. Some obscure incident will be blown all out of proportion and made to serve as the excuse.''

"An incident such as the Moroccan crisis," Churchill put in. "It was only the threat of British intervention there that finally caused Germany to back down.''

Bannerman had been only peripherally aware of the summer's events: the coronation and the equally intriguing crisis that had brought the Continent to the verge of war. Conflicting French, Italian, and German claims in Morocco had again precipitated crisis after crisis until Great Britain had at last been persuaded to stand by France.

"Will the two disasters that have struck the Tunnel recently cause any great delay in completing construction?" Wilson asked abruptly.

Bannerman hesitated and Churchill, taking his hesitation for reluctance, said, "You may speak freely, Mr. Bannerman. No word of what you say here will pass this room. I can assure you of that. All here are trusted friends. And Miss Asquith has certainly lived with plenty of political secrets buzzing in that pretty young head." Violet Asquith gave Churchill an impish grin in reply.

Bannerman shook his head. "I am afraid, sir, that I am not in a position to act as spokesman for the Anglo-French Submarine Railway Company."

Wilson nodded. "I understand perfectly. However, your assessment of the problem is rather critical. You must have some idea how it has affected your company's decision to continue."

Bannerman raised an eyebrow at that. "I am afraid, Sir Henry, that you are asking for reserved information. It would be a breach of confidence for me to make any such comment."

Wilson nodded again reluctantly. "Yes, I do understand. However, we had hoped that you would come to view the needs of Great Britain above the needs of your company, especially as I assure you that whatever you say will not be repeated."

So that was the reason he had been treated to the latest thinking regarding an imminent continental war. Struggling to contain his anger at Wilson's unconscious insult. Bannerman lit a cigarette. "I can tell you this," he said, choosing his words with care. "The project has received two major setbacks that will cause delays. There can be no doubt of that. I have taken steps to see that the delays will be held to a minimum. I have estimated today for the parliamentary committee that tunneling operations will be resumed within three weeks. While the loss of life was great, the physical damage was not extensive."

"Then you see the Tunnel as remaining on schedule?" Churchill asked.

"Nearly on schedule, I believe would be more accurate."

"I referred earlier," Churchill put in, "to a matter of utmost concern to your company and to the government. I see that we have not managed to convince you just how important it is, especially if it should turn out as we both suspect.''

He paused for a moment, as if considering his words carefully. ''You are well aware that public opinion in England is very much against the Tunnel project. The Tory press is most vociferous in its campaign, and certain of our traditional supporters have lately begun to agree with them. If we, you and I, should turn out to be correct in our analyses, and if we do nothing to forestall further problems, there could be serious repercussions, for your company and for the government. As a minister, I have of course a vested interest. But as a citizen of England, you do as well.''

Bannerman was well aware of the discomfort he was causing by remaining silent. And he could feel himself growing angry at being placed in such a position. His stubbornness had a profound dampening effect on the party, and Wilson soon made an excuse to leave. Bannerman followed a few minutes later. Churchill was all affability as he saw him out, following his guest onto the stoop and closing the door behind them.

''See here, James,'' Churchill said, the smile gone and his expression serious. ''There are just the two of us now and this is entirely private. I believe you have been given something to think about tonight. Wilson is a very bright man and his analysis is, I am certain, quite accurate. We both know that an incident of sabotage has taken place, although there is no hard proof. I am not asking you to make up your mind tonight, but please think about this. If they have tried once, they will try a second time. I can offer you, on behalf of the government, troops to protect the works.''

He paused there as if to gauge Bannerman's reaction. Bannerman again felt the unaccountable anger rising and he started to retort, but Churchill stopped him.

''I realize the position you are in. I suspect that you have not yet relayed your suspicions to your Board of Directors, as I have not expressed mine to the cabinet. Yet neither of us can delay much longer. Please think about that and my offer before our suspicions are made public through some agency neither of us can control. Good night now.''

And with that he went back inside, leaving Bannerman to feel that he had somehow made a mistake. He had not made an enemy of Churchill, but he knew that by his reluctance to share information he had attracted an unwarranted amount of attention. The more important problem for him at the moment, however, was how and when to inform the Board that he suspected sabotage. He felt he had managed satisfactorily to sidestep any such suggestion during the hearings, even though several members had tried hard to draw him out. But as he settled into a hansom for the journey back to his rooms, he knew that he could not continue to avoid the situation as he had done Tuesday at the brief Board meeting. The directors were so solicitous of him then that they had kept the business to a bare minimum. But as the rumors grew, which they certainly would now that the Admiralty had reached the same conclusions, their concern for his health and well-being would vanish in proportion to the perceived threat to their collective and individual investments.

chapter══════ 11

V*on Dorn signed the register with an English name and* followed the old woman up the narrow stairs to the bed-sitter above the bar. She mumbled and waved an arm about, as if too weary to be bothered by one more transient visitor, and left.

He glanced around the room and snorted. It was clean and that was all that could be said for it. A narrow bed covered with a worn comforter, a threadbare rug, a cheap cupboard with a cracked ewer and basin, and a single, stiff-backed chair comprised the furnishings. The room reeked of stale air and Lysol. He tugged at the window until it opened and the cold streamed in.

By standing to one side he could see waves beating on the shingle and, directly below, the muddy lane that ran up into the village proper. Kingsdown was certainly no prize—a mean little town of narrow lanes, ancient houses, and unfriendly people. The train down from London had been crowded and there were no first-class carriages available. He had been cramped into a second-class seat for the entire length of the interminable journey. Then in Deal he had searched for half an hour before finding a taxi willing to brave the winter roads to Kingsdown, three miles on.

In spite of everything, he had arrived early. He left his portmanteau on the bed, closed the window, and went down to the bar. Luncheon consisted of lukewarm potato soup, a thin slice of cheese between two soggy pieces of bread, and a glass of stout, apparently the only drink served in the establishment. He managed to choke down the sandwich and stout. The soup was a total loss. When he could stand the waiting no longer, he got his coat and went out.

Kingsdown had been completely isolated by the Tunnel works extending northeasterly into Otty Bottom and onto the

137

slopes of Barrows Hill. Only the single road running north along the beach toward Deal remained; the other two roads leading out to the valley had been closed at the northern border of the Tunnel yards. He went up through the village to the crest of Chalk Hill. A single farmhouse and barn, abandoned to the elements, stood on a knoll. The Channel was visible on the east and the desolation of the Tunnel yards lay before him. A cold wind was blowing off the Channel under a leaden sky. Impelled more by boredom that curiosity, he made his way through the snow-covered fields to the cliff tops, thinking that the walk might clear his head and prepare him for the meeting with that damned fool renegade. Otherwise, he would have to sit in his drafty, evil-smelling room and brood. Since the Tunnel disaster he had heard nothing from Berlin, from either Langenscheidt or von Epping. After two weeks, the silence was becoming ominous.

Long, rolling combers smashed against the base of the chalk cliffs a hundred feet below and involuntarily he stepped back, vertigo and the inexorable movement of the sea causing him to lose his balance. A cargo steamer wallowed a mile or more off the coast as it made for the Nore and London. No other shipping was visible. To the south he saw the great ventilator shafts of the Tunnel marching toward the horizon, their rotating beacons plainly visible in the grayness. Plumes of spray were flung up from the artificial islands on which they stood, as if the waves resented impediments in their long march to the German Sea.

A gradual upward slope lay between him and the main works. The snow was thicker here where it was sheltered somewhat from the wind, and he stared at the level surface in curiosity. It was some time before he realized that he was walking across the golf course he remembered from the maps he had studied so carefully. His watch showed fifty minutes remaining before he was due to return to the inn, and he made his way diagonally across the windswept links. His shoes would be damp all the way back to London but he had not had an outing in two weeks and found to his surprise that he was exhilarated by the cutting wind. He reached the top of the rise and again the yards lay before him, clad in sheltering snow that hid the worst of the damage done to the once beautiful downs.

Plumes of smoke were swept from rank after rank of chimneys. The gray-stone semidetached workers' houses, one exactly like the other, could be seen past the far side of the yard. The dreariness of the spectacle represented industrial Europe at its worst. He had visited the Tunnel works the previous spring on a tour arranged for members of the diplomatic corps by the Foreign Office, anxious to impress the world with the daring of the government's vision. The scale of the project had startled him then, and yet the extent of the plant had doubled since. He estimated now that the yards were nearly two miles across. The number of buildings seemed to have tripled, and the stockpiles of equipment and supplies looked sufficient for an army.

As he watched, a shunting engine gathered steam and began to nose a line of cars away from the great concrete mound of the Tunnel where it projected from the back of the cliffs. The wind swirled grains of sandlike snow about him. A steam whistle blasted across the valley, then fell silent abruptly, as if realizing that its screech was a blasphemy in the winter stillness. Workmen appeared from buildings and the Tunnel like disciplined columns of ants. The sight reminded him of the time and he started back to the village.

Sean McDougal was waiting in the room, greatcoat wrapped closely about him against the cold.

"I would appreciate it in the future," von Dorn said dryly, "if you could pick a more civilized place to meet and one farther away from the Tunnel works as well."

McDougal snorted. "The ol' woman is deaf and too senile to pay any mind to who comes and goes. Her daughter is just as bad and half-witted besides."

Von Dorn rummaged through his bag for the flask. He offered it to McDougal, who shook his head and produced his own bottle. "Don't care for foreign drink."

Von Dorn pulled the chair around to the bed and sat down. "Now that you have brought me here, what do you want?"

McDougal decided to be equally as blunt. "We want to know why it were necessary to kill the woman?"

The feeling that events were slipping beyond his control suddenly made itself felt. First, to be summoned here so abruptly, then to be faced . . . Von Dorn suppressed his apprehension and studied McDougal, seeking a clue to his intent.

"How do you know that I had anything to do with it?" he asked very quietly.

McDougal's eyes widened at the hint of the threat in the German's voice but he refused to give ground. "Finnigan, of course. We want to know why it were necessary to kill her?"

"If Finnigan told you about her, then he also told you why." The lousy little bastard, von Dorn thought to himself. The little fool had reported to that ass in Liverpool, after all. Now even McDougal knew.

"That bloody fool, Finnigan!" McDougal grunted, as if echoing his unspoken assessment. "We want to hear it from you, Mr. Prussian Businessman. Why should she blab to the police when she hated coppers worse than any of us?"

The odor of disinfectant was still strong in the room and, irritated by it, von Dorn stood suddenly, opened the window again, and hesitated, looking down into the road. Two children passed, their voices happy as they kicked a way through the snow.

"We know," McDougal said behind him, "that you was using her to deliver my instructions because you figured that me and Finnigan might take it into our heads to go it on our own. So, it seems a bit strange that you had to kill someone who was so useful. Why, she was the engineering director's own clerk. She must have given good value—in many different ways, according to Tom Finnigan." This last was said with a leer, and von Dorn did not trouble to object or deny it.

"Quite simple, I should say. She was very upset over the men killed. Killed, I might add, because of your incompetence. When I arrived at her flat, she was hysterical. She accused us all of murdering those men. I tried to reason with her but she struck me." He shrugged. "She began to scream and came at me with a kitchen knife. I hit her. I did not think I hit her that hard, but apparently I did. I believe that she had gone insane."

McDougal was silent, and von Dorn knew he was being scrutinized. He allowed his shoulders to sag a bit until he heard McDougal grunt and knew that his story had been accepted. Not that it mattered, he thought cynically. They needed him far more than he needed them.

"What went wrong?" he asked, turning, not giving McDougal a chance to ask questions.

McDougal scowled. "It failed because of your mistake, boyo. 'Twas not blasting gelatin in those mines."

Von Dorn frowned. "What are you talking about?"

McDougal jumped to his feet. "Those mines came from the naval stores at Dover. They was full of cordite."

"Cordite, I . . . I . . ." von Dorn gaped at him. "But no one would use cordite for blasting. It doesn't make sense!"

"You damned fool. They were designed to work that way. Bannerman said the cordite was packed in oversized steel containers."

Von Dorn stared at McDougal, unable at first to comprehend what he was saying. Cordite was a slow-burning explosive, he thought. How could it possibly have caused such damage . . . something McDougal said . . . oversized containers? And then he understood.

"Ah, Christ," von Dorn murmured. "No wonder she thought . . ." He stopped abruptly, aware that he might say too much. Instead, he turned to McDougal. "What is the assessment? Do they think it is sabotage?"

McDougal nodded. "Aye. Bannerman suspects. But he's dithering about the effect it will have on the Board of Directors. So far, he's said nothing except to me."

Von Dorn swore. He needed time to think this through. "Then the government hasn't been asked to conduct an inquiry?"

McDougal shook his head. "No. Not yet at any rate. But Bannerman has had dinner with that bloody Churchill—"

"Churchill? Damn it. How did he come into it?"

"I dinna know. Bannerman visited with him last week. At the great man's house, no less. Churchill tried to pump him for information, tried to get him to admit it was sabotage."

"Damn it all, man," von Dorn exploded. "Why did you not get word to me?"

McDougal laughed at that. "You've murdered our messenger, you bloody fool." He watched as von Dorn strode about the room, hands clasped behind his back. He did not trust this bloody German, but he needed him, the Fenians needed him, needed the arms and ammunition and the money that the Germans were willing to supply. That damned, twice damned cowardly politician, John Redmond, had seen to it that they were cut off from the means of raising more than a few pence in Ireland and now there was that triply damned *Sinn Fein* as well. *"Ourselves alone."* Ridiculous bunch of pansies. They would never amount to anything, yet they and the Nationalist Party had a stranglehold on the Movement and would never let go. And they were content to play about with Home Rule, the bloody asses.

Von Dorn paused in the middle of the floor, unconsciously fixing McDougal with a direct stare while he fought through the tangle of conflicting thoughts. He knew that he was in danger of losing the Fenians; they no longer trusted him. He had murdered one of their own. Killing Margaret had been a fool's play and he had realized it even before he had left the flat. But he could no more have stopped himself at the time that he could have flown, and even now he still felt a sense of excitement at what he had done. Still, he should have gone for Finnigan and let these damned fools take care of her in their own way. The result would have been the same, but they would have done it, not an outsider. The question was now, Did they believe his story? He could not be certain, but he did realize that unless they were given something to distract their attention from him, he would soon see everything— all his plans—go by the boards. And if that happened, his career and perhaps his life would be worth nothing. He needed something dramatic now to sidetrack them, and even as he reached that conclusion, the Kaiser's own words ". . . we will destroy it, completely . . ." occurred to him. He sank down on the bed with a thin smile. It was premature perhaps, but it might serve.

"When new instructions come from Berlin," von Dorn said, still watching McDougal, who sat as if transfixed, "we may well be ordered to destroy the Tunnel. Destroy it completely."

McDougal continued to stare a moment and then, with a grunt, "That's daft, man!"

"Is it?" von Dorn snarled. "You've known all along it might well come to this. Or perhaps you are just too attached to your English after all?"

"Don't talk foolishness," McDougal replied, his voice weary. "I meant only to ask how you intend to go about destroying eight mile or more of cement and brick?"

Von Dorn swore softly under his breath. How he ached for a company of German troops. With them he would bring the Tunnel to ruin within hours.

"And more, why would you be wanting to do that?"

Von Dorn did not reply immediately. He sensed that this moment might well be a turning point in his life. He had felt this way once before, in Morocco. Then too there had been a sense of hopelessness, of events moving too fast, but when he had made his decision, it had all disappeared and the feeling of being in command of the situation had returned. As he stared at the middle-aged Irish engineer, he knew that he could force an end to the silence from Berlin. To do so would call for as bold and unexpected a counterstroke as the attack on the third gun position. If he failed, his career and possibly his life were forfeit. If he won, though, if he succeeded? Promotion, the gratitude and support of the Kaiser? He did not think that too much to expect.

He stood up and clasped his hands behind his back, legs apart, and stared again at McDougal, who suddenly discovered that he had an intense desire to laugh at von Dorn's comical but unconscious parody of a caricature Prussian.

"It must be done. The time for war is drawing close. It will be the decision of my masters in Berlin, but you must inform your masters in Dublin and prepare them to help."

McDougal thought for a moment that von Dorn must be insane, but there was no trace of madness in his eyes.

"Aye, that I'll do," he said slowly, as if reluctant to speak at all. "But the Tunnel? To destroy it completely?" He shook his head. "The price will come high."

"Your country's freedom is at stake as well," von Dorn shot back angrily. "How dare you suggest a price!"

"You great damned fool," McDougal thundered. "You'd be asking us to risk all we've built on a foolish action that'll be of little benefit to Ireland. We need time—four, five, ten years yet—before we can face the English on their own terms. You think a bomb in a silly tunnel will aid us?"

"Of course it will," von Dorn cried. "When war comes, the English must commit their army and when they empty Ireland to do so, you will have your chance. Germany will win, and Ireland's freedom and economic independence will be assured. You must be blind not to see it."

"Oh, aye, I see it all. I see Ulstermen armed to the teeth replacing the damned English. I see our people torn by dissension, fighting among themselves, many even off to help the English in their war. And if Germany loses? 'Twill be another hundred years before the chance comes again. Aye, every foreigner who wishes to defeat the English comes to Ireland with the same siren song: the Spanish, the French, even the Americans, and now the Germans. And the result is always the same: the foreigner defeated and Irish lads swinging from the gallows tree."

He shook his head and glared at von Dorn. "No, Mr. Prussian, you'll not find a ready audience for your daft ideas in Dublin this time. But, I'll pass the word along." McDougal snorted in contempt, wondering why he had ever allowed the Dublin Committee to force him into helping this damned arrogant German.

"If we are to prepare for such foolishness," he muttered after a few moments, "I will need help. I can count on the men I already have but I'll need more. When will I have word on the names submitted to your damned spy bureau in Berlin?"

Von Dorn paused in the act of lighting a cheroot and shook out the match. "What are you talking about?"

"The list of names," McDougal snapped. "The same as I gave you a month and more ago to send off to Berlin. To be checked, you said, although it is beyond me how—" He broke off at the expression on von Dorn's face.

"I sent the approved list to you, two weeks ago. With the plans for the explosion in the heading."

"The bloody hell you did! I received no such list. There was nothing on the letter but instructions, twelve of them and no more."

"Of course not, you fool!" von Dorn hissed. "The list was in the alternate position, beneath the stamp, and the envelope was so coded. If you have messed—"

"There was no envelope," McDougal roared. "No damned envelope. Only a letter from that company in Belgium . . ." McDougal paused, then as his face went gray he stumbled to his feet. Von Dorn reached a hand to steady him, thinking that he was having an attack.

"The stamp," McDougal muttered. "The damned stamp. Was it a fancy foreign stamp, then?"

When von Dorn, struggling to understand what he was getting at, merely gaped at him, McDougal shook off his arm and shouted, "Did the envelope have a foreign stamp, damn you?"

"Yes." Von Dorn backed away. "What are you—"

"She gave it to Bannerman. I saw her. The woman gave him the envelope with a foreign stamp. Ah, sweet Jesus!" McDougal moaned. "She did not know about the codes or how the messages were done up, then?"

"What are you talking about?" von Dorn demanded.

McDougal grabbed his bottle and tipped it to his mouth, but von Dorn snatched it away. "What in hell are you talking about?" he shouted.

"Bannerman collects stamps. Margaret often saved them for him, that's what I am talking about. And now he has the very one with your list. . . ."

Von Dorn was thunderstruck. Never once had she mentioned that the engineering director's hobby was stamps. For God's sake, he thought, was everything now to be jeopardized by a stupid hobby?

"You saw her give it to him?" he repeated as if to make certain.

"Aye. I thought nothing of it at the time," the Irish engineer muttered, staring at his knotted hands. "But he has it now."

Von Dorn turned away, trying to force himself to think logically, coherently. The microfilm was no more than a tiny speck, a piece of dust on the back of a gummed square of colored paper, hard enough even for an expert to recognize. How would this Bannerman ever discover it, recognize it for what it was and decipher it? Impossible. But, as he turned to reassure McDougal, he caught sight of the cringing fear on the man's face, as if he could already feel the hangman's knot under his chin. No, steady, he told himself. Best not to let this chance escape. It could very well be the advantage he needed.

He stared at McDougal a moment, thinking to himself that Bannerman had twice now shown unexpected determination. A way to get rid of him?

146

"I would suggest, Mr. McDougal," he said slowly, his voice cold, "that you had better retrieve that stamp before your Mr. Bannerman discovers what is underneath. For if he does, you will hang. Your name is included in that list. So, for the sake of your own neck, I suggest you retrieve that stamp. At any cost."

chapter ———— 12

*C*onnigham *escaped from the press and noise of the South*-ampton Docks Custom House and paused under the portico to light a cigarette. The North German Lloyd liner that had docked two hours before had unloaded quickly and, taking advantage of the confusion, he had mingled with the passengers flooding gratefully down the gangway. The North Atlantic had been extremely rough and the customs officers were sympathetic, passing the travelers through with only perfunctory checks. There had been no sign of untoward interest in him. The clerk did no more than glance at his passport, hand it back, and wave him through.

The wind off the River Itchen was pushing a thin rain ahead as he trudged across Canute Road to the Terminus Railroad Station. Connigham forced his way through the crowd and into the drafty structure, changed his money, and strode along the lines to the ticket kiosk. A surly individual with bad teeth and clad in a black railroad monkey jacket that was slowly turning age-green, sold him a ticket to Waterloo Station and growled the platform number at him without bothering once to look up.

Connigham went down the line to platform three, where the chalkboard gave the departure time as 10:45. He glanced at the huge clock over the barrier and decided that he would have to endure whatever food was being served aboard the train. He went along the platform until he found a relatively empty carriage.

The ship had endured gale force winds from the moment they cleared Cape Race and the entire crew had little rest. Now the heat of the car and his own weariness combined to put Connigham to sleep before the train had even started.

* * *

He awoke as they were entering Waterloo Station. The sun had finally broken through but had done little to relieve the dreary scene glimpsed briefly before the train ran into the tunnel. He shook his head to clear away the traces of sleep and ran his tongue around the inside of his mouth, wincing at the taste, then gathered up his coat and duffel bag, shuffled with the crowd to the platform, and trudged up through the crush to the concourse. Standing there beneath the clock, he looked around for a pub sign.

Connigham stared at the padlock on the pub, wondering if it was a holiday. He even put a hand against the door and pushed.

"Closed, mate," said a voice from behind. "Closed till four."

"I'll be damned," he muttered, still staring at the door. He heard the voice chuckle. "Been away some time, hey. Closing laws in 1904."

Connigham turned to find a policeman grinning at him. "Sees it all the time. Mostly sailors, like you," the policeman said, indicating the duffel bag and pea coat. "Where you in from?"

Connigham forced himself to remain calm. The policeman was just being friendly. If there had ever been a flyer on him, it had been years before and the copper would certainly have forgotten by now.

"States. New York. Ship docked at Southampton this morning."

The policeman cocked his head to listen hard. "Yer not a Yank?"

"Naw. Canadian. First time in England since the end of the war."

"Ah, after the old Boer, was you? Me Dad, too."

"Not till four, you say? Well, where the devil can a man get a drink around here?"

The policeman grinned as he shook his head. "Nowheres in London till four. If yer that bad off, buy a bottle."

Connigham nodded ruefully. "Been some changes, I see. Well, better get along if I'm to find a hotel. Any suggestions?"

The bobby shrugged. "If you don't mind the expense, the Westminster Palace. Cost you three to four shillings for a room. Take the Baker Street and Waterloo tube to Trafalgar, and walk half a mile along Whitehall, opposite Westminster

Abbey. Underground's all electrified now. If that's too steep for you, there's good inns right along Waterloo Road for a shilling or so a night.''

Connigham grinned. "That's more like it. Thanks very much.''

He went out into the watery sunshine and down the road with no intention of going to either the Westminster Palace or any of the inns along Waterloo Road. If by chance the bobby should remember that he had seen Connigham's face on a wanted flyer, they'd waste their time looking for him there first.

"Where to, chief?'' The taxi chauffeur had that pinched look he recalled as characteristic of many of the London working class—the same bad teeth and feral, almost haunted look. He gave the man directions to the house in Knightsbridge and pushed a pound note through the window into his lap to forestall any objections.

Traffic was hopelessly jammed at the Westminster Bridge and Connigham fidgeted until they broke free. Late sunlight gilded the soot-stained towers of Westminster Palace across the river, and he discovered that he had forgotten how attractive the ancient structure was in spite of the fact that it was the seat of Ireland's greatest enemy. Traffic began to stream across the bridge once more as Big Ben chimed three o'clock.

The driver went straight through the intersection of Whitehall and Parliament Street, horn tootling to warn traffic, and shortly they were into the relative calm of St. James's Park. The light was going here among the bare trees, replaced by a thin mist. Birds wheeled over Birdcage Walk before settling onto Duck Island. The peace of the park was so startling after the heavily congested streets that Connigham nearly had the taxi stop so that he could walk.

The chauffeur eased into the tight circle of Brompton Square five minutes later and stopped before number 6. Connigham gave the driver a six-penny tip and received the man's thanks and a doubtful look. The tall sailor was far from the type liable to be welcomed in Brompton Square.

Connigham ground the cigarette beneath his heel, using the moment to glance around quickly. He spotted a curtain being twitched back into place, then picked up his bag and went up the walk. He twisted the bell and waited. The man who eventually opened the door was dressed in a morning coat and stiff collar, but Connigham guessed he had once seen a boxing ring, from the inside. His nose had been broken several times and there was more than a suspicion of fleshiness about his ears. His coat was tailored but not well enough to conceal the revolver beneath his arm completely. Wild West time, he thought. Clearly Emily had taken to carting bodyguards around with her.

The butler's features rippled in contempt. "Trades entrance to rear. An' we don't give handouts."

Connigham tossed the heavy duffel bag at him, followed as the butler stumbled back under the weight, pushing hard on the man's left shoulder to turn him aside, and with his right hand neatly extracted the revolver from its holster. He kicked the door closed.

"You will tell Lady Emily Wilson-Langdon there's an old friend here to see her. Go on!" he finished, giving the man one more shove.

The butler glared and, without turning his back completely, stalked away to the end of the hall. Connigham looked at the revolver—a nickel-plated Webley Double Action in .44 caliber, an early model 1875 RIC—dropped it into his pocket, and glanced around the hall. Emily was obviously still doing things in style, so she had not managed to spend her way through both inheritances yet.

The house itself was in the fanciest area of London's fancy West End. The hall was a mixture of creamy Italian marble and Indian mahogany, highly polished and gleaming in the waning sunshine washing through narrow windows on either side of the door. Fan-shaped skylights had been let into the walls, and while the middle ground was dusky, the cherub-decorated ceiling fairly glowed.

Several doors opened off the hall, each framed in delicate marble. The first on his left revealed an immaculate library. Connigham stepped inside. The room was large but the floor-to-ceiling bookcases lining the walls made it seem smaller. Heavy velvet curtains were partly drawn and a coal fire burned in the grate. The fire, the smell of oiled leather and French walnut, the rank on rank of books combined to produce in Connigham a feeling that he awkwardly sensed was one of homecoming, and it took him by surprise.

Each bookcase had been fitted with a series of glass partitions that, when pulled outward, slid back to disappear into the shelf above. He lifted a glass panel and removed a book at random. The crackling sound as he raised the leatherbound cover told him that it had never been opened. Entranced, he sniffed the slightly musty smell of old, fine paper with appreciation.

"Put that back, sir, if you please, and tell me . . . ."

Connigham turned with the book in his hand and regarded the woman who had just entered the library. The pug-faced butler was glowering and edging around her, but she held up a hand to stop him.

"Michael . . . ?" Her voice was hardly a whisper. "Michael, is that you?"

"It's me," he said simply, closed the book, laid it on the desk, and opened his arms.

She did not hesitate but ran across the room as fast as her fashionably tight skirt would allow. He took a step to meet her, unconscious that he did so, and whirled her high into the air so that her hair fluffed and tried to escape the pins.

"I cannot believe it." She was laughing. "Oh, my God, Michael . . ." and she kissed him hard, hungrily.

When at last he set her down the butler was staring in astonishment, and Connigham could practically read the thoughts struggling through his torpid brain. But he was much more concerned with the woman in his arms at the moment, and he held her away to look at her. "I'd forgotten just how lovely you really are," he breathed.

And she was. Her gray skirt was as tight as fashion dictated, forcing her to a near hobble, and her blouse was creamy silk, flourished and ruffled but narrow sleeved. Her hair, red-gold in the combination of fire and sunlight, had been done in the new shingled pattern, a mass of curls framing her heart-shaped face. Her eyes, greenish or gray depending upon the light, laughed with her joy at seeing him after three years; her nose wrinkled as she laughed, and for a moment he felt again that curious sense of homecoming.

She kissed him once more and then, remembering the butler, pushed herself away. "Charles, please tell my guests that I will rejoin them in a moment. Oh, and Charles, wait . . . Michael, you will be staying with me, won't you?"

"Emily, there is nothing I'd like better, but you know that I—"

"Nothing of the sort," she interrupted. "Charles, have the

guest room readied for Mr. . . . ." Her expression had suddenly become a frown of concern. "Michael, what name are—"

He put a finger across her lips. "Hush now, darlin' girl. No more to be said. Michael will do. I'll tell you about it all later. But I'd like a wash, a drink, and some sleep in that order."

With a doubtful glance, she turned back to the butler. "Charles, the guest room." Her command was imperious, demanding respect that was inherited rather than earned. "Have Minni prepare a tray and take it up when Michael rings. See that he isn't disturbed and make certain that the other servants know to keep quiet about our visitor. And Charles, Michael is not only an old and valued friend, he is one of *us*. Do you understand?" Her tone was what one might use to instruct a fairly intelligent watchdog and it was clearly appropriate as Charles ruminated a moment, then nodded soberly.

"Very good, madame. Follow me, sir."

She gave Connigham a final kiss that left him breathless, and he followed the butler along the hall and up the polished oak stairs, down the long front hallway to an end room. Charles growled at the diminutive, white-aproned girl who was just about to enter the room, and she gave Connigham one scared glance and fled with her duster.

"You stay in here," the butler rumbled and crossed the room to open the door to the private bath. "Water's hot and the bath is full." He paused by the door and looked at Connigham. His glance traveled from his dirty boots to the battered seaman's cap, then back down again, slowly. His expression still did not change when he said, "I don't know who you are, mate. But if you make trouble for Lady Emily, I'll break your ruddy neck."

Connigham grinned and settled his shoulders, a wordless challenge, but the man only gave him a thin smile. Connigham tossed him the revolver and the butler went out, closing the door. Michael threw open the window then and took a deep breath. The sun had disappeared to the west, leaving behind a flaming sky. The failing light cast a more kindly grace across the rooftops and stark trees. The air was cold but fresh in spite of the unpleasant tang of coal smoke. Summer and winter, it hung over the city like a pall, rising from three million or more grates and stoves.

He stripped off his jacket and shirt, shucked the denim pants and run-down boots, and padded through to the bath, lowering himself into the hot water. Steam rose about him, warming the chill of the North Atlantic from his bones and, still tired in spite of the nap on the train, he leaned his head against the back of the bath and slept.

Chill air flowing into the room from the open window awoke him. The water had cooled, and he shivered and sneezed twice in succession. Swearing at himself, Connigham climbed out, wrapped a towel from the warming rack about him, and hurried into the bedroom to slam the window shut. He poked at the coals in the grate and added more. The fire was slow to catch and, while he waited, he dried himself vigorously.

He dumped his bag onto the bed and found clean clothing—denims and a blue wool shirt, both still damp. Muttering to himself, Connigham draped them across the warming rack in the bath, found a dry towel, and wrapped that around his waist. He noticed the clock. Six in the evening.

A timid knock on the door made him conscious of the fact that he was still wearing only a towel. He opened it to see the little maid who had been frightened away earlier, and she gasped at the sight of his bare legs and chest and almost dropped the heavy tray. Connigham caught it just in time. Face a flaming crimson, she sidled in with her eyes averted, much to his amusement. He eased the door shut behind her and, with elaborate Irish courtesy, asked if he could assist her in any way. She could not have been more than sixteen, he judged, and was so flustered that she could not answer as she laid the table for his dinner.

He bowed, standing between her and the door, grinning the entire while. "Thank you, lass, for yer thoughtfulness." He had dropped into the deepest Irish brogue he could muster. "By all the saints and the Holy Mither as well but ye're a foine-lookin' lass." The towel started to slip and he clutched at it with one hand as it swung away to show a thigh. The girl yelped and scurried for the door, and he laughed as she ran down the hall. Still chuckling, he closed the door and pulled the table closer to the fire.

A crystal wine decanter glinted in the firelight, and he poured a measure into a delicate stemmed glass. The silver platter contained two chops swimming in thick, starchy gravy, half a fowl, and several small potatoes. A grilled tomato completed the course. Afterward, he placed the tray on the floor outside the door, glancing around to see if the maid was in sight.

Then he stood in the middle of the room, wondering what to do next. A bookshelf held a catholic selection, but for once he was in no mood to read. The clock chimed the half hour and he yawned. That decided him. He piled several more coals on the grate, banked the fire, and got into the bed. The bedclothes were chill but he lay there enduring for a few minutes, then reached and turned down the bed lamp. The room darkened except for the glow of the fire and he lay back, comfortable for the first time in weeks. After a moment, he closed his eyes and his mind as he had learned to do years before.

The sound of the door opening brought him awake and he lay still, trying to make out the figure momentarily outlined against the night light from the hallway, then he relaxed as the figure floated toward him. Without a word, he waited as the coverlet was lifted and a soft, round form slid in beside him, one arm going across his chest as soft lips caressed his face. He gathered Emily to him then, his mouth forcing hers open. Her tongue came into his and he shuddered at the velvet touch.

When he didn't answer, Emily turned in his arms and raised herself onto one elbow. It was too dark to see his face clearly, and she traced a finger along one cheek. "I said," she repeated softly, "that it is too dangerous for you, Michael. The police will know you are in London. They always find out. There are so many informers."

When he still kept silent, she poked him with a finger. "Well, answer me. What can you hope to do?"

He shook his head. "I don't know."

"That's all? 'I don't know'? Michael, there are two murder warrants for you. Surely you didn't cross the Atlantic without some idea of what you intend."

He shrugged. "She was my sister, Emily. My only sister."

"But you can't hold yourself responsible for that. You were three thousand miles away."

"But I do."

Emily sat up and drew the blanket around her shoulders. Connigham slid from the bed and added more coals to the fire. It flared and a deep red glow fell across his body, smoothing the cragged muscles. She watched as he worked, wondering about this strange man she once thought she loved and whom she had not seen more than four times in twelve years.

"She *was* my sister, Emily," he repeated quietly, getting back into the bed. "Jack and I left her on her own a long time ago. Both of us are equally to blame, but Jack will never come home. I doubt if he cares much that she's dead. He stopped writing years ago. I was the only one who did, and I never had any money to send her. If I did, she would have given it to the Movement. The bloody Movement," he muttered.

"Michael, she was a grown woman, responsible for herself. She was earning her own way, even had a responsible job."

Connigham snorted. "What's this? Suffragette nonsense?"

As soon as he said that, he could feel her withdraw. He took her face between his hands and kissed her, remembering that it was a suffrage speech which had been the cause of their first meeting. "I apologize, Emily. I know what you are saying is true. She was a grown woman, but still, I ran out on her and so did Jack. And," he said after a moment, "I think there's more to her murder than the press reported. She was with the Movement, and I have the feeling that it's all mixed together, but I don't know how or why. Maybe the police killed her and, if so, I intend to find out."

He drew her on top of him then and pulled the cover up to encompass them both. When she started to protest, he hushed her by pressing his mouth to her until she lay quietly in his arms.

"Emily, what is the real status of the Movement in dear old England? Being stuck across the water is like living at the end of a long tunnel. All you ever hear are garbled echoes."

She stared at the ceiling, wondering how much to tell him, what might involve him more deeply, what might convince him to leave the country again, although she knew him well enough to realize that the latter was a very remote possibility.

"In London, almost nonexistent now. Scotland Yard took nearly all those with connections to the Fenians this past summer, before the coronation. Afraid that something might happen.''

''Informers?''

He felt her head nod against his shoulder. ''Orders came from Dublin to stay quiet, to wait and see. I do nothing more than report social gossip now. That's all they seem to want of me anymore,'' she finished, voice bitter.

''In Ireland?''

''Ah yes, in Ireland.'' Emily laughed, bitterly. ''They still run about the countryside, burning the odd hayrick or police station, getting themselves killed, going to jail, and bragging a lot. We are still alive, but barely so. Home Rule is certain to pass in the New Year and so there's little need for revolutionaries. We are dying, Michael, no longer needed.''

Connigham was silent for a while, thinking about what she had said. The news had reached them in the States as rumors, and as they gained currency, donations had fallen until he himself was barely managing to survive. But he had not put that much credit in the stories, certain that they were exaggerated, certain that something would happen to revive the Movement. Home Rule. And what would that mean? Not even an equal footing in the Commonwealth of which the damned English were so proud. It meant their own Parliament but not freedom. Christ, it would be nothing more than a stooge Irish government paid for exclusively by Irishmen, but doing London's bidding. And the fools were too blind to see that. Ireland's great sin was and always had been her proximity to England; a short boat trip would land an invading force across waters much more sheltered than the bloody English Channel. No, Ireland would never be granted the right to exist as an independent nation; freedom would have to be taken at the point of a gun.

Emily raised herself for a moment and looked at him, then lay her head against his chest, her hair red-gold in the firelight. ''Now again,'' she murmured.

Their lovemaking was quiet and unhurried this time. Afterward, she lay beside him while his hands described gentle circles across her back and buttocks, caressing her skin with his fingertips. The fire had died again to pinpoints of glowing orange coals. After a while, Connigham, certain that she was asleep, drew back the cover to make up the fire, but she laid a hand on his shoulder.

''Stay. Keep me warm.''

He gathered her into the curve of his arm and held her to his chest, and they lay like that until she eased herself away so that her breasts did not press so painfully against his chest. Of a sudden, she was conscious that she, that they both were rapidly growing older. The thought of her fortieth birthday assailed her, no longer so distant as it had once been. And the last twelve years wasted; gone past, never to be retrieved. Why? What was it that drove them both, that held her back from going with him that time to America, that kept her from traveling to Boston three years before when her husband died, that made him as stubbornly resistant as she herself? Was the Cause so all important? And she knew it was and cursed Ireland for it as she knew he had cursed, as thousands, perhaps millions before them had cursed that damnable state of mind that was Ireland.

"An Irishman is worse than a Jew," her husband had said once while witnessing a demonstration in Dublin after the Liberals had put forward their watered-down Irish Councils Bill in 1907. "They're searching for a homeland. The difference between them lies in the fact that the Jew knows where his is, the Irishman does not." And that, she knew, described Michael and herself to perfection.

"Why?" he asked after a while, and she knew that his thoughts had been running in parallel with hers. "Why do they drive us so?"

He was silent then for a long time, and she thought he might have fallen asleep. She would have been content to remain as they were, cradled together, bodies entwined, the harsh world shut away beyond the pale firelight, beyond the warm room. It was an ancient story, she knew; the curse of her race, that sense of tomorrow rising to haunt her. Other people were haunted by the past, the Irish were plagued by tomorrow.

But he hadn't fallen asleep after all, and the world came flooding back. "Sometimes," he murmured, "I think I should let go, let it all go. I read fools like that Russian, Lenin, and I wonder in what vacuum he lives. Give the people a chance to govern themselves, he writes! Hell, they have to be dragged to the ballot box even in a country like America, and nine-tenths of them haven't the vaguest notion of what it's about. Educate them, he says, and they will rise up out of their poverty. Christ. He's either a fool or a liar. His so-called *people* are brutes, beaten down by their ignorance, trampled under by their misery and poverty. And that fool finds it convenient to blame it all on that bogey of the nineteenth century, a conspiracy among the captains of industry. Christ, those bastards are too busy stabbing one another in the back to have the time or energy for a conspiracy." He laughed then and Emily raised herself to study his face, seeing the planes of his narrow features flint-hard in the feeble light. "The people themselves are to blame," Connigham muttered. "They are satisfied to wallow in their discontent, afraid that a change will make things worse. They don't want education, unionization and collective bargaining, social benefits or independence. And the one great conspiracy which does exist, they defend with their dying breath in spite of the fact that the Church has killed and oppressed more people than all the wars of history.

"You have to force them, Emily," he snapped with a vigor that surprised her. "You have to force them to change. And that force has to be so drastic, so astounding, so destructive that they have no more security left and, therefore, no choice but to fight back in spite of their ignorance, their laziness. Maybe then they will realize that they can in fact control their own destiny." He paused a moment then laughed bitterly. "And for what? So that it can be thrown away again by succeeding generations."

At his last sentence, Emily knew that she was listening to the death of a revolutionary. He was finished, burned out, by his own admission. It was no longer the revolutionary dynamic that drove him, but the need for revenge.

When she said as much, he laughed, refusing to take her seriously, yet all the while knowing that she was right. The fire for creating a revolution had long gone out of him. No, he thought, she's right. I do want revenge and I really do not give a damn for Ireland, the Movement, the people any longer. Did I ever, he wondered, and marveled that she understood him so well.

"It is strange, isn't it, Margaret?" he said, unaware of the stab of pain she felt when he called her by his sister's name. "We are lovers, always have been, and yet we have not spent twenty days together in all the years we've known each other."

Emily was silent, and after a moment, thinking that she

was asleep, Connigham shifted her slightly to a more comfortable position.

Did he ever love me? she wondered in the moments before sleep found her. Or has he loved me in place of his sister, all this time?

chapter———13

"*The facts are quite clear, gentlemen. Sabotage is the only* possible answer." Bannerman watched the Board members digest this information. As he expected, Armstrong-Flood responded with a braying laugh.

"I say. This is preposterous, Bannerman. Do you take us for fools?" He shook his head from side to side, jowls quivering. "Preposterous accusation, sir. Suggest carelessness as the real cause." Armstrong-Flood glared around the table. "Your opinion only, sir!"

"It is not my opinion," Bannerman shot back. "It is a matter of fact, as you would see if you had bothered to read my report, sir. It appears likely that someone attempted to delay the Tunnel further and miscalculated the effect of the explosives used. The Tunnel wall was blown out instead, causing the Tunnel head to flood and kill the thirty-one workingmen."

"Now, Mr. Bannerman . . . I think that discussion is in order," the chairman interrupted.

"I beg your pardon, Sir Henry, but I think not. There are only two qualified engineers on this Board and neither of them is experienced with the effects of military explosives. I am." He ignored Armstrong-Flood's outraged gurgle. "The equations are contained in my report and can be verified. The breach in the Tunnel wall was caused deliberately." Bannerman took a deep breath. "In addition, as you well know, I went into the Tunnel head with one of the divers to inspect the damage for myself. While I was inside an accident occurred and I was trapped. Then my air supply was suddenly cut off. Fortunately, one of the crew noticed that although the petrol engine was working the pump was not. Mr. McDougal turned the flywheel by hand to supply air to me. When the pump was dismantled, it was discovered that the linkage between

160

the flywheel shaft and the compressor had been cut nearly through with a file. Under load, it fractured. The flywheel continued to turn and the motor continued to run. Gentlemen, someone cut through that linkage.''

"Surely, Mr. Bannerman, you are aware of the unfavorable publicity that will result if this should be confirmed publicly?'' Benedict Vincent Benet asked.

"I am, sir.''

"Yet you still insist that we do so?''

"I would suggest that the publicity would be much worse if it were discovered that the company had attempted to hide the truth. Lives are at stake, sir, not to mention your own investments.''

Benet gave him an icy smile. "You always seem to be reminding us of our investments, Mr. Bannerman.'' He sat up straighter and went on briskly. "And quite rightly so. You performed an admirable service before the parliamentary committee, sir, by allaying their fears.'' He held up a hand to forestall Bannerman. "I quite understand, sir, that you did so simply because your own investigations had not been completed at that point. But, now that you are convinced that sabotage was performed,''—he tapped the report on the table before him—"you are asking us to accede to Mr. Churchill's request to supply a military guard, sir. And that I do not believe would be wise, as I am certain that the French government would take a very unfavorable view. As you know, there are many people in my country opposed to the construction of the Tunnel. There are even a few organizations that, I am given to understand, have threatened violence. I am certain that the French government would view any move to supply troops to the English side of the Tunnel as a direct affront to France.''

"Then, sir, you are willing to let the sabotage continue?''

"Ah, but I did not mean to imply that. If you are correct in your assumption, sir—as I am certain you are,'' he added hastily to forestall Bannerman's retort, "I think it best that we handle it ourselves. I would favor the hiring of additional guards, the institution of whatever procedures are considered advisable to secure the work site, and suitable inquiries to be made to identify the culprits, providing all is done in such a way as not to attract undue attention from the press.''

Before Bannerman could reply to that, Armstrong-Flood

tapped on the table for attention. "Sir Henry," he growled, addressing the chairman, "I am surprised and concerned that this Board places any faith at all in this nonsensical talk of sabotage. It would seem to me nothing more than a scheme to expend more money at the expense of the investors to cover up certain deficiencies in management of which I have spoken before. We are now facing costly and lengthy delays. I propose that the report concerning sabotage be dismissed out of hand—"

Benet cut the elderly engineer off in mid-sentence by standing. "Thank you, sir. No one is more familiar, I am sure, than you with the ways in which excuses can be invented to cover management delays and errors." He smiled suavely at Armstrong-Flood. "But I have read the report with a great deal of interest and although I am not an engineer, I found the equations easy enough to follow. There can be no doubt in my mind that Mr. Bannerman's conclusions are fully justified. The fact that naval explosives, supposedly emplaced in the Tunnel under great secrecy, were tampered with in itself lends credence to Mr. Bannerman's report. It would also suggest what Mr. Bannerman avoided mentioning, that someone on his staff may have been involved." He looked around the table, and the rest of the Board, mindful of the certain twenty-five percent of the investors' votes that he controlled, nodded sage agreement. Armstrong-Flood, bright enough to see when he was outgunned, remained silent. He leaned to whisper to Sir Henry Keithley, who shrugged him off impatiently.

Benet waited for a reply and Bannerman swore under his breath. Leave it to him to see that. He cleared his throat.

"I am afraid you may be correct," Bannerman said as calmly as he could. "The fact that the explosives had to be removed from one of their sites—a location kept most secret—and placed into a drainage shaft cut inside the heading leaves no other conclusion. Unfortunately, no trace of the order authorizing the work can be found. It may be that it was delivered orally to the gang foreman, who, of course, was killed that night. The shaft could have been cut the night before, the explosives installed, and then detonated the following day when that same work crew was inside the heading. Unfortunately, we will never be able to verify that supposition."

There was silence as the implication made itself felt, and the only decision taken that afternoon was that Churchill's unofficial offer to military troops would be ignored. Further security decisions were to be taken the following Wednesday. At least the matter had not been completely tabled, Bannerman thought angrily as he strode through the halls of Townshend House. A reporter whom he recognized approached, but he pushed past with an angry, "I have nothing to say."

The wind had freshened but the rare bright sun seemed to mitigate its worst effects. He spent the rest of the afternoon on other chores in the city, and it was dark by the time he finished dinner with friends at Rules in Covent Garden and called for a taxi. He briefly considered a visit to the club on the Kings Road, but as he was tired and still annoyed with the Board's reception of his information, decided on his rooms in Draycott Place instead. He was still smarting over the peremptory way he had been dismissed as the directors turned to other matters on the agenda, chief among them the new labor contracts. The doorman helped him into a horse-drawn four wheeler, explaining apologetically that there were no motor taxis or hansoms available at the moment.

Traffic was light for that time of evening and as the growler turned out of Sloane Square the streets leading to Draycott Place were empty. Bannerman, half asleep with the wine and dinner, heard the driver shout and the carriage bucked sideways. The driver yelled again and Bannerman sat up. The door was flung open and a face appeared as someone yelled, "Shoot, you fool!" Bannerman had sufficient presence of mind to lash out with his foot and the face disappeared with a howl. Bannerman was half out of the cab before he sighted two figures running away. The cabby was climbing down from his perch, asking if Bannerman was all right when a policeman ran up, attracted by the shouting.

Bannerman nodded and stood looking up the empty road in the direction the thieves had taken, wondering. Was it coincidence or design? And had he heard right, he wondered? Shoot, he was certain he had heard.

The policeman insisted on escorting him to his flat, and since it was only a few hundred feet, Bannerman paid off the cab and, ignoring curious onlookers, led the policeman to his rooms. As he started to insert the key into the lock, the door moved. The policeman pulled him back and, drawing his truncheon, stepped through the doorway. Bannerman followed and gasped. The contents of every drawer and cupboard had been strewn about. Cushions were torn from the chairs, some ripped open and the stuffing scattered. Curtains had been pulled down and wallpaper ripped away in spots.

The policeman came out of the bedroom, shaking his head, and found the telephone buried in a mass of paper and sofa cushions. He asked for a number and waited, staring silently about the room. Bannerman sat down on the arm of a chair, wondering what in hell was going on.

Inspector David Powell arrived twenty minutes later in response to Bannerman's telephone call. He made a slow turn about the room and whistled gently. "You certainly are one popular fellow lately."

The porter and his wife had volunteered to help clean up the mess, and Powell, after conferring with a detective from the local police station, allowed them to begin.

"Every room but the bedroom," Bannerman muttered. He shook his head. "I just don't understand what the devil is going on."

"Is anything missing?"

"As far as I can tell, no, but then there is little of value here. I keep the flat only for the times I'm in London. No money, of course, and the only jewelry of interest is a pair of ruby cufflinks which I happen to be wearing. Otherwise . . ."

"Then as far as you can tell, nothing at all was taken."

Bannerman shook his head and Powell poked about the room. "What's this?" he asked, pointing at a notebook lying open on a table. "There are two of them."

"Two?" Bannerman glanced around. "There should be three stamp albums." He went down on his hands and knees and peered under the sofa. "That's odd," he muttered to himself and Powell raised an eyebrow. Together, they searched both rooms of the flat without finding the third album.

"What was the value?" Powell asked.

Bannerman snorted. "That album had nothing but modern issues of North European stamps. Not one older than twenty-five years nor worth more than face value. Perhaps a few pounds, certainly no more."

"And these two albums?"

Bannerman shook his head. "North American and Southern European issues. Again, worth no more than the face value of the stamps.''

Powell nodded. "Then why would they take *that* album in preference to these two?" he asked absently. To Bannerman: "Was there anything unusual about that album? Anything that might make them think it was valuable?"

"Other than that it was filled, no. I've collected stamps for years and some are quite valuable, but those are at my hotel in Dover, which has an adequate safe. These are no more than a pastime when I'm in London."

Powell flipped another page. "Well, perhaps it will turn up when everything is cleared away. Otherwise, you must consider yourself quite fortunate that nothing more valuable was taken."

By midnight the flat was at least habitable and the porter and his wife left, promising to have the rest of the damage repaired the following day. Bannerman had declined Powell's offer of a guard and he had departed.

Bannerman poured a large whiskey and carried the tumbler into the bedroom. Placing it on the side table, he opened the clothes press and from the back withdrew a trunk. He found the key on his chain and unlocked it. Removing an oilcloth bag from beneath a pile of old clothes, he drew out a .38 caliber double-action Lightning Model Colt revolver. With the hammer on half-cock, the cartridges slid easily from their chambers as he turned the cylinder and, when it was empty, he slipped his thumbnail in front of the hammer and studied the bore. Dusty and a little pitted, but accurate enough for all that. He found the cleaning kit in the trunk, disassembled the revolver and cleaned and oiled it thoroughly, then reloaded it, and laid it on the table. The charcoal-blue finish gleamed in its sheen of oil.

Bannerman undressed and slid into bed. His mind was a turmoil of thoughts and impressions, and he made no conscious attempt to sort them out, content to let the flow take its random course. But over and over again, the same combinations seemed to float to the surface, so much so that he finally padded naked into the other room and brought back the bottle. Piling more coals on the fire, he got back into bed. The whiskey seemed to steady his mind, and after a while several points were becoming clear. Take them one at a time, he told himself. The explosion in the heading had been deliberate. The fire in Ventilator Shaft Six was questionable, but seemed part of the pattern. Someone had sabotaged his air supply, and his secretary had been brutally murdered. Four incidents within a month! But Margaret's murder? How could it have any possible connection? He could see no relation at all and was inclined to dismiss it as coincidence. As for the pump compressor being sabotaged, McDougal had sent the broken link up to London for his examination, and there was no doubt. It had been cut nearly through with a file.

And now, tonight, the attack on his cab and the ransacking of his rooms. A fifth incident? Was it related to the sabotage? Well, Goddamnit, he thought savagely, if it was, he was ready for them. Someone had clearly yelled to the man who had yanked open the carriage door to *shoot*. He turned his head and the gleam of firelight on the Colt revolver was comforting.

His mind slowly ran down with the level of whiskey in the bottle and by two o'clock it was empty and he was asleep, no closer to an answer than when he had gotten into bed.

chapter ══ 14

. . . my estimate of the Territorial Army as an effective military organization therefore remains low. A single example will suffice. During what were euphemistically called army maneuvers at Woolwich this past week, consisting mainly of spectacles for the edification of the public, such as "tent-pegging" by members of an Indian Cavalry Regiment and a set-piece re-enactment of the Battle at Rourke's Drift, a Territorial unit from North London was to stage a march and countermarch against an entrenched enemy. Unfortunately, half the Territorials were drunk, the other half missing various items of uniform and weapons. The unit was a shambles and the officers dismissed their men quickly before public attention was attracted.

Territorial units which have so far been raised, to replace Yeomanry regiments at Kitchener's insistence, will not, at this time, be a major factor in any European land war. It is my estimate that approximately six months will be required in training by regulars to bring any Territorial unit to the least semblance of order and discipline. The regular army thus remains the only effective fighting force. It currently numbers 50,000.

Von Dorn reread the report, signed his name with a flourish to the bottom, and rang for his aide. When Schram came in, he handed it to him with instructions to dispatch it as usual by the postal service. Von Dorn knew that it would be opened and read by MI.5, the new English counterintelligence service, and he smiled to himself. It was exactly what they would expect him to write and no more than many British officers were saying themselves.

He drew another sheet from the drawer and began the weekly intelligence assessment that would be transmitted in code by

167

diplomatic courier. There were a number of items that should be included in the real report, items he did not care to have seen by Smith-Cumming and his minions at MI.5.

The situation in the northern counties of Ireland was worth watching closely. There were rumors that regular officers would resign if ordered to suppress the new Ulster Volunteers, although von Dorn tended to discount such talk.

As always, there were the aftereffects of the past summer's wave of strikes to consider, the new naval budgets, rumors of the latest friction with Russia over the operations of the tsar's secret police against exiled dissidents in London. Russian-Anglo relations appeared a fruitful source of friction, he wrote, noting that continuing Russian advances into Persia would shortly bring them into actual conflict with England, whose troops were moving up from the south. The target of both powers was the Persian oil fields. It was possible that a wedge for splintering the Entente might just be slipped in here. He wrote steadily for thirty minutes, filling page after page. When he was finished, he would edit it all down into concise, clipped sentences sufficient to fill one typewritten sheet and no more.

Schram knocked once and entered with a buff envelope marked with a red slash. Von Dorn felt a surge of anxiety as he accepted the envelope and swiveled his chair toward the window. With the exception of routine messages, there had been no communication at all from Berlin in over two weeks.

The red slash signified a message from his superior, General Langenscheidt, and he was in no hurry to open it. He had been looking forward to a quiet dinner and a relaxing evening after another hour's work. There was that new club in Chelsea he had recently been introduced into. He had been most impressed with their arrangements and had intended a thorough exploration of their wine cellar and a certain young lady, whose delicate charms were manifest.

Reluctantly, he opened the envelope and read, alarm growing with each clipped sentence. When finished, he sat stunned a moment, all thought of the club gone, then reread the message. He was being ordered, by Langenscheidt, to return to Berlin for consultation, *immediately*. The rest of the message listed a series of questions he was to be prepared to answer. Even his travel plans had been laid on. He was to board the 10:57 train for Dover in the morning, connect with the Dover-Ostende packet and the Ostende-Aachen-Berlin train, arriving in Berlin at 6:30 A.M. Tuesday. He would be met at the train—a euphemism that, he was certain, meant arrest.

The blow was completely unexpected. He had thought to get a message expressing extreme displeasure but when, after two weeks, it had not come, he had concluded that Langenscheidt had been persuaded that now was not the time to challenge von Epping. The message made it apparent that Langenscheidt thought otherwise. That the Junker general had managed to insert himself between von Epping and the Kaiser he was certain.

Von Dorn saw that his hands were shaking. My God, he thought. I'm frightened! He began to pace, that simple act serving to relieve some of the tension and fear building inside him.

If he returned to Berlin as ordered, he would be arrested. He could be court-martialed for direct disobedience, even shot if his assumption that Langenscheidt had outmaneuvered von Epping was correct. If, on the other hand, Langenscheidt was trying to force von Epping to protect him openly, the results could be equally disastrous. It had happened before in the Byzantine world of Prussian politics.

Von Dorn stopped at the window. When he had assured McDougal that Berlin would agree to the destruction of the Tunnel, he knew that he was starting the greatest gamble of his life. And now he was face to face with the reality, put up or shut up, as the poker-playing Americans so aptly phrased it. The question was whether or not Langenscheidt was bluffing. *He* certainly was. Bluffing over von Epping's ability to back his hand. Von Dorn had opened this particular high-stakes game with three copies of a carefully drafted plan for the complete destruction of the Tunnel. These had been sent to Berlin by courier and they could have reached the three recipients—the Kaiser, Langenscheidt, and von Epping—only the previous evening. Either Langenscheidt was confident of his ability to face down the Kaiser and von Epping or he had already done so. Damn, he thought. There had to be a way to find out before he committed himself to that train.

An hour passed before a solution occurred to him. The terminus of the Aachen-Berlin Express was the Friedrichstrasse

Station where he was certain that he would be arrested. Now, for the first time since Schram had entered with the telegram, he smiled. The habit of blind obedience was drilled into every German soldier from the moment he took his oath. Nothing less was expected. But, if he disobeyed his orders by just the least bit and left the train at Potsdam, he could visit von Epping first. If von Epping still supported him, he could then decide what to do about Langenscheidt. If not, it no longer mattered.

Carefully, he drafted the messages: the first to Langenscheidt, acknowledging receipt of the orders; the second to von Epping, detailing the contents of Langenscheidt's instructions as well as his own suspicions, and requesting an appointment. His hands were no longer shaking but his mouth was dry and his surroundings had taken on that diamond clarity he recognized as anticipation of a great gamble, whether behind a rifle, with a woman for the first time, or at the gaming tables. He was also mindful of the danger inherent in this step.

If von Epping abandoned him, he was finished. He could force the issue by refusing to return to Berlin, thus requiring Langenscheidt to instruct the ambassador to remove him from the embassy. It would give him a bit more time, but to do so would involve outsiders, always a dangerous situation as the Kaiser, if the quarrel should become public knowledge, would have little choice but to support Langenscheidt—for the good of the service. And what with the great spy trials in progress in both England and Germany, the press on both sides were actively hunting further scandals. That clumsy fool Heinrich Grosse, rumored to be one of von Epping's agents, was coming to trial at Winchester Assizes on Tuesday next. He had actually been caught inside the Portsmouth Navy Yard making sketches. And to make matters worse, the three English agents, Schultz, Hipsich, and Wolf, were to be tried in Leipzig for spying for the British Admiralty.

No, better it remain in the family, so to speak. His cover, perhaps his life, would depend on von Epping, and on his reading of the Kaiser's support. And that, he knew, was the crux of the gamble. The Kaiser was as changeable as the breeze, never able to make up his mind, it seemed, until forced by circumstances to do so. And the decision then made was often a hasty one, reached without considering all possible alternatives and results. But it had been clear to von Dorn during the Opera interview that the Kaiser was weary of Langenscheidt's constant interference. With a strong feeling of fatalism, he rang for Schram and handed him both coded forms with orders to transmit them immediately.

The afternoon wore on as von Dorn struggled with paperwork. Brief rain showers ranged across the city and several times he started to abandon the office, but he knew that to break his routine would immediately alert the agents Langenscheidt was certain to have watching him. He sent Schram out for his travel tickets and stood at the window, watching a lone horseman cantering in St. James's Park, a late afternoon rider making the best of a miserable day. A policeman strolled past, gloved hands clasped beneath his rain cape, clearly bored as he watched traffic swarming on the Mall. In the Admiralty and government offices, lamps burned, pinpoints in the gathering darkness.

At five thirty he instructed Schram to return to the hotel to pack and left for the club in Chelsea. The very uncertainty of his position and perhaps his life only served to add to his expectations.

Von Dorn descended from the train at the Potsdam Station. He waved away an importunate porter and went out into the cold morning sunshine, carrying his single portmanteau himself. A line of motor cabs stretched along the drive and he went directly to the last in line and stepped in. The man's protests were quieted with twelve marks and the information that he wished to be driven to the Dragoon barracks in Tempelhof. The man started to argue again, but at the sight of von Dorn's stern expression thought better of it. It was, after all, the agreed fare to Berlin.

The trip had seemed inordinately long; the Channel crossing had been quite rough and his belladonna tablets had shown little effect. Snowstorms sweeping across northern Europe had forced the train to a stumbling pace, and the constant jerking and grinding of vans had kept him awake all night.

They left the Potsdam suburb behind as the route led onto the Berliner Strasse. Geometric farmlands, stark in the winter light, fled past, and the motion of the cab along the metaled road lulled him quickly to sleep.

The driver woke him as they approached the Belle Alliance Bridge. During the half-hour drive the sun had disappeared behind clouds and the day now exactly matched his mood. The taxi drew to a halt before the Dragoon headquarters and von Dorn got down wearily. He gave the driver a further three marks and dismissed him.

The cream-colored barracks looked drab in the gray light and a cold wind hurried past with a meager swirl of snow-flakes. Von Dorn walked into the courtyard in company with a group of bundled recruits being shepherded along by an elderly Dragoon sergeant. Past the iron gates, he left them and made his way along the footpath to a series of French doors in the right wing. There he was stopped by an elderly porter wearing the veteran's ribbon.

Von Dorn took a deep breath. It was the moment of truth. "Please inform General von Epping that Lieutenant Colonel Eric von Dorn desires an appointment at his convenience," von Dorn ordered, his Prussian training coming to the fore without conscious thought, suppressing any trace of fear or hesitation.

The porter nodded. "No need, Colonel von Dorn. The general is expecting you." He snapped his fingers and a boy hurried forward. "General von Epping," the porter ordered. The boy took his bag and led him along the endless corridors. Polished wood vied with polished mirror for attention, mas-sive crystal chandeliers cast faceted pools of light along tiled floors; the effect was one of eighteenth-century opulence, yet the building was cold and the odor that infested the halls was compounded of mold, damp, human effluvia and, sharpest of all, paraffin oil.

They passed through a massive hardwood door and the boy whispered to a young officer who sprang immediately to his feet and ushered von Dorn into a reception room.

"The general is expecting you, Colonel von Dorn. One moment while I inform him that you are here."

Von Dorn accepted a cup of tea and sank with a sigh into a carved Vienna chair. Through tall windows he could see the parade grounds where a squadron of Dragoons wheeled among the stately trees. At least he was expected; von Epping was not going to abandon him summarily. He closed his eyes a moment, breathing the heavy aroma of the tea, conscious that he had eaten nothing since a hard roll and coffee on the train early that morning.

"Herr Colonel?"

He opened his eyes to see the lieutenant bending over him. He stood and followed the young officer into von Epping's office.

The general was standing at the window, staring into the gardens. He turned as von Dorn was ushered in, his expression noncommittal, and von Dorn felt the tension clutching at his throat so that he came close to gagging.

"Lieutenant Colonel von Dorn. Please sit down." Von Epping's voice was cold and formal. He motioned von Dorn to a chair while he himself remained standing. The office, in contrast to the rest of the barracks, was spartan in the extreme. Its only concession to luxury was a massively carved desk of the finest French walnut.

"Your report was most interesting, young man, as was the one before it."

Von Epping took a pen from a plain marble holder on the desk top and von Dorn forced himself to remain rigid in his chair. To show any discomfort would be interpreted only as a sign of weakness, an admission of guilt. He waited for the general to continue, but von Epping seemed in no hurry to do so, turning instead to the windows where he began to tap his open palm with the pen.

"Direct disobedience to a superior officer is an extremely serious offense in any rank, doubly so where an officer is concerned."

Von Dorn knew he was waiting for an answer and, for a brief moment, pure hatred flashed at the general's back. "I take full responsibility for my actions, sir," he said in a level voice, fighting back the emotions that threatened to hurl him across the room at the man who was betraying him.

"And well you might, sir. And well you might. Your superior, General Langenscheidt, ordered your arrest immediately upon your entry into the city of Berlin. The charges are direct disobedience, failure to carry out your assignments, acts of war against a friendly nation, and numerous others, equally reprehensible."

This time there was nothing to say and von Dorn remained

silent, knowing he had lost, bitter not at the man at the window who had betrayed him after all, but at himself for even daring that he might win.

When the silence had gone on for nearly a minute, von Epping turned from the window. "You realize, of course, that you could be shot?"

Von Dorn acknowledged this fact, proud that he was able to do so without betraying his fear.

"You also realize that General Langenscheidt is striking at me through you? Two birds with one stone, you might say." He stared at von Dorn as if challenging him to disagree.

Von Epping slapped the pen down on the desk. "Unfortunately for Herr General Langenscheidt, he has miscalculated, perhaps for the first time in his life. He underestimated my influence and, in the last analysis, the Kaiser's determination to see this project through to its conclusion. As that is the case, Herr Lieutenant Colonel, you need not fear that the arrest warrant will be served. Instead, I have news which you may find rather interesting."

For the first time since von Dorn had entered the room, von Epping smiled, while von Dorn could only continue to sit rigidly in the chair, too stunned to believe what he was hearing. "General Langenscheidt has been retired to his estates in East Prussia by direct order of the Kaiser. That was yesterday. And you, my dear sir, have been transferred to my command and promoted to the rank of *Oberst*."

Years of intensive training and discipline took over, and without knowing that he did so, von Dorn jumped to his feet and saluted, face immobile so as not to show the slightest trace of surprise or happiness. But von Epping was not fooled. He came around the desk and clapped von Dorn on the shoulder, then embraced him.

"We have much work to do, *Colonel* von Dorn"—he emphasized the title—"and we have the full blessing of the Kaiser as well. It was he who suggested your promotion."

With his arm still around von Dorn, he led him to the door and opened it. In the outer office, the young officer snapped to attention.

"We have booked your return reservation to London on the midnight train once more. Herr *Oberst*. Slagel here will have

you driven to your hotel. He has reserved rooms for you—
at the Adlon, I believe?''

"Yes, Herr General. And the driver is waiting."

Von Epping nodded, still beaming. "Then, my friend, I
believe you could do with some rest. We will meet at seven
this evening to celebrate your promotion."

The abrupt transition from despair to elation had left von
Dorn shaking with fatigue and just a little stupid. It was all
over in such a hurry; so fast. He could do little more than
stammer his thanks and then Slagel was leading him back
along the corridors and personally helping him into the waiting military motor car. As the motor drove away, a bemused
von Dorn was still trying to come to terms with the fact that
his gamble had paid off.

A driver called for von Dorn at six forty-five. He had been
waiting patiently in the ornate lobby for ten minutes, enjoying
the respectful glances his dress uniform was drawing from
these elegant people, the cream of Berlin society. The efficient Slagel had collected his uniform from his rooms in
Treptow and delivered it to his suite at the Adlon with the
shoulder boards and aiguillette of his new rank attached. That
courtesy and an afternoon's sleep had revived him completely.

The driver, a young corporal, an intelligent face above his
dress uniform, strode into the lobby and looked around, his
demeanor suggesting that even he belonged there. But when
he spotted von Dorn and hurried over to report, his Thuringen
accent immediately dispelled the impression. Von Dorn followed him to the military motor parked before the main
doors. As he settled himself in the back, the corporal lowered
the dividing window.

"I have orders to drive you to the Hotel Fürstenhof, sir."

Von Dorn acknowledged and sat back against the leather
upholstery as they wheeled away from the entrance. A gentle
snow was falling across the Christmas-decorated streets. The
Brandenburger Gate glowed pale cream against the dark sky,
its festoon of flags and Christmas garlands adding splashes of
color. The motor turned left onto the Königgratzer Strasse
and the dark mass of the Tiergarten was on his right, the
government gardens on the left. The various ministry buildings: Labor, Internal Affairs, Foreign Affairs and Reichschan-
cellery were blurred splashes of light in the distance.

The motor slowed as they approached the Potsdamer Platz and its converging lines of traffic. The corporal skillfully negotiated the complicated intersection and a few minutes later stopped before the ornate portico of the Hotel Fürstenhof in the Leipzieger Platz. He turned in his seat.

"General von Epping and his party will meet you in the restaurant, sir. I will return at eleven o'clock to drive you to the railroad station."

Von Dorn went up the broad steps and into the ornate lobby. A porter, spotting his uniform, hurried forward and led him to the wine restaurant. A captain dismissed the porter and escorted him to a curtained cubicle near the back. He announced von Dorn, parted the curtain, and held a chair. Von Dorn stepped into the booth, noting with surprise that von Epping was alone and in mufti. The captain bowed respectfully and inquired if they wished the waiter. Von Epping nodded and when von Dorn was seated and the heavy velvet curtain drawn, von Epping sat back and regarded him minutely.

"I was watching your reactions closely this morning," von Epping began without preamble. "You did well. No protestations of innocence or accusations of betrayal. I was pleased."

Von Dorn nodded, wondering what he was leading up to now.

"Of course, if you had, you would have retained your former rank and been shunted off to an appointment that has recently opened in Shantung."

China service, von Dorn thought. A desirable post but not one necessarily indicative of advancement or suggesting favor. So. He had performed correctly; if not, he would have been rewarded with a handout and sent far from the corridors of power in Berlin.

"The Kaiser . . ." Von Epping broke off at the discreet clearing of a throat beyond the curtain. "Yes," he barked. And to von Dorn as the curtain was switched aside and waiters entered, "I took the liberty of ordering dinner and a wine, as our time is limited. We would not want you to miss your country weekend, would we. Herr Churchill might be disappointed." Von Dorn chuckled as his respect for von Epping's thoroughness grew. He had not yet mentioned the country house invitation in any of his reports.

The efficient waiters quickly laid the table, left the serving dishes, and departed. Von Epping lifted the cover of each dish, sniffing appreciatively at the aromas rising in thick steam.

"You see, we have here smoked salmon, a clear soup, *hammel-braten* and *Lammkotelett*, potatoes, peas, asparagus, onions, mineral water, and wine, an excellent Bordeaux I am certain you will find to your liking. I must apologize for the informality, but we have little time."

Von Epping served the food as efficiently as he seemed to do everything. And his eating habits were similiar. He ate in the American style, first cutting all his food and then carrying it in a steady stream to his mouth—no doubt a relic of his own days as a military attaché, when he had acted as an observer with American forces in the Philippines during the Spanish-American War and later the Moro insurrection.

As they ate, von Epping made small talk concerning the Berlin scene, discussing with humor and insight the usual intrigues in and about the palace. He avoided the subject of Langenscheidt's dismissal altogether, nor did von Dorn ask any questions. As soon as the last course was completed, von Epping rang for the waiters and had them clear away the dishes. A bottle of Napoleon brandy was delivered by the wine steward, accompanied by the captain. The captain's obsequiousness was a better gauge of von Epping's status than his relatively unimportant rank. Berlin's waiters were famous for their ability to judge social, political, and military standings without regard to conventionally accepted trappings. And they were invariably correct. A captain's frown in a restaurant such as this, the Astoria, or the Borchardt had been known to precede by days the fall of a politician or general from a lofty perch. The presentation of a fine brandy was the mark of highest regard and one which von Epping accepted as a matter of course.

"Now, we can get down to business," von Epping said comfortably when all had left. He sat back and inhaled the brandy's aroma, watching von Dorn over the rim of the snifter.

"We have important plans for you, my young friend, beginning with your next assignment." He smiled and selected a cigar, sniffed it in appreciation, and sliced the end with a small pocket knife, conscious of the tension he had created. Not to be outdone, von Dorn followed suit. When their cigars were burning properly, von Epping waved a hand to clear away the clouds of blue smoke.

"I spent several hours closeted with the Kaiser and certain members of the Imperial General Staff," he went on, his voice pitched so low that von Dorn had to lean forward to hear him. This is *it,* he thought, excitement rising in him.

"The Kaiser is convinced that if this damnable English Channel Tunnel had been finished, England would have allowed this past summer's crisis to degenerate into a full-scale war."

Von Dorn nodded. "As you know, General, that was my assessment as well."

"Yes, yes." Von Epping waved the cigar impatiently. "I have read all of your reports." He stared at von Dorn a moment, eyes calculating. "And so, it appears, has the Kaiser."

Von Dorn managed to prevent any sign that he understood the full import of von Epping's comment. Was the man fishing, or did he know that the Kaiser had ordered him to submit duplicates to him? Wheels within wheels, he thought. One intrigue concluded only to begin another.

"His Majesty was most impressed with your perception as well as your ability to carry out difficult tasks," von Epping went on without a pause. "There is now another for you to attend to. The English Channel Tunnel is to be destroyed and you are to see to it."

Von Dorn gaped. He had not expected to hear the command uttered so bluntly.

"Of—of course, Herr General," he stuttered. "It is only . . ."

"You have submitted a plan for doing so, have you not?" Von Epping's voice was ominous. "Surely you would not have done so if you doubted the outcome?"

Von Dorn covered his confusion with a large swallow of brandy, thinking rapidly that it would not do well to be too certain of his ground. "Of course not, Herr General. It is—well, sir, to be honest, I did not expect the plan ever to be used except in the event of general hostilities."

Von Epping nodded, apparently satisfied. "Of course. However, certain events, which I am not at liberty to discuss, make it imperative that the Channel Tunnel never be completed." He regarded von Dorn with a challenging stare.

"I see," von Dorn said slowly. Yet he could well imagine what von Epping was alluding to. For years he had heard rumors of dissension among the various factions of the General Staff. One group, whose most vociferous proponent was Langenscheidt, had fought hard for a rapprochement with England, even at the expense of abandoning the Imperial Navy. The other faction, headed by Admiral Scheer, not only wanted and expected war but demanded that a definite date be named and planning directed specifically to meet it. Apparently the war faction had won. Langenscheidt had been sent into retirement and now he was receiving orders to carry out an act of aggression against a nominally friendly foreign power.

"Yes, sir, I understand." Von Dorn nodded, willing his expression to be that of an officer with no other choice but to obey.

Von Epping gave him a thin, cynical smile. "The Kaiser and the General Staff are of the opinion that should the Tunnel be completed, England would be irrevocably attached to France, and through her, to the rest of the Continent, by economic as well as political factors. At present, as long as her greatest markets are in the Commonwealth, Europe is of lesser importance to her. It is also accepted by the General Staff that war in Europe must come before 1915 if Germany is to succeed. There are those who say we have left it too long as it is.

"If the Tunnel should progress further to completion, the tide of opinion in England could very well turn in its favor as the economic advantages become more apparent. If it were to be destroyed now, particularly with the parliamentary Opposition in full cry, it is unlikely that construction will be resumed. England will thus remain isolated from the Continent and absorbed in her own affairs overseas."

"When, then, am I to carry out this task?" von Dorn asked.

"You will select a time of your own choosing, a time that will offer the optimum chance of success. It is imperative, Colonel, as you so state in your plan, for the destruction to be accomplished before the breakthrough occurs between the English and French shafts. You must seek a conjunction of events and resources that offers the highest assurance of success. When you have done so, inform me of the time and your requirements. They will be met without stinting.''

Von Epping paused. ''We are counting on you to see that success attends your preparations. If so, the rewards will be great—and the penalty for failure greater. You do understand, of course?''

''Of course, Herr General,'' von Dorn snapped, wondering if von Epping was alluding to a high post, possibly that previously occupied by Langenscheidt? It was not beyond possibility. . . .

''Anticipating somewhat your needs, if necessary I can arrange two thousand Mauser rifles and ammunition and the sum of three hundred thousand pounds. I believe your work among the, shall we call them disaffected natives, should prove an ample source of manpower.''

Von Dorn smiled at the delicate allusion to the Fenians, a subject that von Epping should not have known about.

''Unfortunately,'' von Epping went on to say, ''the Admiralty tells me that the English have increased their naval patrols along the west coast of Ireland. The search for an alternative landing site is underway and one will have been selected by the time you are ready.''

The remainder of the evening was devoted to the details of von Dorn's proposed plan, and he soon came to realize that the man sitting opposite had not risen to his present position simply through family connections. Every possible contingency had been foreseen including the outright refusal of the Fenians to help, unlikely as that might be. And although von Epping termed von Dorn's plan a masterful piece of engineering, he did not neglect to review it in detail.

Von Dorn left the restaurant at eleven o'clock and rode through the silent, snow-covered streets to Friedrichstrasse Bannhof. He was, he thought, going to be responsible for the opening shot in what could very well become a full continental war. His entire life had been devoted to just this end, and to garnering sufficient power and status to allow him to play a major role. A porter respectfully took his bag and led him across the narrow hall and up two flights of steps to the platforms. Even at this late hour the railroad station bustled with activity; the odors of tobacco, close-packed humanity, hot wursts and sausages from vendors' wagons mingled with the cold damp, coal dust, and oil as he followed the porter to the wagon-lit at the end of the train. He drew a deep breath in response to his overflowing feeling of satisfaction within. Not for a moment did the possibility of war, of death and agony for thousands, perhaps for himself, deter him.

He paused on the steps and glanced at the great clock beneath the curved glass roof. The hands stood at three minutes to midnight. He had little time to spare.

chapter —— 15

Middlesex Street, or Petticoat Lane as Connigham still preferred to think of it, stretched away into the fog of the midafternoon, a drab vista of shabby colors and patterns as crowds of mid-well to poorly dressed Londoners mingled, surged, ebbed, and streamed in dingy tides among the stalls of the largest secondhand open-air clothing market in the world. He wandered among the stalls, cloaked in the anonymity of the crowds, taking his time, picking the clothes he needed—those not too worn, but obviously used and once of good quality. He gave a stall-keeper a shilling and his old clothes for the privilege of changing behind the curtain into a leather jacket, workman's cap, too large Wellingtons, and heavy dungarees, all of which cost him four shillings. Satisfied, Connigham went down Bishop's Gate past the grimy bulk of Liverpool Street station to Threadneedle Street. A thin rain had begun as he crowded into the Bank underground station in time to board the Central London train for Tottenham Court Road.

Connigham entered Soho Square in a roundabout fashion from Frith Street ten minutes later and found an unoccupied bench. With the deliberate moves of a drunk, he fumbled in his coat pocket until he found a pouch of tobacco and a scrap of paper and methodically rolled a cigarette. The trees and bushes were skeletons in the half-light of the afternoon. The traffic noise was distant, muted by the bare trees, and the rain continued, stippling dark puddles.

A woman entered the Square and paused. She was tall and spare and her ankle-length coat was ragged. The straw hat perched upon a ludicrous mass of curls was better suited to summer than winter.

She wandered aimlessly in his direction, and as she drew closer, Connigham noticed the blank expression and peculiar flat eyes that told him she was a drug user. A rehearsed smile appeared briefly and in an unconscious parody of middle-class manners, she turned, drew her coat about her, and sat down a foot or so farther along the bench. Connigham ignored her and went on smoking, his restless eyes searching the Square.

After a moment, she shifted in such a manner that she was closer to him. Her complexion beneath the dirt and powder was sallow and pitted with acne. A smear of color had nearly missed her lips, and her hands, blue in the damp, cold air, twisted and turned ceaselessly.

"Perhaps you . . . have another?"

"Heh . . . ?" he muttered drunkenly.

"A cigarette, please?"

"Nah. Got no more."

She was silent a moment, recognizing rejection but still compelled to try. "I'm cold. Ain't you?"

When he didn't answer, she sighed. He could see that she wasn't English after all, but darker, almost olive-skinned in the dead light. Italian or Greek, he thought. Someone's bastard.

"Me room 'as a grate. A shilling's all it needs. All I needs." She finished without hope.

When he still did not answer, she got up and made her way across the Square to another drunk lolling on a bench. A shilling, he thought. Christ! For a night's warmth.

The light was fading quickly when the man he was waiting for came into the Square through the north gate. The man spotted him and started forward but something in his manner alerted Connigham. Another figure in a dark overcoat had appeared at the Sutton Street gate and was making an elaborate ritual of lighting a pipe. He shook the match vigorously, dropped it, then clasped his hands behind his back and started along the path. Everything about him screamed police, from the deliberate steps learned walking a beat, to the shapeless overcoat that could conceal a sidearm.

The man he was to meet was moving too fast. His face, which became visible in the gloom as he approached, wore a sickly grin. Connigham shot to his feet and sprinted across the winter gray grass. Entrances were out; they would be full of coppers. Behind, he heard two whistle blasts and cursed at his own stupidity. By coming to the Square early he had made certain that no one was waiting for him, but it had also made it impossible to follow his contact. The contact and the police arriving together told him he had been double-crossed.

Connigham plowed into the bushes along the iron fence and wriggled through the yew hedge, its thick, gnarled branches clutching at his jacket. He jumped, caught the topmost horizontal bar of the fence, and pulled himself up. The jacket snagged on one of the spear points as he rolled over, and there was no time to pull it loose. As he dropped, the leather sleeve ripped with a sharp sound, and he landed in a heap on the far side, turning his ankle. Swearing, he pushed himself up and hobbled down the street, trying to spare his ankle as much as possible.

The light had dwindled to violet-gray dusk when he turned into Bateman Street, struggling to remember the layout of the roads around the Square. He knew that he had to bear west or be caught between the police and the Charing Cross Road, where a running man would be highly visible. His ankle throbbed and the boots, a size too large, were not helping matters. A shout behind caused him to duck into an alley. Dust bins overflowed, creating a noisome mess as he struggled between two ancient buildings. Several openings led down to basement doors, but each was locked. The end of the alley was blocked by a high board fence. Another shout and he turned to see a figure silhouetted against a street lamp pointing in his direction. There was nothing for it but to jump. Connigham caught the top of the fence and prayed that the board would not pull loose. As he threw a leg over, a loud bang and flash filled the alley and a bullet whizzed past his ear. He hurled himself over without looking and landed on a pile of broken boxes, thrashed his way out, and found himself still in an alley, but one opening onto a street. He hobbled to the end as fast as he could manage. The street was filled with people going about their business; no one seemed to notice him or to be running from either direction. He stepped out, hoping to God that the police did not have a photograph, and tried to blend with the crowd.

A few minutes later, Connigham pushed into a crowded butcher's shop and edged through the crush past the counter and into a back room. Someone yelled and he glimpsed a man in a white apron over a heavy coat waving a knife, but by then he had thrust past a startled boy whose arms were full of paper bags and was out the back before anyone could stop him.

He went rapidly along the alley until he came to another street, wishing that he did not look so disreputable. A pound note waved above his head brought a hansom cab to his side. Connigham directed the driver to the Euston Station. When the hansom turned out of the street and he was certain he had outdistanced his pursuers, he drew off his boot, by the time the hansom was approaching Euston, Connigham had wrapped a strip of cloth torn from his shirt tightly about his ankle to contain the swelling.

The night had turned cold and a thin rain was again falling as Connigham paid off the driver. As soon as the cab disappeared into the traffic going toward Regent's Park, he went along Euston Road to Kings Cross Station, the terminus for the Great Northern Railway, several streets away. His ankle hurt less now that he had wrapped it, but the oversized boots were beginning to chafe. Connigham turned into St. Pancras Road and went along beside the soot-covered mass of St. Pancras Station, turned up into Wharf Road, crossing the Regent's Canal before diving into the maze of buildings comprising the Great Northern Railway Depot.

Two days it had taken to locate any of his contacts from the old days. Emily was correct in that respect; no one could be trusted these days. The Yard had rounded up most of the organization during the summer and scared the hell out of the rest. Those who were not lying very low had left London, some even the country.

It puzzled him that Emily had seemed to be able to give him so little help. And she puzzled him as well. In bed she was as open and giving as possible; but otherwise, distant, disappearing for hours at a time. And yesterday, her expression had been grim when she showed him the message from Dublin ordering him to return to Boston immediately. He recognized that moment as a crossroads in their relationship.

"Will you go?"

"When I've done what I came for."

They were in the library, the velvet curtains open and sunlight streaming into the room. She had gone then to the window and stood looking out onto the Square.

"They have given you an order." When he said nothing she turned to look at him. After a moment, she tried again.

"A direct order must be obeyed, Michael. Without discipline we have nothing."

He smiled at that. "We have each other." And for a moment he thought she just might cross the room to him. But she remained beside the window, her hair a mass of spun red-gold in the sunlight, and his body ached with the need of her. That need was in her eyes as well, but she was the stronger, the more dedicated, and when she did not move, he left the library and went up to his room to pack. When he came down again, the door to the library was still open but the room empty.

The idea that had formed in his mind at that moment was now confirmed. There was more reason for Dublin's wanting him out of England than simply his possible capture. What could he tell the police? He had been away for six years. Details of his operations in the States? Hell, they were widely known. He operated openly under American law. He had no doubt that the English wished to hang him for murder as well as to close down the Boston fund-raising operation, such as it was. But for the organization, it would be a temporary interruption at best. There were several others already in the States who could step in and run it more effectively than he. He was not a fund raiser, nor an after-dinner speaker, and the job had come to him by default as he had been the only Fenian in the States at that time. The Dublin Committee had questions to answer, and to ask them he would have to go to Liverpool.

By nine o'clock that evening he had located a goods train making up for Liverpool. He stole along its length, testing the van doors until he found one not yet sealed. Connigham eased the door open and climbed inside, relieved that he would not have to ride the rails. He left the door partly open—a closed, unsealed door was a dead giveaway—stretched out in a corner and was asleep before the train got under way.

chapter———16

A *young naval aide led Powell through the buff-painted* corridors of the Admiralty to an outer office where a good-looking man of about thirty greeted him and nodded to a door, indicating that he was to go right in.

"Inspector Powell, sir," Edward Marsh, Churchill's private secretary, announced and closed the door quietly behind him. The large room was comfortably done up in dark leather and polished mahogany. A deep red Aubusson rug covered the polished floor and an exquisite collection of brass nautical instruments was displayed in glass cases beneath an immense painting of some forgotten ship-of-the-line under full sail. A cased model of a dreadnought stood against the other wall, and Powell had the impression of a well-stocked library—massive bookcases packed tightly with leatherbound volumes of various sizes and colors.

The First Lord of the Admiralty, Winston Churchill, turned from the window where he had been staring into St. James's Park beyond the Parade, hands clasped behind and hidden by the tails of his morning coat. He smiled a welcome and crossed the carpet with his familiar lunging walk.

"David, thank you for coming on a Sunday," he said, shaking hands. "I am most sorry to have to disturb you." He led Powell to a chair beside the desk, then went to the sideboard, where he held up a bottle which glinted amber in the firelight. "Bourbon whiskey?"

Powell nodded and settled into the chair. A small coal fire burned in the grate and late afternoon light filtered through the high windows, relieving the worst of the gloom without dissipating the relaxed atmosphere the twilight engendered.

"First Lord," he finally had to break into the flow of apologies. "Grace and I had no other plans for the day. I was happy to come. If only to see what the Admiralty was like."

187

"Here now, none of that First Lord nonsense. I hear it all day long. Even Clemmie has taken to calling me First Lord when she wants to put me in my place."

"All right, Winston," Powell conceded.

Although the Special Branch inspector was twenty years older than Churchill, they had become good friends in the year they had worked together while Churchill was Home Secretary. As ranking officer in charge of domestic security, Powell had also acted as liaison between Scotland Yard and the Home Office. Unlike many Home Secretaries, Churchill had always shown the greatest interest in the Yard and its various investigating agencies, particularly Special Branch. He had also been instrumental in setting up the new internal security department, known as MI.5 after its office number in Whitehall. Until then MI.6, with the help of Special Branch, had reigned supreme. But Churchill had helped to push the new body through the cabinet, and now, three years later, a nice, triangular relationship had developed that appeared to work quite well.

"And how is Mrs. Churchill?"

"Fine, fine. Both babies are well, and Clemmie is quite recovered from her ordeal. And Grace?"

Churchill thought he detected a faint grimace but Powell nodded. "Quite well, sends her regards. I take it then that you are enjoying the Admiralty?"

Churchill grinned like a small boy and handed Powell his drink. "Yes, quite so. There is so much to be done."

He paused a moment to study a document on his desk, then gathered the tails of his coat and sat down, his expression stern. "David, I must ask you a favor. One which I have no business asking, as I don't think it would find favor with your masters in the Home Office." He looked up to see Powell watching him intently.

After nearly twenty-five years at Scotland Yard and having made his way up from a beat constable to chief inspector, Powell considered himself somewhat of an expert on people. An amateur psychologist, he had made an extensive study of the various schools of human behavior only to place his main trust in the methods proposed by the Austrian, Adler. He believed with Adler that people were motivated by a conscious drive to express and fulfill themselves as individuals, rather than by certain blind instincts as Freud proposed. In almost every instance of criminal activity with which he had dealt, he was convinced that the criminal was searching for a position of superiority, attempting to overcome a feeling of inferiority, or trying to compensate for feelings of hopelessness. Powell had carried his observations further and applied them to the people he came in contact with in the performance of his work, and by so doing he was often able to gain a unique insight into their motivations. In Churchill's case, he had long since concluded that the man was striving to overcome a deep sense of inferiority engendered not by the success of his father, Lord Randolph, but by Randolph's overbearing and often dismissive treatment of his son. That, he felt, was a more suitable explanation for Churchill's apparently limitless energy and willingness to be unconventional, as his father had been. During their association, Powell had come to recognize certain signs indicative of Churchill's state of mind. When he adopted the serious yet humble, man-to-man approach, Churchill was clearly working up to something; but Powell was puzzled by this new, oblique manner of approaching the subject. It was contrary to Churchill's usual practice of charging straight ahead, and Powell thought, with some dismay, that it suggested a very unusual favor indeed.

"I have had a report from McKenna at the Home Office this morning"—Churchill tapped a buff folder on the desk—"which I find quite interesting. It has to do with a man named Connigham. You know the name, of course?"

Powell nodded, clearly puzzled as to what possible interest the Admiralty could have in a renegade Irishman wanted for murder.

"We nearly arrested him last night," Powell said, "but unfortunately he got away in the darkness. It is, however, only a matter of time before we find him again."

Churchill nodded and his fingers drummed on the folder a moment. "How did the Yard know that he had returned to England?"

"Connigham has been under surveillance for quite some time. He left Ireland six years ago after murdering two men. Since then, he has become the Fenians' star fund raiser in the United States and Canada. The Royal Mounted Police and the United States Immigration Service, with the assistance of certain elements of the Boston and New York Police Departments, have kept an eye on his activities over the years.

Certain of the American police consider him a Communist because of his activities on behalf of the labor movement there.''

''Is he?''

''I rather doubt it. His file suggest no deep political commitments even to the Fenians.''

''I see. Go on.''

''We received a cable from Boston noting that Connigham had left the city, possibly en route for New York. There was, however, no following report from the New York police or the United States Immigration Service—we should keep in mind that both employ many Irish.''

''I'm surprised that the Boston police helped,'' Churchill observed.

''I am given to understand that there are two major and rather bitterly opposed factions in Massachusetts politics—those related to the Irish and those not. Our assistance in Boston comes from the non-Irish faction. In any event, as a routine precaution, MI.6 was alerted to brief their people in the customs service. Connigham was identified at Southampton, ostensibly a crew member aboard a German flag steamer. We had hoped to follow him in case he might lead us to any Fenian groups we had not uncovered. However, our man lost him crossing Westminster Bridge in the afternoon traffic the day he landed. It was some time before he was located again. Nearly two days, in fact.''

''Then an attempt to arrest him was made last evening?''

''Yes. It was felt that he was far too dangerous a person to be left free, and far too slippery. Chief Commissioner Sir Edward Henry ordered his arrest. His exact whereabouts, I understand, were supplied by an informant.''

''But he escaped. He appears to be a resourceful person.''

Powell shifted uncomfortably in his seat, aware that the raid had been hastily organized and badly handled and that he should have seen to it himself. The rocket he had received from the chief commissioner still smarted. But Grace had been quite ill and he was damned if he was going to leave her just to arrest some bloody fool of an Irish rebel.

''Have you found him again?''

''Ah, no, but we will. It is only a matter of time. There is a countrywide alert out for him.''

Churchill tapped the report again and leaned back in his

chair to study Powell, as if trying to judge whether this was the proper time.

"David," he said slowly, "I said that I had a request to make."

Powell nodded. "Go on."

"I do not want you to arrest Mr. Connigham." As Powell gaped at him, he continued in an unhurried manner. "Instead, I want you to arrange a meeting with him for me."

The inspector was silent a moment, absorbing the unusual request. Finally, he shook his head. "Winston, do you know what you're asking? The man's a murderer!"

"I understand, David. He killed two men; one an informer, the other an Ulster fanatic who took part in the lynching of his brother-in-law before his wife's very eyes."

"I am sure," Powell said with some asperity, "that a jury will take that into consideration. But the fact remains that one of those men was a police informant and entitled to our protection."

Churchill removed a second folder from his drawer. "This report was delivered an hour ago. It is dated October 5, 1905, and describes the investigation of the lynching. No one was ever arrested or even questioned by the authorities. Like many other anti-Catholic crimes in Ulster, it was merely allowed to die in the files. While I agree that there is never an excuse for murder, I think it would be fitting in this instance to extend a bit of forbearance to Mr. Connigham, especially as the security of the nation may be involved."

This last stopped Powell's protest as effectively as anything could have done. "I beg your pardon?"

Churchill took a deep breath. "I have reason to believe that the national interest of Great Britain is involved, that far more than the parochial interests of a six-year-old murder investigation are involved."

Churchill lowered a rollered map from above the bookcases to expose a huge naval chart of North Atlantic which stretched from the Norwegian coast to the east coast of North America. He picked up a pointer and tapped Ireland. "This bit of land represents a grave threat to England in the event of a general European war and always has. But today that threat has been greatly magnified by modern technology. For instance, Ireland would make an excellent base for hostile submarines."

"Submarines!" Powell exclaimed.

"Submarines," Churchill repeated firmly. "Traveling beneath the surface, undetected and undetectable at the moment, the submarine is capable of firing a torpedo only a bit less powerful than those carried by destroyers and cruisers."

"But you yourself have recently announced that our naval ships have been fortified against torpedoes!"

Churchill waved the pointer impatiently. "Yes, yes, of course, insofar as it is possible to do so. But I am not talking about naval ships; rather about our merchant shipping. We have not been able to develop a reliable method for protecting freight or passenger-carrying steamers from torpedo attack other than the convoy system. How long do you think Britain could survive if all, or even a large proportion, of our shipping was sunk in the Approaches?"

He put the pointer down and clasped his hands behind his back. "We now import over sixty percent of our foodstuffs and the majority of our raw materials, and that makes England extremely vulnerable to such an attack on our shipping. Due to their limited range, enemy submarines in the foreseeable future will be confined to the English Channel and the Approaches. But"—he paused and picked up the pointer to tap Ireland again—"if a fleet of submarines could be based in Ireland, they could range the North Atlantic shipping lanes nearly to Iceland. The time in which to sink our merchant shipping would be extended by several days."

"But," Powell protested, "how could an enemy base submarines in a British possession?"

"Irish Home Rule is inevitable. Two years or ten years. It will come. The question is whether we will maintain friendship with and a degree of control over Ireland. The Home Rule bill to be proposed next year is a halfway measure satisfying no one. It will grant no real independence. It will be only a matter of time before the Irish remove themselves completely from England's influence. If independence must be earned at the point of a rifle, we will surely have an enemy at our back door."

"At the point of a rifle?" Powell shook his head. "Winston, what are you saying? The Home Rule bill is certain to pass in the new sitting. By the end of 1914, Ireland will have Home Rule. Asquith himself has made that statement a number of times."

Churchill's smile was weary. "I wish I could be certain of

that, David. I really do. But will Ireland wait for 1914? Will Ulster *allow* Home Rule? I have had alarming reports concerning the amount of munitions and weapons smuggled into Ireland in the past year, as you must have as well. So much so that I have been obliged to order an entire naval squadron to constant patrol of the Irish coast.

"Germany, it would appear, is supplying a great number of arms to the Catholic South and to the Protestant North at the same time. Her intentions, I am certain, are to form an armed enemy force at our backs in the event of a European war. If her plans should be realized, an independent and hostile Ireland allied with Germany would be the result. And German submarines then, deploying from bases in Ireland, could become a serious menace to us.''

Powell took his pipe from his mouth after a moment, packed fresh tobacco into the bowl, and lit it, stalling for time while he considered Churchill's assessment. As accustomed as he was to the way in which the man was able to assemble widely divergent ideas and bits of information into patterns, nevertheless, such a performance always left him breathless. He thinks at least six steps ahead of me . . . ahead of anyone I know, Powell mused.

"How then," he asked finally, "does our Mr. Connigham fit in? He's been away in the States for six years. How could he know anything of interest concerning the supplying of German arms to Irish nationalists?"

It was Churchill's turn to stall while he sought to assess the impact of his theory on the Special Branch detective. At least, he thought, Powell was asking questions instead of dismissing the notion out of hand, as he had every right to do.

"I do not believe that he knows anything at all about the German arms. Nor do I believe he knows much about current Fenian plans." Churchill turned from the window to face Powell, who was watching him through curls of smoke. "Do you recall a murder in Sedley Place two weeks ago?"

Powell cocked his head. "Yes. I do," he said after a moment. "Woman named Doyle, I believe. Burglar broke in and killed her, probably when she tried to scream."

"Is that how the Yard sees it?"

"I believe so. I happened to be at the Marylebone Street Station the same afternoon on another matter and went round as they were a bit shorthanded."

"Have you followed the case?"

"No, I haven't. But I do recall that she was secretary to the man who is building the Channel Tunnel. Likable enough chap, named Bannerman. His flat was burgled a few nights ago. Asked for me to come round as he knew me." He took his pipe from his mouth. "What are you driving at Winston?"

Beyond the window, a gray dusk had replaced the cold sun. The immense courtyard was nearly empty and across the road, the park and the Mall were quite deserted. Churchill drew the curtains and turned to the folder on his desk.

"Her maiden name was Connigham. She was the sister of Michael Connigham and the wife of the man lynched six years ago in Ulster."

Powell raised an eyebrow. "Is that so?"

Churchill picked up a pencil and began to sketch absently on a sheet of paper. "David, there have been two serious accidents at the Channel Tunnel works in the past month or so. You may have read about them in the press?"

"I should think so. Thirty men drowned through someone's damned carelessness."

"Thirty-one. And it was not carelessness," Churchill answered, but so softly that Powell had to lean forward to hear. "Those thirty-one men were murdered. It was sabotage that killed them." He looked up to see the surprise on Powell's face.

"Why—why—why hasn't Special Branch been apprised of this?" Powell stammered.

"Earlier this month, MI.6 received a report from one of their people in Berlin to the effect that a member of the German Embassy—they were unable to identify the person—had met in Berlin with the head of Germany's secret service and a few hours later with the head of military intelligence. The date of the meeting corresponds with the time that the embassy's military attaché was also in Germany.

"It is my feeling that the sabotage, the consultations in Berlin, the woman's murder, and Connigham's return are all somehow related. To that, I add certain other facts supplied by Admiralty intelligence—German naval reconnaisance of the Channel Tunnel, a high percentage of German merchant ships off the west coast of Ireland, and the identification of a German military attaché in the village of Kingsdown last week—the same military attaché who may have been in Berlin.''

For a moment Powell was annoyed, and he barely suppressed a sharp retort. These vague suspicions were too much like the Churchill caricatures in *Punch* and the Tory press. And he had had to come up to the Admiralty on a Sunday afternoon for this?

"Now see here, Winston, just why do you suppose Connigham will be able to tell us anything at all?"

"As I said before, I do not expect him to be able to tell us anything, nor would I believe him if he tried," Churchill replied, ignoring Powell's impatience. "But I suspect he is in England for a purpose other than Fenian business, David," he said earnestly, leaning forward across the desk. "All I ask is that Special Branch continue to do as they are now, but rather than make a formal arrest, hold him unofficially until I can talk with him. If I am unable to obtain from him what I think I can, then you may proceed with his arrest, trial, and I would presume, date with the hangman."

Powell remained silent for some time; Churchill had warned him that the Home Office would be unlikely to approve. Which meant that Powell would be assuming complete responsibility. He had no doubt that Winston would back him to the hilt, yet that would do little good. *He* was responsible to the Home Office and not the Admiralty. In fact, the Admiralty had no business asking for assistance from Special Branch to begin with, unless the request went through the proper channels. But Powell could understand why Churchill was reluctant to do that. The Whitehall mandarins would have too many questions and an equal number of loose mouths.

Powell sighed. Two more years and he could retire with a pension. Meager though it was, it would keep Grace and him in the cottage they had purchased five years ago in the Lakes District. But, if something should happen to that pension . . .

Churchill sensed what was passing through Powell's mind, yet he remained silent, knowing that there was nothing he could offer his friend that would secure the man's position if he were in the process of making a disastrous mistake. Churchill was confident that he could explain, but knew he could never justify, Powell's actions in Parliament. And it was certain to reach Parliament via one of the Tories' tame backbenchers if they should fail.

Powell knew that his decision would reflect his respect for and faith in Churchill, this half-maverick, half-statesman who had risen so swiftly in the government on the combination of his father's reputation and his own abilities. Public opinion regarding Churchill was split down the middle; the working classes held him in high regard for the social reforms he had managed to force through a reluctant House, but hated him for his role in the Tonypandy affair; the privileged classes, of which he was a member, regarded him variously as a maverick, a messiah, a fool and traitor, and an enlightened statesman of the new breed, according to, but not solely based upon their own political inclinations. There seemed no middle ground regarding Churchill. But he was undeniably intelligent, energetic, and capable. Even his worst critics admitted that much.

Powell also realized that he was indebted to Churchill for his present position, although Winston had never claimed credit nor suggested that he was responsible for the promotion to chief inspector. He knew that debt was now being called, however, politely. He nodded his acceptance.

chapter ____ 17

The train crossed the Mersey and chuffed into Liverpool's Edge Hill goods yard. Connigham stood in the shadow of the van's doorway and watched for the curve just past the long line of warehouses that would conceal the train from the signal box for a moment. As the engine, wreathed in its pallor of smoke, foreshortened and began the reach into the curve, he slid the door open a bit wider. When the lighted tower disappeared beyond the massive shed to his right, he jumped, landing on all fours, rolling quickly to his right to take up the shock, and scuttled into the shadows where he paused to catch his breath. It lacked only an hour until daylight and he wanted to be well out of the yards by then.

Having made his way into the city by tram, he ate a hurried breakfast at the Exchange Railway Terminal, conscious of his torn jacket and generally disreputable appearance. Afterward, he found a secondhand clothing shop in Batchelor Street and purchased a better fitting pair of boots, a denim shirt, and a well-worn cloth jacket, all fairly clean.

He then made his way into the maze of soot-grimed streets in the Dingle district and, after judicious questioning which took the better part of the day, wound up in a scrap yard at the end of Slater Street. Connigham wandered through piles of rusting scrap badly overgrown with weeds to a shack that was itself little more than a scrap yard in miniature. Inside, a bulbous man in a leather apron was leaning on the counter puffing the worst-smelling pipe Connigham had ever encountered. The man regarded him with eyes that were pinpoints among rolls of fat.

"I'm told you can put me in touch with Arthur Boyle."

The man removed the pipe from his mouth and stared into the bowl. "Aye. 'As an office, he does. Keeps 'ter in St. Anne Street."

"I'm on the run."

"Aye? Well, that's yer business then, 'tisn't it?"

Connigham leaned on the counter until his face was inches from the yard owner. "My name is Michael Connigham."

The man wrinkled his face in puzzlement then straightened abruptly as recognition dawned.

"Aye! So ye are," he exclaimed. "And what would ye be wanting with Boyle now?"

Connigham glared at him, and after a moment's further thought, the man drew a polished brass telephone from beneath the counter. If Connigham was surprised at the incongruous appearance of the instrument in the midst of a run-down scrap yard, he gave no sign. The man asked the operator for a number and turned his expressionless face away from Connigham while he spoke a few sentences. A long silence followed during which he turned to watch his visitor, who was silhouetted against the dull light filtering through the dirty scraps of greased paper that passed for windows. Connigham gazed about him at the unbelievable filth of the place while he waited. The dirt floor had once been covered with scraps of board but the mud that had seeped through had half submerged most of them. Pieces of machinery and plumbing fixtures were piled everywhere; the path from door to counter provided the only open space. The air was a mixture of dirty oil, rusting metal, human waste, and damp rot.

"Aye," he heard the scrap man say. Connigham turned as he replaced the receiver and carefully stowed the telephone away in the niche below the counter.

"Yer to go to Canada Docks, number three. There's a Norwegian steamer, *Alesund*. Go aboard."

"And . . .?"

"Go aboard."

Connigham studied the man, searching for any sign of a double-cross in his expression or manner, but the man only regarded him with the same stolid expression as when he had entered. Connigham left without another word. In the distance, the town hall clock struck three. The darkening sky was thick with gray cloud off St. George's Channel and a cold wind whipped through the streets, bringing with it the oil and salt-laden smell of the Mersey. Connigham shivered in his unlined jacket and started toward the docks. Where the

Strand met Redcross Street, he boarded the overhead tram and rode toward the Canada Basin.

Victoria, Trafalgar, Nelson, Wellington Docks. Connigham had worked them all as a young stevedore sent to Liverpool to recruit among the Irish dock workers. But the Fenians had fallen on hard times. By the turn of the new century, the Movement, the violent right wing of the Irish Nationalist Brotherhood, was all but dead. The abortive bombing campaigns of the seventies and eighties had alienated liberal supporters and the moderates had taken to Parliament to achieve their aims. The survivors, then, had become a closed, tight-knit group, mindful of that curse of all Irish revolutionary movements, the informer.

Watching the dreary scene of dockyards and riverfront slums slipping past, Connigham was reminded of the similar dockyards and slums three thousand miles away to which he had been sent in 1905. In the early morning hours, after the shootings, he and Tom Finnigan had met a lorry near Lough Eileen and driven south to Dublin. A few nights later he was placed aboard an American steamer lying in the River Liffey and the following evening was staggering with seasickness between coal bunker and furnace, black with coal dust and stinking with vomit. For a year, they had kept him working on New York's East River docks, feeling his way into the confidence of the large Irish contingent of longshoremen who, with Central Europeans, Jews, and a few blacks, formed the working-class waterfront population.

Fund raising and its attendant requirement, speechmaking, came hard to him as he lacked the glib Irish tongue and so the Committee, that hard-faced, harder-drinking group of expatriate Irish murderers and thieves in the name of liberty, had sent him west to organize the Irish among the miners and cowboys, many of whose fathers had built the vast American network of railways and furnished a third or more of the post–Civil War army. He had found fertile ground among them. The old men without exception had left Ireland to escape waves of famine, poverty, and repression, and still, they had infused their sons with a love of Ireland that Connigham found difficult to understand.

Into Colorado, Nevada, Arizona, then north to Wyoming, they had sent him, lecturing, organizing, and fighting, until the trickle of coins and paper money had become a steady flood with which he bought firearms—lever-action repeating Winchesters, surplus Springfield "trapdoor" army rifles, then surplus magazine-loading Krags from hardware dealers, from drunken quartermaster sergeants and from crooked government officials. He once reckoned that he had bought over ten thousand weapons, seven thousand or more of which reached eager hands in Ireland.

And always, during his years of exile, there were the agonizing hours of loneliness without Emily and, to his surprise, without Margaret. At times, he would find himself staring at his face—all hard planes and angles—in cracked mirrors above dirty washbasins and wondering what in the name of God Emily had ever seen in him. He, a slum dweller with no education to speak of and an accused murderer into the bargain; she, an heiress in her own right and married into one of the most powerful Anglican families in Ireland. Yet she had claimed to love him and her monthly letters smuggled out of Ireland bore that out. Why?

The Liverpool yards appeared to be operating at near capacity judging by the floods of dockyard workers surging along Regent Road. The train was filling up with weary men bundled into black felt coats and heavy work pants with tin pails clutched in rough hands. They shuffled soundlessly aboard, too tired after the ten-hour shift to talk. The lucky ones found seats, the rest stood, eyes vacant, swaying with the movement of the car. The docks and rivers were a forest of masts and steam funnels in the mist. A pall of brown coal smoke hung over all and the Mersey was invisible.

Connigham left the train at Blackstone Street and loitered on the curb across from the dingy American Hotel for some minutes, watching the traffic passing along Regent Road. Then he joined a crowd of workers from the Bramley Moore Dock as they crossed to the hotel's bar. Inside, he made his way to the counter and ordered a stout. One more big Irishman in work clothes excited no comment; if he was a new face, there were new faces every day.

Connigham took his glass to a window from which he could watch the road. It was foolish to suspect that he was being followed; even more foolish to suspect that he was not. The rain that had been threatening most of the day had come on now, and in the lights scattered along the road he could see it pelting down, creating instant puddles. The pub was warm and close with the friendly odor of sweat and beer, and he was reluctant to leave.

Nevertheless Connigham shouldered his way to the door and went out into the rain. It was a good mile yet to the Canada Basin and he started walking. The docks remained pretty much as he remembered. A few more people about, motor lorries rather than horse-drawn wagons predominating, but otherwise little had changed. The same dirty brick walls screened the docks proper from the road, the same dreary line of pubs, chandlers, works yards, coal yards, and boarding-houses lined the other side. The road and footpaths were just as littered and soot- and oil-stained, and the men who trod the road were as sullen and defeated. He was abreast of the Huskisson Number Three Dock now and the entrance to the Canada Docks lay just ahead. He paced steadily on. Lorry after lorry passed in a never-ending stream, the grinding of gears and the noises of engines blending with the harbor's foghorns and the ships' whistles and the rattle of crane engines and anchor chains.

Connigham crossed the road behind a stalled lorry to a point opposite the Canada Docks. Light bled from windows in the Harland & Wolf, Ltd. Shipbuilding & Engineering Works as he leaned against the Home Street corner, where he was protected somewhat from the rain, and waited.

At six o'clock, a series of whistles began to blow throughout the docks and within moments the first flood of workmen crested the gates and overflowed the road. Connigham joined the night shift converging on the same gates and, once inside, followed a group that split to the right, his hands jammed into his pockets, and chin against his chest like the rest of them, to fend off the worst of the rain. It was too miserable a night for the usual chaffering, and they slouched along in silence. Once past the vast, open pit of the Graving Dock with its steam crane raised against the gathering night, the men turned off and he was alone. A dark mass bulked against the feeble lights and Connigham did not trouble to identify it. He hurried on toward the Number Three Dock, skirted a pile of timbers, edged past a horse-drawn car, and followed the tracks to the center of the pier where a dingy tramp steamer was berthed, a faded Norwegian pennant dangling from the stern.

Connigham climbed the rain-slick gangway to the main

deck. As he hesitated, a surly oaf in a heavy knit sweater and dark cap shouted down from the bridge in Norwegian. Connigham shrugged. With a grunt, the man motioned him up. Connigham found the ladder leading to the bridge and started toward the Norwegian silhouetted at the top. The man backed away as Connigham gained the bridge and rumbled something that he translated after a moment's thought as "What you want?" pronounced with a series of *v*'s. He gave his name and the man shrugged and pointed below. When Connigham started to ask another question, the man only shook his head, jabbed his finger at the deck again, and began to curse in Norwegian.

Connigham left the bridge and went back to the main deck. He stood for a moment, undecided, then suddenly angry as well as tired and hungry, he stamped into a passageway. A hatch opened and a bearded, bleary-eyed man looked out. "You Connigham?" he asked in passable English and, without waiting for an answer, led the way down a deck to a tiny cabin barely six feet deep and four wide. He shoved open a door and lit an oil lamp, backed out, and motioned Connigham in.

"They come soon," he muttered and started to leave.

Connigham grabbed his arm. "Something to eat?"

The man started to shake his head, then, as if the steadily tightening grip on his arm had something to do with his decision, nodded reluctantly.

"Soon."

"Very soon."

Connigham released him and stepped into the cabin. There was barely room to move once the door was closed. A mussed bunk covered with a torn wool blanket that had not been washed in years occupied nearly the entire space. The place smelled of unwashed bodies, urine, and rusting iron, but Connigham had been in worse places. He hung his jacket and cap next to the blower through which a wisp of warm air moved and lay down on the bunk.

The cook knocked on the hatch twenty minutes later and handed in a battered billy can and a steaming cup of tea. Connigham took the food and turned to set it on the bunk. As he did so, he heard the lock click. When he tried the door, he found it securely fastened. For a moment he was angry enough to kick the thin wood slats apart, then thought better of it. There was nothing more he could do until Boyle arrived and they talked. He had to find out where he stood.

Connigham sat down on the bunk, suddenly more depressed than he could ever recall. He bit his lower lip and stared at the door, trying to ignore the sense of failure that had been threatening to overwhelm him of late. After a moment, he uncovered the billy to find an unappetizing mess of cold stew congealed in its own fat. The tea at least was hot, if weak, and when he finished, he stacked the containers on the floor and stretched out again on the bunk with a cigarette.

Connigham came completely awake as soon as he heard a key in the lock and was sitting up when the door opened. A heavyset man with a bushy mustache stared at him for a moment. Connigham returned the stare and the man crowded into the cabin. Another remained in the passage. Both were big, well-muscled, and had about them the confident air of prize fighters slumming in the toughest section of town. Connigham ignored them as a third man, short, dumpy, and reeking of goodwill, crowded into the cabin.

"Michael," he breathed. "It's been a damned long time. Stand up, lad, and let me look at you."

Connigham scowled and stretched out a hand. "For Christ's sake, Arthur, drop the damned politician act. We grew up together, remember. I hauled your ass out of more fights than I care to remember."

Arthur Boyle, Member of Parliament for Liverpool's Dingle District and covert head of the Fenian Movement in England, subject only to the orders of the Dublin Committee, roared with laughter and shook Connigham's hand hard enough to set him jiggling on the bunk.

"Michael, of course I remember," he cried. "You were a great help to me then, lad, as you have since been to the Movement. We are all proud of you, boyo. Very proud."

"So proud that you'll only meet me on a dirty tramp steamer, Arthur?"

Boyle laid a finger along his nose and risked a quick glance over his shoulder. "Ah, but that is security, Michael. I had to come along to the docks for a meeting tonight. What better opportunity, heh?" He chuckled and wedged his bulk securely into the doorway as if afraid that Connigham might escape.

"After all, Michael, you're a wanted man. Ah, yes and the police, now, would love to put their hands on you, wouldn't they?" He shook his head. "Now then, I don't understand why you felt the need to leave the safety of the United States, Michael? I surely don't."

"The hell you don't, Arthur," he observed mildly. The two bodyguards shifted, one tensing visibly. "And who the hell are these morons, Arthur? Since when did you start traveling with chimpanzees?"

Boyle smirked. "Ah, and you've been a long time away, Michael. You don't realize the precautions we must take these days. I represent a very touchy constituency. The Irish are not loved in England, Michael, and there are those who would do me harm. Unionists."

He pronounced the word *Unionist* in the confidential voice of a man using a forbidden word to a friend.

"You've no idea how strong *they* have become since certain people have begun to encourage them. Ah, and they have organized. They are after us now. And you as well, boyo. But then you haven't answered my question, have you Michael? Why did you return to England?" This last had a sharp edge to it.

Connigham fished a cigarette from his pocket, lit it, and dropped the match on the metal deck. He blew a streamer of smoke at Boyle and smiled as a flicker of annoyance crossed the fat man's face.

"They tell me, Arthur, that you've become a very powerful man. There have been times even when I thought I detected your delicate hand in some of the instructions I received in Boston. More than a few times, in fact. I'd say that you are getting on in the world." He smiled and Boyle inclined his head modestly. "But to become a big man you must know *what* is going on around you. To stay a big man, you must know *why*. Would you say that was correct, Arthur?"

Puzzled as to where this was leading, Boyle nodded.

"Well, if you have gotten to be such a big man," Connigham hissed, "why the hell didn't you know that my sister had been murdered, you son-of-a-bitch? And *why?*"

Boyle jumped back involuntarily and one of the guards started to reach for Connigham, but Michael was on his feet and facing him, his knife a bare fraction of an inch from the man's windpipe. "Call him off, Arthur, or I'll cut his throat."

Connigham did not raise his voice but his expression left no doubt as to his intentions. Boyle signaled to the bodyguard and Connigham released him when the man dropped his hands to his sides. When he stepped back, Connigham noted that the man's eyes were full of hatred and he smiled lazily at him.

"Well . . . Michael, what . . . can I say. Of course I knew of the unhappy circumstances, but . . ."

"But what could you do?" Connigham finished for him, not taking his eyes from the guard as he folded his knife and slipped it back into his boot. "You might find out who did it, Arthur? Or don't you have any influence in London?"

"But of course, we did investigate, Michael!"

Connigham resumed his seat on the cot, ignoring the protest. "Doesn't the fact that she was one of us make any damned difference to you? Or perhaps you just felt that you owed neither of us anything? Does Dublin agree with you, Arthur?"

"Now wait, Michael." Boyle rubbed a fleshy hand across his face. "You are going too far. I did institute certain inquiries. In fact, we have a copy of the police report which states that she was murdered by a burglar."

Connigham shook his head. "That was in the Boston paper, Arthur, and you know as well as I do that the police are only guessing. Someone hushed it up. Otherwise, why didn't the press report that she was my sister? They would have put it in the Boston papers, if they had known. I'm an important man there, Arthur. Not nearly so important as you, but important enough so that the papers would take notice."

"She used her married name, of course," Boyle snapped, beginning to lose his temper.

"For Christ's sake, Arthur, don't be a damned fool. Even the drunkest reporter would pick up on that. Margaret wrote me eight months ago that she had joined the Movement. She was one of us, and when one of us is killed, we find out why and someone suffers for it. Isn't that right, Arthur? Remember what you told me one cold night in Belfast. And then you sent me out to risk my neck while you stayed warm and dry at home, never lifting a finger to help afterward."

Boyle scowled. "That is not true, Michael. There was nothing we could do. You were to have taken them elsewhere, not shoot them down in the Shankill Road in front of a dozen

Prod witnesses.'' He peered at Connigham angrily. "Damn it, Michael, we have made an inquiry into your sister's murder and are satisfied it had nothing to do with the Movement. What I want to know and what Dublin wants to know is, Why are you in England? Permission was not given for you to leave the States. In fact, you were ordered the day before yesterday to return and—''

Connigham swore at him. "The hell with your permission. I came to England to find out what happened to my sister. You tell Dublin that this is a personal matter and to mind their own business.''

Boyle regarded him for a long moment. "You know about me, Michael, and that is something the authorities do not. Therefore, you are a liability. Do you understand!'' He went on without waiting for an answer. "The situation in England is very fluid at the moment and we cannot risk calling attention to the Movement now. We have had a disastrous setback, I don't mind admitting, this past summer, and we cannot afford any renewed attention. Therefore, Michael, you will return to the States immediately. This ship sails at ten in the morning for New Orleans. You will remain aboard. You are not to leave the United States again without permission from Dublin. Do I make myself clear, Michael?''

Connigham was well aware of the ruthlessness of the Dublin Committee. They would not hesitate to have him killed if they thought it would further the cause in even the slightest respect. He nodded, so angry that he did not trust himself to speak. Boyle broke into a fatuous grin that did not fool him for an instant.

"Ah, Michael, and good it is to know that you understand. I realize that it was anguish for your only sister that drove you to this rash move. Believe me, I championed you in Dublin when they were all for sterner measures. I pointed out your long and effective service in America and before that, in Belfast and here in Liverpool as well.'' He beamed upon Connigham. "You must realize, Michael, that this is necessary. Scotland Yard did us great damage this past summer. We have had to rebuild from the ground up, and that meant bringing in trusted people and establishing them. Now, Lady Wilson-Langdon has been a great help in this matter. A great help. So, knowing your feelings for one another, I've made certain that she knows why you have had to leave England so quickly, without the chance for a proper good-by. But the Committee has asked me to tell you that she will be paying a visit to New York next year, or perhaps the year after, to conduct a discreet fund-raising campaign. I am certain that if it is possible, the Committee will grant you permission to see her.'' He finished his little speech with a grin that let Connigham know just how much he had enjoyed delivering this piece of news. ''In fact, I will make it my business to see that they do.''

Connigham knew now that he had been properly whipped into line and served notice that his private life was nonexistent. He could only expect the worst if he did not obey, while, on the other hand, the Committee might just possibly be generous if he did what he was told like a good little soldier.

He considered kicking Boyle squarely in the belly and heaving him over the stern for the harbor police to find the next morning. And he would have done so, bodyguards or no bodyguards. But there was something strange here. Boyle was far too anxious to get him out of England. He was not the only person who knew that Boyle was more than a respectable Member of Parliament, even if he did belong to the Labour Party.

Boyle's face hardened. ''Remember what I said, Michael.'' He jerked his head at the two bodyguards and they filed out. The taller one gave him a superior grin and slammed the door. The latch did not click. After a moment, he heard a chuckle and bootsteps going down the passageway.

Connigham sat for a few minutes, struggling to bring himself under control. When he thought he had done so, he opened the door and peered into the dim passage. Empty. But he knew damned well that the door had been left unlocked for a purpose. They were testing him. If he stayed below and sailed with the ship in the morning, well and good, and he would be forgiven his breach of discipline. But if he tried to leave the ship, he was a dead man. He smiled to himself and stretched out on the bunk. He had no wish to be forgiven.

When he tilted his watch to catch the dim light from the passage, it read ten minutes to four. The ship was unnaturally quiet, and he had come to the conclusion that the crew was all ashore or asleep, leaving Boyle a clear playing field if necessary. He pulled his cap down snugly and slipped out into the corridor, easing the door shut behind him. At the ladder, he stepped back into the shadows cast by the swivel-mounted oil lamp on the bulkhead and waited, listening. Again, nothing but the unusual silence. He went up the ladder quickly and was through the open hatch and out onto the deck concealed behind a windlass in a matter of seconds. He could not be certain from this angle, but the bridge appeared deserted. The drunken sailor who had shouted at him hours before had either passed out or gone ashore.

Crouching low, he made his way along the deck opposite the docks until he reached the end of the deckhouse, where he paused to make certain that the afterdeck was deserted. The rain that had begun earlier was still falling steadily, hissing into the oily water, stilling the tiny wavelets that usually surged in the sheltered basin. Feeble electric lamps glowed along the dock, and on the opposite side of the basin was a newer cargo vessel, sketchily outlined by its own electric lighting system. Preparations for an early departure were underway he decided, noting the stir on board and the occasional sound of a shouted order that carried across the basin.

Satisfied that the Alesund's deck was deserted, he made his way to the stern winch, where he crouched beside the machinery that held the mooring lines taut.

A long row of sheds edged the far side of the dock, a massive cement pier nearly a quarter of a mile long and half that wide. Rusting piles of machinery, channel buoys, cranes, and a thousand other objects that made up the detritus of a dockyard were strewn haphazardly along the dock itself. The weak electric lamps depending from poles did more to increase the darkness than relieve it. The steady moan of foghorns echoed up and down the Mersey and in the distance Connigham could hear a drawbridge clank into activity. An answering whistle came faintly and his mind, falling into old patterns, identified it as a tug.

He started at the channel end of the sheds and worked slowly along, probing the shadows on either side of the meager electric lamps. Directly opposite the gangway and some twenty yards across the dock was a small wooden shack. The door was open and, as he watched, he saw the flare of a match as someone lit a cigarette. It was unlikely that the dock authorities would waste a watchman's wages here in the middle of the night. There was nothing to steal. He finished his study of the sheds and patiently repeated it before returning again to the shack. If that was his guard, the man had picked an excellent spot, he thought. He could not only watch the gangway but either end of the ship.

He settled back into the shelter of the winch and thought about his predicament. He could accept Boyle's story, go back to the cabin, and sail in the morning, and he might as well, as he knew that Boyle had no intention of investigating further. And that puzzled him. Why? If Boyle was afraid that Connigham might betray him, why let him come to Liverpool? Far easier to have sent some muscular boyos to London to escort him to Southampton or Portsmouth and put him aboard a ship, or better yet, shoot him. Or was Emily the reason why they had done neither—offering him, instead, a chance to go on his own. Be that as it might, there was a reason they wanted him out of the country and quickly, and that reason was not the ridiculous one given by Boyle. And then there was the matter of the police in London. Was it as simple a matter as an informer? Or had the word been given to the police? He would not put that past either Boyle or the Dublin Committee. Were they afraid of what he might find out about Margaret's death? But why? And Emily had tried to discourage him as well. Was it because she feared for his safety? And if so, where was the threat—from the police or from the Movement? Social reporting, she had described the work that had been parceled out to her. And he did not believe that either.

He shuffled to the far side of the stern and studied the dirty water below. A single hemp line stretched from the winch to a bollard set well back from the ship. The cable fell in a long catenary, dipping below the edge of the dock before snubbing itself around the mushroom-shaped bollard. Was the rain heavy enough to provide concealment, he wondered? With a bit of luck it might be. But how to work his way past the shack? The sheds were at least fifty yards distant. The ship was moored in the second position; a harbor fireboat was tied up between the *Alesund* and the channel and, like the *Alesund*, it appeared deserted. The fireboat might provide a measure of cover as he climbed onto the dock, and its stern mooring line, looped around the same bollard, would provide a handhold.

But once on the dock, he still had to work his way across

to the warehouses, and the end of the dock was empty and uncluttered. The quay across the channel that divided the basin from the Mersey proper was brightly lit, and he would be silhouetted against that light.

Connigham made his decision, the tension already beginning to build. He had to go now, to take his chances. He needed all the time he could manage to get clear of the dockyards before someone discovered him missing and alerted Boyle.

Without further hesitation, he slipped through the stern railing, reached down, and got one hand and then the other onto the mooring line. The hemp was rough and rain-slick. Connigham took a deep breath and fell forward, hands swiveling around the wrist-thick line; for a moment he hung beneath, feet swinging across the filthy channel water thirty feet below. He let his forward momentum carry him through the short arc and at the last possible moment, kicked upward and got an ankle over the wet line so that he hung, back down but still hidden by the curve of the stern.

He slid down as quickly as possible without tearing the skin from his hands, kicked loose as he encountered the rat guard, and began to work his way around the metal cone. His belt snagged on the turned metal edge and he almost lost his hold. Swearing softly, Connigham waited until the line had stopped swaying, then clamped his legs tighter and reached one hand around the guard, inching his body down until he was doubled around the cone. As his fingers scrabbled for a hold, the rain eased off and a light flashed from the far side of the channel. Connigham froze. If it happened again, it would surely attract the attention of the man in the shack and he would be a sitting duck. He squeezed himself as far down as possible, let go with his left hand and lunged forward with his right. For an instant before his fingers caught the slippery hemp, he swung loose but his legs held him long enough to bring his left hand up, and he locked both arms around the line and slid the remaining ten feet to the lowest point of the curve below the edge of the dock.

Shaking as much from fear as exertion, he hung with arms and legs locked about the line, fighting for control and for the energy to reverse himself and work up to the edge of the dock. The fireboat's stern line provided a secure foothold and a moment later, he was peering over the edge.

The dock had been built by sinking caissons into the river-bed and filling the intervening space with rubble. Once the fill had risen above the channel surface, huge wooden forms were erected around the perimeter and filled with cement. When the forms were stripped away, an indented ledge, one foot deep and five feet below the top of the dock had been left. Connigham transferred himself onto the ledge and worked along to the end where a pile of timbers had been piled haphazardly.

Moving slowly, staying as low as possible, he lifted himself onto the dock and wriggled forward until he was lying full length on the wet cement. A ship's whistle blasted the night: a tug maneuvering a steamer into the channel. He cursed in frustration; the activity would only draw the guard's attention in his direction. The rain began to fall harder and for twenty minutes he endured it, shivering against the cold of the cement as it drew heat from his body. It seemed an interminable time before the pounding of the tug's engines faded and Connigham was able to move toward the sheds, slowly, testing each step. Twice he tripped over tangles of discarded cable before the dim shape of the sheds came into view and he covered the remaining few feet in a rush to crowd into their shelter.

The few pole-mounted lamps on the dock cast no usable light in the heavy downpour—at once advantage and disadvantage. Using the rusting machinery and scrap for cover, Connigham began to work his way toward the shack. A pile of anchors baffled him for a moment in the dark until he felt his way along the rusted shaft of one and found the fluke. It was then that the rain began to ease and as it did so, the dim horizon crept back until he could see both shack and steamship beyond.

The shack was less than ten feet away. He slipped the switchblade knife from his boot top and hefted it thoughtfully. Whether he killed the guard or not, they would kill *him* if he was caught.

Connigham waited, studying the shack from a rear angle. After a while, he heard a yawn. The door opened and a figure emerged. The man had a cigarette cupped in one hand to hide the glowing end from the ship. The red coal gave him a target and he smiled as he inched forward, holding his breath so as not to betray himself. When he was less than four feet away, he lunged, left forearm clamping the man's face. The guard arched his back, but Connigham leaned forward, pushing him off balance as his right hand drove the knife into his kidney and twisted. He withdrew the knife and slashed the blade across the exposed throat. The man shuddered and stumbled to his knees. Connigham stepped into the shadows where he could not be seen while the man collapsed forward gurgling and scrabbling at the muddy cement as he bled to death.

Connigham remained where he was for a full minute before kneeling beside the body. He went through the man's pockets and found a wallet containing a thick wad of bank notes and two keys. He tossed the keys and wallet away and jammed the notes into his jacket pocket. In the waistband of the man's pants was a heavy pistol and he grinned at the familiar feel of the slab-sided Colt 1902 Model automatic. It could very well have been part of one of his shipments.

Connigham dragged the body into the shack, stripped the trousers off, and changed them for his own wet ones. He struck a match and checked the body—it was the man who had remained in the passage when Boyle had come into the cabin. The pistol was fully loaded; eight copper-jacketed .38-caliber cartridges nestled in the magazine. He slid it back into the butt and jacked a round into the chamber, eased the hammer down, and slipped the pistol into his belt. Time to go, he thought. Past time. Connigham stepped outside and listened; nothing but a distant foghorn and the sound of rain drumming on the dock. The ship was a dark hulk, imperfectly silhouetted in the lights of the steamer behind.

The docks ran out at right angles from a quay that edged the Regent Road beyond the brick walls. Gates for lorries were let into the wall at intervals, but most were blocked by heavy wooden doors. Only at a few points were the gates open, and each of those was guarded by a night watchman. Between the wall and the edge of the quay were piles of machinery, bollards, winches for mooring ships, cranes, and sheds for the many services required by the second busiest port in England. At intervals along the quay, the way became a tangle of cables and ropes snaking from the bows or sterns of steamers and sailing ships loading or unloading cargoes.

He had reached the sheds when he heard a grating sound, a piece of metal being moved in the darkness. Connigham faded into the shadows and waited. For just an instant, there was something, a shadow where there should not have been one. Boyle had been smarter than Connigham had credited him.

He backed away, showing himself briefly against a lamp above the door to a freight office to draw the man out, but whoever he was, he was too experienced for that ploy. Connigham continued to move back, feeling for each step. Halfway across the open area he turned and dove into cover so quickly that it took the watcher by surprise. There was a sharp crack of a pistol shot and something struck the cement and whined away into the night.

Not caring how much noise he made now, Connigham ducked and twisted between the stacks of crates and machinery. The man had no choice, and he came out of the shadows, but too quickly for Connigham to catch more than a brief glimpse. Connigham heard a footstep echo from the brick wall and he knew the man had found an opening in the crazy-quilt pattern of machinery, refuse, and freight to place himself in a commanding position to control the only escape route. A moment later he heard a low chuckle and a voice called softly, the brogue exaggerated, "Give it up, man. Ye'll not leave here alive. I'll see to that."

Connigham knew that he might very well be right. Having gained the advantage of the wall, the man could keep him tied up in the dockyard until it was light enough to see or until help arrived.

He risked a quick look around. They were beyond the sheds now; a four-foot pathway led along the Graving Dock to the end of the pier, where the lighted quay half a mile across the channel offered no help at all. The Graving Dock. An idea began to form.

He eased away from the shadowed building and skirting the open edge of the huge dry dock, moved along to the crane mounted on the edge of the dark abyss. He had spared the Graving Dock only the briefest of glimpses as he passed the previous evening, but he remembered the crane and the two sets of steps leading down into the dock from either side.

The Graving Dock was immense, one of the largest dry docks in the world, 925 feet long. At the channel end were two massive iron doors closing off the waters of the basin. As he remembered, a huge rectangular steel box was under construction, and he had spent enough time in ships to know that it was a steamer's engine compartment. A jungle of scaffolding had been erected about it and, big as it was, it filled only a small portion of the vast pit. If he could get down into the Graving Dock, he could work his way along to the channel doors without being detected in the pitch black interior. From there, if he was lucky, he could find steps or a service ladder leading to the top, while Boyle's guard was still searching the Canada Basin for him.

A cable dangled into the dock from the crane, but in the darkness it was impossible to tell how far down it reached. The dock was sixty feet or more deep and it could be a long drop. The crane had been swung so that the cable dangled only a few feet from the edge. He wiped his hands on his trousers, sat down on the edge, leaned out, and grabbed the cable. Below, the shackled bight clanked against the wall. He froze at the noise and it struck again, the sound echoing in the huge cavern. The cable did not reach the bottom; there was no way to tell how far above the dock floor it ended, but the noise had committed him. There was nothing for it now, he thought, but to go. The cable was coated with grease and the rain only made it that much more slippery. He went down at an increasing rate, struggling to get his feet onto the cable. Just as he did, they were knocked away by the steel shackle that formed the bight. He let go before the steel slashed his hands and fell, knees bent to take up the shock.

Connigham landed hard, driving one knee up to hit his chin and snap his head back. One foot landed higher than the other and he sprawled, again twisting his bad ankle and banging his head against the floor. He lay stunned, half in, half out of the drainage channel; afterward he thought that he might have knocked himself unconscious for a few minutes, but he was never certain. A band of lighter darkness grew, and it was some moments before he understood that he was on his back looking up at the sky. Rain pattered on his face and the smell of brackish water and mud assailed his nostrils.

After another few moments, he tried to stand, but his ankle gave way. Teeth clenched against the pain, he managed to get to his feet on the second try and leaned against the wall for support. After a minute or two, he found that he could walk, but with a pronounced limp, and his ankle hurt like the devil.

To stay in the open was to invite a bullet. He would never be able to make it to the channel end of the Graving Dock before it occurred to the man above simply to walk along and wait for him. The steam engine compartment under construction was near the rear of the dock, its afterend tangled in scaffolding. Connigham, with his good foot, felt for the far edge of the drainage channel, found it, and hobbled forward, hands out in front of him. The bottom of the Graving Dock was wet and water stood in puddles. He nearly fell once when his foot encountered a discarded timber and his weight came down hard on his bad ankle. He managed to choke off the shout of pain but it was some minutes before he could continue.

After what seemed an eternity, he felt the icy metal of the engine compartment with outstretched hands and leaned against the timber supports gratefully, wondering now how he was going to entice his pursuer down after him.

"Connigham, you son-of-a-bitch, I'm coming after you!" The shout echoed and reechoed through the depths of the Graving Dock until it was impossible to tell from which direction it had come. It had been meant to panic him, but instead, Connigham began to smile.

The man would come down through the scaffolding, behind and above, and wait for him to betray his position. Connigham moved out into the open space between the engine compartment and the far wall, feeling terribly exposed but forcing himself to stand his ground. The man would not dare use a torch. Its light would betray him before he could locate his prey. Connigham reached what he thought was the center of the pit and scanned the lighter band of darkness above the bulk of the compartment. The merest hint of movement and he shifted his gaze slightly to the right to make use of his peripheral vision; there it was again. Something *had* moved. The fool had forgotten that the sky would be lighter from inside the dock.

From the corner of his eye, Connigham could follow the man's progress until he disappeared into the void of scaffolding. He was coming down that way, there was no longer any question about it. Connigham concentrated on the base of the scaffolding, counting seconds and trying to envision the man's progress as he felt his way through the maze of timbers. Connigham was certain that he must come out near the engine compartment, otherwise he could too easily lose his bearings.

Two minutes passed, five, ten, and Connigham was having

trouble keeping count of the seconds. The tension, as he crouched on the muddy floor, Colt pistol held loosely in his right hand, hammer back and index finger resting along the slide, was becoming unbearable. Yet he forced himself to remain still, a dark mass against the dark cement.

And there it was, above the hissing of the rain, a gentle clink, boot against metal. A moment later, the barest suggestion of movement. He smiled slowly and stopped counting. All he had to do now was wait.

Time crept by and still he did not relax, remained crouched, eyes moving slowly back and forth against the utter blackness that was the engine compartment, patiently waiting for the next sign of movement or the faint sound that would mark the man's progress. He was in control now, anxiety suppressed, knowing he was safe from detection in the black void.

The moment, when it came, was anticlimactic. The man reached the end of the engine compartment and made his mistake then, as Connigham had known he would. For a moment, he was a dark blur against the lighter cement wall, a bit of darkness detached from the black-painted bulk of the engine compartment. The man was not fifteen feet away. Connigham forced his subconscious to take control. "Don't try and sight the weapon, you bloody fool," he could almost hear his instructor in small arms screaming at him as he faced the target against the surging waters of Galway Bay. "Let your damned instinct aim for you. What in hell do you think you are seeing in the dark?" And he did so now and squeezed the trigger with the gentlest of pressures.

The report slapped against the walls, blotting the man's scream as he stumbled forward and fell. Connigham dove to one side after the shot and rolled several times until he was in the drainage channel. After a few moments, when he had heard no other sound, he got to his feet and cautiously approached the area where he thought the body lay.

The man shuddered when he stirred him with his foot and he struck a match, shielding it with his body, right hand holding the Colt against the man's head. It was the bodyguard with the bushy mustache. He was sprawled on his back, eyes open, and as Connigham brought the match to his face, the pupils contracted.

"Help—me." He heard the whisper faintly above the rain. The bullet had hit him low in the abdomen but must have gone through to sever the spine as his legs were twisted at a strange angle.

"Help me," he mouthed again.

"Sure, boyo, sure," Connigham whispered, and pressed the muzzle against the man's forehead. There was just enough time for the lips below the mustache to form the word *no* before the pistol roared and the match went out.

chapter———18

Bannerman gave up in disgust, dumped the papers into his briefcase, and kicked it into a corner. He was fed up with the estimates. He had spent the past two days revising them and cursing the government bureaucracies and company rules that required him to spend so much time on useless paperwork. He stamped around the two-room flat until he calmed down, then fixed a large whiskey and soda and carried it back to his desk. The Westminster clock on the mantelpiece chimed eight, much too early for bed. He glared at the briefcase again, resenting afresh Margaret's death. The estimates were among the many things she had done for him. Standing morosely at the window staring out into the rain, he lamented, and not for the first time, the fact that there was so little to do of an evening in Dover.

He decided to indulge himself. It had been weeks since he had looked at his stamp collection and, feeling not the least bit guilty, Bannerman fetched the new North European volume purchased in London to replace the one stolen and the box of stamps from the desk drawer. He began to catalog and mount each one, whistling softly as he worked, the familiar routine soothing and relaxing him. He was unaware that his headache had stopped or that sore shoulder muscles were loosening. The pale squares of paper and the sticky stamp hinges occupied his attention fully as he searched the volume for preprinted imprints or cataloged the unlisted ones. He had nearly finished the North European issues when he recalled the stamp Margaret had given him. What the devil had he done with it? Then he remembered folding the envelope and slipping it into his wallet. Thinking that it was probably still there, he stretched and started to the bedroom. A loud knocking interrupted him halfway across the floor and, his mind still on the stamp, he went to answer it.

A man as tall as he but broader through the shoulders was standing in the hallway. His shock of reddish-brown hair had been plastered across his scalp by the rain and his worn clothes were soaked. For a moment, Bannerman took him for a workman from the yard.

"Are you Mr. James Bannerman?"

"Yes," he snapped, already annoyed at the interruption. "What do you—" He was pushed aside and the man stepped in, kicking the door closed behind him.

Bannerman stumbled back, aware of his idiotic carelessness, wondering if he could reach the revolver in his briefcase.

"My name is Michael Connigham," the man said and limped across the floor to glance into the bedroom.

Bannerman edged toward the briefcase. "So?"

Connigham turned and shoved his hands into his jacket, apparently paying no close attention to him.

"Margaret was my sister," he continued in the same emotionless tone.

"Who?" Bannerman demanded.

"Margaret. She used the name Doyle, her married name."

Bannerman tilted his head to one side as if to see better. "Margaret was your sister?" He repeated the question, and then, aware of how idiotic it must sound, he motioned vaguely toward the fireplace. "Then you've just come back from India?"

Connigham nodded his thanks and stepped to the coal fire, spreading his hands to the heat. "No. From the States. I'm the other brother. I don't suppose she would have said anything about me. Wouldn't have wanted the police watching her."

"The police?" Connigham's statement confused him even more and to cover it, he went to the sideboard and took down two glasses and a bottle of brandy. He handed one to Connigham, who drank it down quickly.

"The police? I don't understand," Bannerman said as he refilled the glass.

"I'm wanted for murder, by the police. I've been away from England for six years."

A confused mix of impressions were jockeying for attention and Bannerman sank down in the overstuffed Morris chair. "I think you had better take that jacket off before you catch your death, and tell me what this is all about."

Connigham shrugged out of the jacket and hung it over the back of the desk chair which he drew up to the fire. He sat down opposite and Bannerman noted a large, scabbed abrasion on the left side of his chin.

"There isn't much to tell. I've come to England to find out who killed her."

"Good Lord, man, it was in the papers. You didn't have to cross the Atlantic. The police report says—"

"I know all about the police report," Connigham interrupted. "And it's a damned lie. Whether they know it or not," he added as an afterthought.

Connigham lit a cigarette and regarded Bannerman narrowly through the smoke. "Margaret wrote me twice about her position. She said you were a good man to work for and fair, that you took an interest in her welfare." He sat back and waved the smoke away. "I need you to tell me about her, about her life and her friends, where she went and so on."

Bannerman hesitated. "I'm not certain I can help you," he said slowly. "Margaret was a very private person. She didn't speak much of herself or her friends. She told me there was a relative in London, an aunt, whom she visited. Of course there wasn't, as it turned out."

"And you never suspected that it was not true?"

Bannerman shrugged. "Why should I? Her life was her own business. She went up to London at intervals and what she did there, whom she saw, was her own business."

"She worked for you for nearly a year and you learned nothing about her?"

"Not even the fact that she was Irish. I only gathered as much from her accent. She told me she had no other family but a brother in the Indian Army. So you have rather taken me by surprise. I'm not even certain yet that you are her brother."

Connigham nodded but offered no comment. They stared at one another for several moments before Bannerman shrugged nervously. "I really do not see how I am going to be able to help you. Just why is it you think that there was some other reason for her death than the one the police have given?"

"You have no idea whom she saw or what she did when she went up to London?"

Bannerman answered with a flash of annoyance. "No! I've already told you I do not."

"It wasn't to meet you?"

"Good God, no!" Bannerman, startled by the question, felt a twinge of guilt as he recalled the real reason behind his visit to her flat that Sunday evening. "Look here," he said, "I can understand the strain you must be under, if you really are her brother, but that's no reason to be insulting."

"There was nothing insulting about the question," Connigham answered mildly. "It would have been perfectly natural in the situation."

"Well, it was not!"

They stared at each other, two antagonists. Finally, Bannerman shifted his position and, with a trace of truculence, asked, "If you think that she was murdered by someone other than a burglar, why don't you go to the police? I can give you the name of the officer in charge of the investigation."

Connigham grinned at that and seemed to relax. "I could hardly go to Scotland Yard, now could I?"

"Yes, I had forgotten." A very curious person, he thought. "You say you have been charged with murder? What were the circumstances?"

Connigham waved a hand as if dismissing the matter as of no importance, but Bannerman would have none of it. "I think that when a man forces his way into my flat, announces that he is wanted for murder, and asks for my help, the very least he can do is to explain."

"That need not concern you," Connigham snarled. "It has no bearing on what happened to my sister."

Bannerman was taken aback by the fierceness of Connigham's reply; and angry now, he stood up. "Then I think that you had better be on your way. I see no way in which I can help you."

"Sit down." Connigham said, his voice flat and emotionless again. Bannerman, moved more by curiosity than apprehension, did as he was told.

"How many times in the past three months did Margaret go to London?"

Bannerman shook his head. "I can't tell you that. I had other concerns. . . ."

"Try."

Bannerman glared at Connigham but leaned back in the chair and thought about it, trying to order the events of the last few months chronologically. "I think," he said slowly, "she went up on the evening of the third and fourth Fridays, or perhaps Saturdays, of November. Before that, it was sometime in October, I believe. I don't recall the date. . . ."

"First, middle, or last of the month?"

"Last . . . I believe. Perhaps the last weekend or so. And then before that, once in mid-September. As I said, she did not go regularly."

"And you did not think it odd, as she claimed, to visit an aunt that frequently?"

Bannerman shrugged. "Why should I? I've already told you, as long as she did her job properly, which I can assure you she did, what she did with her private life was no concern of mine."

"And what was her job, specifically?"

"That," Bannerman replied, scratching an ear and grinning ruefully, "is rather hard to pin down. Initially, she was to be my clerk. Keep my appointments, do my correspondence and filing work. However, it was not long before she had assumed control of the entire office. Rather an office manager in a way. In fact, I was contemplating promoting her to that very position. She was quite efficient."

Connigham nodded. "That would imply that she knew a great deal about your work?"

"Yes, she did. I am sure that technical details were beyond her, but she did not stop trying to understand. She asked quite intelligent questions."

"Then, except for the technical details, she probably knew exactly what you knew about the Tunnel and its progress?"

The question surprised Bannerman, and it was a moment before he answered. He had not thought about it in quite that way, but he supposed that Connigham was at least partially correct.

"Well, I don't know if you could say everything, but she certainly knew a great deal," he answered slowly.

Connigham nodded to himself and sat staring at the fire.

"I say, just where are these questions leading?"

Connigham did not answer, but continued to gaze into the fire as if he might find the answer there.

After a moment, Bannerman asked softly, "You had not seen her in those six years since you left England, had you?"

Connigham came to with a jerk. "No," he said, as if distracted. "Not since leaving Ireland."

"You were very fond of her, weren't you?"

Connigham seemed to consider the question. "Yes," he said slowly as if the answer were a surprise to him. "I was."

"Tell me about her."

Connigham looked at him as if he did not exist and Bannerman thought he might refuse. But after a moment, Connigham said, "She was the only one he didn't touch. I suppose he knew that if he did, Jack or I would kill him."

For a moment Bannerman's annoyance at this irrelevancy almost overcame him, but something in the man's face stopped him from interrupting. It may have been the exhaustion, heightened by the firelight, that carved deep hollows in Connigham's cheeks and under his mouth, or it may have been the softening of his harsh voice, the fact that it had taken on a hint of sadness. Bannerman studied the man as he talked, the words coming faster now, as if his simple question had acted as an emotional cathartic, deepening his accent at the same time until the brogue was so thick that all traces of American intonation were lost.

"Besides, I don't think it ever entered that drunken sponge of a brain to do so. He nearly beat Ma to death and Jack and me as well, but he never touched her. Jack was bigger, but when he was drunk Da was strong as an ox. Berserk, the priests called it. He'd come home on Saturday night, swaggering in his constabulary uniform and smelling of whiskey worse than any pub. And it wasn't good, honest whiskey either but lousy poteen; what they call rotgut in the States. Only it wasn't his gut that was rotting but his brain. Everyone was afraid of him and that damned great revolver he carried. If his dinner wasn't on the table or something else had gone wrong, he'd start shouting at Ma, and from shouting he'd go to hitting. More than once the police were called; but they were his own friends. They never took him away and after he'd stopped shouting and they had left he'd go for me and Jack as if it were our fault. He'd beat us with that dirty leather belt of his until he was exhausted or passed out from the whiskey and there wasn't a thing any of us could do about it. Margaret would crawl under the table and scream and scream with no one paying her any mind. And it wasn't only Saturday nights either. Any night would do. The priests would come round and talk to him, man to man, and get him to take the pledge, but that wound only last so long as he didn't pass a pub. And the priests would come in the daytime to warn Ma against exciting him. Jesus,'' he muttered, ''they would warn her time after time. Life was a cross, the reward would be in the next. But never would they offer to help . . . the bastards.''

He was quiet for a moment and Bannerman could feel the tension in him. His voice had grown distant as he talked, and Bannerman wondered as he watched the man staring into the fire whether he was sane or not. Were these all the delusions of a maniac? Once again, he eyed the briefcase across the room.

''He was a good policeman, they used to say. None better than old Seamus Connigham. All the old women loved him because they didn't know what he was like at home and wouldn't have believed it if they did. Blamed it on the drink, they would have. And thought that was excuse enough. The same excuse Ireland has always had for stupidity.

''One night Jack wouldn't take it anymore. He was laying for Da when he came through the door. Before he even had his revolver off, Jack knocked him down. He kicked him, kicked him twice,'' Connigham said with relish. ''Then he beat him unconscious. Jack didn't say a word the whole time. Just hit and hit and hit and when he finished, he left. Like that, without a word to anyone. Ma dragged Da to the bed, but she couldn't get him in and I wouldn't help. Margaret had run after Jack and I went looking for her. Found her in a church, damn it! In a church! She was praying to the bloody Virgin.''

His anger was palpable now. Bannerman could feel it in his voice even though it was barely raised above a murmur. ''I couldn't get her to come. I had to carry her from the church and her screaming and the priest trying to stop me. When we got home, the old man was staggering about not knowing what had happened. He lay abed for three days then until he was almost sober, and crying and weeping the whole time at what he had done. He apologized over and over to Ma and to me. I think it was the first time that he was sober in ten years or more. And then the shakes got him and it was as bad as if he were drunk except that he was so weak. His mates covered for him. He had the influenza they said and the doctor afraid of pneumonia. But he went back to the beat after a week, still shaking but no longer screaming at ghosts and divils and animals come to kill him. He never said another word about Jack. Never as long as he lived. Wouldn't let his name be mentioned even by Margaret, even when she cried herself to sleep for months. Jack was her favorite, you see. He was sixteen then and I was only thirteen. There had been another brother a year older than me and a sister a year older than Margaret, but they went early of the lung sickness. So Jack was more a father to her than her own father. And *he* deserted her. He had always stood up for her, protected her, even from the nuns. They daren't whip Margaret as they knew if they did, Jack would get back at them. He was never afraid of them.

"The old man died a year later," he murmured. "A stroke. He came in one night, all pale and shaking. He took off the revolver and holster and turned to my mother, watching from the stove to see if he were drunk. He said her name, just once, 'Maire,' and his mouth stayed open and his face blanched and he fell straight down, dead. The doctor put it down as a stroke brought on by overwork, for the pension. It was nothing more than enough to keep us alive. I found work as a butcher's boy and that brought in a little more, and Ma took in washing, the Irish widow's fate, they calls it.

"She died a year later. The government had took away the pension just the month before. Said there had been a mistake, that Dad had been three weeks short of the time. I was able to earn my way then. The priests took Margaret and put her in a fine house near the park so she could work as a domestic. A *domestic*, they called it. A slave was what it was. Every dirty job the other servants were too lazy to do. Until I found out about it.

"Do ye know what I did then?" It was a rhetorical question and Bannerman knew it. For some reason, he was fascinated, reading into the man's words the horror and the degradation left out, the brutality of a drunken father, the moral weakness of an older brother who had deserted them, a mother who had literally starved to death to see that her children ate. It was familiar. The radical press and the weekly illustrateds were full of such stories. For years the government, whether Liberal or Tory, had been embarrassed by Dublin's Liberties, the worst, most appalling slum in Europe. What was it he had read somewhere, the author quoting a Russian refugee newspaper editor named Lenin, who haunted the British Museum Reading Room writing turgid political and economic tracts that no one could read, let alone understand. The man had claimed that a great revolution of workers and poor would sweep out of the Liberties and across the world.

"I went to the priests, though God knows why," Connigham went on. "They had never helped before, never wanted to. The pastor was a big man, holier than the bishop even, and he would not listen to me. 'I'll hear nothing against them, do ye hear,' he shouted. 'Ye're nothing but a dirty little slummy too lazy to work.' And he tried to beat me with his belt. But by then I was as big as he and I beat him instead. They put me in jail for a year. A priest beater, I was labeled. Whenever the guards had nothing better to do, they beat me. Do you know how badly a priest beater is treated in an Irish jail? Hell, even the chaplain will have nothing to do with you."

"But when I came out, ah, it was another day. I got Margaret from that fancy house and took her to Belfast and once she was settled, I went back. I found the head warder going home drunk one night and beat the living hell from him. He knew who 'twas beat him, but I put the fear of God into him and he never told."

His voice trailed away for a while and Bannerman waited, appalled at the hatred in this man. The anger, he understood, had only grown with time, feeding upon itself, and he knew the outcome of the story. It was inevitable because Connigham was the type of man all too often found in construction gangs, the type of man who could not be bent or beaten—except by himself.

"We went to Belfast because there was work there, so they said. And there was—at half the Protestant wage. But it was still more than we could have earned in Dublin by half. I found us a room in the Bally Murphy and got a job on the docks. Margaret went into the mills. Between us then we had sufficient to eat for the first time in our lives. We had Sundays to ourselves and I would wait for her to come from the church and we might walk in the hills above the city if the weather was fine or go to a lecture if it was not.

"We lived there five years. Five years," he repeated to himself, "and she grew into a young woman. Ah, not a beauty as I had hoped. She was too thin from her childhood and her skin was not good. Not enough vitamins, the mill doctor told her. But she was pretty enough and had beaus to come round. And she married a local lad, a nice young man who worked at the same mill but had got to be foreman, a position unheard of for a Catholic.''

He told the rest of the story in a flat unemotional voice, and Bannerman knew that much was left out, parts too painful for him ever to speak aloud.

''Bob, he was her husband, was one of those innocents who never understood how one man could hate another. He was as devout as any old widow and the pride of the parish priests. But he had joined the Gaelic League to learn the old language, study the old ways, and that was the kiss of death in Belfast when the hatred was on. He and Margaret had been married for three years when they came for him in the night, a drunken bunch of Prods who had heard he was a Gaelic Leaguer and a foreman besides. They took and lynched him that night, right up the road from the house, hung him from the lamppost on the corner. And Margaret saw it all, they told me the next morning.''

Connigham turned to look at him and Bannerman was astonished at his calm expression. He could have been narrating another man's story, something that had happened a thousand years before, for all that it seemed to have affected him.

''I found two of the men involved,'' Connigham said, holding his eye. ''I found one in a pub in the Shankhill and shot him where he sat. The other we took later. He was a police informer, and I've been on the run since.''

Bannerman did not know what to say. A welter of foolish responses was available, but he managed to reject them all as he watched the man sitting across from him. He knew that his initial assessment had been correct. Telling his story had been an emotional catharsis for Connigham. Bannerman would have taken any odds that he had never done so before. He glanced again at Connigham and saw the way his eyelids were shut tight, shielding his eyes; from what? From the pain of living? His very expression suggested fear, and the anger that always followed. But there was nothing that he could say to Connigham. Not only did he not have the words, but the ideas, the rationale were lacking.

''I'd suggest you leave the country tonight,'' Bannerman

offered, not knowing what else to say. "The police must know you are here. Perhaps if you return to the States and work for a better understanding of the Irish cause instead of rousing further rebellion, you might accomplish something worthwhile. Certainly killing will not." It was a lame put-off and would have no effect on the man at all, he knew, but it was the best he could do. He braced for an outburst.

"Aye," Connigham said gently. "I know all the arguments." He stood up, slipped into his jacket, and gave Bannerman a pitying stare that summed up his contempt. "I'll not bother you further."

With that he was gone, the door closing softly behind him. Bannerman looked at it for a long time. After a while, he poured himself another drink, wondering what else he could have done. The man had revealed himself to his core, and he had dismissed him with meaningless platitudes. The telephone mocked him. He reached for it, hesitated, then shook his head and gulped the brandy. He would not call the police. He could at least do that much. After a while he got up and removed the revolver from his briefcase. As he slipped it into his coat pocket, Bannerman resolved not to be without it again. There were, after all, limits.

chapter —— 19

The men crowded Bannerman's small office to capacity.
Rain lashed the windows, a steady drumming that ran like an
undercurrent to their nervous murmuring. The smell of wet
wool and perspiration was overpowering. Bannerman watched
them shed jackets and mackintoshes and find seats along the
narrow table that had been placed at right angles to his desk.

This was not a usual staff conference but a meeting with
trade union officials. An unusual meeting urged on him by
McDougal, who was sitting near the door, to deal with such
wild and varied rumors as the project closing down; his
resignation; loss of government support; design flaws in the
Tunnel conduits; sabotage—all the rumors that were always
present in a large engineering works but were never a problem until things began to go wrong.

And now he was in the position of having to lie—or at least
withhold the truth—and he did not like it one bit. All during
the hot, troubled summer, they had experienced few of the
labor problems that plagued the rest of the country. Wages
paid by the Anglo-French Submarine Railway were better
than elsewhere in England, and working conditions in the
main safer than in the collieries or factories. And then, too, a
matter of national pride was at stake; the Board of Directors
had cleverly orchestrated the natural rivalry that had developed between the English and French crews to see who would
reach the midpoint first.

But he doubted if it would be much help now. Even though
he had discussed his findings concerning the explosion only
with McDougal and the Board of Directors, it was inevitable
that rumors of sabotage would arise among the engineering
staff and the work crews. Then too, there had been speculation in the press the past few days, primarily in the *Times*,
and he was certain that he had detected Churchill's hand.

McDougal was convinced that the condition had become serious enough to warrant postponing his trip up to London for the Board meeting and, reluctantly, he had agreed. Sir Henry Keithley had been hard put to conceal his glee over this turn of events when Bannerman spoke to him by telephone. Keithley agreed that the meeting with the workers' representatives was potentially quite serious and offered the terms of the new wage contracts approved the week before as an issue which he could use if the discussion appeared to be going against the company.

"Rest assured, Mr. Bannerman, we shall keep the best interests of the project, and your assessment of the situation, before us in our discussions tomorrow."

"I am certain you will, Sir Henry," Bannerman had replied, trying his hardest to keep the irony from his voice. "Just remember, if you please, that security must be increased."

Bannerman had rung off knowing exactly what the outcome of tomorrow's meeting would be without him there. Yet he also knew that if he postponed the meeting now to attend the Board, it would seem as if he were scurrying off to London for instructions.

They were all seated now, waiting for him to begin. "Gentlemen, it would appear we have a situation rapidly growing out of hand. I refer of course to the unfounded rumors that are rife. . . ."

At the far end of the table a heavyset man with a trace of beard spoke up. "Aye, Mr. Bannerman, we do agree. There are the rumors to be discussed. But there are other problems as well."

Bannerman knew the man only by reputation, Jonah M. Mereside, a union official sent down from London the previous month. Mereside was a paid employee of the union, not the company. Strange, Bannerman thought, how far the trade union movement had come in England in the past decade. At the beginning of the century, the man would have been an employee of the firm whose workers he represented and no owner or manager would have deigned to speak to him, let alone sit at the same table. Bannerman decided on an immediate offensive.

"Gentlemen, before we get to those matters"—he smiled around the table—"the Board has authorized me to announce their decision on the new compensation contracts presented in

October. The directors have considered your demands and while they cannot justify to their stockholders the full ten percent across the board pay raise requested, they have approved certain categories for a ten percent rise. In general, the remainder are to be raised six percent.''

A clerk distributed folders containing the details and the murmur that followed caused Mereside to hesitate as he was about to stand.

Seeing his opportunity, Bannerman got to his feet first. "As you know, we have fallen severely behind schedule, incurring additional expenditures. The company expects some difficulty in raising the capital necessary to deal with them. Not,'' he added with a smile meant to take them all into his confidence, "that the company is in danger, but raising capital these days is quite difficult, as I am certain you are all aware. Therefore, I hope you will understand that the Board feels it would be unwise at this time to go the full ten percent. I am certain however, that you will all agree with me that the six percent rise is quite handsome.''

The nods and grins along the table told him that they had expected a fight to obtain that much. Mereside, however, was not fooled. Before Bannerman could continue, he slapped a hand on the folder.

"Completely unacceptable, Mr. Bannerman,'' he snapped. "And you may inform your directors of that.''

A chorus of protests broke out, with several of the lesser officials, particularly those elected ones who were also employees of the company, demanding to know why.

Bannerman knew why, and he struggled to remain in the dominant position. "Mr. Mereside, I find your attitude—''

But that was as far as he got. Mereside had twenty years' experience behind him.

"Because it is a trick,'' he shouted. In the abrupt silence that followed his accusation, he pointed a finger the length of the table.

"Any fool can see it if he but takes the time. The mucking crews have been raised ten percent. Electricians and mechanics six. By penalizing skilled workers, your directors seek to disrupt the trade unions' united front.'' He turned so that he was speaking along the table. "Think a moment. What will the skilled trades say when they learn that the unskilled have been allowed the full requested rise and they have not? At the next contract's negotiation, we will be faced with open dissension; there will be no united front and the employers will defeat us piecemeal.''

''Aye then,'' one of the representatives shouted, ''what would you have me mucking gangs do, turn down the rise?''

Mereside turned angrily to the man who had spoken but was prevented from replying by a chorus of voices raised in the man's defense. Mereside sat down and Bannerman guessed by his composed features that he had expected nothing less. The man was a professional, he thought.

''As for working conditions,'' Bannerman continued, ''the company feels that our safety precautions are the most advanced in the world today. Our pension plan for injured workmen is extremely generous, as you are aware, and settlements for the widows and families of those killed on the job are unique. After the recent unfortunate affair, the families of the men killed already received their £50 settlements. As for—''

Mereside had seen his opportunity and was on his feet again, leveling a finger at Bannerman as he spoke one word, loudly. ''Sabotage!''

Bannerman stared at him as if nonplussed. ''Sabotage?''

''Aye, sabotage. The 'recent unfortunate affair,' as you term it, was the result of sabotage! And what has the Board done to see that none such will happen again to kill more of the lads?''

Bannerman shook his head. ''I am sorry, Mr.—Mr. Mereside, is it? But how have you come to the conclusion that sabotage was involved?''

Mereside leaned back, tucking his thumbs into the pockets of his vest, expression grim. ''I've me own contacts. It's said that the government offered the army as guards but was refused. And now, sir, you inform us that the directors do not see how the safety of the workers can be improved. Well, sir, I can tell you frankly that it can be improved by allowing in the army. In fact, sir, can you tell us why the army was not allowed in?''

Bannerman shook his head in mock surprise. ''I am astonished, Mr. Mereside, at your information. I am not aware that the company had been approached to allow soldiers to guard the Tunnel. And for what purpose, sir? Who would sabotage the Tunnel? The French?'' The question brought polite laughter which Mereside promptly quashed. "And, I would also think that the unions have little love left for the army after this past summer."

"This is no joking matter. Thirty-one men lie dead in the Tunnel heading—victims of sabotage."

"Now, see here, Mr. Mereside. Just how do you come to the conclusion that the men died as the result of sabotage? It seems to me that you lack the qualifications to make such a judgment. Are you an engineer, sir?"

"I am not, as you well know. But it takes no fancy degree to see that those men were not killed when they struck an undetected fault. And if they were," he added slyly, "then the system for detecting such faults is totally inadequate and must be improved."

"Ah, Mr. Mereside, I do not mean to denigrate your abilities or judgment, but you must admit that what you imply can only be evaluated by skilled engineers. Perhaps your union would be willing to suggest representatives to a panel to do so. I will then nominate an equal number of engineers from my staff. I am certain that the Board of Trade will supply a referee who will cast the deciding vote. Such a procedure should assure a fair and impartial evaluation."

"Ah, Mr. Bannerman." Mereside chuckled. "A generous offer, but wasteful of time and perhaps more lives. Whether or not sabotage caused those deaths is of secondary importance. The heart of the matter is the manner in which the excavation is being conducted. Correct me if I am wrong, but at the time of the accident, the excavation machine was approximately 180 yards ahead of the newly grouted section, just twenty yards short of the limit agreed to by you at a meeting of the Board of Directors on November 13 last. And that revised limit," Mereside said, his voice dropping so that everyone about the table had to concentrate to hear him, "is 150 yards beyond the limit established by the designers as a safe margin, it is not, Mr. Bannerman? Perhaps that great distance between the grouted section and the work face contributed to the so-called recent *unfortunate affair*."

Bannerman did not allow himself to rise to the bait, did not allow Mereside to see how disturbed he was by the mention of the November 13 meeting and his cowardly compromise.

"Nonsense, Mr. Mereside." He snorted. "As any of these gentlemen with their years of experience can tell you, chalk subsoils are among the safest of all tunneling mediums. That is why the margin between the work face and the bricked sections was extended. At the moment we have no explanation for the blowout in the heading three weeks ago. The evidence we have suggests subsurface movement that may have caused a fissure that resulted in a blowout. The damaged section of the Tunnel will be sealed off in another week, at which time it will be pumped clear. Until then, all else is conjecture and does more harm than good as it merely produces unfounded rumors which, may I remind you, were the reason for the meeting today."

Bannerman could see that his appeal to their expertise over that of a newcomer had gained support among the older union representatives. His suggestion of a review panel coupled with the welcome news of the new pay contracts achieved without interminable wrangling had done much to disarm the rest.

Mereside, realizing that he did not have sufficient support to force the issue, fell back to his previous position. "We will nominate our panel members," he snapped. "But we will demand that the panel consider whether or not sabotage has been done or if the disaster was the result of careless disregard for workmen's lives." He paused and studied Bannerman. "There are certain of us who are of the opinion that demolition charges, emplaced to destroy the Tunnel in the event of war, were removed from their chambers and taken into the heading where they were exploded. Our analysis suggests that only naval cordite could have caused such a breech."

"Indeed, Mr. Mereside?" Bannerman broke in, a chill feeling of betrayal breaking over him. Where in God's name had Mereside got that information? But he knew the answer almost as soon as the question formed itself in his mind. Armstrong-Flood. It could only have been he. He was the only man on the Board who hated him enough to jeopardize the entire project just to discredit him. He tapped his pencil on the desk top and stared along the table to meet the man's expectant stare. Mereside would never dare admit the source of that information. Could not possibly. He tossed the pencil down as if annoyed.

"And what qualifications do you ascribe to your analysis, may I ask, as you have already admitted to having no training as an engineer? Perhaps you are an expert on explosives? If you are correct, then it becomes a matter of national security and the facts must be placed before a suitable investigating board."

"Aye, Mr. Bannerman," Mereside acknowledged pleasantly. "We should do just that. In view of your agreement that this is a serious matter, I propose that rather than the Board of Trade, the panel operate under the authority and responsibility of the Home Office, with suitable representatives of the military forces present as well."

Mereside smiled and Bannerman knew instantly that he had been outmaneuvered. This is what Mereside had been after all along: a Home Office investigation into the possibility of sabotage rather than an ineffectual Board of Trade investigation of another industrial accident.

"I agree, Mr. Mereside, that the Home Office is better equipped to handle such an investigation," Bannerman replied, straining to keep his anger under control. "I will make the request today."

"And work will stop immediately until the investigation is complete?"

"That is patently ridiculous," Bannerman exploded. "The men must feed their families. How could they do that without work?"

"Conditions are unsafe in the Tunnel," Mereside returned stubbornly. "No man can feed or care for his family if he is dead."

Bannerman could see by the stricken expressions around the table that Mereside had gone further than anticipated.

Bannerman shook his head. "I must warn you, Mr. Mereside, the company cannot stand such a shutdown. I have mentioned the heavy expenses already incurred. And should the men refuse to work, they may soon find themselves permanently unemployed, as the company would consider it incumbent on behalf of their stockholders to hire replacement workers."

"And be damned to them if they do," Mereside flashed. "The other trade unions will stand by us for certain. We'll bring the project to a complete stop for—"

"And is that what you're after, Mr. Mereside?" Bannerman's quiet voice knifed through Mereside's rhetoric. "To demonstrate again the power of the trade unions? Don't you consider that enough was made of that this past summer? Is that your final statement then? Will you call a general strike if the project is not shut down immediately?"

Mereside was engulfed in a wave of arguments and when he finally managed to answer, his angry face acknowledged his defeat. Yet Bannerman knew as well as he that it was only a temporary setback.

"In view of your threats, a general strike is not in order at this time. However, we serve warning, here and now. Another accident, whether sabotage or callous disregard for the workers' safety, and we damned well will strike!"

Mereside thrust the batch of papers stacked before him into a worn leather folder and strode angrily from the room. The rest of the union officials filed after him. Bannerman knew well enough that Mereside, outsider or not, would have their backing if one more serious accident occurred. The general strike he had failed to obtain this time could very well be his for the asking then.

McDougal had sat silently to one side, alternately glowering or grinning as the arguments had raged. He shook his head when the room had emptied.

"You're taking one hell of a chance, then, James."

"And what the devil would you have me do? Shut the damned works down for two or three weeks while they confirm what I already know? The Board would never stand for that. And when the investigating panel reaches the same conclusion, what then? The company will have collapsed."

"Aye," McDougal said after a moment. "Aye, you are right there, James. But we are talking of men's lives. It is fair to ask them to go into the Tunnel, knowing that at any moment more of them could be killed?"

"Men are constantly being killed in tunnels," Bannerman snapped angrily. "Tunneling is a dangerous job. They know that when they go in. No one stands behind them with a gun, forcing them inside, do they?"

"Ah, but don't they, James? Perhaps not with a gun, but aren't they forced to go inside to feed their families?"

"Hell, Sean, what's come over you?" Bannerman hesitated then, his voice turning sullen at having said things he did not believe and would not have said if he hadn't been angry. "They can find other work. Every man employed in the works is fit and healthy."

McDougal stood up slowly as if feeling his age of a

sudden. "Aye, you are right, James. Don't mind the rantings of an old man. But, if there should be another accident . . ." He let the thought trail away.

Long after McDougal had gone, Bannerman sat staring at the empty table, knowing that the Irish engineer was correct. He knew beyond a doubt that it was sabotage that had killed those men and that if he had refused to compromise with the Board, they would be alive now.

chapter ___ 20

DECEMBER 16, 1911. SATURDAY EVENING

The manor house rising above the long wood on the east slope of Malmouth Hill, though partly Georgian, partly Victorian, plainly owed a great deal to its Tudor forebears, however well disguised. Massive chestnuts swept up the curving drive to the park and a riot of shrubbery obscured the house to the level of the windows. It had been an interesting hunt over varied terrain; the fox had gone to earth twice, both times flushed by the dogs. Von Dorn had lost the others in a stand of heavy cover and, with darkness coming on, turned back.

He handed his horse to a groom and stamped mud from his boots as he went up the steps. A maid opened the door with a curtsey and handed him a hot toddy from the spirit-lamp grill in the hallway. Sipping it, he wandered into the library to find that he was not the first to return. The room was half full of booted gentlemen in red and pink coats and ladies in sweeping hunting skirts and tight monkey jackets, laced and braided to put the best Hussar regiment to shame. For a moment he watched from the shadows near the doorway, swept by a wave of nostalgia that he was at a loss to understand. He was not English, yet for a moment he felt as if he belonged.

Von Dorn, with his sandy hair and teutonic good looks, was considered a "catch" in the current vernacular, and his weekends—the few that were free of embassy duties—were well filled with invitations from which he could pick and choose.

Carrying his toddy glass, he moved forward into the room, aware of the impression he was making on the younger—and not a few of the older—ladies present. To be invited to Lord Wolton's Berkshire country home for the weekend was to be "accepted." And he was enjoying the fact that this was not the first time this winter hunting season that he had been so invited. The servants, from the house to the outlying reaches of the estate, now knew him by sight as well as reputation. And since the other guests carefully noted the demeanor of the servants when gauging the relative acceptability of their fellows, his standing was secure.

Talk of the day's hunt would monopolize conversation right up to the moment they mounted again on Sunday, he knew, and accordingly von Dorn fortified himself with another toddy and plunged in, stopping first near the windows to listen to Sir Garnet Simon lisp his way through a description of how he had put his horse to a fence, forcing the poor beast a bit past his mark, "but then that's what it's all about, by gad, heh?" During the intricate pavane of the cocktail hour, he found himself among a simpering group of ladies, and, ignoring the glare of a suddenly deserted young blood, von Dorn flirted outrageously, a ploy that he had discovered often excited the mothers more than the daughters.

There was one lady, however, who held herself aloof from the others and who, therefore, aroused his curiosity. He recognized her name as soon as they were introduced: Lady Emily Wilson-Langdon, widow of an English aristocrat, a high muckety-muck at Dublin Castle for a number of years. As he recalled, the man had been killed two or three years before during a hunting expedition in the American West. She was, he supposed, about his age, yet she concealed it well. You had to look closely to see the tiny lines around the eyes, the infinitesimal sags of skin about the chin and neck where the tone was beginning to go. But the magnificent auburn hair, which was worn in a riot of curls and had clearly never seen the touch of the cosmetologist's dye brush, distracted all unwanted attention. Von Dorn was a connoisseur of women and in consequence, an expert on their arts. Her cheeks were still flushed from the chill afternoon and her lips were red and full. Deep brown, almost black eyes regarded him gravely, if from a neutral standpoint, and he knew that he had his work cut out for him this weekend. He sensed that while they exchanged well practiced pleasantries, she was as interested in him as he in her and his intuition was confirmed a moment later when she laughed and maneuvered herself so as to place them at a private angle, still within the group but not of it. She smiled at him in such a way as to leave no doubt that it was done on purpose.

Before their conversation could proceed past the opening moves, their host arrived to announce that dinner would be served at eight, a polite suggestion that they retire to exchange hunting clothes for evening wear. Von Dorn finished his toddy, only half-listening. He was more interested in watching the gentle sway of Lady Emily's hips as she followed the other women from the room. Lord Wolton noticed the direction of his glance and swung round to catch a last glimpse of her as she disappeared into the gloomy corridor.

"Fetching, wot?" he demanded, showing yellowed teeth in a cadaverous grin. "Keeps a house in Knightsbridge, of all places. Can't imagine why. Good seat though. Take a horse anywhere a man would." He stepped closer and half whispered, half chuckled: "Had you placed across from her at dinner tonight, old boy."

Von Dorn gave him a dazzling smile of thanks and escaped.

Dinner that evening was an extravagant affair. Von Dorn, however, paid little attention to the various courses served. Lady Emily Wilson-Langdon, seated directly opposite as Lord Wolton had promised, occupied the majority of his attention. In fact, she occupied the majority of attention from every man present. Her form-fitting, ankle-length, emerald green grown, perfect contrast to her auburn hair in the golden candle light, relegated the other ladies present to insignificance. She carried on a lively conversation with her two partners but her eyes were on von Dorn most of the evening and he found it hard to remember that he had an obligation to his own dinner partners as well.

He was relieved to see that the guests now included the First Lord, who had been notably absent earlier. He would have been very unhappy if he had rushed back from Berlin for nothing. Churchill had driven down from London with apologies for having missed the day's hunt but bringing the news that Lloyd George, the Chancellor of the Exchequer, had been injured that morning when a suffragette supporter had thrown an object through his carriage window.

It was obvious that the assembly, including two peers and several quite wealthy landowners, were having grave difficulty in properly expressing their sympathies. Quite a few would not have been unhappy to hear that the rock had knocked his head off. Churchill, appearing blithely unaware, went on to describe the scene and resulting melee. It was only when von Dorn happened to glance up that he caught a flash of the well-known impudent grin. The Chancellor's extreme liberalism—from his support of the Boers during the late war to his recent "people's budget," and now the National Insurance Bill just sent to the House of Lords, had done little to endear the "Welsh red" to the aristocracy. Most equated him with the Jacobins of the French Revolution and talked as if tumbrils were already trotting up chestnut-lined drives to haul them off to the guillotine.

The talk was steered politely into other channels by their host, and Churchill resumed eating with a satisfied expression on his face. Someone mentioned the spate of recent shipping accidents including the liner *Mauretania's* having been blown adrift from her moorings in Liverpool by a gale the week before, requiring her sister ship *Lusitania* to be pressed into service to replace her.

Churchill wiped his mouth with the napkin and beamed around the table. "I have," he said, "some quite excellent news. We heard this morning at the Admiralty that *Lusitania* has completed a record run to New York, docking yesterday afternoon at four p.m. local time. She is expected to depart on the eighteenth and, barring further unforeseen incidents, should arrive in Liverpool sometime on the twenty-second. She is sure to equal or break *Mauretania's* record of last year."

This announcement was greeted with a great deal more interest than Lloyd George's misfortune. For years the nation had actively watched the progress on the Cunard Line's two great passenger vessels as they vied with one another to shatter the North Atlantic crossing time.

Lord Wolton asked Churchill if there was further news regarding the *Delhi*, which on Wednesday night had gone aground off the Moroccan coast. "The Princess Royal, the Duke of Fife, and their daughters were taken off by HMS *Duke of Edinburgh*, which, assisted by the French naval vessel *Friant*, was able to rescue all two hundred and twenty passengers," he replied and waited for the applause to die away. "Unfortunately, three French bluejackets were drowned when one of the lifeboats capsized."

Von Dorn found himself wondering what Churchill was doing at a country weekend as the guest of a died-in-the-wool

Conservative. Yet here he was, the man that many in the country, Tory and Liberal alike, termed brilliant but unstable and tarred with every appellation ranging from Lloyd George's tame lackey to soldier-of-fortune. Without doubt he had made his mark in government, at the Colonial Office, the Board of Trade, the Home Office, and now the Admiralty. And during the past four years, in partnership with Lloyd George, he had introduced and campaigned for many needed social reforms in city after city across the country, holding up as an example Germany's social security retirement pensions and workmen's compensation.

Von Dorn caught his eye, and Churchill nodded a greeting. They had met a few times but not socially. When the Englishman traveled to Germany in 1909 at the invitation of the Kaiser, von Dorn had acted as his escort for a day. Still, he was surprised that the man would have remembered him at all.

The talk eventually came round to the current political situation, both domestic and foreign, as von Dorn had known it would. Someone from the Foreign Office was reviewing the course of the past summer's war crisis, and he forced his attention away from Lady Emily's distracting expanse of décolletage.

"And so you see," the man was saying earnestly, "the Entente policy *is* paying off quite handsomely." He turned with a thin smile and a half bow toward Churchill. "A policy, I might add, originated by the last government."

"I never claimed that all Tory policies were full of mischief." Churchill chuckled. "Merely the majority."

There was laughter at his response and the Foreign Office man went on. "I am certain that had we not supported France there would be a war at this very moment."

Von Dorn sipped his wine, aware that everyone was anticipating his reply. But he smiled as he replaced the goblet.

"I am in full accord with you, my dear sir."

That answer took the Foreign Office man by surprise, and in the lull, von Dorn took charge of the conversation.

"Just as there are certain interests in the War Office and the Admiralty," he said with a polite nod toward Churchill, "who view war with Germany as inevitable, so we in Germany have those who consider war with France and Russia inevitable. And," he added in a discouraged voice, "given the current distribution of political alliances, that war could include England as well, as an ally of France. The Kaiser must contend with the war faction, just as your cabinet must here. None of us is entirely free to do as we think best,'' he ended with a polite shrug.

"Then you condemn the stance of Germany during the Algeciras crisis, Herr von Dorn?'' The Foreign Office man smiled.

"Condemn! My good sir, of course not. Ill-advised perhaps, but certainly I am in no position to condemn anything my government does, just as you are not.''

He risked a glance across the table and saw Lady Emily form the word *bravo* with her lips. Near the head of the table Churchill chuckled loudly. "I say there, Moore, I believe Herr von Dorn is one up on you.''

Churchill leaned forward so that he could address von Dorn directly. "Then you feel that the Kaiser is being victimized by certain members of the Imperial General Staff, my dear sir?''

Careful, von Dorn told himself. "Hardly victimized, sir, for certainly they are convinced they are doing what is best for Germany. Influenced would be a better word. I know the Kaiser desires peace as much as the late King Edward did. Given time, I am certain that this will become most clear.''

"But in the meantime Germany goes full speed ahead with her naval program. How do you reconcile that with a sincere desire for peace?'' Churchill asked.

"Ah, but is Germany alone in such a naval construction program? I believe that three new dreadnoughts of the *Queen Elizabeth* class have been launched this year alone by Great Britain: *King George V, Centurion*, and *Ajax*. And *Audacious* and *Queen Mary* will be launched in January and February of the new year. Am I not correct? And England already maintains the strongest navy in the world. The Americans and Japanese are also building new fleets. Such expenditure around the world is enormous. Can Germany then allow herself to be placed at a military disadvantage? Can any nation who wishes to protect and expand her commercial interests?''

"Your point is well taken, sir. Of course, I answer that we act only in the face of Germany's determination to build the world's strongest navy. We would gladly stop if Germany would. But your remarks interest me very much,'' Churchill continued. "This Pan-German influence, or war faction about which we hear so much is considered in many quarters to control the Imperial General Staff as well as the Foreign Ministry."

Von Dorn smiled. "I can assure you, First Lord, that in my opinion such is not the case. Certainly, they exercise a strong influence in the Wilhelmplatz, but they are by no means the only faction to do so. The—for want of a better term—peace faction still strongly desires accord with England. They ask only that German aims and objectives be accorded a fair hearing."

"Am I correct in suggesting that you associate yourself with this faction?" Churchill asked.

Ah, the fox, von Dorn thought. "I am sorry to disappoint you, First Lord, but as a military representative of his Imperial Majesty's government I am not at liberty to express a preference for one political party over another."

"Well said, sir," Churchill applauded.

"You would seem to be a contradiction in terms, Herr von Dorn."

Surprised, von Dorn turned to find Emily smiling at him from across the table.

He inclined his head politely. "And how do you mean, Lady Wilson-Langdon?"

"First you deplore the militants surrounding your emperor and then go on to justify your nation's intense program in naval shipbuilding. It would seem, sir, that you are both proud of and, at the same time, appalled by the new militarism."

Von Dorn's smile had a brittle quality that was obvious to all. "I am, after all, a citizen of the German Reich. I see it as no crime to take pride in one's country. As for the 'new militarism,' as you term it, I do not see it restricted to Germany. I believe that a recent number of *Blackwood's* put forth a scheme for combining the office of Secretary for War with that of the First Lord of the Admiralty. Surely such a proposal appears quite warlike to foreign observers and provides the impression that England is preparing for war. Yet it is justified merely as an efficiency in the strengthening of Great Britain's worldwide interests."

"And are Germany's ambitions worldwide?" she asked.

The question was innocent enough, but von Dorn was quick to see the trap being laid for him.

"Of course. We have proclaimed them often enough. But Germany is no threat to Great Britain or France in the traditional colonial realms. Our economy is not geared to the support of, or from, a major colonial empire as are those of Britain and France. Germany is relatively self-sufficient in foodstuffs and most ingredients required for manufacturing. Our major markets are domestic and continental. Our desire is then to expand those markets to other parts of the world, where there is still room for imperialist policies—the Pacific, China, and so on. Therefore"—he gave them all a disarming smile—"we need an army and navy only large enough to secure our own borders and those of our few colonies."

Churchill interrupted at that point. "It would seem then, Herr von Dorn, that there are differing interpretations as to what constitutes an army of sufficient size to defend your borders. The German army is currently composed of fifty-two first line divisions and twenty-five second line. Surely, these are two to three times the number required?"

"Not at all, First Lord. You must not forget that to the east of Germany lies Russia, whose first line divisions alone number one hundred and thirty."

"Then I would be correct in assuming that you view the major threat to Germany's existence as coming from the east?"

"Ah, and there you are asking for an opinion better left unstated. But yes, I will take the plunge. It is quite clear that the main threat to Germany's existence has historically been the Russian Bear. As our population increases, the virtually empty lands to the east become increasingly attractive. This is a matter of historical knowledge, and passions inflamed by a thousand years of warfare cannot quickly be subdued. However, we in Germany have tried. Over the past forty or fifty years, Germany has sought accord with Russia. And that accord has been denied us. That, too, is a matter of historical record."

"You must then be distressed with the formation of the Triple Entente?" Emily asked softly. Too late he saw that she had trapped him anyway. His smile indicated his respect for her debating skills. But he had been schooled in the Prussian cockpit of Berlin and learned long ago that when all else fails, the truth is often disarming—even if you lose the battle, your adversary is left with a positive appreciation of your sincerity.

"To be frank, I was. As the military attaché from my country to yours, I had hoped the alliance would go the other way, or at the very least, that England would remain neutral. The military combination of France and Russia has always been Germany's nightmare. With England into the balance, the scales are, in my opinion, tipped against Germany."

The admission had the desired effect. She smiled, leaning forward just a trifle to indicate that no harm was intended by her victory.

"And what, my dear sir, do you foresee as the effect of the Channel Tunnel on Germany's domination of continental markets?"

Von Dorn realized with a start that Churchill was addressing him. He tore his eyes away from Lady Emily. "I don't really know," he replied slowly, as if deliberating the question for the first time. "I am a military man and know little of foreign trade or business."

"Come, come, sir." Churchill chuckled in a good-natured manner. "Surely you must have some knowledge."

"Well," he said, as if the subject were completely new to him, "I would imagine that British manufacturers would give German goods a run even now. If, as is claimed, the new Tunnel will lower the cost of British goods, it would seem that Germany's advantage—a central position and an excellent railway system—would count for little. If such is the case, I would suppose"—and he paused and grinned slyly—"that Germany will be forced to erect tariff measures to protect her economy." He finished to general laughter in which Churchill joined. The subject of tariffs had long been a bone of contention between the Liberal and Conservative Parties and in 1904 had been Churchill's reason for crossing the floor.

The dinner party had reached the brandy and cigar stage at that point and broke up to general merriment, all feeling that the handsome German military attaché with his curiously non-Prussian attitudes—a refreshing change from the monocled, dour, spit-and-polish individuals who seemed to emanate from number 9 Carlton House Terrace—had scored well. Lord Wolton beamed on the ladies as they departed and the gentlemen were ushered into the library, certain that the dinner conversation would furnish gossip for weeks to come.

Churchill took the chair offered, lit his cigar and watched the elegant figure of Eric von Dorn moving smoothly from group to group. For some reason the man set his teeth on edge. He was patently a phony but slippery as an eel. There was no doubt that he was doubling as a spy; a military attaché was expected to do so. But was von Dorn limiting himself to the methods employed by a gentleman and allowed by convention? They were nearly the same age; von Dorn seemed so mature and sure of himself that Churchill wondered how he had shown in comparison.

Since going to the Admiralty, he was continually being shocked by the shoddy state of Britain's defenses. As Wilson had been pointing out for years, they were practically nonexistent, and in his day and age that could very well be a death sentence.

France, Russia, Germany, the United States, Japan. Each could become England's staunchest friend or deadliest enemy. It involved choosing for allies those who had the least to gain and the most to lose by antagonizing Great Britain. Of them all, the United States was perhaps the best choice. Her interests seemed to lie increasingly in the Pacific—the latest indication of that was the arrival yesterday of General Homer Lea at Penang, probably to act as adviser to Sun Yat-sen. If the United States could be persuaded to accept the burden of keeping the peace in that area, she might very well act as a counterbalance to the cocky Japanese.

Emotionalism had to be totally divorced from the choice of allies, he had discovered. During the past summer, he had watched Lord Grey agonize over the decision to intervene on the side of France, knowing full well that war with Germany, a war the French passionately desired—as long as England and Russia would assist—could result. Cooler heads had prevailed at last in Berlin. But the next time?

Was von Dorn really as amiable as he seemed, Churchill wondered as he noticed him laughing over some joke with Moore from the Foreign Office. He strongly doubted it. There was that disturbing intelligence report sent over yesterday from MI.6. A thorough shakeup of the German intelligence community was in progress, it seemed. The last of the Bismarckians, Langenscheidt, had been retired to his Saxon estates, leaving the Imperial General Staff clearly in command. And von Dorn? There had been that hurried trip to and from Berlin, where he had been seconded to the General Staff and returned sporting a promotion. Churchill had written a strong minute to Haldane at the War Office requesting that the situation be watched carefully, but he was not much loved across Whitehall Street, where Kitchener had so much influence. Probably nothing would come of it, officially. He drew on his cigar. Thank God for David Powell.

Shortly before one o'clock there was a general exodus and von Dorn joined it. He had flirted outrageously with Lady Emily across the billiard table when the ladies and gentlemen mingled again in the game room. He had been at pains to maintain his position opposite her as she leaned over the table to shoot. The polite but intense jockeying of the bloods for position had become outrageous, and many of the ladies had retired in a huff, taking eligible daughters along.

There had even been time for a quiet conversation with Churchill that had produced nothing. Their verbal sparring, begun at dinner, had continued and, as a result, neither had learned much of value.

Von Dorn avoided his host's invitation for a final brandy, which he knew could very well last until dawn. His room, one of the favored guest rooms, he had been pleased to note, in the quiet north wing of the house, was ready, the covers turned back and bed warmer in place. He made a mental note to leave a sizable tip, more so than usual, for the maid had not only cleaned his boots but polished them to a soft glow. His hunting clothes had been laid for the morning and a decanter of cognac rather than the usual brandy placed on the night stand. As he lifted the decanter, he noticed the calling card. *Lady Emily Wilson-Langdon* was printed in a thin Spencerian script on a cream-colored card of the finest linen stock.

Von Dorn grinned at the card. Forward little bitch. He tapped his thumb with it, considering. He had thought to make a second approach in the billiard room, but except for the immense smile and even more immense view of curving white breasts with which she had favored him—and anyone else in view—she had avoided all approaches and he had written her off as a flirt. Apparently, he had been mistaken.

Von Dorn listened at the door, then opened it and peered out. The gloomy hallway stretched away into the shadows at either end. Lord Wolton was not one to waste money on lighting empty hallways, and the single electric lamp high up at the far end provided little illumination. An Aubusson rug swept the length of the corridor, leaving a border of highly polished wood on either side that caught dull reflections from the lamp. He turned the card over. Written in a fine hand was the notation *Next but one, on the right*.

As he stepped into the corridor, von Dorn heard the murmur of voices and a suppressed giggle. Ah, the English, he thought, unconsciously assuming the superior attitude of the continental. They were so moralistic in public, but in private, worse than any Frenchman. He walked quickly to the red walnut door, turned the latch handle, and stepped in with a quick glance over his shoulder to see that he hadn't been observed. But he was looking the wrong way and did not notice the single eye peering from the doorway farther along the hall. The door was closed quietly, and Churchill laid his cigar in the ashtray and climbed into his high bed.

Von Dorn crossed the room, smiling at the woman sitting in the pillowed majesty of the canopied bed, silk night shawl covering what he supposed were bare shoulders. The feather comforter was pulled halfway to her chin. He indicated the decanter on the table against the dresser.

"May I pour you a drink?"

She smiled and nodded, but remained silent. He poured and sat down on the bed and Lady Emily, extending a graceful, bare arm, took her glass and sipped it, watching him over the rim. Her eyes were very dark in the reduced lighting and he found himself so drawn into them that he started when she spoke.

"Our mutual friends in Dublin have some information for you."

The bold statement astonished him. "Our friends in Dublin?" he repeated stupidly.

She smiled at him and placed the glass on the bedside table, the cover drifting downward to reveal a bit more warm flesh. But he was too taken aback by her words to notice.

"Oh, yes, Colonel von Dorn. Are you surprised then?"

"What in the name of God are they thinking of, the damned fools," he snarled and bolted to his feet.

"Please don't be angry," she patted the bed. "I have been associated with the Movement for many years. I am quite trusted."

He considered that for a moment. "Even before your husband died?"

She laughed softly. "Oh my, yes. Long before I met him, in fact. I was the typical, spoiled-rich-girl-rebelling-against-her-parents'-wishes, I suppose. Charles was of great value to the Movement, although I must admit he was never aware of his contribution."

"And this information," he said, sinking down again on the bed, "is of sufficient importance for them to inform you of my part in the affair—and for you to reveal yourself to me?"

Lady Emily chuckled at the double meaning, a deep throaty sound that excited him. "Yes. As you can well imagine, I guard my association with the Fenians carefully. But as there was no one else to communicate *certain* types of information from Dublin, I was chosen. Finnigan will continue as your regular contact, as before."

Von Dorn nodded but something she had said piqued his curiosity. "Certain types of information?"

"Let us say those concerning a certain incident. It is not though wise to trust Finnigan with quite that much."

"Ah, I see. I take it then that my proposal was viewed with interest?"

Lady Emily smiled but her eyes did not match the soft curve of her lips. "A great deal of interest. Dublin's opinion is that your plan verges on madness and does not concern our ultimate aspirations. However, the incentives offered are appealing."

"I see. And where does your information fit in?"

"The first bit concerns the Tunnel project and might affect your plans," she said. "McDougal has reported that the trade unions are making difficulties over the—ah, shall we say accidents, that have occurred recently. They have forced the company to agree to an investigation by the Home Office. It is certain now that the government will be asked to furnish troops to provide security at the conclusion of the investigation, about the start of the new year."

Von Dorn nodded, expression thoughtful as he absorbed the implications of this news. That made it all the more urgent that they act swiftly. He tapped the glass against his teeth, the alluring woman beside him forgotten for the moment. If the army were to guard the Tunnel, there would be little or no chance to infiltrate. . . . Damn the trade unions. They were an unlooked-for complication that would force him to move sooner than he wished. He would cut short the weekend, pleading business at the embassy after Schram telephoned in the morning. Damn, he thought. He had less than three weeks to act.

Emily could feel the pressure of his thigh against her leg but his absent expression suggested he was far from aware of her at that moment.

"And the second bit of information?" he asked finally.

"Yes, and this is a bit more complicated. The woman whom you killed?" She noted the swift darkening of his face but he did not protest. "You should know that her brother, Michael Connigham, is searching for her murderer. Connigham is a member of the Movement. He has been in America for six years, the result of two murder warrants against him in England. He is a ruthless man, believe me. He went to Liverpool to make contact with Arthur Boyle and was ordered to return to the United States. He disobeyed, killed two men who were watching him, and escaped. We believe he has since returned to London."

She leaned forward and placed a hand on his arm, holding the eiderdown against her with the other. "I am to warn you that Michael Connigham is a dangerous and resourceful man. He is being hunted and will be taken eventually—by us or the police. But until then, be very careful."

"You talk about this man as if you know him."

Emily nodded once. "I do," she said, her voice sharp, sharper than it should have been, and von Dorn studied her with new interest. "I have known him for a long time. He grew up in the Dublin slums and he is a dangerous man. Just be careful."

"What does he look like?"

Emily described Connigham quickly. "There are no photographs of him, of course, but he looks very much like his sister."

"You knew her?"

"Many years ago."

"And you consider him dangerous."

"Insane, possibly."

Von Dorn was surprised at the tone of her voice. "I don't understand?"

"Michael Connigham is a violent man. Very violent. He was raised in the Liberties. You have heard of them?"

"Who hasn't?"

"His father was a drunkard, his older brother deserted the family, and his mother died of starvation. His sister's husband was murdered by Ulster Protestants, hanged while she was forced to watch. Michael killed two of the men involved and left Ireland. He is full of bitterness, and I believe that he always felt he too had deserted his sister."

"And you think his sister's death has pushed him over the edge?"

She nodded. "Yes."

Von Dorn watched her, trying to detect any sign of disapproval, but there was none, just a tightening around those almost perfect eyes that could have meant anything. Von Dorn caressed her bare arm with his fingertips. "And you do not disapprove of this woman's elimination?"

"She could not be allowed to go to the police."

Von Dorn laughed at that. "I see you are made of sterner material than I would have thought."

"Perhaps."

Von Dorn shrugged. "Well, I will not worry too much about an insane Irishman, I should imagine."

Emily smiled and he could have sworn she was mocking him. "Let me tell you a story about Michael Connigham."

Von Dorn half bowed. "Please do, dear lady."

But there was no answering humor in her expression. "When Michael heard about his brother-in-law's murder he went to see Arthur Boyle in Dublin. I never knew exactly what brave Arthur told him, but when Michael returned to Belfast, he went directly to one of his friends, Tom Finnigan."

"The same Finnigan?"

"Yes. Somehow, they found out that one of the men who had a hand in the lynching often went to a certain pub. That was sufficient for Michael. He and Finnigan selected three others. They went down to the pub, which was in the Shankhill, armed with revolvers. Two men guarded each end of the street while two went in through the back. Michael went in alone through the front door.''

Finnigan, for once not needing to embellish it, had later told her the story, how the pub was warmly lit of a January night with the rain falling steadily outside and a huge fire burning in the grate. How the men at the bar and sitting against the walls had stared at Michael in surprise and at the sight of his revolver had raised their hands without being told.

The barman had made to ask him a question but at the sight of Michael's face thought better of it. He came round the bar quickly when Michael motioned and stood against the wall, his hands high over his head, sweat beading on his forehead and running off the ends of his mustache. The Ulsterman they were after sat rigidly at a table, the terror of the damned on his face.

Michael had just stared at him and Finnigan had counted the seconds as the man crumpled under the onslaught of those flat eyes. Two minutes by the clock passed and still Michael said nothing. Finally, the man had started to stand but his knees buckled and he collapsed back into the chair.

"I want the name of the man who told you about Doyle," Connigham said finally. He spoke quietly, almost apologetically into the dead silence that held the men in the pub.

The Ulsterman tried to speak but could not. His mouth worked but no sound came out. Connigham picked up glasses and a bottle from the bar and brought them to the table. He pulled the chair out and sat down and poured two glasses.

"Go on. Drink it." The Ulsterman reached for the glass but his hand was shaking so badly that he knocked it over. Patiently, Connigham righted the glass and filled it again. He also placed the revolver on the table between them, butt turned toward the Ulsterman, and seemed to forget about it. Every eye in the place went to the revolver. It was lying right beside the glass but when the man reached, it was for the drink and not the gun. This time he managed to get most of it to his mouth and gulp it down. The liquor seemed to steady him a bit. His hands were still shaking but he appeared in better command of himself. Connigham poured the glass full again.

"Now, tell me the man's name."

The Ulsterman took a deep breath. "I cannot tell you that. You know as well as I do. 'Twould betray a trust.''

Connigham gave him a half smile before he said, so softly that they had to strain to hear, "Do you think I give a damn whose confidence you betray? You lynched my brother-in-law. Now you know who I am, don't you?"

The man's eyes were pools of terror as he nodded.

"You know that you are going to die tonight. You can make the dying easy or you can make it hard. But you will tell me." These statements were delivered in the same emotionless tone as if Connigham were reading from a list.

The silence stretched, Finnigan had said, and in his only flight of rhetoric he had described it as brittle glass suddenly shattered when the Ulsterman spoke. "Brian Strain."

Connigham nodded then, as if he had expected nothing more. He stood and picked up his revolver. He contemplated it for a moment, then slowly raised his eyes and pointed the gun at the Ulsterman, who ducked down and covered his face with his hands. Connigham shot him with no sign of hesitation or emotion, as if he were shooting a coney, then the three of them left the pub without a word. The motor car they had come in was waiting at the curb and they piled aboard as doors were flung open and shouting began along the street.

They had driven directly to the home of Brian Strain's mother, where one of the men knew he could be found. He was brought out, sobbing and begging for his life, but Connigham was implacable. He was shot through both knees and finally, the back of the head, and his body was left where it had fallen, the marks of the informer plain to see.

"Do you understand now?" Emily asked. "Michael Connigham is a resourceful man. Resourceful and intelligent. And he never worries about the odds. To go with only four men into the heart of the Shankhill is as foolish a thing as a Catholic can do. Yet he never hesitated."

Von Dorn chuckled. "You are suggesting then, my dear lady, that if I underestimate him, he will kill me."

"Yes."

"It would seem that you do have my best interests at heart. For a time this evening I wondered. Your performance at dinner was not such as to lead me to believe that you cared in the slightest."

Emily nodded. "It was necessary that we appear to be adversaries so that the others would not suspect—that we were perhaps more?"

She leaned back against the pillows, letting the eiderdown slip so that his breath caught in his throat. "Perhaps we could combine business with pleasure," she suggested without a hint of coyness, and reached to turn down the lamp.

He drew the shawl and then the eiderdown away, smiling at the smooth perfection of her body revealed in the dim lamplight, and leaned forward and kissed the hollow between her breasts. But she put a warning hand on his.

"One more thing," she said quietly. "Dublin is most interested in the shipment of rifles you have promised."

Before he could say anything, she went on. "They have asked me to tell you. The rifles must be delivered before Christmas Day. The money as soon as possible. If not, they can no longer provide further assistance as they will be busy seeking arms from an alternate source. I have also been instructed to tell you that we do not wish to see them landed to the Ulster Volunteers—even by accident. We have a prior claim, as it were."

He chuckled and tried to pull his arm back but her grip was like iron. Surprised, he did not force the issue. "Business with pleasure, didn't you say?"

But there was no amusement in her voice as she repeated, "Christmas Day," before releasing his wrist.

chapter———21

Inspector David Powell followed the same boyish naval aid down the same corridor and into the same outer office for the second Sunday in a row. Grace had not protested when he told her he had to go out; she never did. But he knew her well enough to realize it made her unhappy. They had such little time together lately and her health seemed to have declined abruptly in the past month; he was beginning to fear the worst in spite of the doctor's hearty and repeated assurances. "Suspect she's just a bit run down, old man. Needs a tonic to perk her up. Perhaps a season of sun in Italy or Spain?"

Powell had no doubt that it would do her the world of good promised, but he did not see how the devil he was to manage it on his paltry salary. He was due at the doctor's office tomorrow to hear the results of the tests, and all week he had been gripped with the frightening certainty that the doctor already knew the answer.

His musings were cut short as Eddie Marsh hurried in with an apologetic greeting.

"Chief inspector, forgive me. I did not realize you had arrived so soon. Have you been waiting long?"

The two men shook hands and Marsh opened the door to announce him.

Churchill came across the room full of profuse apologies for disturbing his Sunday evening for the second time in succession. Powell waved the apologies away and as Churchill went to pour him a whiskey, noticed that he was wearing a Norfolk jacket and tweed trousers. It must be important if Churchill had returned in such a hurry that he had not bothered to change from his country clothes. The room was brightly lit as if to banish the gloom of the winter evening beyond the windows. It had rained steadily all afternoon and the drop in temperature indicated that it might very well turn to snow before the night was out. Powell thought again of the Mediterranean sunshine.

Churchill brought the whiskeys and took the chair opposite, stretching his legs to the log fire with a sigh. "I like a good wood fire. Can't abide the coal ones."

Powell nodded, sipping the whiskey, mind still preoccupied with his wife's failing health. Their drafty Hammersmith flat was certainly no place for her in winter. She had never before complained of the cold, but this autumn she had taken to wearing a shawl indoors. The first time he noticed, it had shocked him. The sight of that shawl brought home to him as nothing else had the fact that they were both aging. He remembered effortlessly a time not so long before, it seemed, but in reality nearly thirty years ago, when he had walked a beat through Hyde Park, one of the choicest patrols in the West End. A fine spring day with the trees fully in bud and air soft and the irritating smell of burning coal banished by the soft breeze blowing from the southwest with the distant scent of the Kent hop fields. But of course that was all done now. With so many motors about . . . She had appeared at the end of the walk leading in from Stanhope Gate. With the sun behind, her golden hair piled high in a mass of curls was a blazing halo and he caught his breath. . . .

Churchill was leaning forward, a hand on his knee. "Are you feeling all right, David?" From the tone of his voice, Powell realized that Churchill must have been talking for some time.

Powell shook his head ruefully. "My apologies, Winston. The fire . . ." He took a deep breath.

"Is everything all right, David?" Churchill asked again, concern strong in his voice.

Powell forced a grin he did not feel. "Of course. Just a bit tired, that's all. Long week. Please, go on."

"It was not important, David," Churchill said, still watching him. "Please, if you are not feeling well, tell me. I can have the medical officer up. . . ."

"Winston, I am fine," Powell said, trying to keep the annoyance from his voice. "I am fine," he repeated. "It was just the fire and the whiskey."

Churchill sat back and regarded him soberly. "If you say so." He gave his friend a searching glance, then crossed his legs and chewed a moment on his cigar, still not convinced.

"Have you been able to locate our Mr. Connigham?"

Powell nodded. "Yes, we have. Our watch on Bannerman in Dover paid off. Connigham visited him, as I thought he would." He removed a thin notebook from his coat pocket and flipped through the pages. "It was Tuesday night last. They spent two hours together. Conningham left and returned to London by train. We have kept him under surveillance since, in spite of what appears to be aimless wanderings."

"Do you know where he went after he escaped your men last Saturday?"

Powell shook his head. "No, I am afraid we do not. We did not spot him again until Dover."

Churchill thought about that, wondering where the man could have gone in the interval. It was all very interesting, he decided. "My dear David," he said after a while. "I want you to think about this. Our friend, Mr. Connigham, disappears for several days and then, much as you expected, shows up in Dover where he has a nice conversation with the employer of his murdered sister. The same employer, I might add, who pooh-poohed the very idea that sabotage might be involved in those Tunnel disasters and then refused to agree to a military guard. He then returns to London, where, according to your report, he begins to wander the city. Perhaps searching for someone or something."

"A justifiable assumption," Powell murmured.

"Quite right." Churchill paused as if struggling with several ideas at once. "Now then," he said slowly, putting his thoughts into words and letting the process clarify the jumble of information contained in his mind, "let us suppose that Mr. Bannerman is a party to this sabotage."

Powell reacted in surprise. "Are you serious, Winston?"

Churchill waved a hand impatiently. "This is for the sake of supposition, at this point. Please bear with me. Suppose Bannerman was involved. He would certainly be in a position to obtain the maximum from any incident of sabotage. But there is no motive for him to do so. To the contrary. Even if the Tunnel were destroyed and he remained undetected, his reputation would still be damaged. No, I believe that Mr. Bannerman can be ruled out.

"Now then, for Mr. Connigham. Why has he returned to England? Because his sister has been murdered is the obvious answer. Is he, in fact, involved somehow? Is he the saboteur?"

Powell shook his head. "How could he be? From what you have told me, the first instance of sabotage occurred while he was still in the States."

Churchill nodded and leaned forward to tap his knee in time with his words. "What if you were the saboteur and you wished the blame placed on a certain group. Who better than the Fenians? Of which our Mr. Connigham is a member. Especially now with the Home Rule bill to be introduced in the new year." He sat back, satisfaction evident.

Powell nodded thoughtfully. "I see what you are driving at. If you wished to redirect suspicion, then you make it appear that someone else is responsible. But why murder the man's sister? I should think that would be rather a long shot as a drawing card."

"Perhaps, although if you read through Connigham's file you come away with the impression that it would be just the thing. He certainly seems a headstrong, impetuous man, and the post office list shows a regular correspondence between them over the years."

Powell nodded. "I take it then that you suspect the Ulster Volunteers or a group with similar aims."

Churchill shrugged. "I am not certain at the moment. I suppose those fools are the most logical choice. Some of them are certainly capable of an action such as this—both murder and sabotage."

"And how does all this square with your theory of German subversion in Catholic Ireland?"

Churchill took a pen from the gold desk set and examined the nib minutely before answering. "I am not certain that it does, yet I am not certain that it does not."

"I find that a bit confusing."

Churchill gave him a feeble grin. "So do I, David. But certainly if sabotage could be laid at the door of the Fenians, the chance for Home Rule would be destroyed."

"That is certainly true. But how does your theory of German involvement fit in?"

"Perhaps better than it seems at first glance. If Home Rule is prevented, Germany would have little trouble persuading the Fenians, and many others in the Catholic south, to take up arms against us in the event of war."

"I see," Powell murmured. "Thus tying up British forces in Ireland."

"Precisely."

"That is why you see Connigham as a scapegoat?"

Churchill nodded and Powell had a sudden premonition of the coming years that left him shaken and cold, so that unconsciously he stretched his hands to the fire.

Churchill nodded again. "Germany may desire to kill two birds with one stone—the destruction of the Tunnel and Civil War in Ireland. Certainly, they would derive a great deal from both accomplishments."

Powell said nothing as he continued to stare into the fire. Churchill waited a moment then went on. "There was an interesting discussion last evening at dinner. Eric von Dorn was present."

Powell nodded, taking his eyes away from the fire reluctantly. "I reviewed his file after our discussion last Sunday evening. Seems a quiet sort of chap. Great one for the social scene. Considered very eligible, I understand. Nothing in his file to indicate any untoward activity, but then it's not very complete."

"My impression exactly. Yet at times, he seemed just a bit too naive for someone in his position. Nothing specific that I could put my finger on."

Powell waited, sensing that there was more.

"There have been reports, unconfirmed so far, that a major power change has occurred in Berlin." Churchill briefly described the contents of the secret file he had reviewed on Friday. "The point is, at dinner last night von Dorn denied any sympathy with the war party despite the fact that he apparently owes them his promotion," he concluded.

"Perhaps they are trying to gain his sympathy?"

"Von Dorn is not important enough to warrant special attention. He could easily be replaced. His family is without high social standing or influence."

"Perhaps then he has accomplished something or has made contacts that are very important. Important enough to make him invaluable."

Churchill nodded. "I rather favor that supposition myself. Is there any surveillance on Herr von Dorn at present?"

Powell shook his head. "No, at least not from Special Branch. I could quiry MI.5. It's a little more in their line."

Churchill nodded. "Perhaps, David. I just don't know. There is just this feeling and I can't seem to rid myself of it."

Powell smiled at that. "Winston, you should be at the Yard."

"Why is that?"

"A good policeman often feels that way. A hunch. Sometimes it is even valid."

Churchill grinned sheepishly. "Perhaps I am making too much of it?"

"Not at all."

"Then what do you do when you find yourself in a similar situation?"

Powell shifted in the chair. "I've found that often the most advisable course is to provoke someone to action."

Churchill hesitated. "Precisely what I have concluded. It would seem to me that there are too many unanswered questions, too much speculation. I think that it is time we take a hand in the game and, as you say, provoke someone to action. When can I meet with Connigham?"

"Do you still think it wise not to inform the Home Office?"

"I do." Churchill coughed. "I do not feel I can yet discuss this matter with McKenna. Our relations are still a bit strained, and although I know he would agree to this course of action, it would place him in an untenable situation if it failed."

And me as well, Powell thought, but kept the thought to himself. "Then sometime this week, at a favorable opportunity, we will arrest him, unofficially, and take him to a safe meeting place. I will endeavor to notify you as far in advance as possible."

Churchill rubbed his hands together and grinned. "Good, David, good. The prospect of action is always exciting."

Powell grunted a reply, remembering the last time Churchill had uttered those words the year before while still Home Secretary. Powell had notified him that a gang of Letts had robbed a jewelry store, killed three policemen attempting to arrest them, and holed up in a loft at 100 Sidney Street. He had requested a company of Scots Guards from the Tower of London who were armed with rifles to assist the lightly armed police. Winston had not only sent the company, but had gone to the scene himself. He and a newsreel photographer had come under fire. The press, Tory and Liberal alike, had a field day with the old soldier-of-fortune charges that had pursued Churchill since his Boer War days, when as a newspaper reporter he had been captured by the Boers and imprisoned for bearing arms.

"There is one other possibility," Churchill muttered. He got up and walked to the fire and, half turning to Powell, leaned on the mantel.

"Yes?"

"The Ulster Volunteers may not be involved at all. The Fenians, I am certain, would be happy to see Home Rule fail; it would only bring them new recruits and revived importance."

"I do not see that it really changes matters one way or the other."

"Perhaps not . . ." Churchill shook his head and straightened. "Extremely confusing, isn't it?"

For a moment, Powell thought he looked quite lost.

chapter ___ 22

The motor bus clattered away in a flurry of dust and noise,
leaving Connigham standing alone beside the Mile End Road.
He sauntered over to a deserted shop, lit a cigarette, and
regarded the street. In the fading light of the winter afternoon,
it was even worse than he remembered. Shop fronts were
empty, boarded here and there, gaping in other places. Dingy
one- and two-story brick hovels huddled beside classical buildings of the seventeenth and eighteenth centuries. The roads
were filthy and cluttered with refuse of every description, but
at least the people thronging the street were no longer starving
and in rags. Some strides in improving the conditions of the
lower classes seemed to have been made in the past few
years. There had even been a reduction in the number of
homeless haunting the benches of Shepherds Bush of late.

Traffic was heavy, horse-drawn wagons and motor lorries
fighting for space. The din was beyond belief and the smell
worse. Even the muddiest, most refuse-strewn lane in Boston
or New York, he knew, could never come close to matching
the squalor of Whitechapel. And this in the greatest city of
the most prosperous nation on earth.

He pushed away from the wall and turned into White Horse
Lane, shouldering his way through the crowd where necessary,
ignoring the urchins dodging about his legs and the whining
beggars stationed along the curb. He was not interested in the
social politics of the English poor and he was inured to
squalor from his own childhood.

It had taken the several days since his return from Dover to
find Jemmy, and the contact had been vague as to his exact
whereabouts.

"Dunno, guvnor. Jemmy, 'e's a strange one. Niver know
where 'e's to be found twicet in the same day." But the

pound note had fastened the man's attention so that, soaked in gin as he was, he was able to provide general directions.

He cut through the dour mess of Rectory Square, crossed Stepney Green quickly, turning to see that he hadn't been followed, and ducked into a dingy street called Copley, which was little more than a dirty alley. He found Tillotson Road and, shortly, the crumbling brick front and cracked, filthy glass with its barely legible signboard proclaiming tobacco and sundries. He pushed the door open and winced at' the smell that flooded out to meet him.

The paint or wallpaper, he could not tell which, was peeling away in dirty strips. Years of rain had drained down the walls, turning them a uniform rusty brown. A single candle mounted on a pie tin burned in the gloom at one end of a counter beneath whose fly-blown glass a few packets of cigarettes and tins of tobacco could be seen. The shapeless mass at one end stirred and he recognized the toothless crone as Jemmy's wife. She stared at him from one good eye; the other was filmed by a cataract and half hidden in a massive growth.

"Where's Jemmy?" His voice was hoarse and the smell of the place nauseated him.

The crone continued to stare while her thoothless mouth worked soundlessly. Finally, she used the stick clutched in one hand to bang the wall behind her and Connigham glanced at the torn blanket hanging from two nails. It stirred a bit as if in a breeze.

"Come on out, Jemmy," he said wearily, "I know you're there."

The blanket was pushed aside and an old man shuffled out, clutching an iron bar in both hands. He shrank against the wall and stared at Connigham. If there was fear in his eyes, it was not detectable beneath the placid acceptance of whatever might happen. His attitude proclaimed him one of the poor who had lost all hope. But Connigham was not fooled.

"Cut the act," he growled. "You know damned well who I am."

The ugly little man worried the idea for a moment, then jerked his head once in a parody of a nod, his toothless mouth working like the woman's.

Connigham smiled. "Of course you do, Jemmy. It's me.

Michael Connigham. You remember me? We used to be great friends years ago."

The man considered the information again and jerked his head as before.

"God damn it. I've no time to play games," Connigham snarled. He stepped forward and wrenched the iron bar from the boneless hands, and the man dropped to his knees, huddling into himself, hands raised to protect his head. The old woman began to gabble and Connigham kicked at her.

"Shut up, the pair of ye," he snapped, lapsing into the brogue. "I've no time for yer games. Stand up or I'll kick ye to death."

Jemmy got to his feet with alacrity and brushed at his rags. Standing erect, he was still a head shorter than Connigham.

"So what do ye want then, Michael?" Jemmy glanced around, eyes shifting from corner to corner of the room, dispensing with the senile old man pose. He pushed past Connigham to peer through the filthy window.

"Good God, man, do 'ee know what a chanct yer taking? Dublin 'as promised a 'undret poun' for yer 'ead, dead or alive. A 'undret poun'!"

Connigham nodded. "Aye, I know. And the police are after me as well. But ye won't deal wi' them, and the hundred pounds don't interest a man like ye, do they?" Connigham snorted. "Ye know what would happen if ye tried to turn me."

Jemmy nodded and, half-resuming his protective coloration, crouched back across the littered floor, nodding and bobbing his head. Connigham glared around. "Christ, this place is a pigsty. It smells like a pigsty. Why the hell don't you ever clean it?"

The old man giggled at that, showing toothless gums, but did not answer. A miser, that's what he was, Connigham thought. He probably had a thousand pounds or better squirreled away somewhere, but he would die in the same squalor in which he had lived all his life. Jemmy was a parasite; he lived on society, had never done a moment's honest work. He lived by selling: people, information, goods, whatever. Nor was he particular about his customers, with one exception. He had never been known to sell or trade information to the police, and for this reason, he was used and trusted—within limits. By virtue of this unique acceptance, Jemmy knew everything of value in the London underworld and many things about the world beyond that could turn him a penny. He heard things; people came to sell him information much as they might go to a pawnshop to sell articles of property. And Jemmy bought, bought cheap and sold dear. People who had nothing else to sell, not even their bodies, could always earn a shilling or two if their scraps of information were of value.

Connigham placed a five-pound note on the dirty counter and watched Jemmy begin to salver. He reached a tentative hand toward the note but Connigham slapped it away. "Now, Jemmy, ye've to talk to me first, boyo. Talk to me, and maybe the fiver will be yours."

"I already have," he whined. "Told you Fenians 'er looking . . ."

Connigham swore. "You stupid bastard. You think I don't know that?" He shoved both hands into his pockets and stared at the dirty little man, wrinkling his nose against the cloying odor that emanated from him. He wondered if the man had ever had a bath in his life.

"I want to know who killed my sister," he said slowly.

Jemmy shuffled away from Connigham. He had a mind that retained everything he saw or heard. He could dredge up an obscure fact overheard a decade before and repeat it with unerring accuracy. Now he reviewed quickly what he remembered about Connigham—the man had saved his life once, in the streets when footpads had set upon him. But gratitude was an emotion missing from Jemmy's twisted life. Connigham was a murderer. He remembered that. Had shot two Prods in Belfast.

The old man turned, his eye winking at Connigham. "Aye, I 'eerd yer sister was kilt. 'Eerd it 'tware burglar. Wasn't no one special, only Charlie Osgood. Course't 'e's daid now, kilt by a costermongers wagon, 'e were."

Connigham stared at him, certain the old man was lying. He was about to say so when Jemmy came near and pawed at his arm.

"Ye did save me life onct, Michael, aye, and ye—"

Jemmy got no further.

"Ye lying bastard." Connigham kicked him into a heap in the corner. A huge hand reached down, yanked him up by the rags he wore, and slammed him against the wall. His head struck the bare lathwork so hard he came near to blacking out. He had been hurt numerous times before but never so badly as when Connigham shook him with both hands and he flopped, feet clear of the floor and arms windmilling like a rag doll. Bone grated against bone, he could not breathe, and his head threatened to topple from his shoulder before Connigham flung him against the wall again.

Connigham knelt down. "Now, Jemmy-me-boyo, no more lies," he said softly. "I want to know who killed me sister, Margaret."

Jemmy's chest hurt badly and he knew something had broken. He found it hard to breathe and even harder to talk, but Connigham slapped him twice and threatened to slap him again.

"Aye . . . aye . . . can . . . only . . . Finnigan . . ."

Connigham rocked back on his heels instantly and stared at him. "Finnigan?" He pulled Jemmy to him. "Do ye mean Tom Finnigan?" His voice was so soft and deadly that Jemmy stopped gasping.

"Aye . . ."

Connigham stumbled up and stood with his hand braced against the wall, head down and gasping for breath himself. He stared at the old man, who had both hands pressed against his meager chest as if to prevent its splitting apart. A trickle of blood had appeared on his lips.

"No," he whispered. "No, you're lying!" This last was a scream, and he swooped down to snatch the bundle of filthy cloth and bones from the floor. In his madness, he did not hear the sound behind as the old crone swung the iron bar. The glancing blow still struck with shattering force, and Connigham went to his knees, dragging the old man with him. In the pain that flashed through his skull, Connigham barely felt the next blow across his shoulder. Dazed, he pushed and rolled to the side, struggling to keep clear of the flailing cudgel. She was not strong enough to kill him, but if the old man should help her . . . Connigham scrabbled behind the counter where she was hampered by the narrow space and had to poke with the bar at his face.

Connigham caught hold of it then and twisted the rod from her grasp. Pushing himself up, he swung it viciously, catching her across the forehead, and she fell without a sound, her skull shattered.

Connigham slumped across the cracked glass of the case in

a daze, hypnotized by a single dirt-encrusted packet of Players' cigarettes. Jemmy whimpered in his corner, still hugging his chest, and the sound brought Connigham back to reality. He staggered across the floor and knelt beside him.

"Jemmy"—his voice was almost begging—"not Tom Finnigan?" But Jemmy was too far gone to understand more than that the man had killed him. Connigham wiped a bloody hand across his face and stared at the deep gash in the thumb web where the iron bar had caught him. The old man whimpered again, and his eyes opened. He fastened them on Connigham and cackled. "Aye, 'twas Tom Finnigan. He done it, so I 'eerd."

Rage exploded deep inside; the old man was lying again, laughing at him. Even when he grabbed the scrawny neck and choked him, Jemmy's eyes continued to mock him with the name of his oldest friend.

Von Dorn met Tom Finnigan in Red Lion Square, and they walked slowly about the perimeter, ignoring the heavy mist that the cold was turning to an icy fog. The tall buildings on either side, stained with the coal smoke of generations, frowned at them through the bare oaks.

"Do you have all that?" von Dorn demanded.

"Cours't I do. Think I'm some kinda swell, for bleeding sake?" Finnigan cupped the cigarette in his hand and spat. "Four charges, four pounds blasting gelatin at each anchor between the balcony and the fan blades. Electric detonation so all charges goes off together."

"All right. Do not leave anything out and tell him it's to be done this week. The sooner the works are struck, the better. Then report to me on the effects. Use the telephone number."

With that, von Dorn walked rapidly away, not wanting to prolong the meeting. It was not likely that he would be recognized in this part of London, but the fewer chances the better.

Finnigan watched him go, marveling at the arrogance of the man, and here it was less than a month since he had come begging him to save his life. And at the thought Margaret's white body was in his mind again, that body that he had so long wanted. Even now after she was dead and in her grave, her icy rejection could cause him to writhe in embarrassment, and with sudden insight he wondered if it was her disdainful rejection—as if he were some uncouth animal—after all he had done for her that kept him from hating the German. He would have enjoyed the sight of that white body blackening in the fire, curling, descending into the same hell he wished for her soul. But that fool had barged in and spoiled it. Finnigan was no killer, and there had been no time to get the man out so that the fire could do its work.

He paused on the curb to light another cigarette and stared at the flame a moment. Aye, it would have been somethin' to see.

chapter 23

DECEMBER 20, 1911. WEDNESDAY.

The urgent hooting began again, its now familiar pattern spreading shock in ripples to the farthest reaches of the works. Men dropped their tools and began to run, swearing in frustration and anger. Whistles screamed across the frozen landscape, bouncing and echoing from the tons of supplies and stockpiles of steel and iron that lay rusting under the glowering sky.

Bannerman smashed a fist onto his desk and stormed from his office, snatching up a duffel coat as he went out and across the yard at a run. Men saw him coming, saw the expression on his face, and moved away as he crossed the duckboards to the gatekeeper's shack. An emergency crew was already loading a van as a shunting engine backed from the Tunnel entrance. He did not spare it a glance but pushed through and into the shack, where the gatekeeper turned from the telephone and handed him a hastily scrawled message. A moment later, the duty engineer burst in, saw Bannerman, and crossed to the desk to read the message over his shoulder.

"Where's McDougal?" Bannerman snapped.

"He's out today, sir. Touch of the grippe. Sent word that he would—"

"Read this damned thing to me," Bannerman snarled and threw the scribbled note back at the gatekeeper.

"Ah, yes sor, it says, plate—ah, plate fallen from roof, Number Six Ventilator shaft. Apparently weakened by fire. Four men trapped beneath—"

Bannerman did not wait to hear more. He rapped out a series of orders for heavy-duty jacks and braces to be sent down and ran out to the van, where it had just been coupled to the shunting engine. He checked that cutting torches and wooden timbers for bracing had been loaded and vaulted into the cab. The engineer looked at him for orders and Bannerman swore. "Go, damn you. What are you waiting for?"

The rest of the crew scrambled into the van as the engine jerked the train forward and into the Tunnel, leaving behind a flurry of purposeful activity as the duty engineer began to marshal a second crew.

As the train sped down into the gloom, Bannerman quickly told the crew foreman what little he knew. By the time he had finished, his anger was so great that he could not even think coherently, and it was some minutes before he had calmed enough to realize it. He took several deep breaths, forcing the anger down, bringing it under control. The despair that was as much fear held him in thrall, and it was all he could do to keep from lashing out, from pounding the railing which he was holding so tightly that his hands were white. The engineer felt his anger and shrank away to the far side of the cab.

Was this an accident or more sabotage? His fist clenched tighter and the rage surged forth again. The strain was visible on his face, features stretched in a rictus of anger. Plate had fallen from the ceiling, from inside the ventilator shaft, the gatekeeper had said. Weakened by the fire a month ago? But why had it fallen now? The ventilator shaft had been in partial use for nearly three weeks. There had been no other problems, no sign of structural weakness. He swore under his breath, cursing the slowness of the engine. They passed several gangs of men trudging toward the entrance or huddled in the safety shelters, waiting for the shunting engines to pick them up.

They reached Ventilator Six twenty minutes after entering the Tunnel. Below the shaft, a twisted mass of plate, tangles of iron reinforcing rod, and cement rubble formed a dam to further progress. It appeared that half the ceiling had fallen, leaving gaping holes through to the chalk itself. Even the brick lining of the shaft had torn away from its anchors, exposing the grouting around the bore.

The engine ground to a stop and Bannerman went forward to survey the pile of rubble that had filled the shaft and cascaded into the Tunnel. The gang foreman was lying against the wall, a red-stained bandage across half his face.

Bannerman knelt beside him. "What the hell happened?" he demanded.

The foreman shook his head gently in spite of the pain and

tried to speak. Bannerman had actually reached toward the man in his anger, to shake him into consciousness, before he realized what he was doing. He jerked his head back. What the hell is the matter with me? I'm going insane, he thought, stumbling to his feet. One of the workmen, misinterpreting, steadied him.

" 'E'll be all right, guvnor. Just a bit of a blow to the 'ead. Looks worse than it is." The workman, a wiry little Cockney, shook his head. "Proper do 'twere, guvnor. We was up on level three, inside the shaft, when we 'ears this loud grinding, as it were, going on below. The plate pulled away. Fell straight down it did."

"The men . . ." He had to stop and repeat the question. "The men trapped beneath?"

"Aye. Four men. 'Eard them pounding a bit ago. Nothin' we can do wi'out equipment. Some o' them plates weighs more'n a 'undret stone."

Bannerman pushed away from the knot of men, angered afresh at their respectful expressions, their trust in him. He examined as much of the debris as he could, pausing now and then to push an iron pipe into an opening and listen. Hearing nothing, he clambered onto the pile of rubble and repeated the process. A few feet below the ruined ceiling he caught the first sound of hammering coming from far down under the smashed cement and twisted plate. But it was the sound that followed that chilled him to the bone as he leaned into a crevice formed by the junction of two plates tipped together, almost at right angles: the sound of gushing water.

The fire reservoirs! Apparently the force of the falling plate had smashed through the flooring, severing water mains, and now the conduits were flooding. The four men were trapped in the main conduit and would drown if the mass of rubble above did not first crush them to death. As if to underline the urgency, the plate on which he was standing shifted, and he was almost thrown into the crevice. Bannerman stumbled to one side and jumped, caught somthing above, and clawed his way up as the plate began to pivot, slipping down at the same time until it jammed into the crevice. He slid down the rubble to the Tunnel floor and ordered two men back up-Tunnel to the water mains to shut down the flow into the conduit space.

The second shunting engine arrived as Bannerman was organizing the emergency crew. Heavy jacks were removed from the vans and manhandled into place below the few ceiling plates which still dangled from the shaft. Bannerman estimated that some two hundred or more tons of broken cement and iron plating had fallen so far. He moved quickly, directing the placement of additional lights, the rigging of a tripod hoist, and bracing where possible to prevent further falls. When they were ready, he gathered the two crews and described his plan. They would proceed carefully, bracing the rubble at each step to make certain that it did not collapse further to crush the men below. Water was the greatest danger. If the flow was strong enough it could undermine the rubble, making the heavy bracing timbers useless. The mass was already unstable; not much force would be needed to settle it further. Therefore, he planned to go directly after the men, down through the crevice in which he had heard the water. The two blocking plates would have to be shifted aside first. Once that was done, they could lower ropes and bring up the trapped men.

The crane hook was reeved through the tripod block, the other end attached to a shunting engine, and two men climbed onto the rubble and worked their way up to where the two plates formed a wing. They chose one plate, wrapped the steel cable around it, then backed off and waved for the slack to be taken up. As the cable came tight, the shunting engine began to labor and the distinct smell of ozone filled the Tunnel. Men ran to the engine with lengths of timber to block it in place, and sand was scattered to increase friction between the engine's wheels and the metal tracks. The plate began to lift, tilted, slammed against another, and came free. The engine backed away, the driver watching his dials with a worried expression until he could lower the plate clear of the mass.

Bannerman placed a hand on the engine cover and swore under his breath. Already overheated. The first plate had been removed easily enough, but the second was jammed into place by several large chunks of cement with twisted talons of reinforcing rod protruding, all of which would have to be laboriously cleared by hand. The plate itself was resting on more rubble, and it rocked continually beneath their feet, increasing the difficulty of removing the rubble. For three hours they worked while the sound of rushing water grew louder beneath them. The gate mechanism in the reservoir's main water point had been smashed and until it could be got at, there was nothing they could do to reduce the flow. And they could not reach the gate without first clearing the rubble.

Finally, they were able to maneuver the cable around the plate, but as the strain was taken up the overworked engine slipped and the two-thousand-pound plate slammed down onto the mass, causing a cascade of rubble down into the crevice. Screams of terror and pain rose clearly from below. Bannerman trotted back to the engine.

"It's no good, sir. She won't hold. Engine's overheated and the insulation's startin' to burn."

"Try one more time," Bannerman snapped. "If we can get this one away, we can move the smaller pieces by hand."

The engine driver nodded and slid the switch lever to the right. The motor began to whine and the shunting engine jerked back against the cable. Bannerman could see the smoke begin to pour from beneath the bonnet. Without thinking it through, he ran forward and clambered up the leading edge of the tilted plate, wriggling forward, ignoring the warning shouts from below. The edge of the massive plate had lifted just high enough for him to peer under. He twisted, got hold of his torch and shone it into the opening, working it around until he caught sight of a dark shape that turned slowly to look at him. One eye gleamed. Behind him, the whine of the engine had become a scream. He shouted. "Brace here . . . bring something to brace this place . . . I can see them."

Two men ran forward with a timber baulk. Others joined them, and they manhandled it toward the opening. Bannerman edged out of the way, grabbed the end of the beam as it swung, and pushed. If he could just wedge it in, the plate could settle back and there would be enough room to go in under and bring the men out. The man beneath the plate thrust an arm forward, reaching toward the opening. He had one shoulder through when the shunting engine motor burned out and the plate slammed down, one edge catching the timber and flipping the wooden beam as if it were a matchstick. Bannerman was thrown down the incline, his eyes riveted to the iron plate as it swerved and began to slide ponderously after him. He hit the base of the incline, jamming against a girder, and the plate followed him with all the inexorable power of an avalanche. It was as if it were happening to someone else; he was aware of everything at once; men rushing forward, two thousand pounds of iron grinding toward him, edge on. He wanted to close his eyes, to shut out the sight of the razor-sharp edge bearing down, but he could not take his eyes away. Curiously, time stretched to a standstill in which everything had a gemlike clarity and moved with agonizing slowness, as if trapped in some clear, viscous fluid. There was no fear and he was amazed at that; there was merely the fascination of death approaching. The leading edge of the plate ran up on a steel support with an ear-splitting screech. The girder refused to give way beneath the awesome load and the plate hesitated, then revolved lazily, one edge slicing past his head, slammed into the same girder holding him and came to rest not two feet away. The jolt of vibrating steel almost snapped his spine.

Bannerman lay still, not believing that he was alive. Then the first hands reached under the plate to drag him out.

By midnight, the worst of the damage was known. The four trapped men killed, six others injured, the water main destroyed, and flooding continuing. The gangs farther up-Tunnel had all been evacuated through Ventilator Shaft Seven, and work had come to a complete halt. They had retrieved the mangled bodies an hour earlier, and additional work crews had come down-Tunnel to relieve the two original gangs.

Bannerman leaned against the burned-out shunting engine, exhausted beyond belief. He had completed his assessment earlier and phoned it through to McDougal, who had arrived at the works office in spite of his illness and was directing the supply and dispatch of the emergency crews. Power cranes had been brought up and the clearing operation had begun, but the Tunnel floor had collapsed for fifty feet along the track bed, the reinforced concrete unable to withstand the strain of tons of falling iron and masonry. The electrical mains through which the power lines ran were repairable, although it would require a week or more to do so, and the flooding was on the way to being halted. Power was out except for emergency lighting, which Bannerman had ordered shut down to conserve batteries as soon as he was certain that everyone had got out through Shaft Seven. A single auxiliary electrical circuit hurriedly being laid along the wall would supply current to provide reduced lighting and run fire point pumps farther along. He sipped at a cup of hot tea, grateful for its warmth. He could feel the familiar accelerated heart rate, the acid feeling in the pit of his stomach, the tenseness that he knew was fear. He tried to ignore it by staring into the dark vault of the ventilator shaft above. The familiar whisper of air and the hum of turning blades were gone. A single plate, spinning end over end as it fell, had smashed the junction box containing the electrical switching for the fans. That was another bit of repair that needed doing.

Bitterly, he flung the contents of the cup away as the gang foreman in charge of the repair crew approached. The man removed his cap and wiped a sweat-soaked face with it. His skin was the color of the gray chalk that had settled over everything and rose in choking clouds whenever anything was shifted.

"We'll be taking the bodies out now, sir. Nothing more you can do here. Why not get a bit of rest."

Bannerman started an angry retort, then realized that the suggestion was sensible. There was nothing he could do now except brood on his own bitterness and fear. He nodded.

"The shunting engine's going up for another load, sir. You could go wiv' it."

Bannerman stared at the rubble blocking the Tunnel completely; it seemed for a moment to form an open mouth in which the jagged pieces of cement were snaggled teeth protruding in a taunting grin. He turned away abruptly and went to the wagon behind the blanket-wrapped bodies.

Bannerman lay on the cot in the small shed attached to his office which he used as a sleeping quarters when the pressure of work kept him too late for the long drive to Dover. Sleep, however, eluded him as he listened to the wind moaning across the downs; souls of drowned sailors, the locals would have said. Well, he thought, you could add to them the souls of workers killed in the Tunnel, and his mind shied away from the appalling total to date. In the space of two months, thirty-seven men had been killed and the Tunnel's record had fallen from the safest ever excavated to one of the deadliest.

He had spotted a jagged chunk of grouting, blackened and pitted, as the gang cleared the rubble; the grouting could not have been damaged by the earlier fire, protected as it was by four tiers of brick and the iron plating. An explosive had to have been used, probably just sufficient to blast the grouting away from the wall and sever the iron anchor bolts. After the fire damage, the weakened plating would have literally peeled away.

And that was what ate at him so that he could not be still. Who? Who? Who? Who was killing his men, destroying his Tunnel, destroying him? Who and why? And he had only aided the unknown saboteur with his indecision, his cowardice in the face of the Board's insistence that he bend to their will. He had made the wrong decisions again and again. He had been wrong when he allowed the Board to browbeat him, to call his bluff over the grouting. He had made the wrong decision when he had allowed the Board to hide the evidence of sabotage after the blowout in the heading and when he had not fought for increased security.

He turned restlessly on his bunk, seeking a comfortable position, but the pain in his back and a twisted knee only added to the tension keeping him awake. He ground his teeth and sought to blank everything from his mind. Grimly, he struggled to force his thoughts away from the Tunnel and all it represented. And as he struggled, the hours wore on until, finally, he slept and his subconscious released a flood of dreams to taunt him.

chapter —— 24

Connigham stood on the curb across the road from Brompton
Square, lost in the Christmas crowds swirling among the
stores that lined the Brompton Road. The temperature was
thirty-four degrees and the wind was blowing under a sky as
clear and diamond-hard as only an English winter sky can be.
The money Emily had given him combined with what he had
taken from the two dead guards in Liverpool was running low,
and the worn jacket purchased in the Liverpool secondhand
shop was no match for the wind. Yet he remained undecided.
Emily's dedication to the Cause was something that he had
never fully understood; there seemed no reason for it. She had
been raised with every advantage, had made an excellent
marriage, and inherited two fortunes. She was a part of the
London social scene, slightly scandalous yet all the more
desirable for it. She had been welcomed into King Edward's
circle and, according to the rumors, was also approved by the
staid sailor king—as he was coming to be called—George V.
But it was the strength of her love for him that he wondered
about. The years had passed so quickly and their time together was measured in weeks.

They had last met in Wyoming in 1908, on a ranch sprawling along the Lodge Pole River which belonged to an expatriate English son of an eminent peer, one of the remission men
plaguing the American West. Connigham was passing the
hard times as a ranch hand, and had given up any attempt at
fund raising.

Emily's husband, Sir Charles Wilson-Langdon, was tour-
ing that summer and the sight of her that August evening had
come as a distinct shock as he rode in from a week of fence
mending, filthy, bearded, and soaked in sweat. Aye, he
thought, it had been a memorable evening, one that had
carried him across the three intervening years. Connigham

had asked her more than once to join him in the States and her excuse had been that she was too valuable to the Movement by virtue of her husband's position. But even after he was dead the answer had remained the same.

Always the Movement. He had deserted his sister because of the Movement, made a fool of himself over a woman because of the Movement, killed because of the Movement, and now he was certain that his sister had been murdered because of, or even by, the Movement.

The policeman saluted with a finger to his helmet, interrupting Connigham's daydreaming. "You seem to be lost, sir?"

Connigham gave him a wide smile. "Ah no, constable. Waitin' fer me mate. 'E's a bit overdue and I'm freezing me bum."

"I see. Then you'll be movin' along?"

"Sartainly, sartainly. Soon's 'e shows." To back down would be fatal Connigham knew, and it was exactly what the policeman was testing for.

"Not then, now! Move along."

Connigham jammed both hands into his pockets. "Look 'ere, mate. "I knows me rights. I ain't doing nuffing wrong waiting 'ere for 'im. Ain't me fault 'e's late."

The policeman eyed him a moment longer. "All right. But if yer 'ere when I come back, I'll run yer in for vagrancy, understand?"

"Sure, mate. Got a cigarette?"

The policeman snorted in disgust and walked away. As soon as he disappeared into the crowd, Connigham turned and walked up the Brompton Road. He shivered as the wind freshened and increased his pace. He dared not, after all, he decided, take the chance that Emily's devotion to the Movement might be greater than to him, and he was certainly in no position to test her. Jemmy had warned of, confirmed rather—probably the only truthful thing he had said—the price on his head. Even if Emily would not betray him, he knew her butler would. The man was aching for a chance to try him on.

But he needed help to find Finnigan and he wondered if Emily knew that Finnigan was somehow involved in Margaret's murder. But why? What could Margaret possibly have done, what kind of a threat could she have been? He rejected the idea that she was an informer. Besides, the execution of an informer was a ritual that was always carried out as a warning to others, and it had not been so in her case. Why then was the Committee so anxious to get him out of England? Why did Jemmy name Tom Finnigan as her killer? There were too damned many questions that made no sense.

Connigham found it impossible to believe that Finnigan would have murdered her. Even as a child he had looked after Finnigan, weak, ugly little runt that he was, because Tom was his only true friend. And Finnigan had gone north to Belfast with them, had been with him the night he found that Prod in the Shankhill. And he had been sweet on Margaret before she married, and Margaret had mentioned him occasionally in her letters as looking out for her. Connigham shook his head. Old Jemmy was not above lying if it favored his circumstances.

Across the busy road with its tram and omnibus traffic, the horse cabs, taxis, and private motors, might possibly lie the answer. But if Emily knew, would she tell? Or had reinforcements been sent from Liverpool in case he appeared again?

He growled in frustration, startling an elderly woman accompanied by a younger, quite pretty girl dressed in a stylish tube coat and hobble skirt, both followed by a weary footman laden with packages. The woman muttered, the girl smiled from beneath her high cloche hat and feather, and the servant ignored him.

The South Kensington tube station was just ahead, and he was tired and cold. The thought of the grubby single room he had taken earlier in Renforth Street near the Albion Dock was far from inviting, but he needed time to think. Connigham went along toward the end of Thurloe Place, shivering in the worn leather jacket.

He pushed his way into the station and joined the queue for his ticket. A man stepped into line behind, jostling him, and then Connigham felt something press against his back. At the same instant a hand grabbed his right arm above the elbow and he looked up to see a second man smiling at him.

"No trouble now, Connigham. We've orders to bring you quietly."

He tensed and half turned but a third man pressed close, forcing a knee between Connigham's legs to throw him off balance. A hand slipped beneath his jacket and removed the Colt from his belt.

"No trouble now," the smiling man repeated. "We've several others along, all armed."

Connigham recognized the futility of his position and allowed himself to be led aside where he was handcuffed and taken out to a motor waiting in Onslow Square.

The room had once been painted dull green but the accumulation of years of dirt and neglect had turned it gray. They had not taken him to a police station, of that he was certain. The building lacked the noise and bustle, the burring telephones and the smell of Lysol that filled every police station he had ever visited, willingly or unwillingly. As soon as the motor turned onto the Fulham Road, curtains had been drawn, and complete silence had been observed by his three captors throughout the seemingly interminable drive. At first Connigham had tried to keep track of where they were going by the sounds about him. He was certain they had driven along the Fulham Road and turned south through Chelsea. The sound of a ship's whistle to his left suggested that they had crossed a bridge, Battersea or Albert, into South London. Later, they had apparently crossed the Thames again but he could not have said where.

When the motor car finally stopped, he heard the squeal of hinges as a door was shut and he assumed they were in a garage. He was taken into a narrow hallway of graying wood and down a corridor, up a flight of steps and along another hallway to the room in which he now sat. They had shoved him in and the door was closed and locked.

A small table and two chairs comprised the only furnishings. There were no carpets and no wall fixtures except for an old gas point now converted to an electric lamp. There were no curtains on the single shuttered window.

His shoulder muscles were cramped and he tried to wriggle his arms, but the jacket hampered his movements and Connigham gave up. The fact that he was still alive and in this room told him that they were certainly not Fenians. Otherwise, they would have gone on until they found a stretch of deserted country road and sped him on his way with a bullet. No, he was certain that they were police; they dressed, talked, and smelled like policemen. Connigham gave up further speculation as futile after a few minutes. They had extracted him from the tube station so neatly that not a single curious glance had come their way. Clearly, they wanted his arrest to go unnoticed and so they would tell him in good time.

Connigham had fallen asleep in an uncomfortable posture, head back and resting on his shoulder. His neck ached fiercely and he rolled his head in a circle, wondering what had awakened him. The single lamp continued to burn and there was nothing to indicate how long he might have been asleep. He heard a murmur of voices and a moment later the door was unlocked. A man peered in—a youngish-looking man with a full, almost chubby face—withdrew a moment, said something to someone in the hall, then stepped in and shut the door. The man stood by the doorjamb studying Connigham as if he were an unknown specimen beneath a powerful glass. Connigham in turn stared back, noting the expensive cut of the man's suit and the homburg dangling from one hand; but it was the man's eyes that drew him. They were blue and completely without expression. After a moment of intense scrutiny, the man reopened the door and motioned. The detective who sat next to him in the motor came in.

"Remove the restraints, if you please, David."

The man looked as if he were about to argue, then changed his mind and stepped behind Connigham. He felt hands fumbling at his wrists and tensed to take the sudden squeeze that he knew would come when the cuffs were jammed tighter as a warning to behave himself.

But the pressure eased immediately and he could not help his astonished expression. The man with the homburg grinned and drew up the other chair as the police detective went out.

"We can be quite civilized, you know. You are Michael Connigham?"

"You know damned well I am. Who the hell are you?"

The man laid the homburg on the table between them and leaned back to unbutton his overcoat. "My name is Winston Churchill."

"Winston-bloody-Churchill?" Connigham pronounced in astonishment. "I don't believe it!"

Churchill shrugged. "I do not care whether you do or not. You are an accused murderer. Shortly, you will be taken before a magistrate's court and bound over for trial. With the evidence against you and the witnesses available, two of whom will be brought to London from Belfast, I think you will hang in very short order."

Connigham laughed. "If that's what you believe, then why did you have me brought here? Not to satisfy your curiosity, I am sure. What possible interest could the navy have in me— or have you given up the Admiralty already for another post?"

Churchill smiled. "The Admiralty is not interested in you. But the government is. And I am a member of the government. We are most concerned with certain problems in Ireland and how they affect England."

"A little late for that, isn't it?" Connigham asked sarcastically. "It would seem to me that you have had all of eight or nine hundred years in which to be concerned."

Churchill ignored the comment. "Look here, Mr. Connigham, you are in a very dangerous situation. I suspect that it will be to your benefit to hear me out."

Connigham shrugged.

"There is an organization known as the Irish Republican Brotherhood. I am sure that you are very much aware of them, having been a member of their extremist wing, the Fenians, for several years now."

"That's no great secret," Connigham observed, and Churchill inclined his head in agreement.

"Of course. But what we are concerned about is the fanatic makeup of the Fenians. Home Rule is a certainty—" He held up a hand. "Please let us not debate pros and cons at the moment. The bill satisfies neither side, but it will be a start. You will have heard of armed groups forming in the North and calling themselves the Ulster Volunteers?"

Connigham nodded, waiting to see what he was driving at.

"The Ulster Volunteers have one avowed intention, and that is to prevent the Home Rule bill from passing and, if they cannot, to prevent it from being implemented. They are prepared to use whatever force they consider necessary and are arming themselves as quickly as possible." He waited for Connigham's reaction and when there was none, he frowned and went on. "We now know that some of their arms are coming from Germany."

"I would expect that to be so." Connigham's tone and manner suggested a complete lack of interest.

Churchill sat back in his chair and studied the man opposite. He was puzzled by his reaction to the circumstances. The broad shoulders were as erect as ever, and the hard, lined face remained expressionless.

"We know that the Fenians have also obtained arms from Germany."

Connigham shook his head. "I had not heard that before, but I would not be surprised."

"Even though your position in the United States is to raise money and, whenever possible, arms for the Fenians?"

"Is it?" Connigham asked innocently, and rubbed at his wrists where the cuffs had cut into the flesh.

Churchill stood up and began to pace the room; leaning forward as he usually did when thinking, he appeared to be charging the walls. "However, I suspect the reason you are in England has nothing to do with the Fenians. Am I correct?"

Connigham raised an eyebrow.

"A young woman was murdered here in London three weeks ago. Her married name was Margaret Doyle and she was your sister. You have come to London to find her murderer."

Connigham gave a snort and shrugged. "If you say so."

Churchill studied him a moment, then went to the door. When he returned, he carried a large envelope. He stopped beside the table and tapped his thumb with the packet. As if reaching a decision, his mouth worked in a grimace, and he extracted a photograph and placed it on the table.

For a moment, Connigham could not catch his breath. The room seemed to recede in a mist as he stared at the marble-cold face in the photograph. The eyes were closed and the expression relaxed in death, yet the traces of pain were still there, in the downward curve of the lips and the strain lines at either side of the eyes. Someone had artistically spread the mass of hair around her head, yet it only emphasized the death-mask characteristic of the face. The large bruises were still visible about the neck and shoulders. The photograph was underexposed and grainy, but it was Margaret plainly enough.

"That is a photograph of the dead woman taken before the autopsy."

Connigham stared at him, fighting to control the fury that had taken possession of him. But if Churchill was aware that the prisoner was on the brink of exploding, he gave no sign. Instead, he blinked, rather sleepily.

Connigham's voice was hoarse as he asked, "What possible interest could you have in my sister's murder?"

Churchill regarded him for a moment, wondering if perhaps he hadn't made a mistake after all. There was violence in the man, far more than he had expected, and it lay just beneath the surface. He wondered if Connigham were not too unstable to be of use. But the need was desperate and he made his decision.

"Somehow your sister's death may have something to do with the troubles in Ireland, perhaps with the Ulster Volunteers. Was she a Fenian?"

"How should I know that? I left Ireland six years ago. I have not seen her since."

"No communication of any kind?"

When Connigham shook his head, Churchill drew a sheet of paper and read a list of dates beginning in 1905. "Those are the dates the post office recorded letters from her addressed to you." Churchill resumed his seat. "As you may have surmised, I have taken quite a bit of trouble to have this conversation. I do it because I feel there is a major threat to the security of Great Britain."

Connigham stared at him in surprise. "Now, why in hell should I be concerned about England? I don't give a damn if the entire British Empire disappears in a puff of smoke. In fact, I'd be glad of the chance to light the fuse."

"Don't be a fool," Churchill snapped. "You are certainly more intelligent than that. You know as well as I do that for the foreseeable future, Home Rule or no, Ireland and England are tied together economically, if in no other way. If England's security is threatened, then Ireland's is as well. If total independence should come tomorrow, how long would it take Ireland to construct an effective army and navy to prevent invasion by a foreign power?"

"Ah, the old English nightmare. The perennial excuse for holding Ireland in subjugation."

"And never more valid than since the end of the Napoleonic wars," Churchill retorted.

"And you think that my sister was vital to the security of the empire?" Connigham snorted. "Then you are a bigger fool than I thought."

Churchill ignored the gratuitous insult. "No. But the reason she was murdered may be of importance."

"I don't understand. What are you trying to say?"

Churchill took a leather case from his suit coat and offered a cigar to Connigham. When he shook his head, Churchill selected one and clipped the tip with a gold-plated cutter. He lit the cigar and dropped the match onto the table. For a moment he poked at it with his finger, expression thoughtful, as if trying to decide how much to tell him.

"Like you, I am concerned with the reason for her murder. I do not believe, although there are some at Scotland Yard who disagree, that she was murdered by a housebreaker. I suspect that your sister was murdered because she knew or did something she should not have. You are familiar with the Tunnel being constructed beneath the English Channel?"

Connigham nodded, confused by the sudden switch in topics, then caught himself and asked warily, "What has that to do . . . ?"

Churchill interrupted impatiently. "I suggest we stop playing games with one another. You know as well as I that your sister was employed as the private clerk to the engineering director of the Anglo-French Submarine Railway—you in fact visited him on Tuesday night last. In such a position, she would have been privy to much information concerning the actual construction taking place."

"I suppose so," he conceded. "Then that fool of an engineer went to the police after all." Connigham chuckled. "I didn't think he would."

"He did not." Churchill exhaled a long stream of smoke. "You were spotted coming out of his hotel."

"I've been followed?" Connigham asked, thinking of his visit three days before to Jemmy.

"Yes," Churchill conceded. "For part of the time at least." He paused a moment to order his thoughts. "During the past few months there have been a number of unexplained accidents at the Tunnel. Men have been killed. The accidents were not accidents but cleverly concealed instances of sabotage. The perpetrators made use of information that could only have come from someone with access to private and confidential information contained in the engineering files."

Connigham thought about that for a moment. If it was true, why hadn't Bannerman mentioned such a connection? But, and the thought brought him up short, was Churchill suggesting that the Movement was involved?

"You think that the Fenians are responsible?" he demanded.

"Possibly. And so, your sister may have been responsible for obtaining information to aid the saboteurs."

Connigham digested that for a moment. "And that is what you meant," he asked slowly, "by knowing too much? How does that tie in with the Prods?"

"It is also possible that members of the Ulster Volunteers tried to force her to divulge information about the Tunnel for their own use."

"Why, for Christ's sake?"

"I admit that I am speculating," Churchill answered. "The Home Rule bill will pass in the coming session. There's no doubt about that. Perhaps they wish to divert attention by a spectacular series of incidents during the bill's reading or even to blame it on the Catholics. Certainly Germany would be only too happy to assist either side."

"Germany?"

Churchill nodded. "I will tell you a state secret, and I hope that you will be circumspect enough to keep it a secret.

"This past summer, as Home Secretary, I was responsible for seeing that the coronation was carried off without incident. There were rumors that the Irish Brotherhood might attempt to disrupt the ceremonies; possibly even kidnap the king. This last was of course absurd, but the chance could not be taken. Therefore Special Branch conducted a roundup of all known Fenian and other radicals of any persuasion. During the course of the investigations that followed, circumstantial evidence was developed that linked the German Embassy to the Fenians. At the time we suspected that only small amounts of money had been passed to the Fenians through members of the embassy staff. No arms were involved. Similar information was uncovered linking Germany to the radicals in the Ulster counties.

"Certain known Fenians and Ulstermen were left free, but a careful watch was maintained in the hopes that they would lead us to others not yet in our files. To some extent this phase of the operation has been successful."

He paused here and took a second folded sheet of paper from his pocket and laid it on the table, but kept a hand on it. "I have here a list of those names identified as Fenians."

My God, Connigham thought, he's like a spider, spinning webs within webs. "What do you . . . ?" He could not finish the sentence.

Churchill obliged. "I want you to examine this list and then tell me if you recognize any of the names. I then want you to go to each person and determine if that person had any connection with your sister's death."

Connigham pulled the chair closer to the table. He could not believe what he had just heard. "I don't understand."

"It is quite simple. In return for your assistance, I will guarantee you, in writing, safe passage from England to any country of your choice. You will be given a British passport in whatever name you choose and a thousand pounds to cover expenses." The First Lord held up a hand. "The money is not intended as a bribe, but to assist you in resettling. I ask only that you find the man who murdered your sister. Provide me with that information and he will be arrested and all charges and warrants against you will be dismissed."

Connigham shook his head. "This is ridiculous. If you are so certain it is one of these names, then why not arrest and question them yourself?"

"For two reasons, Firstly, I do not know that the murderer is on the list. But you are resourceful enough to establish whether or not he is. Secondly, I am certain that every name on the list would have what the mystery writers call an unbreakable alibi. In place of Sherlock Holmes, I have only you, Mr. Connigham."

"Scotland Yard has agreed to all this?"

"Scotland Yard has not. That is why certain precautions were taken in bringing you here. The men who arrested you did so unofficially and at my request."

Connigham reached for the list but Churchill kept his hand on it. "Do I have your agreement?"

"Hell, no. What kind of a fool do you think I am? I'd sooner hang than help this damned country."

"Your sister's murderer, Mr. Connigham. Would you have him go free?"

"Shit, what makes you think I believe you?"

Churchill sighed. "A man can be so many kinds of fool, there is no enumerating them. Mr. Connigham, you came back to England to find the man who murdered your sister.

You know it and I know it. Now, if you wish that man to go free . . .''

"How do you know it was a man?" Connigham sneered. "It could have been a woman."

Churchill studied him for a moment, his expression softening. When he spoke again, his voice had lost its superior tone and become far more sympathetic. "There was a piece of information, Mr. Connigham, which the police kept back from the press. It is often done to spare the family and the memory of the deceased."

"What information," Connigham whispered, fearing the answer.

"Your sister Margaret was raped before she was murdered. The bruises and, well, other indications, leave no doubt that she was raped." He watched Connigham's face drain of blood as the man stared at him in total shock. Churchill removed a silver-mounted flask from his coat pocket, uncapped it, and handed it to Connigham.

The tall Irishman stared at it a moment and shook his head. "All right," he said finally, his voice barely more than a whisper. "I agree to your terms."

Churchill pushed the piece of paper to him. Connigham unfolded it. The list had been handwritten and Churchill's messy scrawl was hard to read. There were ten names, arranged in alphabetical order. Finnigan's name was number three. His hands shook as he read the address opposite each name. When Churchill saw his eyes go to the bottom where a telehone number had been written, he said, "You may use that telephone number to reach me at any time of the day or night."

Connigham folded the paper and slipped it into his shirt pocket. Churchill handed him an envelope. "I suspect that you will need this. It contains two hundred pounds. Consider it an advance on the thousand."

There was nothing more to say and Churchill stood up. For a moment it seemed as if the First Lord would offer to shake hands, but he apparently thought better of it and went to the door. He paused with his hand upon the knob.

"It certainly should not be necessary to warn you against attempting to go your own way. You will, of course, be watched closely."

When Connigham did not reply, he opened the door and went out.

* * *

The wireless operator pressed the earphones tightly to his head with one hand and began to scribble on the pad. Von Dorn stubbed his cigarette out and went to stand behind him. When the message ended, the operator tapped an acknowledgment and spun his chair to the typewriter, rolled a sheet of fresh paper into the carriage, and pecked out a series of blocked codes. He then reread the typewritten sheet against the scribbled message form and handed both pieces of paper to von Dorn.

Von Dorn left the wireless room and hurried along the oak-paneled corridor to his office where he instructed Schram that he was not to be disturbed for any reason. He closed the door and unlocked his safe for the code book.

It took ten minutes to decode the message, headed by von Epping's personal cipher. As he did so, his mood swung from elation to annoyance.

158961 — AZ — 2 19.12.11 Steamer Karlsruhe *departed Kiel with shipment. Adverse weather west of 10° longitude. Encountered engine trouble. Will put in for repairs. Expected arrival 21.12.11 dawn. Standby reference TM 327—565, tower. Christmas Plan confirmed.*

Von Dorn scowled at the message. The first problem was to identify the landing site which, from the map reference letters, he knew to be somewhere on the east coast of England. Christ in Heaven! How was he to move two thousand rifles across England and then to Ireland? He banged his fist on the desk. Adverse weather. Longitude 10° was the Irish west coast. The British navy was still keeping up the pressure then, but for God's sake—England's east coast! Well, the Fenians would have to deal with their own damned transportation problems.

Von Dorn yelled for Schram and the man popped into the room immediately.

"Yes, Herr Oberst?"

"Have you located Finnigan yet?"

"No, sir. He is nowhere to be found. He was to have returned from Dover this morning but if he has done so . . ." Schram shrugged his meager shoulders.

"Then keep trying, damnit. In the meantime, go down to

the library and bring me the one-inch Ordnance survey map that covers area TM.''

Finnigan's disappearance was less a problem at the moment, he thought, than that of persuading the Fenians to cooperate. For the first time, he would be calling upon a major part of the network, all levels, clear to the Dublin Committee, for assistance—a sort of dress rehearsal. He could only hope that the bribe really would induce their cooperation. Von Dorn quickly wrote out a list of tasks for Schram to see to in his absence, then drafted a telegram to Boyle in Liverpool, notifying him that Eric Schneider would be arriving that evening.

Schram returned with the map and was sent out again with the telegram. Von Dorn unfolded the map to find that it covered an area on the Suffolk coast from Colne Point north to Woodbridge and East Bergholt to Orford Ness. The main port in the area was Felixstowe, and he saw at once why it had been chosen as a haven for the *Karlsruhe* with its simulated engine trouble. A merchant ship departing the Kiel Canal for ports along the European coast as far south as Spain would shape a course for the English Channel. Once out of the German Sea and into the Channel, haven was offered in both Hollesley Bay and Harwich Harbour, north and south of Felixstowe in the event of severe gales or, as in this case, mechanical trouble. Von Dorn found grid thirty-two, laid a ruler along its north-south axis, estimated seven-tenth of the grid square east and drew a line. He repeated the process along the east-west axis fifty-six, estimating five-tenths of the grid. The pencil lines crossed beside a black dot labeled Martello Tower. Perhaps a good choice after all. But he knew just how misleading a map could be.

Stretching northwest, the curve of Hollesley Bay would shelter them from heavy seas while the Martello Tower would provide an elevated point for signal lamps, perhaps the highest along the coast. He checked the map again. Two of the hundreds of towers that had been erected during the Napoleonic wars to provide early warning of French invasion forces were shown within the area of the map. The map reference singled out the southernmost in the Felixstowe area. The section of coast on which it stood was labeled golf links. Curious, he took down the 1910 edition of Baedeker's for Great Britain and looked up Felixstowe in the index. It was listed as page 499 but when he reached the page he found only a brief entry noting that it was a seaside resort sixteen miles from Ipswich, had a population of 5805, and had golf links at the mouth of the River Orwell. He checked the map again. There was an obvious misprint in the book. The links were shown on the map adjacent to the mouth of the River Deben. Von Dorn shrugged, knowing the Admiralty planners in Berlin would use the same Ordnance survey maps he did. It was probably the best plan that could be improvised in such a short time, and he could imagine the consternation his coded message of Sunday afternoon must have caused at von Epping's headquarters in Tempelhof and in the War Department. Since Sunday he had not been out of the embassy in Carlton House Terrace. Schram had set up a cot in the office for him, and he had practically taken over the wireless room to deal with the spate of details flashing between London and Berlin. The information that army troops were certain to be sent to the Tunnel upon the conclusion of the Home Office investigation had galvanized Berlin into agreement with his choice of dates—Christmas Day, when the majority of British army and naval officers would be absent on Christmas leave. And, as von Epping had promised, every request had been met without argument.

He reviewed again the plan that had been the catalyst for his hurried trip to Berlin the week before. The main thesis was that a small, armed commando unit could force a way into the Tunnel during the early morning hours of a Sunday or holiday when only a small maintenance crew was at work. If the Tunnel doors could be closed and their controls wrecked so that they could not be opened from the outside, the commando unit would be virtually impregnable for twelve to eighteen hours.

The idea had come to him while reading an article in a French aeronautical magazine reporting studies conducted in Russia by a scientist named Sikorsky. The Russian had been engaged in following up technical studies of wing loading and design begun by the Wright brothers in what was called a "wind tunnel." It had long been known that different shapes varied the speed of air flowing over a curved wing surface that produced the lift necessary to raise the flying machine from the ground. In a related series of studies, Sikorsky had shown photographically the effect of airflow through various types of tubes, indicating that a constriction at one end increased flow and therefore pressure. That in turn had reminded him of a study by another Russian scientist, Ziolkovsky, who had increased the efficiency of a rocket motor by introducing a nozzle at one end of the tube.

He had spent several days studying the plans Margaret had procured for him and applying the equations developed by Ziolkovsky in 1903 and refined by Sikorsky to calculate the effects of airflow through the Tunnel if suddenly compressed to pressures consistent with those found at the bottom of the English Channel.

The equations had shown that if the air within the uncompleted shaft could be compressed instantly to a minimum of 12,208.8 pounds per square foot, the result would be an almost solid mass of air smashing through the Tunnel. If the Tunnel remained closed at one end—that is, before being joined to the French shaft—and if the air mass could be given added impetus at periodic intervals, it would be forced up-Tunnel, destroying everything in its path—in effect, turning the Tunnel into a compressed air bomb. He had studied the steel doors closing off the end of the Tunnel, checking and rechecking their maximum specifications before concluding that they would not be sufficient to contain the air hammer, would in fact act as a diaphragm, causing the pressure inside the Tunnel to build until they blew out with all the destructive force of a bomb.

But to succeed, the plan depended upon several factors: first, it must happen before the breakthrough into the French section occurred or the effect of the air hammer would be dissipated long before it ran the full twenty-four-and-a-half-mile length of the Tunnel; secondly, a way had to be found to compress the air in the Tunnel instantaneously; third, they needed a way into the Tunnel without being detected; and finally, their intent had to remain undetected until they were inside and the steel doors had been closed. He had solutions ʿor all but this last condition and it worried him more than anything else. There were too many loose-mouthed Irish renegades involved—by necessity.

He threw down his pencil and went to the windows overlooking the Mall, where the wind was hurrying pedestrians along and thrashing the bare trees at the lowering sky.

The plan was a thing of mathematical beauty and as an

engineer he had no doubt that it would work if he could just control those four factors. Von Epping had been right in his assessment of the political situation. Agitation was mounting against the Tunnel among the public and in the press, even from Liberal papers. His plan of carefully escalated incidents was paying off handsomely. Many Liberal members were turning against their own party. So far it seemed that Asquith was holding the Irish to his side with the promise of the Home Rule bill, and their eighty-five members still gave the government a clear majority; but with the Tunnel destroyed, the outcry would be so great that even the cabinet would have to vote against resuming construction or see the government fall.

Yes, von Dorn thought. They were smart to do it now, when there was no hint of war, when Germany appeared thoroughly cowed after the summer's crisis. With the destruction that would be achieved, it could never be suspected that Germany had had a hand in the disaster. The addendum to the plan that he had added and that von Epping had so delicately approved would implicate the Fenians beyond a shadow of a doubt. The Home Rule bill must surely fail then, and conditions in Ireland would be perfect for raising guerrilla bands that would divert England's attention and troops from their alliance with France and Russia when Germany marched after the roads dried in the spring. A lovely Christmas present to the Kaiser—and to himself—it would be, and he grinned at the thought.

"God damn you for a fool, Finnigan," McDougal hissed. He glanced around the windswept lumber yard. "You'd better do it right this time or I'll personally break your bloody neck." Exasperated, he jammed his hands into his pockets and shook the rain from his hair. "Now you listen to me. I don't care what you have to do to get that envelope, do you understand?"

Finnigan grunted and stayed well out of reach of McDougal's big hands. He was wet, cold, and thoroughly cowed. And disgusted as well. To be sent down from London at a moment's notice and to have to put up with this abuse to boot was more than he could bear. By God, he thought savagely, if that flaming fool touches me again . . .

"I knows what you want," he muttered, "but don't lay a hand on me again, you bloody bastard."

McDougal started toward him but Finnigan scampered back. "I'm warning you. Don't touch me again."

McDougal stopped at the sight of the revolver. "Put that away, you daft fool," he hissed in contempt, "before I shove it down your dirty little throat."

Finnigan crouched back against a pile of lumber, the pistol still centered on McDougal's midsection. "No. Come near me again and I'll kill you, and that's the last I'll say on the subject."

McDougal gave in then, recognizing that time was being wasted. He would deal with the little weasel another time. "All right, lad, all right." His voice was placating now. "You needn't worry . . . unless you don't get that envelope."

"Aye. I'll get it. But it is your fault that I have to be here as it is. You had to show what a damned hero you are and turn the flywheel and save his bloody life."

"Enough," McDougal snapped. "I had no other choice, then. Now listen to me. It's a white envelope with a Belgian stamp upon it. The postmark will be Ostende. Do you understand that?"

"Belgian stamp, Ostende postmark. Aye, I understand. The same as we looked for in London."

"Then make certain you get it this time. He'll either have it with him, else it will be at his flat in Dover. When you get it, kill him."

Finnigan nodded. "And yer certain he'll be driving across the downs tonight?"

"Aye. An hour ago he said he would leave after the meeting. Don't miss this time!"

McDougal turned on his heel and stalked away, leaving Finnigan raging at him from the shelter of the lumber pile. My God, McDougal snorted, what he had to put up with at times. Dublin must be out of their collective minds, he thought, to put such trust in a man like Finnigan. If ever there was a fool and a coward, surely it was Finnigan.

Bannerman left promptly after the meeting. He had been at the Tunnel since four o'clock the morning before, with only two hours' sleep the entire time. It had been a long, tiring emergency meeting, and the strain of holding his temper, of forcing himself to deal calmly and correctly with the union officials had nearly driven him to total exhaustion. But, it had served. A strike had been averted, if narrowly. He knew that he had to get away from the works, so much so that he was willing to endure the five-mile drive across the stormy downs. Bannerman closed his office door and sprinted down the steps and across the half-submerged duckboards to the motor car. As soon as the door was closed, the chauffeur put the engine in gear and started toward the main gate. As rain slashed the canvas roof, Bannerman muttered a curse and shifted the Colt revolver to a more comfortable position in his belt.

He was too tired even to think about the events of the past two days. Instead, thoughts came and went in disjointed bits and pieces: the ravaged ventilator shaft, the blanket-covered bodies brought up from the conduit, the medical officers' shocked expression at their appearance. And then the endless postmortems that followed while he sat and listened, all the while thinking about the scorched lump of grouting now hidden under his desk until he could take it to London.

The gateman speaking to the chauffeur distracted him, and he opened his eyes to see that they had reached the main road. The motor started forward again and bumped over the last stretch of gravel to the badly eroded, metaled surface of the Dover Road. The motor accelerated and as they left the lights of the works behind, he leaned back again and closed his eyes.

The drive normally took fifteen to twenty minutes, but tonight the rain and the high winds held them to little more than ten miles an hour. They were blown from side to side, and at times the roadway was flooded straight across with water pouring into the drainage ditches. The motor car slowed and Bannerman peered ahead through the windscreen to see a lantern waving. The driver slid back the glass panel. "Looks as if ta road's out, guvnor," he shouted above the noise of the engine and the wind, and Bannerman cursed the thought of having to return to the works.

As they drew closer, they could see a barrier across the road and four men in rain slickers, three standing beside the barrier, the fourth waving the lantern. The men near the barrier were leaning on shovels and, as the motor came to a stop, they straightened and began to walk toward the car. The man with the lantern approached the chauffeur's side.

Bannerman heard him explain that the road had been washed out ahead and that they would have to wait until it was repaired or turn back. The peculiar action of one of the road gang caught his attention. The man sauntered toward the motor as if to examine it more closely, then apparently changed his mind and walked past. Another had come up beside the foreman and the third had gone to stand near the bonnet. Bannerman craned to see what had happened to the first as the foreman and chauffeur continued their discussion. Something bothered him. Perhaps it was an exhaustion-induced awareness of his surroundings, but the actions of the work gang were not those of men soaked to the skin and thoroughly miserable. Then he realized what it was that had bothered him. They had no portable shelter. No one in his right mind would stand beside the road all night in the driving rain without shelter. He turned just in time to see the first man glance back at the motor and start across the road.

Everything came together for him then, and with an oath, he yanked open the far door and jumped out. The man who was now in the middle of the road shouted as he saw Bannerman and reached for his gun. Bannerman dove toward the drainage ditch on the far side and landed waist deep in water. Above the rain and wind, he heard feet pounding on the metaled surface. There was a sudden gleam of the lantern as the foreman jumped away from the motor to see where Bannerman had gone; the lantern showed the first man running toward him with a pistol.

For an instant, shock held him and then he was moving instinctively and with deliberation as he had that day in the Transvaal. The Colt .38 revolver was in his hand, his thumb cocking the hammer back, and he aimed at the running figure less than twenty feet away. The revolver jerked upward in recoil, the man hesitated in midstep, staggered to his right, and sprawled headlong. But Bannerman had turned by then and fired at the man with the lantern, who was moving toward him from around the bonnet of the motor car, two quick shots in succession to drive him off.

It happened so quickly that the chauffeur had no time even to duck. The lantern sailed up and over the roof to smash on the pavement, the paraffin in the tank flaring to light the three men racing toward another motor car parked on the dark verge further along. He fired twice more at them, emptying the revolver.

Bannerman climbed from the ditch and trotted back to the man he had shot. His weapon was nowhere to be seen, and Bannerman knelt down and felt for a pulse in the throat but his fingers encountered a sticky mass of blood and tissue. A lucky shot, he thought. The man was dead. He got to his feet and swayed for an instant, then staggered forward, going to his knees and ducking his head until the dizziness passed. An arm went around his shoulders and the chauffeur helped him to stand; he tilted his head back to let the cold rain beat upon his face.

Between them they got the body to the motor and dumped it in the boot. The chauffeur went back once more to search for the weapon while Bannerman huddled in the seat, trying to stop his shivering.

The chauffeur returned with a Colt automatic pistol. It had slithered to the edge of the drainage ditch. Bannerman was absurdly pleased to note that the man's hands were shaking as badly as his own when he handed over the pistol. But he had fought the bastards off himself; and the more he thought about it, the more pleased he became. In the morning, he would telephone Sir Henry Keithley and demand a meeting of the Board immediately after the Christmas holidays. It was time he laid down a few ultimatums—and stuck by them this time.

chapter 25

The house was compressed between a deserted factory and a dilapidated warehouse, the single remaining casualty of too-rapid commercial development sixty years before. Sleet beat upon its sharply pitched roof and the wind whipped at broken windows. The brick had gone black with generations of smoke and what woodwork remained was a weathered gray, no trace of paint or color remaining. At one time, when this section of London had been a fine residential area, it had been a proud home, but that was before the soap factories, tanneries, scrap yards and, lately, the factories had sent the gentry fleeing south toward Croydon and Wimbledon. Connigham waited inside the deserted factory, leaning against the wall, and watched the house. He had been here since just after dawn, when he had paid off the cab at the end of the Old Kent Road and taken great pains on his roundabout journey northward into the maze of streets and roads that comprised Rotherhithe.

It had been difficult to find the address listed on Churchill's scarp of paper among the tenements beyond Barkworth Road. The house could only be approached through a narrow, refuse-strewn lane that twisted its way among the crush of flats and factories that had grown like a cancer across London south of the Thames. The former hunting grounds of England's magnificent kings were now the refuge of England's wretched poor.

He had recognized Finnigan instantly as he came through the lane an hour earlier, hurrying a frowzy, complaining woman along. They had gone inside but there had been no light or movement that he could detect. Finnigan had not changed, he saw even in the half light, nor would he have expected him to. Occasionally, Connigham left his window post to scan the approach to the factory. He was certain that

299

he was being followed, just as he was equally certain that he had managed to lose the man somewhere in the maze of streets. It made no difference either way. That ridiculous fool Churchill would soon discover he was not intending to play the game the way he was expected to.

A blanket had been stretched across the single window of the house and he could see a glimmer of light behind it. Once he heard a faint, drunken laugh followed by a woman's high-pitched giggle ending in a hiccup. That decided him, and Connigham went out and across the alley. Without ceremony, he kicked the door in. It slammed back against the wall, twisting off one hinge. Connigham stepped inside and the stench was appalling: a compound of ancient tanned leather, sweat, various bodily fluids, and alcohol. The single candle guttered wildly. The room was filthy beyond description, the bed against the wall little more than a pallet, a single blanket half covering the naked man and woman tangled together. In one corner, a stove glowed red hot and coal had fallen from the scuttle. Empty bottles lay everywhere.

The two people on the bed stared at him, both slack-mouthed with shock. The woman was middle-aged, hair badly dyed and stringy with dirt and oil. Even from where he stood he could see the dirt on her skin and the black cavity of her decaying mouth. The man was in little better condition. His skin was sallow and lifeless, eyes blank with alcoholism. He was thin, consumptive, and afraid.

Connigham crossed the room, snatched a small revolver from the floor beside the bed, and flung the woman's dirty shift at her. "Get out," he shouted and, when she did not move, grabbed a handful of hair and heaved her from the bed. She found her voice then and began to scream as he hauled her to the broken door, planted a boot on her backside, and catapulted her into the alley. She slithered into a puddle to lie still a moment under the lash of the sleet. Then she began to scream again, raving mindlessly, over and over, and the sound of her screeching caused the last vestiges of Connigham's sanity to snap. He dashed out into the rain. The woman saw him coming and tried to get to her feet, but the sleet defeated her and she flopped back into the puddle. Connigham snatched the ragged shift from her, twisted it around the revolver still in his hand, pressed the muzzle to her head, and fired. The report was curiously muffled, hardly more than a dull pop.

Her back arched in a single convulsion and went limp. Without bothering to see if she was dead, he went back into the house where Finnigan still lay on the bed in shock, not having moved an inch.

Connigham kicked the end of the bed, causing it to collapse, pulled the little man to his knees, and shoved the revolver into his face. For a moment, they stared at one another along the gun barrel. Finnigan's eyes black with fright, Connigham's face twisted with hatred.

"Tom Finnigan, old friend, do you remember me?"

When Finnigan did not answer but continued to stare, paralyzed with his terror, Connigham hit him with the revolver barrel.

"Michael Connigham," he told him. "Do you remember your old friend, Michael?" Finnigan's eyes closed, as if it were more than he could bear.

"Do you remember me?" Connigham demanded. "Do you remember me in Dublin and Belfast, Tom Finnigan? Do you remember how we grew up together, how I looked after you . . . ?"

The man's head jerked up and down once and his hands clutched feebly at Connigham's arms, but Connigham shoved him away in disgust. Finnigan lost his balance and fell against the bed, and as he did so, he made a curious mewling sound that enraged Connigham to the point where he lost complete control. He kicked him in the ribs, then kicked several more times as Finnigan scrabbled away until he was jammed between the bed and the wall, whimpering softly.

"Do you remember Margaret?" Connigham shouted and knelt in front of Finnigan. "Do you remember the little lass in the white communion dress that Sunday? Do you remember?" He was shouting now, squeezing the man's throat in his hands, the revolver on the floor forgotten. He realized that he was choking Finnigan, and he flung him away and sat back on his heels to watch as Finnigan struggled for breath. He could never remember such hatred as he had for this man who had once been a friend, who had betrayed him and murdered his sister.

His voice was calmer as he began to question the terror-stricken man. Why? Connigham demanded over and over as Finnigan gasped out the story of Margaret's love affair with the German, her work relaying information between the German and the Fenians at the Tunnel.

"And where have you been, Tom?" Connigham demanded when he finished. "Have you been hiding? I've been looking for you for days. Maybe you knew I was looking for you? Maybe someone told you?"

Finnigan made an attempt to sit up straighter but Connigham pushed him back.

"Were you hiding from me, Tom?"

"Ah no, Michael." Finnigan shook his head so hard it wobbled on his scrawny neck. "God, no. I did not know ye had come back. Name of God, I didn't. I was in Dover for the Movement," he went on, a trace of pathetic eagerness in his voice.

"And what would you be doing in Dover?"

"You see, Michael"—he tried to put an eager hand on Connigham's arm but it was knocked away—"Margaret was that upset over the boyos killed in the Tunnel explosion, she was going to the police—that's why the German killed her. But he made a mistake. There was an envelope with a stamp. Something about it can identify some of us . . . I was supposed to get it back from the man—"

"Margaret was going to the police? Why?"

"I told you. Because of all the men who were killed. They were mostly Irish."

Finnigan began to cough, a long choking cough that ended with a thin stream of spittle dribbling down his chin. Connigham looked away in disgust. It was incredible. Churchill had been right after all, and at the thought of the First Lord his anger grew again.

"You bloody little bastard. You're lying to me," Connigham screamed. "Why did you kill her?"

He slammed Finnigan's head against the wall.

"No! No!" Finnigan spat a piece of tooth in a spray of blood. "I didn't kill her," he whispered. "She was dead when I got there. The German did it. He sent me to . . ." The sentence ended in a thin scream as Connigham struck him across the bridge of the nose.

"You're lying," Connigham shouted and yanked him upright so that his head flopped on his shoulders. "You raped her and then you killed her. Why? Why?" He caught his breath and stared into the terror-filled eyes. "My God, Tom, you loved her. You wanted to marry her once. Why did you kill her?''

"Rape . . . my God, Michael . . . Michael. You must believe me. Niver did I touch her. Niver. Not even when I found her . . .'' He couldn't go on, and tears ran down his unshaven cheeks, his mouth twisting in a parody of grief and terror so that Connigham flung him away.

"It . . . it . . . were the German there. He killed her. She threatened him. Was going to . . . police. Tell them about . . . Tunnel and him . . . he killed her . . . by accident, he said. But . . . but . . .'' He could not force himself to use the word.

Connigham felt some of his anger draining away now. He stared at Finnigan for a long moment before he retrieved the revolver. He looked to see that two rounds had been fired from the five-shot nickel-plated Smith & Wesson. Connigham went to the doorway and stood staring at the woman's body huddled in the puddle, her face fallen into the mud, stringy hair spread around her shoulders and across one dirty cheek. He shivered a moment and turned back. Finnigan was hunched into himself, in a fetal position, shoulders jerking with sobs. He felt Connigham staring at him and raised a bloody face to stare back.

"What is his name?'' Connigham asked, his voice dull.

Finnigan made a pathetic attempt to retrieve some dignity by pushing himself into a sitting position and dragging a blanket to cover his naked body. "I . . . I . . . never knew his real name . . . only that he was German. He used a false name . . . Schneider. I . . . never knew . . . real name.'' Finnigan choked back a sob.

Connigham considered that for a moment. "Does Dublin know about this?''

Finnigan closed his eyes for a long moment and Connigham waited, not really wanting to hear the answer.

"Aye,'' Finnigan whispered.

"Do they know who he is?''

Finnigan nodded, his head wobbling on his shoulders. "Aye.''

And there it was, he thought. They did know and they had tried to keep him from finding out, knowing what he would do. Better that they had killed him that night. Finnigan had put his hands to his face and was sobbing, his body wracked with the violence of his fear.

Connigham raised the revolver and Finnigan looked up as the hammer clicked back. Finnigan's mouth started to open as Connigham pulled the trigger and the crash of the exploding cartridge echoed in the room. His old friend's head snapped back under the impact and his body shook once and was still.

Connigham turned without a sound and walked into the sleet, past the body of the woman, and down the alley into the deserted factory building. Outside, he could hear only the distant sounds of traffic. Once the high-pitched squeal of an engine whistle came to him. He went through the factory quickly, pausing at the doorway to survey the street beyond. The sleet was giving way to rain and heavy clouds seemed to press along Barkworth Road, framing the line of dirty yellow industrial buildings. He remained for several minutes, trying to cope with what he had learned.

Dublin did know, he thought. Knew all along. There was no possibility of his crossing to Ireland, Churchill would have seen to that. But there was someone in England who would know who the German was. Boyle. Arthur Boyle would tell him who had killed Margaret, and for a moment, he was overwhelmed with anger and sadness and longing.

For a long while, von Dorn had been afraid that the storm would become a full gale, but toward two o'clock the wind seemed to slacken and then veer to the northwest. He closed the rickety wooden door against the rain and went back into the foul-smelling interior of the Martello Tower and resumed his seat against the wall. Four of the twelve men present were sitting around the blanket playing an interminable card game by the light of the half-shuttered lantern. Several more were doing guard or observation duty, and the remainder were sleeping. The cardplayers' voices were subdued and they seemed to be playing by rote, stopping once in a while to listen to the wind keening about the dank tower and thrashing the surf on the shingle beach.

Von Dorn leaned his head back against the wall and closed his eyes. For a moment, the urge to let go, to allow the comforting warmth of sleep to cover him, was overwhelming. The vertigo began and he forced his eyes open and, to make certain, dug into his jacket pocket for the packet of cigarettes.

He lit one, wincing at the harshness. He had smoked so much in the past two days that the tissues of his mouth were raw.

He never slept well on trains, and eighteen of the past twenty-eight hours had been spent in a succession of railway carriages going from London to Liverpool to Ipswich and finally, after a two-hour wait, on to Felixstowe in a rocking, jerking narrow-gauge car with straight hard seats. He was only in time to engage a room at the Grand Hotel and snatch an hour's sleep before tramping three miles through the rain to rendezvous at the Tower with the four lorries arriving from widely separated points in England. Since then, they had waited out the hours in the damp, ice-cold Tower, whose only virtue was that it kept off the rain. He could sympathize with those long-dead coast watchers who, a hundred years ago, during the Napoleonic wars, had manned the towers that stretched along the English and Irish coasts, waiting for the invasion that never came.

Von Dorn cursed the rain and that ridiculous fool Boyle. Twelve men and four lorries for two thousand Mauser rifles! And those fools in Berlin! Only someone warm and dry beside a fire could have selected *this* as the landing site for the rifles. Looking for a map, seeing the golf links hard by the sea, Felixstowe must have seemed a logical choice. But the planners had not reckoned with the general inaccessibility of the town. There was only one main road leading to the coast from Ipswich, sixteen miles inland. Sandbars protected the beaches and the area was well populated with year-round houses. And to top it all off, there were two coast guard stations and a naval base within five miles. If the *Karlsruhe* were delayed past dawn, there would be no possibility of landing the shipment with safety. Von Dorn swore again under his breath.

A pair of legs dangled over the observation platform and a face peered down just as von Dorn sneezed violently, missing the first words.

". . . three long and two short. Directly out to sea. Gave 'em the recognition signal."

Von Dorn muttered an acknowledgement and blew his nose. He unhooded the lantern and checked his watch: 3:30 A.M. The men gathered up their mackintoshes and lanterns and followed him out into the rain. They stumbled down toward the beach, cursing the slippery shingle. Von Dorn found that the wind was so strong he had to lean into the rain beating in from Hollesley Bay. In response to his shouted instructions, the men dispersed up and down the strand at hundred-yard intervals and uncovered their lanterns. Von Dorn stationed himself in the middle.

Then began the interminable wait on the exposed beach as the rain drove at them in cold fury. Fifteen minutes passed before they were able to discern a light approaching from the sea. It flickered on and off as the boat rode up and down on the waves, and von Dorn shook his head, wondering at the stupidity of it all. That arrogant bastard Boyle had laughed in his face when he had told him of the orders from Berlin. Laughed at him! He had stood up then in cold fury and asked for his hat and coat, and the Irish bastard had realized that he had gone too far. The Tunnel meant nothing to Boyle; merely another chance to tweak the Lion's tail. But two thousand rifles and £300,000 in credits were another matter. And how he had screamed, von Dorn recalled with pleasure, when he was told that he would have to transport the rifles to Ireland himself. Von Dorn had not been able to resist the final touch, pointing out that it was the Fenians themselves who were at fault. Every ship off the Irish coast in the past months had found British gunboats waiting, informers no doubt responsible. If they wanted the rifles and credits, then that condition had to be met.

In addition, Boyle was to see to it that eight men from the list approved by Berlin—all with military training—were detailed to him at Dover. They were to be ready at dawn on the twenty-fourth and remain available as long as needed. He, von Dorn, would be in complete charge of the operation and those terms were to be made clear to McDougal, who was to take von Dorn's orders just as if they had come from Boyle or, better yet, from Dublin.

After a great deal of argument, Boyle had agreed. Von Dorn had taken pains to make him understand that unless his instructions were carried out to the letter, there would be no further assistance from Germany. He had waited then while a coded telegram was sent across the Channel to Dublin. The answer had come back in the early morning hours, confirming agreement to the terms. Von Dorn had then gone directly to the Exchange Station and taken the next train east toward Ipswich.

During a lull in the roaring surf, they heard shouts and a moment later saw a spill of lantern light. With a great rush, a lifeboat shot out of the darkness to ground on the shingle. For a moment, its stern swung as the frustrated waves sought to pull it back, but von Dorn and two others raced into the next surge of water, caught hold of the gunwales, and managed to hold it while the weary sailors climbed overside. Between them, they dragged it further up the shingle.

Without need for orders, the men fell to unloading the boat, and a few minutes later, a second lifeboat grounded a hundred yards away. Von Dorn worked back and forth between them, organizing and directing his working party, now augmented by the six-man crew of each boat, as, stumbling and cursing, they carried the heavy crates to the crest of the beach and down and across the boggy golf links to the maintenance road where the four lorries waited, engines ticking over because he did not dare chance one of them not starting up again.

This was the most dangerous phase of the operation, the point at which they were most exposed. Discovery would find them scattered across the beach and the golf links with no way to put up an effective defense in the dark.

It took an hour and a half to unload the forty seventy-five-pound crates of rifles and the fifty smaller metal boxes of ammunition from the boats and stow them away in the lorries. When the last crate was out of the second boat, von Dorn dismissed the two crews. He had a brief glimpse of one lifeboat cresting the surf line. He did not know if it had capsized or made it through, nor could he wait to find out. The last crate was lashed into place, and von Dorn went along the line checking the lorries. As each was released, it lurched forward along the soggy, potholed maintenance road. Von Dorn followed them on foot, knowing that if one became mired, it would have to be unloaded and abandoned. There would be no time to drag it free. But all four trucks reached the graveled Ferry Road safely.

It was still dark when von Dorn eased open the hotel's rear door into which he had earlier jammed a folded postal card. He crossed the hallway quickly and went up the stairs to his first-floor room. The fire had died to a bed of coals and, shivering violently, he added logs and plied the bellows until flames leapt toward the flue. Then he stripped quickly, threw his soaking clothes on the floor, wrapped himself in a blanket, and huddled before the fire in the Morris chair.

He must have slept, for a loud pop from a log startled him awake. The room was much warmer now and von Dorn got up, aching with weariness, and placed the washbasin on the floor; he wrung as much water from his clothes and coat as possible, then hung them before the fire to dry. He placed his boots on the hearth where they were within reach of the heat but would not scorch.

Still wrapped in the blanket, he got into bed and huddled under the feather tick. In spite of his shivering, he felt hot. His nose was running and he cursed his luck. All he needed to make his day complete was a bad cold.

Before falling asleep again, von Dorn opened his pocket watch: 6:21. He had left word the night before for the desk to wake him at eleven; that should give him sufficient time to catch the 12:55 train to London. He settled back, reviewing the events of the past few days. The lorries should be leaving Ipswich by now. Each would take a different route: one to Glasgow, one to Liverpool, one to Plymouth, and the last to Bath.

Ten rifles and two hundred rounds of ammunition for each had been repacked into a wooden crate addressed to a removal warehouse in Dover. It had been left at the local freight yard, where von Dorn had parted company with the last lorry and tramped across the town to the hotel. His final thought as he fell asleep was that it made little difference now if the police did find the lorries loaded with weapons. His needs were taken care of.

Dense cloud filled the sky, but it was not raining as yet in Liverpool. Conningham stood at the foot of the road, looking along to the great house at the end. The double iron gate was shut and lights shone in the windows. Occasionally, he saw the silhouette of a man pacing back and forth. A guard, he thought. He wondered if they suspected that he was coming.

He had taken the most direct route to Liverpool, the 10:35 train from Euston Station. Churchill's advance was at least allowing him to travel in style. The new suit and overcoat he had bought were as effective a disguise as any. He no longer looked like an unemployed laborer but rather like a mildly prosperous lower-middle-class businessman. When he tried to remember all that had occurred in the past two days, Connigham found there were great gaps of time for which he could not account, and he pressed his hands to his aching head and tried to stop the fierce pounding, but it was no use. The headache—which had never really stopped since Jemmy's wife had struck him with the iron bar—had begun in earnest shortly after the train left Euston. He had endured the long ride in agony and could recall only a canal that had paralleled the right of way for many miles and innumerable country towns and stations, one after another, each marked with signboards made illegible by the train's speed.

Connigham kept close to the shrubbery as he retraced his steps to the opposite end of the road. The long blocks in this section of Liverpool which surrounded Princes Park were graced with the houses of upper middle-class merchants and professional men. Each mansion was bordered by a high wall, and entry could be gained only through the wrought-iron gates which had been erected in imitation of lordly manor homes.

He had scouted the back of the house which Boyle occupied before the cold December twilight had failed. Where many of his neighbors had allowed trees and shrubbery to grow up next to the wall, Boyle had made certain that his gardeners kept the foliage cut well back; too many secrets, Connigham thought bitterly, to chance a burglary. He studied the eight-foot brick wall. Bare of overhanging foliage, it stood in stark contrast to those of its neighbors. The garden wall belonging to the house next door was more inviting.

He found the tree he had marked earlier and, with a quick glance about to insure that he was unobserved, Connigham jumped and caught a branch protruding from the main trunk. He pulled himself up, climbed two branches higher, and eased himself to the top of the wall, peering down at the empty yard beneath. A formal rose garden had been pruned so severely that only stumps showed. Graveled walks ran in and out of shadows cast by scattered oaks and beeches and only one light showed high in the back of the house: a servant's room? As he watched, a figure appeared, drew curtains, and the glow faded.

Connigham dropped silently to the yard and waited to see if there was a guard dog. There was not, and he made his way along the wall in the shadows of the whippy brush. He reached the wall common with Boyle's mansion and pulled himself up to where he could observe the rear garden. Here, too, gardeners had pruned everything back for the winter. The clouded sky was pale with the yellowish glow reflecting from millions of the city's gas and electric lamps. The house was a blur to his right, pinpointed by lighted windows on the ground floor. Connigham eased down into Boyle's garden and the concealment offered by a massive beech. After a few moments during which nothing moved, he trotted across to a small pergola some fifty feet from the main structure. He could now see that the house was three stories high, the type of gingerbread Victorian structure that had sprouted in the 1880s and '90s as the newly rich felt the need to display the wealth flowing from railroads, shipping, textiles, banking, and all the other fruits of imperialism and industrialization. The first and second floors were surrounded by balconies and a continuing flight of steps led from one story to the next. Connigham ignored the steps; they were too accessible, too liable to be attached to an alarm system. Boyle was not the kind to take an unnecessary chance.

Only one light glowed above the ground floor and that was on the top. A porch half encircled the house, and by climbing onto the railing, he could reach up and grasp the wainscotting of the balcony above and pull himself up. He felt certain that Boyle would have his room on the first floor; the man was so fat that to climb further could very well place his heart in serious jeopardy. He made his way along the balcony, peering through windows until he found a service cupboard. The window was locked but by inserting his knife blade between the sashes he was able to slip the catch. He swore softly when he ran a sliver of wood into his thumb.

Connigham eased through the window and, shielding his torch with two fingers, examined the room. Laundry was stacked in bags on the floor, and cleaning equipment—sacks of soap powder, mops, a vacuum cleaner, and dusting cloths—filled the shelves. He shut off the torch and opened the door a crack.

A wide landing encircled the entire floor. A massive stairwell filled the center and oriental rugs woven into long runners covered the parquet. The walls were covered with polished oak paneling and two feeble green-shaded gas jets cast just enough light to heighten the feeling of richness. Boyle had come a long way on the backs of Irish workers, Connigham thought.

He pulled a bag of laundry to the door and settled down to wait. His watch showed ten past one. Rain began to patter against the window and he shivered a bit, but the cupboard was warm enough and gradually the shivering left him. Occasionally he heard the murmur of voices below or the sound of a door opening and closing. Otherwise, the house remained silent.

At two o'clock, the sound of a door opening below was followed by the rising swell of voices. Connigham jerked awake from the doze he had fallen into and leaned to catch what was being said, but the murmuring passed out of his hearing. A few minutes later a door slammed and he heard someone mounting the stairs.

An exceedingly attractive woman paused at the top and called back down, then turned with a flourish of skirts and an annoyed sigh and went along the corridor to the end, where she disappeared into a bedroom. Boyle certainly had come a long way. But the woman was an unexpected complication; if Boyle made for her room, he might well remain there all night.

As if in response to the thought, Boyle himself puffed into sight on the stairs. He paused at the top to catch his breath and shut off the electric lights below. Then he stared along the corridor a moment, muttered something, and gave his head a rueful shake before lumbering into what Connigham assumed was his room and closing the door. Ten minutes later, the fan of light along the floor disappeared. Connigham settled back to wait until his watch showed three o'clock.

He pushed the cupboard door open and listened carefully, then stepped out into the hall, pulling the door to but leaving it unlocked. He stayed close to the walls where the floor was less likely to creak and moved to the top of the steps. Hall lights were on below, but the rest of the house appeared to be in darkness. Connigham went down two steps and spotted the legs of a guard. The man was slumped on a divan, arms folded and sound asleep.

Boyle's door was unlocked. Connigham eased himself into the room and stood pressed against the door. A tiny gas jet glowed at the far side of the room, casting sufficient light to see Boyle asleep on his back, mouth open in a muted snore. The room was heavy with dead air and the odor emanating from the chamber pot beside the night table. A book lay open on the bedstand and as he crossed to the bedside he saw that it was a Bible. Connigham snorted.

Boyle's pendulous cheeks had collapsed into flaccid masses that quivered with every snore. The sight was disgusting, doubly so to Connigham. The man had lied to him and tried to kill him. He took Finnigan's nickel-plated revolver from his pocket and leaned forward to jam the muzzle into the gaping mouth. Boyle woke with a start. The pressure of the revolver against the roof of his mouth made him scrabble back gagging until his head rapped the intricately carved headboard.

Boyle's eyes were open but filled with sleep and it was a few moments before he understood what was happening. He gurgled around the barrel and his eyes went wide with fear as he made out Connigham's features. Fully conscious now, his face turned dark with a sudden rush of blood, and Connigham eased the pressure lest he have a stroke. Boyle struggled for breath, but when he tried to turn his head away, Connigham pushed the revolver against his teeth.

"Arthur, easy, easy. You and I must have a bit of a talk now," Connigham soothed him. "If I take the gun away, you'll not be yelling and carrying on, will you?"

Boyle managed to shake his head, and Connigham, still smiling, withdrew the revolver and rested the muzzle on the bridge of his bulbous nose. Boyle's eyes crossed and his forehead went slippery with huge beads of perspiration.

"My God, Connigham," he managed to choke out at last. "My God . . ."

"Yes, Arthur?" Connigham's voice was polite.

Boyle swallowed several times and closed his eyes. "Michael, what the hell . . . are you doing?" His voice was broken and his whispers little more than gasps.

"I've come all the way down from London, Arthur, to talk just to you."

"You were . . . you were . . ." he began, but his voice failed.

"Supposed to return to the States? Is that what you're trying to say, Arthur? Surely you are not unaware that your boyos failed and that both of them are dead. Why, I understand there is even a very large reward for me. Was that your idea or Dublin's, Arthur?''

When Boyle did not answer, Connigham nodded. ''I thought as much. Who told you I was in England? Was it Emily?''

He regarded the terror-stricken man on the bed a moment with a half smile. ''You know, Arthur, I heard a very disturbing rumor in London. The rumor says that you know the name of the man who killed Margaret. That you helped to cover up the murder, that you approved of it and''—he paused and smiled in a friendly way—''perhaps even ordered Margaret to be killed?''

Boyle moaned, and when he tried to shake his head Connigham rapped him on the forehead hard with the revolver barrel. ''No, don't even think of moving, Arthur.''

Boyle's mouth worked as he gasped for air. ''No, Michael. No, as God is my witness, I did not order your sister killed.''

''Ah, but the man said you did.''

''He's lying,'' Boyle gasped. ''The—''

''He also said that you were after killing me because I wouldn't do as I was told.''

''I had no choice,'' Boyle mumbled. ''No choice. They told me to do it. They said that as you wouldn't leave, you were to be killed. You were a liability—''

''To whom, Arthur? To the Movement? No, I think not. But to you, yes! Because you knew that I would find you out and when I did, I would kill you.''

''Michael, believe me, I knew nothing of Margaret's death until the next day.'' Tears were running down Boyle's flabby cheeks and his mouth drooled saliva in his fear. ''Mother of God, Michael, you've got to believe me. I didn't know!'' He gasped as Connigham ground the muzzle into his forehead.

''You lousy bastard, you're lying again. You knew who did it and you ordered them to. Finnigan told me before I shot him.''

''Finnigan! The dirty little son-of-a-bitch! He lied to save his own life.''

''Ah, that's where you are wrong,'' Connigham chuckled. He was enjoying the man's terror. ''Tom Finnigan was a dead man the moment I found him and he knew it. He had nothing to gain by lying.''

"Finnigan, the little shit. He was always a liar. He—"

"He told me the truth," Connigham replied mildly. "You are the one doing the lying."

"No, Michael, no. I'm telling you the truth." Boyle was blubbering now and his words were blurred in a welter of sobs.

"Then who," Connigham snarled, "did kill her?"

The question brought Boyle up short and he went rigid. "Tell me," Connigham said quietly. "It may be your only chance, man."

The implacable face above him offered no hope, no sympathy, yet there was ingrained in Boyle, by a lifetime of conspiracy, the need to remain silent.

"I don't know," he began but the words were choked off in agony as Connigham jammed the revolver barrel into his mouth and struck him in the throat with his hand. He hit him a second time, slamming his fist against the collarbone and Boyle's body convulsed, half rising from the bed. His eyes glazed with pain.

"I'll ask you again," Connigham told him in the same quiet voice. "Give me the name of the man who killed Margaret."

Connigham became a blur as tears of pain filled Boyle's eyes, but he managed to control his terror, keeping it at bay, something to be considered, recognized, but no more. He could see clearly what would happen if he gave Connigham the name he wanted. The entire enterprise would come crashing down. Years of planning, of skulking and hiding, of fighting for what he believed right, would be dashed to pieces in an instant. Yet he knew that he was not strong enough to resist Connigham much longer. If he could only scream loud enough to attract those damned, worthless guards . . .

Connigham was watching him so closely that he could almost read Boyle's thoughts as determination crept across the flabby, sweat-soaked face, and for a moment he could admire the man Boyle had once been. He forced the revolver a bit further into Boyle's mouth as a reminder, and Boyle knew then of a certainty that he was finished.

"Who did it, Arthur? Tell me and it will be all over."

Boyle closed his eyes a moment and breathed a prayer, something he had not done in years. He was finished, whether he told Connigham what he wanted to know or not. But the man's insanity could not be allowed to destroy Boyle's life's work. He opened his eyes and looked into Connigham's pitiless face, no longer afraid now. Connigham withdrew the revolver to allow him to speak and Boyle spat and opened his mouth to scream.

Connigham whipped the pillow from beneath his head and jammed it down over his face. He tossed the revolver aside and held the pillow down with both hands, mouthing obscenities, totally out of control, as Boyle struggled, tearing at him with impotent hands, legs and body thrashing until, with one final, convulsive heave, he was still. Connigham held the pillow tight a few minutes longer, the last of the anger draining from him, then he pushed himself from the bed and staggered to a nearby chair and slumped into it, face in his hands, gasping for breath. When he raised his head, Boyle's crumpled form mocked him.

How long he sat there, mind a blank, he never knew. Connigham was past even self-recrimination. He had killed the only man who knew the name of the German who had murdered his sister. After a while he got up and retrieved the revolver. He did not bother to look at Boyle's body but went out into the hall, half hoping someone would see him.

The cupboard door was still unlocked, as he had left it, and he closed it behind him and climbed out through the window and stood on the balcony, breathing deeply of the cold night air. The headache was back again and much worse, and he rubbed his temples gently.

The rain had stopped and clouds glowed softly with the city lights. He stumbled to the corner of the house, climbed down, and crossed the lawn the way he had come, moving as if in a trance.

He huddled on a bench in the Lime Street Station, staring at one of the huge Witchurch clocks, willing the hands to move faster. The interior of the railway station was filled with stinging coal smoke and the noise was unbearable. His head throbbed; the pain was agonizing and he shut his eyes, trying to force it to disappear.

When he opened them again, it was as if a great silence had enfolded the station for a moment; a train moving to the end of the barrier blew out a gout of steam that expanded with a curious roiling motion toward the soot-stained arc of the glass roof. A man in a dark suit, umbrella tucked under his arm, one hand gesturing, gave him an incurious glance. A newsboy threw down a twine-wrapped bundle of papers, a guard chalked a notation on a schedule board, and the noise erupted around him again.

What is the matter with me? he wondered and clasped his hands to his head, enduring. Emily's name kept running through his mind but, for some reason, the face was Margaret's.

Connigham pounded on the front door of the Brompton Square house, ignoring the shocked looks of two passersby. A maid flung the door open, her expression of angry annoyance disappearing when Connigham thrust her aside and stormed into the hallway. He spun, grasped the maid by the arm, and shook her hard.

"Where is your mistress?" he shouted, but the girl was so frightened that she began to babble. He pushed her away and she fell against a table, knocking a delicate gold-washed vase to the floor where it shattered. Connigham was halfway along the hall when the butler burst out of the pantry and saw him. His hand shot to his jacket but Connigham was on him in two strides, grasping his coat collar, whirling him off balance, and flinging him onto the floor. As the butler struggled to his feet, Connigham kicked him viciously in the temple with his heavy boot. The man flopped and lay still, and he kicked him again.

Connigham took the steps two at a time and slammed open the door to Emily's room. She had been reading by the fireplace and at the sound of the scuffle below had started out of her chair. Connigham's backhand slap knocked her across the bed and, without a word, he straddled her body, slapping her back and forth across the face.

"You knew all along who killed Margaret, didn't you?" he bellowed. The attack had taken her completely by surprise, and in a daze, she sought to understand the words Connigham roared at her.

He shook her hard. "You knew who murdered Margaret, you little bitch, but you didn't tell me. If I had come back after that first time, who would have been waiting here for me, some of Boyle's people? Or that damned poor excuse for a butler?"

He was shouting at her, shaking her so hard that the pain was driving everything else from her mind. It was impossible to think coherently, and his words made no sense.

Connigham flung her away and she collapsed onto the floor. He stood over her, gasping for breath. Emily had not yet dressed and was wearing only a thin robe which had torn as he pulled her from the bed, exposing one slim leg to the thigh.

He leaned against the bedpost, trying to regain control of himself, but it was no use. He flung himself around with a groan. He had loved her, the little bitch, and she had betrayed him, had even conspired in Margaret's death. He started for her, but she scrambled away, pushing herself around the bed. He lunged and she got to her feet, twisting and fighting, and ran across the room. Connigham stumbled on a fold of rug and fell across the table.

Emily snatched up a heavy brass candlestick and swung it down with all her strength, but Connigham saw it coming and began to twist away so that it missed his head and splintered the table top. She struck again but this time the heavy brass was almost too much for her, and instead of killing, the blow raked the back of his head. Connigham slid off the table onto the floor, screaming with the indescribable pain which blinded and deafened him, paralyzing him so that he was conscious of nothing else.

Emily leaned on the table, choking and shaking with fear. Blood seeped from his head to soak the pale blue carpet, and she gagged and staggered from the room for help. The hall was deserted and, hanging onto the railing, she stumbled to the stairs and started down. Halfway along, she tripped on the hem of her torn robe and fell, tumbling over and over down the steps. A maid peered into the hallway, gasped when she saw her mistress sprawled at the bottom of the staircase, and fainted.

Groaning, Emily pulled herself up. Her vision was blurred and she was having trouble making her limbs obey. Her first thought was for the butler, and she stumbled down the hall toward the pantry where she found him. She went to her knees beside his body, hands buried in her face, sobbing. After a moment, Emily touched the blackened bruise on his temple. The skin was jellylike beneath her fingers, and she vomited hoarsely in great wracking heaves.

When she had finished, she got to her hands and knees and
waited, panting; then, with the aid of a chair, she struggled to
her feet. Emily had impressions of the room whirling about
her as she staggered along the hall to the library and collapsed
into the desk chair, her empty stomach retching violently.
When the spasm eased, she found herself shivering uncontrol-
lably, so violently that she slid from the chair and lay moaning softly on the floor while the tremors shook her like
convulsions.

A watery beam of sunlight had penetrated the velvet drap-
eries and her eyes were drawn to it as it made its snaillike
way across the carpet. Visions of Dublin, her husband, her
father, of Michael Connigham were inexplicably caught in
that glowing bit of molten gold. Michael as he was all those
years ago in Dublin, when he had appeared from the hostile
crowd to beat up a drunken bully who had climbed onto the
platform screaming obscenities at her and at the suffrage
movement for which she spoke. He had split the man's head
with one blow and, judging the temper of the crowd and the
constable wading toward them, had yanked her from the
platform.

It was during the long walk through the rainy spring evening to her home in Phoenix Park that she learned he was on
the run for the killing of two men in Belfast and why. Charles
was away in London on ministerial business, most of the
servants were on Easter holiday, and it had been simple
enough to spirit him into the old, disused carriage house.

The memories slipped past as if on a cinema screen, but
flowing smoothly from one to another until, suddenly, the
pleasant gold haze vanished and the pain came flooding back.
She could stand now, but shakily, bewildered, still partly
caught up in the glow of memory. The telephone had been
knocked askew and she straightened it before lifting the receiver.

Connigham rolled onto his side, hands pressed to his head.
He managed to get to his feet and stagger drunkenly to the
washbasin. It was empty and, holding a towel to his bloody
head, he shuffled along the corridor to the stairs.

The butler still lay sprawled at the far end of the main hall.
A maid crouched away, hands pressed to her mouth, when
she saw Connigham on the stairs. He ignored her and wob-

bled toward the front of the house. Emily saw him through the open library door. The telephone receiver was in her left hand and she stopped speaking instantly. Connigham stepped inside and shut the door, his pain forgotten for the moment.

"Who is he, Margaret?" he asked, his voice soft, almost caressing.

Margaret's name registered with Emily even through her fear. "I'm not Margaret, Michael." She closed her eyes a moment at the realization that he was completely insane. "I'm Emily. Don't you remember?"

Connigham smiled. "Of course. I know who you are. Please tell me his name?"

She took a deep breath. Connigham stopped just inside the doorway. Her husband had always kept a gun of some kind in the desk drawer, but her hands were shaking too badly to reach for it. "Whose name, Michael?" She tried to force a smile, to gauge his reaction. For a moment he looked confused, and her panic receded a bit. She needed time to calm down, to regain control.

"I . . . I . . ." He took a deep breath, then suddenly sprang across the room at her before she could blink. He brushed the telephone away and his hands found her throat. She screamed and he dragged her forward across the desk, choking her. He twisted and pressed her down, edging around the desk so that her back was jammed against the blotter. A great storm of sound filled her head and a red haze suffused her vision. The pressure of his hands eased, and she gasped and coughed and then he was choking her again. He did it twice more before he whispered, smiling to her.

"I want his name, Emily. You knew all along. You betrayed me and now I'm going to kill him."

"Oh, God," she moaned and tried to move away from the press of his body, digging feebly at his rough hands around her throat.

"Please, Margaret. You must tell me his name. I must find him." His breath rasped against her face, and his voice had become a wheedling whine. His hands closed about her neck again, squeezing together and once more the searing pain tore at her chest.

His voice was stronger, steadier when he spoke again. "I can keep this up for hours, Emily, and worse. In the end, you'll tell me. Spare yourself the pain. Just tell me who raped and murdered my sister?''

The word "rape" did not at first register with her. *Rape.* *He* had done that to her? The hands began to clamp down again but she gasped out, "No." The hands moved away.

"Michael . . ."

"Just his name, Emily."

"Von Dorn," she gasped finally. "Eric von Dorn. He . . ."

Connigham smiled down at her, brushing a hand gently across her cheek. "And you wouldn't be lying to me now, would you, Margaret darling?"

She shook her head, terror-stricken at the insanity in his eyes. "Oh, God, no, Michael. I didn't . . . I . . . he is the . . . attaché . . . military attaché at the . . . German Embassy."

Germany! It was too much for Connigham, and the last thing he remembered was choking her, screaming at her.

Connigham found himself on Brompton Road. He leaned against an iron railing and stared about him. Several people were watching, and a man was asking if there had been an accident. He took a deep breath and forced a smile and thanked the man, trying to explain that he had slipped on the ice and cracked his head. The man took charge then, telling the others gathering about that he would see to him. He led Connigham to the road, flagged a hansom cab, and gave the driver an address in Sloane Street.

"We'll have my doctor look at you, old man. Fix you up in an instant, he will." The man smiled and continued to talk, but Connigham heard only a disjointed word and phrase as the pain ebbed and surged. He was barely conscious of the horses' hooves and the man's worried voice urging the driver to a faster pace.

The cab stopped at last, and he was helped up an endless walk that danced and tilted beneath his feet. A white-gowned woman opened the door, and he was taken into a dim hall smelling vaguely of disinfectant. Sights and sounds whirled about him: a man with a pointed beard, a narrow doorway that loomed and receded, a hard white table, helping hands tugging at his overcoat and suit jacket, a gasp of surprise, the sting of a needle, and nothing more until the pain began to recede.

*   *   *

He tried to move and the pain stabbed at him again. Two men were talking; one, with the pointed beard, gestured toward him, the other he thought he recognized as the man who had come to his aid.

Connigham heard a word and suddenly the pain seemed less important. He was beginning to understand what they were saying.

". . . have any choice. Must be reported to the police."

"I agree," he heard the other say. "Even though he looks like a gentleman, there is no telling how he came by that blow to the head."

Through slitted eyelids he saw that the man who had brought him to the doctor's office was holding the revolver. Good God, he thought, if they called the police, it was finished. Churchill would have what he wanted but he . . .

He groaned faintly and both men came to the table. The doctor reached a hand to slip back an eyelid and he struck out, catching the doctor in the throat with a doubled fist. He came off the table so quickly that the other man had no time to react before Connigham jammed him back against the cabinets. The man gasped and swung a blow with the revolver but missed, and his momentum carried him forward to sprawl across the examining table. The resurgent pain nearly caused Connigham to black out as he pushed himself away from the cabinets. His hand encountered a heavy glass jar and he swept it up and smashed it against his benefactor's head.

The noise brought the sister rushing into the room, but Connigham was waiting for her. He caught her around the waist, shoved her face against the table, and hit her hard at the base of the skull.

Connigham leaned on the table then, breathing hard, fighting to control the pain. His hand brushed the ice pack that had fallen away and he pressed it to the gash. After a few moments, he was able to straighten up and the room remained stationary. He eased himself down on the table and waited until the pain became a dull ache. After a while, the medicine cabinet attracted his attention and he got up gingerly. He found some pain killers—heroin tablets—and a tin of ether and placed these on the counter, then tore a towel into three strips. He soaked each one with ether and tied them about the faces of the three unconscious people, then he secured their hands and feet with bandages. He needed time, time to figure out what to do next, time to let the pain in his skull diminish. As it was, each movement was agonizingly painful. When he finished, he swallowed one of the tablets—he did not dare take more—and staggered along the hallway to the front door and eased it open. The surgery hours were embossed on a brass plate fastened to the door, and he saw that patients were not scheduled to call for several more hours. He shut and locked the door and went back to the surgery, eased the sister onto the floor, and with a groan lay down on the table and closed his eyes.

When he awoke, Connigham could see through the narrow window that it was approaching dusk. He raised his head tentatively and, while the slashing pain was still there, it was no longer as intense. He sat up then, slowly, and felt carefully around the back of his head. The doctor had shaved away hair and cleaned and bandaged the long gash. The bandage was stiff with dried blood but at least it was dry. He swung his feet to the floor and stood, swaying a moment. The doctor grunted and wriggled and Connigham could see that he was awake and had been working at the bandages. When he rolled the man over, the doctor glared. Connigham found the ether tin and poured more of the sharp-smelling fluid onto the gag. The doctor tried to twist away, but Connigham held his head until he was quiet again, then poured more onto the gags of the other two and stood up. Dizziness assaulted him, and he had to hang onto the surgical table for several moments before it passed.

Someone rapped at the front door, startling him. He looked at the wall clock beside the medicine cabinet. It was four o'clock. He had slept for nearly two hours. Connigham found his revolver where it had fallen onto the floor and went into the corridor. Darkness had filled the narrow hall and it was impossible for him to be seen from outside. He went along to the back of the house, found the kitchen, and beyond it a small pantry with a door that opened out onto a narrow alley. He studied the alley in the gathering gloom. Blocks of flats formed two anonymous walls on either side of the cobbled drive. He went down the rickety steps and along to the street, wondering how long it would be before someone took it into his head to go for a policeman to find out why the doctor had not yet opened his surgery.

Time was running out. But enough yet remained. He had the name. Von Dorn. For a moment he had to think why the name was so important to him.

chapter————26

V*on Dorn eased down into the bath and groaned with* pleasure as the heat eased his bone-deep ache. He coughed, a deep racking cough that stretched and hurt his lungs. When the spasm had passed, he breathed deeply and huddled further down into the water seeking warmth. These damned English, he thought. Why in hell had they never thought it necessary to heat bathrooms. He lay there until the water cooled, reveling in its warmth, trying to forget the misery of the past forty-eight hours.

When he shouted for Schram, the little sergeant hurried in with a warmed towel and von Dorn went along to his rooms while Schram drained and cleaned the tub for the next guest and fetched along his damp clothes. The fire was roaring and von Dorn drew a chair close and lit a cigarette. When Schram came in, he poured a brandy without needing to be asked and then went about unpacking the suitcase.

The telephone burred, startling him, and von Dorn realized that he had almost fallen asleep. He turned to see Schram beckoning urgently. Von Dorn took the telephone receiver and before he could say a word, Emily's voice, shrill with hysteria, came on.

"Thank God, thank God. I've gotten to you in time, Eric. Oh, my God. Listen to me. He's killed my butler and tried to kill me."

"Emily," von Dorn snapped. "Get hold of yourself. You are not making sense."

He heard her gasp and there was a moment of silence. "Eric." Her voice was calmer now. "You must listen. You must understand. There is not much time. He is here now. He's murdered my butler and almost killed me."

"Who, for the sake of God?" he shouted. "Who? Make sense."

"Michael Connigham."

"And who is Michael Connigham?" he roared, struggling to recall the name.

"Eric, listen to me. He is the brother of the woman you . . . Margaret Doyle's brother. I told you about him at Lord Wolton's. He's gone quite mad. He knows what happened that day. . . ."

"Emily"—he forced himself to remain calm—"are you quite certain about this? You haven't made a mistake?"

"Eric, listen to me. Arthur Boyle is dead. He was murdered last night in his own bed. I received a telephone call just this morning. Then Michael came. . . ." She broke down a moment, then caught herself. "He is upstairs in my bedroom now. I struck him . . . I . . . oh, no, God . . ."

There was a long pause in which, faintly, he could hear her voice. Then something banged against the telephone and he heard a thin scream. There was an incoherent shout and the line went dead.

Von Dorn stared at the receiver before replacing it on the hook, unable to think clearly for a moment. What in the name of God was happening? It did not make sense. Someone was . . . the screaming. . . . He made to pick up the phone again and call the police, but his hand released the instrument. My God, how could he do that? They would demand his name, want to know why she had telephoned him. And she had said that Arthur Boyle was dead. Was Margaret's brother responsible for that as well?

He looked up to see Schram staring at him. "Is there anything the matter, Herr Oberst?" he asked politely.

Von Dorn struggled to force his exhaustion under control. He had planned to stay the night in London, then start in the morning for Dover. But that was impossible now. If Connigham knew who he was, where to find him . . . had she said that Connigham knew who he was? It made no difference; he could not chance it. Von Dorn made his decision quickly. There was a seven o'clock train from Victoria. He would take that to Dover.

"Schram," he snapped. "I have changed my mind. I will leave tonight. Lay out my traveling suit and pack a bag. Include my stoutest pair of walking boots. I wish to take the evening train tonight, and we have less than—" He went to the mantelpiece and looked at his pocket watch. "Less than seven hours. Snap to it, man!"

If Schram was surprised, he did not allow it to show but went swiftly about the process of selecting clothes and re-packing the single leather bag, while von Dorn shaved and dressed himself. Thirty minutes later, he locked the door behind them and followed von Dorn as he hurried down the hall to the lift.

They spent two hours at the embassy clearing up immediate affairs and selecting documents for destruction. Von Dorn wanted nothing left behind that would be in any way com-promising. It was not likely that they would be returning; he had von Epping's implied assurance of a better posting and perhaps a promotion as well. He hesitated over the lists of German and Fenian agents, then dropped both onto the pile to be destroyed along with his code book. If necessary, both could be resupplied to his successor by Berlin, but he did not see that they would be needed. The agents were to remain incognito until called upon.

At four-thirty von Dorn hurried down to inform the ambas-sador, who was preparing for a state dinner later that evening, that he had been recalled to Berlin a day earlier than expect-ed. If the ambassador suspected that there was more to it than a change of travel plans, he did not inquire. He preferred to face his opposite numbers in the Foreign Office with a clear conscience. The ambassador contented himself with wishing von Dorn a happy Christmas.

Von Dorn breathed a sigh of relief and returned to his office to give Schram his final instructions: he was to remain in the embassy for the night and take the morning train to Dover as planned. As an afterthought, he opened the safe and took £400 in £20 notes and made certain that he had a spare clip for his service Luger in his pocket.

It was after five when he left the embassy, giving the taxi driver Sloane Square as his destination. There would just be time for dinner and a bit of relaxation. It was also a private place from which to telephone Emily's house in Knightsbridge to try and determine what had happened there.

Connigham surveyed the front of the German Embassy at number 9 Carlton House Terrace from beneath the statue of John Fox Burgoyne. Snow drifted lazily and lights had come on throughout the city. A lamp near the corner cast a pale yellow sheen over the film of snow that had already gathered. A horse cab slopped past and was followed by an electric brougham. Few pedestrians were about at the dinner hour. The garden beyond the wrought-iron fence across the street was lost in shadow beneath the bare trees that lined the perimeter. A gardener swept the last of the autumn leaves into a catcher and piled them onto a smoldering fire.

Connigham's head throbbed painfully; he had taken the last of the heroin tablets but it seemed to have had no effect.

No one had gone in or out of the embassy for thirty minutes now, and he took a deep breath and crossed the road to the edge of the garden directly across from number 9, where he leaned against the wrought-iron fence a moment until a ripple of dizziness passed. The revolver nestled in his jacket pocket and he slipped a hand over it to hide its outline as he crossed the road and went up the steps to the massive mahogany door. He swayed a moment in the doorway and put a hand out to steady himself. The blow to his head had done more damage than he had suspected. A while ago his ears had begun to bleed.

The receptionist, a prim, tight-lipped woman in pince-nez, looked up from her desk with a supercilious stare at the quality of his clothing. It was when she saw his face, drawn and gaunt, that she became wary and folded her hands to wait for him to speak. A porter stepped from an anteroom to watch him closely.

"May we help you?" she asked, putting as much hauteur in her voice as she could manage, her slight German accent barely noticeable. She looked him up and down and her lip actually curled in disdain.

Connigham chuckled at that in spite of his pain and dizziness, and she had the grace to blush. "I wish to see Eric von Dorn immediately." It was taking every ounce of strength he could muster to face this woman without trembling, without collapsing from weakness.

The receptionist looked at him again to make certain that she had understood correctly. The man's accent had the curious transatlantic touch that was becoming more common in London, but something else as well. She was also aware that von Dorn was more than a mere military attaché, and there had been even stranger people to call on him or that little weasel of an aide in the past.

"I am not certain . . ."

"I am." He took a deep breath. "Tell him that I am here and I am short of time. He will understand. Tell him that I am sent by Mr. Arthur Boyle."

"Your name, please!" She waited and, when he did not answer, she snapped her fingers for the porter, scribbled a short message and sent him off with it. She indicated a line of chairs against the wall. "Please be seated."

Connigham took a seat, remaining stiffly on the edge. The dizziness had returned and the hall began to rock gently. For a moment, he was afraid that he might be sick. Resolutely he stared around the hall in an effort to take his mind away from his nausea and pain. The ceiling rose to a rounded vault of gilded plaster above luxurious marble walls. He was trying to remember for whom and when the row of mansions along Carlton House Terrace had been built when the porter touched his arm.

There was concern on the man's face as he asked in a heavy German accent, "Are you all right, sir?"

The words seemed to come from far away even though the man's face was quite clear. "Yes. Yes, I am," Connigham muttered and made to get up.

The porter helped him but he shook off his hand. "Herr Colonel von Dorn is not in at the moment," the porter said, "but his aide, Sergeant Schram, will see you."

For a moment, blackness nearly engulfed him and he fought to hold himself upright until it passed, then nodded stiffly. Connigham followed the elderly porter as he toiled up two flights of steps to the second floor and down a hallway to a paneled door at the end. Inside the outer office, he signed for Connigham to wait and knocked on another door. It opened almost at once and a man even smaller than the porter peered out. His pop eyes darted curiously at Connigham, taking in his wrinkled suit and stained overcoat, and he said something in German to the porter who left immediately.

"You are from Mr. Boyle?" he asked in nearly flawless English.

Connigham nodded. "Where is von Dorn?" he demanded.

Schram shook his head. "I am sorry, my good man, but Colonel von Dorn is away from the city for the holidays. May

I help—'' He got no further as Connigham shoved him back into the inner office and kicked the door closed behind. Schram looked at the revolver Connigham was pointing, his expression comical in its surprise.

The inner office smelled of burning paper and in the fireplace Connigham saw a pile of papers still smoldering. Below an open wall safe a loose-leaf notebook lay on the floor, a number of pages still intact. Connigham picked up the remains of the notebook and slipped it into his pocket. Two thin stacks of currency remained in the safe and he pocketed both.

Schram started toward the telephone on the desk but Connigham pointed the pistol at his head. "I want to know where this von Dorn is?" Connigham tapped him on the nose with the barrel to emphasize his point.

"I . . . I do not . . ." He started and screamed as Connigham slashed the gun across his face. Schram crumpled to the floor, burying his head in his arms.

"Once more. Tell me where he has gone?" Connigham's voice was impassive, but the room was beginning to float and the edges of his vision had darkened again. He staggered once but the edge of the desk steadied him.

Schram slobbered and tried to crawl away. Connigham followed, kicking him over and over, until the man was reduced to a blubbering mass of terror, then knelt to grab a handful of hair and slam his head against the walnut desk. "Tell me or you will be surprised how painful it is to die," he told Schram in an even voice. There was no anger in him now, only a tremendous weariness and the need to have it over and done.

The little man tried to pull his head away, and Connigham rapped it back against the desk one more time. Schram's eyes fastened onto the pistol muzzle wavering before his eyes and burst into tears. He pawed feebly at Connigham's arm, his words incoherent.

"Again," Connigham shouted, slamming his head against the wood.

"To Dover . . . by train. Victoria."

Connigham thrust the man away and stood up. "When?"

"Seven o'clock train. To Dover."

"Why?" he shouted. Schram shook his head, sobbing, and Connigham banged it against the desk again. When Schram went limp, Connigham stared at the man with pitiless eyes and placed the pistol muzzle against his forehead. Feeling its coldness, Schram opened his eyes and groaned.

"One more time. Why has he gone to Dover?"

Schram hesitated, then the words gushed from him. "To destroy the Tunnel. To blow it up. Rifles . . . landed at Felixstowe. Rifles and explosives. He will blow up the—"

"Shut up," Connigham roared. "I don't care about that." He straightened and leaned on the desk until the dizziness had passed again.

"Did he kill my sister?"

Even in his terror, Schram was surprised by the question. "Kill your . . . your sister. Are you mad . . . ?"

Connigham knew the man's surprise to be genuine. He had heard all he wanted in any event and he turned and looked about the room. An overstuffed couch and chair were set near the fireplace for informal conversations. A large pillow graced either end of the couch and he picked one up and wrapped it around the barrel, taking care that it would not jam the hammer. He walked back across the room to Schram, who was watching, paralyzed with fear, and shot him without a second thought. The muffled report could not have been heard beyond the room, he decided, and without glancing at the body, he went out, locking both office doors behind.

He went down the curving steps to the main hall and went out, ignoring the receptionist's call to wait. He knew that she would telephone for help, but it would take several minutes to break down the two heavy doors and find the body. Which way to go then—down the Duke of York steps to the Mall or along Waterloo Place? Victoria. He must go to Victoria, but for the moment the reason escaped him. He put a hand to his aching head where the pressure was growing and, without thinking, trudged on. He reached the Pall Mall corner and turned automatically to his left. A motor taxi had stopped just ahead and a man and woman were stepping out. He brushed past, ignoring the man's angry comment at his rudeness.

The chauffeur slid open the window and shouted at him to get out, that he was off now. Connigham snatched from his pocket the first banknote that came to hand and flung it through the open panel. The chauffeur stared at the £20 note and closed the window, but had to open it again to ask the destination.

"Victoria Station," Connigham told him and slumped in

the seat as the motor started into the traffic. The interior was cold and he shivered. The cold leather seat felt good against his aching head though, and he closed his eyes to shut out the dizziness.

The chauffeur had come around to the side of the taxi and was shaking him by the arm. "Hey, guvnor, this yer's Victoria. Yer can't sleep in me taxi. Not even for twenty quid."

Connigham shook off his hand and stepped down onto the littered pavement where he stood a moment, confused by the bustle. He put a hand to the side of the taxi to steady himself and the chauffeur backed away muttering about drunks. He got back into his cab without offering Connigham his change and drove off quickly.

By the time Connigham had passed through the entrance toward the platforms, he was feeling somewhat better. The dizziness and nausea seemed to have receded. He stepped out of the scurrying throngs and leaned against a partition to try and orient himself. He located the schedule board, but for some reason he was unable to read it or the large clock above, and the electric loudspeaker was a jumble of painful static. Puzzled, Connigham started toward the ticket windows but had to stop to remember what he had come for. A ticket to Dover, he recalled. But why Dover?

Without knowing how he got here, Connigham found himself staring at an angry clerk who was demanding a bill smaller than a twenty-pound note.

"I . . . I have nothing else," he stuttered and, suddenly angry himself, smacked his fist down on the marble ledge.

"Give me a first class to Dover, and be quick about it, or we'll take it up with your superior."

The clerk slipped a cardboard rectangle from the stack and slid it and a sheaf of bills through the grille. Connigham ignored his invective and slowly counted the bills, then turned, staggering a bit, and made his way across the concourse to platform one. He found a bench near the gate and sat down, gasping for breath. His face was soaked with perspiration but his vision had cleared. He could read the chalkboard in front of the gate now. He looked for and found the huge clock over the barriers. It was six fifty. There was something else he had to do and he struggled to remember what it was. Behind, near the entrance, a forlorn Salvation Army band thumped away on a medley of Christmas carols which were largely ignored by the hurrying travelers.

Powell had gone from the house at Brompton Square straight to Churchill's office at the Admiralty. The First Lord paced before the fireplace now, hands clasped behind his back, a worried frown creasing his face.

Again, there was that nagging thought that Powell had aged badly within the last few weeks, and Churchill was at a loss to understand why. He knew the man better than to think it was merely tension caused by the present circumstances, but Powell was visibly going downhill. His shoulders had taken on a defeated slump they had never had before. In fact, his bearing had always had a touch of the military about it.

"I don't think we have any other choice, Winston," Powell was saying. "The man is completely out of control. We suspect that the two bodies found in Stepney were his work. The dead man was a notorious informer and contact with the criminal underworld as well as with the Fenians. We know he is also responsible for the man and woman murdered in Rotherhithe; the man was one Tom Finnigan, a known Fenian left free this past summer. As you may recall, his name was also on the list you gave Connigham. And one of the maids has identified Connigham as the man who murdered Lady Emily Wilson-Langdon and her butler this afternoon." Powell delivered the list in a monotone, as if too tired even to be indignant. "We have also traced his movements to Liverpool on the twenty-first, the night the MP Arthur Boyle was murdered."

Churchill shifted in the chair, wondering that he could detect no trace of disapproval in Powell's voice. "And he has disappeared again?"

The Inspector nodded. "Yes. But a related matter reported to the police may put him on Sloane Street at four o'clock this afternoon. Apparently, he was badly injured by Lady Wilson-Langdon before he strangled her. There was a great deal of blood in her bedroom and traces of blood on a heavy candelabrum. The blood was a different type from hers or the butler's. She must have struck him quite forcefully, then gone to the library to telephone. Connigham, it would seem, recovered enough to follow and strangle her. The receiver was off the hook and the wire ripped from the wall. I surmise she was in the act of telephoning when he found her.

"Afterwards, Connigham apparently went out into the street. A gentleman found a man fitting his description further along the Brompton Road. Connigham told him he had slipped and fallen and as he appeared to be badly injured, the man called a cab and took him to his own doctor.

"At five o'clock, an hour after the surgery should have opened, a patient brought a policeman who broke in and found the gentleman, the doctor, and the sister unconscious and bound. Connigham, it seems, overpowered and robbed them and made good his escape. The doctor stated that the man he treated appeared to have sustained a concussion and possibly was bleeding internally."

"An extremely busy and resourceful man is our Mr. Connigham," Churchill observed. "You feel as well then that he is responsible for Boyle's death?"

Powell sank wearily into a chair opposite. "I am not certain, Winston, to be perfectly honest. I spoke to the chief superintendent of the Liverpool CID by telephone. It was known that Boyle had one or two bodyguards with him at all times, but the man on duty last night heard and saw nothing, of course. Nor did any of the servants or the other occupants of the house."

"I knew Arthur Boyle," Churchill mused. "Born in Ireland, elected to a safe Labour constituency in Liverpool. Not a brilliant man, but steady."

Churchill stared deep into the fire thinking. After a while he tapped his chin with a finger. "It occurs to me, David, that Connigham's only *real* concern was to find his sister's murderer. If he is in the process of doing so"—he looked over at Powell—"is he following a trail of some kind? Are all of these people, including Lady Wilson-Langdon and Arthur Boyle, involved with her murder?" There was in his voice a hint of disbelief at his own supposition.

"Or is he completely mad?" Powell asked.

Churchill shook his head. "But how or why would he have access to Boyle and Lady Wilson-Langdon? As you say, there is a connection among the other murders as they were involved with the Fenians. No, David, I think we must assume that they were, as well."

Powell disagreed. "If you are correct, then the Fenian

organization is much more widespread than Special Branch suspected. Or MI.5, for that matter. We must only have trimmed the tip of the iceberg this past summer. The widow of a high-ranking Irish government official and a Member of Parliament?'' He shook his head again. ''It surpasses belief.''

''Especially if we can, in fact, prove a connection with Germany.''

The silence drew out before Powell sighed. ''Yes, I must agree, Winston. But the question now is, Where has he got to?''

Powell trudged down the Admiralty steps and onto the Parade where his motor was waiting. The chauffeur held the door and he sank gratefully into the cold seat. He could easily have walked the short distance to the Yard, and up to a week ago, he would have done so without a second thought. But he was just too weary and exhausted to do it now. Powell knew that he was no longer giving his best to the job, but the image of his wife, propped up in her hospital bed, intruded too often for concentrated attention. There was something that he was missing here, something that with thought would have become clear, but he no longer cared, no longer even tried.

Grace had been taken to Middlesex Hospital two nights earlier where pneumonia was diagnosed, a fact that he had concealed from Churchill only after a great deal of thought. He was no longer concerned that his own role in this affair might reflect unfavorably on his career. If Grace died, the pension would be meaningless. The doctor would not so state, but it was clear enough from his manner that Grace had not much longer to live. The pneumonia was only the beginning of the final stage. As the doctor had suspected all along, the problem was cancer of the lung. Inhalation treatments seemed to have helped a bit, for when he visited the gray, depressing building that afternoon she had been half-sitting in the bed, eyes bright and skin flushed, looking healthier than he had seen her for a long time. The doctor had made it clear to him, however, that it was the fever that accounted for her color. Her concern was for him and, as in the past, she had insisted that he discuss the details of his case, knowing that just the process of verbalizing was helping him to order his thoughts and gain new insights. As he talked, Grace seemed to perk up, and he realized for the first time in their marriage that she lived vicariously through him. Much too shy and frail all her life, she gained her experiences through his. And Powell knew it would have been the same if he had been a postal clerk instead of a policeman.

Looking at her thin, wasted body that he loved so dearly, he had accepted finally that she had not much longer to live. And as if to confirm that she knew it as well, Grace had urged him to continue with the investigation instead of wasting his time in hospital with her. She needed to know how it all came out, she told him, laughing and covered the cough that followed with a handkerchief that did not quite conceal the trace of blood on her lips.

The details of the case, Powell knew, would do more to keep her in a healthy state of mind than anything else, and perhaps to prolong her life as well. It was selfish to feel that way, but the doctor had assured him that the drugs would prevent pain until her body would no longer respond to nerve impulses. And now that he thought about it, the times of her greatest animation and interest had always coincided with his most difficult cases.

Powell had left the hospital in a mild state of shock, having learned more about their marriage in that too-brief visit than in all their previous thirty years together. He could feel the overpowering desolation growing in him.

The green-shaded lamp cast a pool of light across the bound folder. The phone rang and Churchill sat back and pinched the bridge of his nose to relieve the ache, wondering irritably why his secretary had not answered it. On the third ring, it dawned on him that it was the private telephone and he snatched the receiver from the hook. "Churchill here," he snapped.

"Listen to me carefully." It was Connigham's voice and Churchill pressed the electric buzzer under his desk. A moment later the door opened. Eddie Marsh took in the situation at one glance and crossed the room to the other telephone where it stood on a table beside a bookcase. He lifted the receiver carefully as he sat down and opened his note pad.

"Connigham, where are you?" Churchill demanded.

"Shut up!" The voice slurred for a moment, then paused as Connigham drew a deep breath. "You shut up and listen to what I have to say or I'll ring off. The man who killed my sister is Eric von Dorn. He is the military attaché with the German Embassy."

Churchill could not restrain a muffled exclamation at this verification of his theory.

"It all has to do with your damned Tunnel," Connigham continued. "My people *were* involved." This last was said with only the slightest trace of hesitation and, with that peculiar insight into people which he possessed, Churchill realized that it was the strain of this knowledge that was breaking Connigham.

"Where are you now?" he interrupted, his voice terse.

Connigham's laugh was hollow over the telephone. "Never mind that. Just shut your mouth and listen. A shipment of rifles and explosives was landed from a German freighter near Felixstowe. I don't know when. They intend to destroy the Tunnel. There is a document that will identify the people involved. An envelope or a stamp of some kind. Finnigan was to get it back from Bannerman." In the background there was a burst of noise that obscured Connigham's next words.

"Wait!" Churchill broke in. "What do you mean, they intend to destroy the Tunnel."

"What do you think I mean, you damned fool." There was the sound of heavy breathing from the other end, and Churchill and Marsh exchanged puzzled glances.

"They are going to destroy the Tunnel," Connigham repeated. "I don't know how. That's your problem. Von Dorn murdered Margaret. He used her flat. There were cameras there. You won't find him before I do, so don't try."

"All right," Churchill shouted to make himself heard. "You've done what we asked. Now I'll see that you are taken out of the country . . . ." But he was shouting into an empty line.

"A railway station?" Marsh asked. "It sounded like an engine whistle near the end."

Churchill nodded, thinking furiously. "I believe you are right. Get Inspector Powell on the telephone quickly. Tell him to send men to Victoria, Charing Cross, Cannon Street, and London Bridge Stations. Those are the only ones with connections to Dover, I think. Check to be certain. They must find Connigham. Then call the Foreign Office and the Home Office Secretaries. Ask them to come here as quickly as possible."

Eddie Marsh nodded and hurried out, and Churchill tapped the pencil he was still holding on the desk. What would come of it all now, he wondered.

Von Dorn found a seat in a crowded first-class compartment and tried to relax, mentally cursing the fate that seemed to dog him just as he was on the verge of success. The man who had answered Lady Emily's telephone was from the police. There was no doubt about it. The man had refused to answer any questions, and von Dorn had replaced the receiver quickly. He had left the club earlier than he had intended and directed the cab along the Brompton Road. Several vehicles were just leaving Brompton Square, one a London County Council ambulance. He still did not know for certain what had happened, but his decision to leave London a day early was confirmed. Finnigan had disappeared and that fool Boyle had managed to get himself murdered, and in his own house as well. Von Dorn realized that, with the exception of McDougal, he was now completely isolated from the Fenians.

Doors slammed as the guard strode the length of the train. Von Dorn started, surprised by the noise. He opened his eyes to see the guard passing on and, across the aisle, a young couple exchanged smiles. He frowned in annoyance. He was bone weary and his chest was beginning to hurt. He could not remember ever having been so tired. The promise of his own bed had been all that had sustained him during the day, and now even that was denied him. He popped a Valda pastille into his mouth and sucked on it until the menthol began to ease his throat.

The train started with the usual jolt and the familiar sooty brick walls began to glide past. Here and there a lamp cast a pool of light across the snow-patched gravel and railroad tracks. As the train ran out from the enclosing arms of the station, the vista of nighttime London opened before him in a sea of electric lights. A bridge was outlined in bright pinpoints against dark waters. Snow was beginning to fall in earnest as the train crossed the Thames. It was going to be a long night, and all he had to look forward to was a few hours of uncertain sleep snatched on the bumpy train before they arrived in Dover.

*   *   *

Connigham slid open the door to the next car and staggered through. A blast of cold air swept in and, behind him, he heard annoyed mutters from disgruntled passengers. The train was crowded with holiday travelers, and there were no seats left. The aisles were jammed with men, women, and whining impatient children. He ignored the growls and evil looks as he forged his way through the carriage. Connigham was uncertain for whom he was looking but, irrationally, knew he would recognize the man when he found him. He pushed and shoved his way through car after car, staggering as much with the movement of the train as his own dizziness, peering into each compartment. A suspicious conductor demanded his ticket and Connigham gave it to him, ignoring the warning that he was in the wrong car.

When he entered the first-class carriage, the uncrowded aisles, the well-dressed people, the lighted compartments, and the lack of noise combined to disorient him for a moment. He pushed on through, peering into each compartment, ignoring the hostile glares that followed him. A young mother leading two small children was struggling with the door to the next carriage. He reached past her shoulder and yanked it open. She gave him a distracted smile and ushered the children through. But the small boy, dressed in a sailor suit, insisted upon holding up a carved wooden dreadnought for Connigham to examine. The boy's face glowed with excitement as he tried to explain what the ship was, his words tripping over one another in his eagerness. Connigham felt his expression freeze as he stared at the child. The mother's smile, which had softened as she reached for the boy's hand, vanished when she saw the look on the ill-dressed and perspiring man's face. The little boy evaded her hand and went on chattering, brandishing the ship at Connigham, who could only stare at him, trying to understand what he was saying. His thoughts were confused; the boy was talking to him, waving a toy ship, but he could not understand why. That woman, why was she staring at him so oddly? The train crossed a series of switching points and he lurched against the wall, a loud roaring growing in his ears, a noise so painful that he could not stand it, and he closed his eyes.

The mother finally managed to get hold of the boy and, giving Connigham a very odd glance, tugged the children with her along the aisle. The noise receded as abruptly as it had come and Connigham opened his eyes. He saw the three hurrying along the aisle, the boy still looking back at him. He tried to call after them, to form the words, to apologize, to make her understand that he had no experience with small children, but no sound would come.

Von Dorn looked up from his book to see, through the compartment door, a tall man in a soiled overcoat standing in the aisle. Part of a blood-soaked bandage was visible beneath the man's hat and von Dorn stared, seeing Margaret's features in the hard face. Connigham turned to him and, for a long moment, they stared at one another as the train slowed to enter the Bermondsey yards.

Why was that man staring at him, Connigham wondered. Everyone was staring at him. He looked at the man again, seeing the close-cropped blond hair, almost a military cut . . . and he understood then why the man was staring. He had found his sister's murderer.

Von Dorn's bemusement vanished as the man's expression changed and he glanced at the other passengers in the car. The young couple across the way were engrossed in one another, the elderly man read a newspaper while his wife looked out into the night, a middle-aged military officer was already asleep opposite. There was no help, and Connigham was reaching for the compartment door handle with his left hand, a small revolver just visible in his right.

Von Dorn lunged past the young couple, his boot catching and tearing the woman's skirt, and jammed down the handle of the outside door. It would not open and, desperately, he thrust his shoulder against it. It swung out and then, dragging him with it, and for an instant he swung free, still clutching the handle as his feet scraped gravel. He let go and the train went on, squares of light flashing past while he twisted and tumbled down the embankment.

Connigham slammed the compartment door open, wrenching it from its track, and pushed and shoved the passengers out of his way as they clustered about the open door, yelling to one another. Someone grabbed his arm and he turned to see a soldier struggling to pull himself up, shouting at him. Without thinking, he lashed out with the revolver, slashing the man across the face. The officer fell and other faces, white with fear, melted away as he lunged for the door in time to see a man get to his feet and begin to run. Without hesitation, he jumped, body automatically recalling hard-won hobo skills. Connigham relaxed and rolled down the embankment to stop half submerged in a shallow icy puddle.

He could no longer feel the searing pain in his head, and the gasping lungs belonged to someone else. He floated outside the stumbling, staggering body as it labored on, swearing and cursing, turning to skirt a pile of timbers, jumping a line of tracks. He was not even aware that he was seeing the running German through a long narrowing tunnel edged in darkness.

Von Dorn turned once to see the figure following him. As tired as he was, he wondered if he could outrun him. A bare bulb beneath a crinkled metal shade swung erratically in the wind, flicking shadows about. As he ran again, the night was silent but for the distant sound of an engine getting up steam and the lonely cry of a train whistle.

A signal lamp changed from red to green ahead, and he ran toward it as exertion drained away the panic. There was still time, he knew, even though he must now find another way to Dover. There was still time.

Connigham was running doggedly, head down, breath coming in great lurching gasps. Ahead, his quarry continued to run as strongly as ever. He had ceased to hear now, even to think of anything but raising legs, to which huge blocks of lead had been attached, for one more stride. The dreamlike trance was gone and he knew he was reaching the end of his endurance, knew subconsciously that he was dying, but that no longer bothered him. Ahead was the man who had raped and murdered his sister. His sister, his only sister. The sister he had deserted, he and his older brother, the bastard. He knew that he could not force himself to run another yard; his legs refused to obey, his feet banged against one another, the muscles too weary to keep them in line, but somehow he kept on, driven by something he was no longer able to understand—something, a face, a name that lurked just beyond memory.

Von Dorn tripped and sprawled headlong. The force of the fall stunned him for a moment. At first Connigham could not believe it, and his cry of victory was little more than a gasp as he forced himself on. The German crawled onto his hands and knees and tried to stand, but lost his balance and fell again. The ground was warm and safe and he lay still for a moment, lifting his head just enough to see the distant figure still coming on. His lungs were rattling with each breath and he struggled again to get up, fumbling the Luger from his coat pocket as he did so. His breath was coming in great heaves and he tried to bring the rear and fore sights into alignment, but it was too dark to see. His thumb moved the safety and he fired once, blindly.

Connigham heard the snap of the bullet as it went past, and he lurched to one side and stumbled to a stop. With surprise he found that his own revolver was in his hand. He raised it; von Dorn was caught in a pool of light, brightly outlined against the darkness, and he took his time as he had been taught, bringing the barrel up rather than down, until the sights came into line. He took a deep breath into his starved lungs and, in spite of the agony, released part of it and held as he squeezed the trigger. The hammer clicked against an empty cylinder just as a fist thudded against his chest. He dragged the muzzle up again, not believing that the revolver was empty, seeing the sights come into line; but for some reason von Dorn was no longer in view beyond. The sights began to swing to the left, slowly at first and then faster until he was staring along the barrel as it swept past a line of distant vans, dipping lower and lower, and finally he was looking up at the swinging lamp. He could not see the revolver any longer and the pain in his head had gone. He blinked once as someone walked toward him. The figure was in shadow and he wondered who it was. He was warm now and a soft blanket covering him pressed down gently, comforting. A face stooped over his and he thought for a moment it might be Margaret's and began to smile, but it was Emily's face that shimmered for a moment as if in a pool of water, then began to recede. He continued to smile after the life went from him.

Von Dorn got stiffly to his feet, wondering at the smile. His second bullet had taken the man in the chest. Without curiosity, he stared down at the face below, the gaunt, worn face heavily stubbled, now relaxed in death. The smile made him wonder how he could ever have thought the man looked like Margaret. Beyond a general similarity about the eyes, he thought grudgingly, there was none, or at least not enough to remark on.

He drew a deep breath and looked around. There were no shouts, no lights coming toward him. The Bermondsey rail

342

yards were huge, and he doubted if the sound of the gunshots had carried far. For a moment he thought of trying to drag the body into some kind of concealment. But he was exhausted and his lungs ached from the long run. Let it stay here, he decided. No one would find it until morning, and by then he would be in Dover. He started back the way he had come, intending to find the rail line and follow it out of the yard. Somewhere he would find a cab or taxi. He could still be in Dover by morning.

chapter ———27

The *closed Rolls motor came across the downs on the* Deal-Dover road, chasing the pale morning light. A tenant at Kings Farm waved as it went by and continued on about his chores. The stubble lay under a thin layer of snow, and Churchill shivered once in spite of the rug he had wrapped about him. Powell shifted his position with a half snore, half snort and settled down again, and Churchill regarded him for a moment with affection, then turned back to the window, searching for a first glimpse of the Tunnel works. So far all he had seen was downland beyond the wire fences bordering the road.

A mile on, they passed through the village of Ringwould, now taken over entirely by the company as a dormitory for its married workers. Slate houses, one as dreary as the next, had obliterated any trace of the ancient village that predated even the Saxon invasion. Most of the thatched houses had been torn down to make way for mass-produced block buildings thrown up in depressingly geometric rows, each with its picket fence and tiny plot of garden.

The first sign of the Tunnel works came into view beyond the village. A high barbed-wire fence of the kind he had seen throughout the American West on a lecture tour years before ran across the downs and disappeared into the horizon.

The chauffeur slowed the motor and, up ahead, he could see a road turning off toward low hills. They negotiated the turn and came upon a barrier in front of which two Royal Marine guards stood ramrod stiff in the early morning cold. As the driver halted the vehicle, the Marines did not move except to lower their bayoneted rifles a trifle as if readying themselves. An elderly gatekeeper shuffled out and the chauffeur handed

343

him a pass, which he in turn presented to the young officer who had followed from the lodge.

The officer glanced at the note, came around to the side, and peered in as Churchill lowered his window.

"Good morning, First Lord," he saluted. "Had word you would be arriving. Shall I just phone through to the works, sir?"

"Thank you, Lieutenant." Churchill nodded. "Bit chilly this morning, isn't it? When did you arrive?"

"Yes, sir. It is, sir. An hour ago, sir. Ordered to occupy the site and allow no one in or out, sir, without a pass signed directly by you. Bit of a flap in the yards, sir. Don't take kindly to being ordered about by the Marines."

"No, I don't imagine they do." Churchill smiled. Beside him Powell stirred and opened his eyes.

"Thank you, Lieutenant." Churchill waved and the young officer stepped back, saluted smartly again, and motioned for the gate to be opened.

As they started down the metaled track between the hills leading toward the works, Churchill scanned the sky. Powell stretched and settled back against the cushion, occupied with his own thoughts for the moment.

The weather report at Deal had suggested a strong gale in the Channel before the end of the day. And certainly the lowering, roiling clouds ahead lent credence to the forecast. The wind had already begun to blow, and Churchill could hear it keening beyond the windows. The motor bumped and rattled along the road, the driver doing his best to avoid the worst of the winter potholes.

Connigham's phone call had stirred up a hornet's nest. Churchill had narrated Connigham's conversation from Eddie Marsh's notes to both the Home and Foreign Secretaries. Once McKenna and Grey had heard the entire story, Lord Grey had summoned the German ambassador, Count Paul von Wolff-Metternich, who arrived twenty minutes later, direct from his state dinner. They had all adjourned to Lord Grey's rooms in the Foreign Office and, after remarking that midnight was no time for diplomatic subtleties, Lord Grey launched immediately into a summary of the information Churchill had provided.

Von Wolff-Metternich blanched as the story unfolded and groped behind him for a chair. When Grey had finished, the German ambassador sat stunned, staring over hands folded about his ceremonial sword hilt before he shook himself back to attention. He stood, staggering slightly, and McKenna moved to help. But the German waved off the restraining hand.

"Gentlemen, I am absolutely appalled at what you have told me!" He glanced from one to another, as if appealing for understanding. "I must insist that you provide proof of your accusations if you wish to continue. I must also protest at the manner in which they have been put. That a member of my staff should even be considered capable of such a dishonorable course of action!"

"Then you will question Colonel von Dorn yourself, your Excellency?" Churchill asked.

"You may be assured, First Lord, that I will do so."

"Immediately, tonight?" Churchill pressed.

"As soon as he returns from Berlin. He was to leave this evening on holiday," the ambassador answered stiffly.

The three cabinet ministers exchanged glances. "Perhaps you could speak to his aide," Churchill suggested.

Von Wolff-Metternich appeared about to protest but, at the sight of Churchill's grim expression, shrugged and asked for a telephone. The call was placed and the ambassador turned his back, every line of his body advertising his disdain.

Count von Wolff-Metternich was considered by Lord Grey to be a member of what had come to be termed the peace party in the German government. Strangely enough, he carried a great deal of weight with the Kaiser and the Imperial General Staff, and Churchill was wondering if perhaps they might not have offended an important ally.

When the call was put through, a sharp exchange in German took place. The ambassador's face went white, and the receiver fell from his nerveless fingers. McKenna helped him to a chair as Grey poured a brandy. The liquor seemed to revive him somewhat for he stared at the three of them with consternation, mumbled an apology, and rushed from the room.

Ten minutes later, Special Branch informed McKenna that all curtains had been drawn at number 9 Carlton House Terrace and a large young man was pacing up and down the walk, refusing to answer questions.

Leaving Grey and McKenna to argue precedents, Churchill returned to his office, where he phoned the admiral com-

manding at Dover and ordered him to deploy a company of
Royal Marines to the Tunnel works at dawn. He then arranged for Powell to meet him at Tower Bridge, where a
torpedo boat was standing by. They boarded at 1:15 and by
7:30 A.M. had covered the ninety miles down the Thames and
through the Nore to Deal, where a navy motor car from
Dover met them.

Churchill nudged Powell and pointed. They had breasted
the hill and before them, sprawling along the valley, newly
fallen snow hiding the worst scars, was the muddy tangle of
the works yards. Against the far side of the valley, the steel
doors loomed half open and black in the diffuse light. A
shunting engine was just disappearing into the Tunnel, and
stick figures of men plodded along the tracks; of a sudden the
scene below popped into scale and they both gasped, as did
every visitor at this point. The size of the engineering works
dwarfed even the Panama Canal.

It was a weary and angry James Bannerman who ushered
them into his office where they unwound mufflers and shed
overcoats. A clerk brought steaming mugs of cocoa and,
when the man had gone, Bannerman dropped into the chair
behind his desk and regarded his two visitors, still red-faced
from the intense cold.

"First Lord, Inspector. I'm certain you did not come all the
way down from London to pay a social visit. Perhaps you
have an explanation for the Royal Marines who seemed to
have assumed control of the works?"

Powell and Churchill exchanged glances, and Powell took
the plunge. He gave Bannerman the entire story through to
the time they had left London. "We do not know," Powell
finished fifteen minutes later, "just what happened to
Connigham or the German military attaché, von Dorn. As
soon as definite word is received, it will be telephoned through
to us here."

Bannerman was silent, absorbing all that he had heard.
Finally, he opened a drawer and drew out a bottle of whiskey
and three glasses. Without asking, he poured each half full.

"Two nights ago," he said, "I was waylaid by four men
on the Dover Road. I strongly believe that they were attempting to murder me. I shot and killed one man but the other
three got away."

Churchill and Powell exchanged glances.

"I put through another request to my Board of Directors for additional security. It was turned down on the grounds that, in view of the investigation now being conducted by the Home Office, the public would be unduly alarmed and the investigation prejudiced. They mean, of course, their investors."

Bannerman sipped at the whiskey, then pointed to the dust bin beside his desk. "I had written my resignation with every intention of posting it this morning. As you can see, I did not."

Churchill nodded and his expression said that he understood perfectly. "Does it surprise you," he asked, "to discover that your secretary was involved in the sabotage attempts?"

Bannerman shook his head. "Last week I had a visitor who told me something of what was going on; enough so that I was able to guess a bit of the rest. And while my visitor did not say so, I was left with the impression that Margaret belonged to this same revolutionary group."

Powell nodded. "We wondered how much he might have told you."

"You were aware that Connigham came to my flat?"

Powell nodded.

"Then that makes me an accessory, does it not?" Bannerman asked.

Churchill smiled and shook his head. "I would not be concerned about that. No harm has been done. You would not have helped by reporting the fact."

"All right then, gentlemen, you have come to Dover for a specific purpose. What is it?" Bannerman demanded, the edginess creeping back into his voice.

"We are certain that another act of sabotage will be committed," Churchill said, "probably within a matter of days."

Bannerman grunted and rubbed a hand across his forehead. "Do you know by whom?"

Powell nodded. "We think so. Connigham supplied certain information leading us to believe that the Fenians, with German help—possibly that of the military attaché—are involved."

"I see," Bannerman replied slowly. "And that is the reason for ordering such a strong military guard without consulting the directors beforehand?"

Churchill nodded. "I have done so on my own initiative. If I am wrong, I will absorb the blame. But if necessary, I can persuade the Home Office to invoke a state of emergency."

"But you have no information as to what kind of sabotage?"

Powell shook his head and started to answer, but the telephone rang at that point. Bannerman listened for a moment, then handed the receiver to Powell. The room was quiet but for the hiss of burning coal, the scratch of Powell's pencil, and an occasional monosyllable. After a few minutes, he handed the telephone to Bannerman and read silently through his notes, organizing in his own mind the information they contained.

"Well?" Churchill demanded finally.

"It seems," Powell said, "that our Mr. Connigham has been found. Dead. Shot through the chest in the Bermondsey rail yards. The medical examiner estimated that death occurred between six and eight yesterday evening, which suggests that he was on the seven o'clock train from Victoria. The Dover police are being alerted to question the train crew and any passengers they might still find. The bullet taken from Connigham's body was submitted to the ballistic laboratory and they state that it was fired from a nine millimeter Luger pistol, the standard sidearm of the German military. It would seem, however, that there is no trace of Colonel von Dorn. Given the number of holiday travelers, the ticket sellers at Victoria would require photographic memories to recall an individual who purchased a ticket."

Churchill sipped at the whiskey, thinking about Connigham, wondering if in fact there was something more than the murder of his sister that had finally driven him to his death. He could not rid himself of that image of Connigham at the end of the interview; for just a brief moment, he had seen on the man's face an expression of hopeless frustration far beyond any emotion that might have been occasioned by his arrest.

"Then I think," Churchill said slowly, "that we must assume Colonel von Dorn has escaped and might now be in or near Dover."

At eleven o'clock, the telephone rang again for Powell. When he hung up, a trace of animation showed in his manner.

"It seems that Connigham had several pages of a notebook

in his pockets containing a partial key to the German intelligence cipher and a listing of German and other continental citizens residing in the vicinity of London and all employed by a German company, the *Präzision Maschine Gesellschaft*. Although such a company is registered, their only business premises appear to be a flat at number 4 Sedley Place.''

"Good Christ! Margaret Doyle's flat."

"Correct, Mr. Bannerman. I believe, sir,"—Powell turned to Churchill—"we have a list of German espionage agents. That will certainly bear further investigation and quickly.''

Churchill took the cigar from his mouth and contemplated the glowing end. "Perhaps it might be better to leave them unmolested for the time being.''

"Winston, what . . .''

"Consider how valuable they might become in the event of war. Possibly they could be persuaded to pass along certain information to their masters . . . information of our choosing?''

Powell nodded thoughtfully. "I see what you mean.''

"Was there anything else on those pages?''

"Yes.''

"Well?''

Powell took a deep breath. "There were three other names listed. Tom Finnigan, Arthur Boyle, and Lady Emily Wilson-Langdon.''

Churchill grunted. "I was afraid of that.'' His teeth clenched on the cigar and he thought for a moment before picking up the telephone and putting a trunk call through to London. On his authority the lines were cleared, and in a moment he was instructing Eddie Marsh to notify the Home Office and the Treasury to arrest von Dorn on sight.

Bannerman, who had been staring at the window for some minutes, said slowly, "I do not understand Margaret's role in all this.''

"Neither do we, for certain, but I think we will find,'' Powell answered, "that she played a double role. You mentioned to me that she was more an assistant than a secretary. I would assume therefore that she knew a great deal about the workings of the project and may have had access to many of the same documents as yourself.''

Bannerman nodded, and Powell continued, "It is my guess that she acted both as a spy and a courier, carrying messages and information between von Dorn in London and whoever his agent is here. The usual German practice is for the courier not to know whom he or she is contacting.''

Bannerman turned a puzzled glance on him. Powell shrugged. "Quite simple really. The courier merely places the message in a prearranged spot. Sometime later, the recipient comes to collect it. Often the courier knows neither the receiver nor the sender, but in this case she evidently knew von Dorn. Well enough at any rate for him to strangle her while she was nude in her own flat.''

Bannerman flared. "I beg your pardon, but your insinuation is insulting. She could have been surprised while readying—''

"For a bath?'' Powell broke in. "The bath was dry.''

Bannerman struggled with that for a moment, but Powell went on. "Did it not occur to you to wonder how Mrs. Doyle could afford a flat here in Dover and a second one in a relatively expensive area of London? The fact is, she could not, even though she occupied the flat off and on for several months. The fact was uncovered quite some time ago but was not brought to my attention until just now as, the case having been closed by CID, it was considered of no importance.''

"I see,'' Bannerman said after a while. He was remembering the woman and her air of disdain that he had put down to shyness, and the times that he and McDougal had tried to jolly her. "Then she was the go-between—between the man who planned and the man or men who carried out the plans?'' he said in a bitter voice.

Churchill agreed. "Connigham said there was a message that would identify whomever it was here at the works. He mentioned a stamp in connection with Mrs. Doyle and von Dorn, but the context was unclear—'' He broke off as Bannerman sat bolt upright in his chair.

"For God's sake!'' Bannerman snatched his wallet from his coat pocket, rummaged through it, and extracted a folded envelope. He spread it open on the desk. "The missing stamp book!'' he turned to Powell. "Perhaps this is what they were after that night in London. Remember, they took the Northern European volume.''

Powell bent to look at the stamp.

"The day before Margaret returned to London,'' Bannerman

rushed on, "she gave me this envelope, as it had a Belgian commemorative."

"Have you a glass?" Powell asked.

Bannerman gave him the large magnifying glass he used to study blueprints. With a pencil, Powell turned the envelope this way and that, flipping it over and then upright again.

"I suspect," he murmured to himself, "that when the handwriting is checked, we will find it belongs to Colonel von Dorn. The stamp was posted at Ostende on November 12. I would assume, this year, although that part is not clear. Can you tell me on which day she gave it to you, exactly?"

Bannerman flipped through his appointment schedule. "It was the day after the explosion in the heading. Yes, here it is, the twenty-fourth of November. She went up to London the following morning, Saturday."

Powell used his handkerchief to pick up the envelope and blew at the end to open it. With his penknife, he carefully peeled the flaps apart and examined the interior with the glass, angling the paper to catch the light. "To see if there are any scratch marks from the pen nib," he explained, "in case an invisible ink of some type was used."

He smiled at Bannerman's expression. "Yes, Mr. Bannerman. They really are used. And they were invented quite some time before Mr. Conan Doyle thought of them."

Powell tapped his teeth a moment in thought, muttering to himself, then bent again to peer at the stamp. "Do you have a geyser for hot water or is it boiled as required?"

"I believe the clerical staff keeps a kettle going on the outer office stove in winter. Why?"

Whistling softly through his teeth, Powell picked the envelope up with his handkerchief and went out. Churchill and Bannerman exchanged puzzled glances and followed. The clerical staff, reduced to two for the Christmas weekend, watched as Powell held the envelope over the kettle, playing steam over the stamp. From time to time, he loosened a portion with his pocketknife. When it came away, Powell turned it over to show them. At first neither man noticed it until Churchill, bending closer, started to pick at the black speck with his finger. Powell pulled the stamp away and motioned them back into the office.

Seated at Bannerman's desk, he slipped the knife blade

under the speck and lifted it from the paper. Glancing around the desk top, he noticed the calendar. "May I?"

Bannerman nodded, still not understanding what he was up to. Powell removed the celluloid window from the calendar and cut it in two with scissors.

"Fortunately, there are only a few days left in which to use the calendar." Churchill smiled, trying to lighten the mood.

Powell sandwiched the speck between the two pieces of celluloid and peered through the glass.

"Ah! This, gentlemen, is called a microdot. It is made by a photographic process developed in Germany. A full-size document is reduced photographically again and again onto a special negative material called microfilm, until the desired size is obtained."

Bannerman stared at Churchill and shrugged. "I've heard of microfilm," Churchill replied, then, turning to Powell, "but it was my impression that you could reduce a negative only so far before the silver particles in the emulsion begin to interfere with and obscure the image."

Powell nodded. "That is correct, but this is a very special film with quite small particles of silver salts. Fine-grained, I believe is the proper term. We became aware of it a few years ago at Special Branch. But this is the first time I've actually seen it used. This also explains Connigham's reference to photographic equipment and the traces of chemicals we found in Mrs. Doyle's lavatory."

Bannerman broke in, "Is this the document Connigham said could identify the saboteurs, do you suppose?"

Powell studied the film sandwiched between the two strips of celluloid. "Perhaps. But we must find a way to enlarge it. It's completely unreadable as it is."

Bannerman glanced at the film in Powell's hand and snapped his fingers. "Come with me, gentlemen."

They gathered coats and followed him from the office and across the yard where the wind was flinging crystal-hard snow in long streamers. They stamped up the steps of a clapboard building and pushed into a deserted office. Bannerman turned the light switch.

"This is our geological laboratory," he explained. "You will find several microscopes on the bench against the wall."

Powell went across the room to the bench as Churchill stepped back into the outer office for a bucket of coal to light the stove.

Two hours later, the last telephone call from the Dover police came through. Powell jotted notes, hung up, and checked the names he had been given against his list of twenty-seven. "All but nine, then, have been accounted for," he said. "Surveillance is being arranged by Special Branch for the eighteen we have located." Powell looked at both men and his expression was difficult to read. "There seems to be no particular reason why the names on the microfilm were selected. None of them is known to Special Branch and only one has a police record, for public drunkenness some years ago in Manchester. There seems to be nothing extraordinary about any of them except they are all Irish, employed at the Tunnel works, and many, but not all, have done military service. I am afraid the nine missing include Sean McDougal. The Dover police have visited his rooms and they found that all of his personal effects have been removed and an envelope with an extra fortnight's rent left behind."

Bannerman turned away from them to stare blindly at the schedule board behind his desk. The shock of finding Sean's name on the microfilmed list was fading and in its place was a growing anger at his betrayal; and beyond that, the first real traces of fear. McDougal knew the Tunnel as well as he.

"Mr. McDougal's disappearance would seem to confirm our previous information, would it not?" Churchill said slowly. "Perhaps this is a providential opportunity. Mr. Connigham indicated that von Dorn intended to destroy the Tunnel. Now, think a moment as to what that might mean. Is it possible utterly to destroy eight miles of cement and brick? Not with the explosives available to them, certainly. But how else? By flooding?"

Bannerman shook his head. "More easily than that. So many delays have been encountered that we are now running behind our contractual dates and the penalties have been severe. We are teetering on the edge of a labor strike, and if the project should shut down for three or more weeks, the company will be forced into bankruptcy. We narrowly avoided a lengthy shutdown a month ago after the airlock blowout." Churchill swore in exasperation.

Suddenly Bannerman snapped his fingers. "Of course!" He turned to the desk and shuffled through the blueprints until he found the schematic of the airlock and pinned it to the wall.

"That is the simplest and the most effective course open to them," he went on, reasoning it out as he spoke. "If the airlock is breeched, massive flooding results. To continue work, the breech would have to be filled, and the Tunnel pumped out. Added to the time already lost and the cost of the pumping and penalties involved, the company would have no choice but to shut down. And a single charge, properly placed, would easily destroy the airlock."

"And as a member of the cabinet, I can state unequivocally that the government could not support in any way the continuation of the project. Given the present trend of public opinion, it would be suicide to do so."

"You are suggesting then that the Tunnel need not be destroyed physically to destroy its usefulness?" Powell asked.

Bannerman nodded. "And Sean McDougal is as aware of that fact as I am. If a major catastrophe should occur and the company is bankrupted, it could be years, if ever, before the damage could be repaired and the construction continued."

"That suggests to me then," Powell went on, "that having failed once before to stop the project by making it look as if an accident had occurred, the Germans are now throwing caution to the wind. By using the Fenians—or those who could be called Fenians—they avoid any stigma of sabotage themselves and, as a bonus, drive a further wedge into Anglo-Irish relations. They have nothing to lose and everything to gain, it would seem."

"A frontal assault then, using trained soldiers, done on a holiday when few people are about." Churchill laughed aloud. "Then we have them. It is only a matter of gathering them in like grouse."

He went to the telephone and instructed the clerk to ring the admiral commanding at Dover. When he had him on the line, Churchill ordered a company of Royal Marines sent immediately to the Tunnel works. Still grinning, Churchill replaced the receiver. "I think we can stop worrying, gentlemen. Within the hour we will have sufficient force to stop even the most determined assault."

*   *   *

The carbide headlamps were no match for the blowing snow, and winds that promised a gale were already snaking through the medieval streets. Von Dorn glanced toward the harbor, still hidden in the pre-dawn darkness. A storm could help or hinder depending upon its strength and direction. He put the thought from his mind. Time enough to worry about that later. He found the narrow street exactly as shown on the map McDougal had drawn for him and turned into it, but snow had banked across the entrance and he shut off the ignition switch and sat for a moment in the darkness listening to the wind. A single street lamp swung wildly above the road, flinging shadows across the interior of the Rolls he had stolen in London.

It had taken Von Dorn almost an hour to work his way out of the Bermondsey rail yard in the blinding snow and then persuade a cab driver to take him across to the West End. He had concluded that it would be the height of idiocy to attempt another train to Dover. God only knew who else Connigham had talked to after he had, von Dorn assumed, murdered Emily. But that in itself had given him an idea. Emily had driven down to the Berkshires for the country weekend in a new Rolls motor car. Standing now across from Brompton Square, he could see that the house was dark and the police gone. Thoughtfully, he walked up the road to the corner and along the side street until he found the mews where a single lamp glistened on the film of snow that covered the rear court.

It was simple enough to break the old lock on the carriage house door and drive away. But it required nearly two hours to divine a way through the warren of city streets to the Dover High Road, so that it was midnight before the suburban lights faded. For what seemed an interminable time, he drove on through an endless black tunnel broken only by the occasional village and, once in a while, a sign indicating the slowly decreasing mileage to Dover. Snow swirled hypnotically in the light of the carbide lamps and twice he was forced to stop and shake off the warm sleep that threatened to overwhelm him by marching up and down and bawling drinking songs at the top of his lungs.

The puzzle of how the Irishman had connected him with

Margaret's murder and tracked him to the Dover train nagged at von Dorn. Connigham had to have had help, and he wondered if Emily had perhaps given it to him. Her manner that night had been assured when she spoke of Connigham, and von Dorn suspected she knew him a great deal better than she had let on. But in the end, he had killed her. Why? Because she had betrayed him and he had found out?

At six-thirty A.M., leaving Canterbury behind, he saw a sign that gave the distance to Dover as sixteen miles. The snow had continued to fall gently all night, piling up on the road, but not enough to impede progress so long as he held his speed to a steady thirty miles an hour. Von Dorn had a few anxious moments on some of the steeper grades, but the heavy motor car was equal to the task. The road was a flat, smooth expanse of virgin snow, and he could have been alone in the storm-ridden world.

But as von Dorn neared Dover, the wind began to rise. Snow smoked across the road and the wheels had a tendency to slither toward dimly seen ditches.

It was a full hour after leaving Canterbury that he came to a stop at the top of the steep descent into Dover. The wind was strong here, and the heavy car rocked on its springs. Snow whipped across the windscreen, adding to his difficulties. Von Dorn took a deep breath and, with the engine in its lowest gear, began the descent carefully, gingerly, holding the motor to what he judged was the center of the road. The engine raced as it fought to restrain the heavy motor car, and von Dorn could see the temperature gauge, set in the polished walnut fascia, creeping toward the red end of the scale. The snow was thick across the road, a smooth blanket filling the cut made down through the chalk cliff.

Grimly he clutched the wheel, making minute adjustments, left hand darting to the throttle to increase or decrease his speed. The winding road became an endless nightmare and the wind mounted as the motor rounded the sheltering bulk of the cliffs and was exposed to its full force. Snow clashed at the windscreen, huge wet flakes driven off the Channel. He pumped the wipers to no avail and was finally forced to open the window and thrust his head out to see where he was going.

It seemed forever but in reality it could not have been more than five minutes before von Dorn reached the foot of the descent and the protective bulk of the cliffs closed around him once more. He brought the car to a halt and lit a cigarette with shaking hands.

McDougal had sent him a crudely sketched map of the most direct route to the warehouse in Dover. There was a single main road running into and through the town to the Promenade and then a series of complicated turns into back streets that would bring him to the removals warehouse in the very shadow of Dover Castle. He picked his way through the silent, snow-shrouded streets, losing his direction only once.

Exhausted beyond belief after the long night's drive, cold and hungry as well, he trudged up the road to the alley shown on the map. A sign, partially obscured by snow, the rest illegible from weathering, was fastened to the sliding door of the warehouse. Von Dorn banged on it and waited, stamping his feet against the cold.

A judas door opened, and McDougal peered out warily.

"For God's sake, man," von Dorn snarled, "open up."

Ignoring the hostile stares of the men scattered about the room, he shoved past the Irish engineer and crossed to a wood-burning stove in the center of the greasy cement floor.

McDougal followed him to the stove. "Well?" he demanded.

Von Dorn placed the sole of his right shoe against the hot metal and grunted as the heat began to penetrate. He switched feet, sighing with relief.

"We will proceed this evening," he finally answered McDougal's question, struggling to keep his exhaustion from showing. "I assume that you have taken care of everything?"

"Aye. The rifles've been cleaned, the explosives packed away, and the boat captain has agreed."

Von Dorn nodded absently and, still chaffing his hands together, strode to the lorry parked against the wall. The side panels had been repainted to read LUDEN'S GREENGROCERS, DOVER. He pulled open the rear doors and saw the single rifle crate lying tied beneath the bench. He took a rifle from the box, opened the bolt, withdrew it, and squinted through the barrel to see that the cosmoline had been properly removed and the action lightly oiled. He slipped the bolt back into the receiver and jacked a round into the chamber. The bolt closed smoothly and he turned the cutoff and opened the bolt again. The cartridge flipped straight out; he caught it in midair, released the cutoff, moved the bolt to full open, and pressed the cartridge back into the magazine. He nodded at McDougal, closed the bolt, and put the safety up.

"They will do," he pronounced and handed the rifle to the Irishman. Von Dorn turned with his hands on his hips and stared around at the eight men scattered about the warehouse.

"I would assume you have told them what is expected?" He turned at McDougal's grunt. "I also assume that no liquor is being allowed. For anyone." He added the last for McDougal's benefit and, before he could respond, turned toward the piles of equipment stacked to one side of the lorry.

Von Dorn first examined the ammunition bandoliers to see that each pocket contained a clip; then he looked over the coils of hemp rope. The British army knapsacks and Mills belts showed wear but were in sound condition.

"Something more than the usual Irish carelessness," he commented wryly and pointed to the petrol motor and the winch. "Start it up."

A man snickered and whispered something to a companion and McDougal swung about. "Hold your bloody tongue," he roared. His face had gone brick red with anger, and he turned on von Dorn.

"Look here, you damned fool," he hissed. "What do you think you're playing at. You don't come marching in here ordering me about like a navvy. You want to see if it runs, start it yourself or ask politely."

"Is that so, Mr. McDougal? Well then, would you please oblige me and have it started up?"

McDougal glared, then motioned angrily, and one of the men sauntered over and knelt beside the engine. He checked the level of fuel, turned the petcock to full on, and depressed the plunger to prime the engine. The man stood, grasped the crank handle, and swung it once. The engine sputtered into life. As soon as it settled into a steady roar, he engaged the winch and the empty drum began to revolve.

McDougal made a chopping motion with his hand and the racket died away. Von Dorn drew out his watch and, with a studied gesture, snapped it open.

"We will leave at ten thirty P.M.," he said. "Have all this packed away in the lorry—if you please. I will sleep until then. Wake me sharply at nine thirty. Now, I would like some food and a bed.''

McDougal studied the German's departing back as he followed one of the men to the door on the far side of the warehouse, and he wondered at von Dorn's arrogance. Clearly, he resented them, but why McDougal could not fathom. Not that it made a particle of difference, he thought with relish.

chapter———28

The *bluff-bowed Dutch coaster thrashed past the break-*water to meet the long combers rolling down through the narrow gut of the Channel from the German Sea. Two belladonna tablets had quieted both stomach and nerves and von Dorn, standing in the cramped wheelhouse behind the heavy-set captain, could watch the heaving seas with equanimity as the bow came round to the heading that would take them to Ventilator Shaft Number Six.

McDougal, on the other hand, was extremely unhappy at the seas flooding the decks each time the coaster put her bow into a wave. An occasional flash of white water and the impression of heaving seas could just be seen in the glimmer of their running lights. But the violent motion of the boat alone would have been sufficient indication of the gale working up somewhere in the desert of the Arctic Ocean—the third such within a month.

In spite of his anger, McDougal preferred the noxious company of that bastard Prussian to the eight seasick men crammed into the stinking afterhold. McDougal was no sailor and knew little of the sea. But you could not live for long in the British Isles without gaining some appreciation of the power and destructive force of winter gales. The English Channel, perhaps the world's busiest international waterway, was a well-charted maze of conflicting currents and navigational hazards; but when the northwesterlies swept down from the Arctic, only madmen would venture from sheltered harbors. And they were mad, McDougal thought, if they really believed that they could survive those monstrous seas in this boat, even madder if they thought they could destroy eight miles of cement-reinforced iron and brick of the Channel Tunnel with ten men, ten rifles, and a few pounds of explosives.

360

* * *

Less than an hour before, von Dorn had finally conde-scended to share the details of the plan with McDougal, and he had exploded with anger when the German had finished.

"First, there's eight mile and better to walk, for God's sake. Secondly, you bloody great fool, if you had asked me first, I could have told you the Tunnel is blocked top to bottom below Ventilator Shaft Six and not a hope in hell of clearing it before New Year's Day. Thirdly, you are insane if you think we can ourselves place sufficient explosive in the Tunnel and the shafts, all six of them, to destroy the walls. Finally, how will your ship know where to find us."

Von Dorn, striving visibly and cursing Finnigan, who was to have brought him a report of the damage, stalked to the table where a chart of the Tunnel was spread, corners held in place with dirty tea mugs. He studied it for some time, then pointed to Ventilator Shaft Six, where McDougal had scrib-bled random lines to indicate the blockage.

"Then we will enter through Number Six rather than Num-ber Eight. I assume that there is sufficient room between rubble and roof to reach the Tunnel floor? When we leave we will merely fire a signal rocket from whichever shaft we use as an exit, as arranged."

McDougal scowled at his tapping finger. "Aye," he an-swered reluctantly. "But how do you plan to get the men down? The ladders have all been torn away."

"We'll go down the same way as the crates, by the winch."

"Well, I . . ."

"It can be done," von Dorn insisted.

"Aye, maybe." McDougal agreed slowly. "But for God's sake," he burst out, "demolition charges in every shaft? It can't be necessary . . ."

"But it is. Each shaft must explode in precise sequence to allow the seawater to drop to the base of the shaft with sufficient force to compress the air in the Tunnel and drive it toward the entrance. The forces thus generated will be suffi-cient to rupture the Tunnel walls."

McDougal's long experience as an engineer had enabled him to grasp the details of von Dorn's plan instantly and while on one level he might be filled with admiration for the man's brilliance, he could and did hate him for his arrogance and assumed superiority. We'll see, Mr. Military Attaché, he thought. We'll bloody well see who gives the orders in the end.

"The time allowed is limited . . ." McDougal's final protest was half-hearted at best, and von Dorn's answer was half sneer, half insult.

"It will be sufficient. Even for Irishmen."

The fishing boat gained the crest of a wave and poised momentarily before her bow fell with a sickening swoop that nearly emptied McDougal's stomach and smashed into the following wave with sufficient force to bring her up short. McDougal lost his hold and cannoned against the front of the wheelhouse. The captain muttered something unintelligible and von Dorn laughed.

It seemed an endless time to McDougal before they picked up the revolving beacon atop the ventilator shaft through the driving sleet. The captain swept the boat's single spotlight across the artificial island to examine the breakwater and approached so as to utilize whatever lee its bulk to windward would provide. McDougal staggered out onto the deck to rouse his thoroughly seasick crew from their nauseous hold.

The fishing boat rounded to in the quartering seas and came up into the dubious shelter of the stone quay. McDougal drove the weak and retching men onto the island, where they huddled against the sleet and waited for the world to stop pitching and tossing; but McDougal was not giving von Dorn further excuse for insults, and he hurried them to start unloading the equipment and hauling the crates up the path.

While McDougal struggled to open the ventilator shaft hatch and get his men inside, von Dorn congratulated the Dutch captain on a job well done. He removed his wallet and the man's eyes gleamed.

"Please ask your engine man to come to the bridge," he said slowly in English, dignifying the miserable closet into which they were jammed. Anticipating a further cash reward, the captain gave a quick command into the speaking tube. Von Dorn smiled at him as he held the wallet in his right hand, the notes he had removed in his left. The door slid open and a short, ugly man covered with grease pushed into the wheelhouse, an expectant smile splitting his perfectly round head.

Von Dorn slipped the wallet inside his jacket and yanked

the Luger from his waistband. The two shots were deafening inside the wheelhouse but lost in the rising violence of the storm. The captain collapsed instantly while the engine man stumbled back through the open door. Von Dorn followed him out and shot him in the back as he scrabbled onto the quay. The man fell back as the boat lurched and disappeared into the dark waves.

Von Dorn thumbed the safety catch on the Luger, slipped it back into his belt, and without change of expression stepped back into the wheelhouse. It took only a moment to loop a loose-fitting cord around the wheel so that it would have some play, but not enough to turn the boat completely about. With luck, it would describe a wide circle long before the Dover cliffs were in view and, somewhere within that circle, the boat would swamp and sink without a trace. After removing the bow mooring line, he engaged the motor and let the bow swing out, then dashed to the stern and vaulted to the quay. When a wave drove the boat slightly back, von Dorn lifted the stern mooring line from its bollard and let it fall into the sea.

The coaster, gathering way slowly, pitched violently as it came out from the sheltering lee of the ventilator shaft. Von Dorn stared after it, protecting his eyes against the sleet with cupped hands. The stern running light winked at him once before disappearing into the rain. Pleased with himself, he started up the path toward the shaft. McDougal would never know. Margaret, Arthur Boyle, Emily Wilson-Langdon, Michael Connigham, and now the two Dutch sailors—everyone who could identify him except Finnigan were dead. No one would believe Finnigan if he should talk and with Schram already out of England, there was nothing and no one to connect the sabotage of the Tunnel to Germany. Except, of course, for McDougal. Von Dorn smiled at the thought.

The very violence of the wind seemed to infect him with enthusiasm so that in spite of his aching chest, he literally bounded up the last steps to the gaping hatch set in the iron-plated side of the towering shaft.

It required an hour more than von Dorn had allotted to rig the winch and lower the first crate of supplies from the top balcony of the shaft. Von Dorn had insisted on going down first and McDougal was only too happy to let him, hoping

perhaps that the cable would break. Von Dorn's offhand
comment as he climbed onto the crate that he had sent the boat
away had come close to causing McDougal to have an attack
of apoplexy.

"And how are we to leave, ye daft fool?" he roared.

"A German merchant vessel will take us off at nine-thirty
A.M. on Christmas morning. We could not very well have had
a boat hanging about, now could we? Suppose it had been
seen? Certainly someone would have wondered what a Dutch
coaster was doing here. Use your head, for God's sake!"

"And what if we're forced to leave before then? Supposing
they're waiting for us down there?"

"Nothing will happen," von Dorn had replied as patiently
as he could. "And there is no possibility of anyone expecting
us to come down through the shaft. Even you did not know
until two hours ago." The implication was clear enough to
McDougal, and he snarled and walked away.

"And we will not leave until the task is completed," von
Dorn shouted after him. "Do you understand?"

The crate jerked upward and was swung over the railing.
Von Dorn glanced up at the block-and-tackle arrangement to
make certain that it was running freely and then the crate on
which he was standing dropped past the balcony railing. Six
hundred feet below lay the mangled remains of iron plate,
broken cement, and protruding reinforcing rods that could
skewer him, and for a moment his courage all but failed.

Those electrical circuits repaired after the previous month's
fire had been knocked out again in Wednesday's incident and,
as a consequence, the shaft was pitch black. Von Dorn fumbled the electric torch from his pocket and swung its beam
across the iron walls. The torch did little more than show a
tiny portion of the vast cavern through which he was plum-
meting, but he felt the better for its presence. When he turned
it downward, metallic headlights glinted and he tugged sharply
on the signaling cord to tell the winch operator to slow his
descent. He went down at a snail's pace, past the first of the
three fan assemblies.

The downward plunge began again, and he went on through
the darkness, trying to estimate the speed of his descent by
counting the reinforcing rings flickering past his torch beam
every one hundred feet.

When he judged he was near the one-hundred-foot level,

von Dorn slowed his descent and carefully examined the shaft. The winch had been rigged to lower the crates close to the shaft wall in order to pass the fan blades. The number three fan had been severely damaged on Wednesday and von Dorn did not care to find himself spitted on any twisted projections of metal. His torch flickered across the walls where great chunks of iron plate and cement grouting had been torn away from the chalk face; apparently, the weight of falling material had been sufficient to carry everything cleanly before it, including the control balcony at the fifty-foot level.

Von Dorn signaled to slow his descent even more, shifted the torch to his left hand, and wrapped that arm around the cable. In his right hand, he held the Luger. McDougal had assured him that all work except essential maintenance on the surface had been discontinued until the first shift on the twenty-sixth in order to provide the workers with a Christmas holiday, but one could never be too careful.

The crate teetered as it contacted the irregular slope of rubble on the Tunnel floor, and von Dorn signaled the winch operator to stop. Work crews had cleared sufficient debris to allow him to clamber down the mound, cursing and dragging the heavy crate with his left hand while he kept the Luger ready in the other. The Tunnel was indeed deserted. He stood in the gloom cast by the feeble emergency lamps, staring up-Tunnel to where it dwindled into a converging tube of blackness. In reality, it was an optical illusion as the upward curve of the two-degree slope prevented him from seeing more than a hundred yards ahead or behind.

By the time he had the crate open and the rifles and explosives stacked, the second crate was descending with two men aboard. Von Dorn drew out his pocket watch. Thirty-five minutes. Far too long, and there was a third crate and seven men yet to go. Four more trips, during one of which explosives would be placed in the shaft.

It actually took six hours to bring them all down, six hours during which van Dorn fumed and fretted. He was certain that their entry would go undetected, but every hour's delay increased the chance that something could go wrong.

McDougal was the last man down, controlling his rate of descent with a line tied to the throttle. The winch motor would continue to run until the petrol tank was exhausted. If they were successful, he would never have to worry about its being found. If not, it would scarcely matter to him.

McDougal assembled his men and started them up-Tunnel without reference to von Dorn, who followed half angry, half amused. This was no time to become involved in a foolish contest for control, he decided. As long as McDougal did as he was told, there would be no trouble. They marched steadily along the gentle incline, McDougal wisely keeping their pace slow to conserve strength. They passed Mile Four before McDougal was certain of his suspicion. He halted the men and drew von Dorn aside.

"There is something very odd."

"What the devil do you mean by that?"

"The Tunnel has been emptied." He took out his massive key-wind watch. "There should have been a maintenance crew by now. There was one scheduled till six o'clock this evening. Do you suppose they know we are about?"

Von Dorn thought a moment, then shrugged. "Perhaps. But it will make it that much easier for us if we encounter no one. No possibility of a warning being sent up."

McDougal shook his head, clearly restraining a sharp answer. "Aye, but it also means they are waiting for us."

Von Dorn sneered at that. "We are approaching from inside the Tunnel. Clearly they do not suspect. Any attack they may anticipate would be from the outside. Otherwise, the ventilator shafts would have been guarded."

McDougal nodded. "Aye," he agreed doubtfully.

"Then please order your men to continue. I believe we still have four miles to go and I would not want your concern over our time schedule to grow more acute."

Churchill peered at the tea mug in front of him, saw that it was empty, and considered briefly going across to the stove for more before deciding that he was too tired. Powell was still studying the diagram of the Tunnel that Bannerman had sketched for him, comparing it with the engineering drawings. Finally he sighed and leaned back.

Bannerman grunted at the interruption and threw down his pencil. He stood up from the drawing board, where he had also been studying blueprints, and went across to the stove. "There is no other feasible way to get inside than through the front, gentlemen," he stated. "No other way at all."

"And you say," Churchill asked without lifting his head, "that we have taken every precaution?" He was weary beyond belief, having had little sleep during the night on the hard bench in the outer office and even less the night before.

Bannerman stared at him but did not answer for a moment. Every workman had been withdrawn from the Tunnel and a strong guard had been concealed about the main entrance. Just inside the Tunnel, partially hidden by the half-closed doors, was a machine-gun emplacement. Two companies of Royal Marines had been posted to wait for von Dorn to walk into their trap.

"I think we have taken every precaution."

"Would you wager your life upon it?"

Bannerman shook his head. "No."

"Then we have overlooked something. Your friend Mc-Dougal knows that Tunnel as well as you."

"Better," Bannerman snapped.

The First Lord turned to the wall where a nautical chart of the Channel had been pinned. The coast from Selsey Bill to the Goodwins curved smoothly north like the shoulder of a shapely woman, indented slightly by irregularities in the great cliffs. The line of the Tunnel had been sketched out into the Channel to disappear beyond the edge of the chart. Somehow, somewhere within that chart lay the key to how the sabotage party would approach the Tunnel. He was certain of that, just as he was convinced they would not have left this part of the plan to chance.

A frontal attack in force? That was the most obvious and normally would have been the most successful. But Connigham had spoiled that game. The question was whether or not von Dorn realized it. He had been trying to put himself into the German's mind for several hours now in an effort to rationalize the next moves from the information he thought von Dorn possessed. But the only conclusion it led him to was the fact that he himself had insufficient troops to cover the six square miles of the Tunnel yards. It would be four o'clock in the afternoon before the army would be able to supply even one more company of regulars.

The First Lord of the finest navy the world had ever seen, that had reigned supreme since the days of Queen Anne, sat staring helplessly at a nautical chart of the English Channel coast while he sipped the tea Bannerman had brought him, wondering just what it was that he had overlooked.

Bannerman had been standing behind him, also staring at the chart, and as Churchill turned away, his eye caught the pencil marks indicating the ventilator shafts stretching in a line east-southeast from Hope Point. He started to speak, then dismissed the thought. The gale was far too strong in the Channel for them to land on one of the artificial islands through which the great shafts protruded. He noticed Churchill watching him and recalled his early thoughts about the similarities between them when it came to considering every possible precaution.

"There is just one other way," he said, his voice suddenly hoarse with premonition. "The ventilator shafts. They could reach the Tunnel floor through one of them, but the storm . . ." His voice trailed away.

Churchill hesitated only a moment, then hurried across the room. As he reached for the phone it rang, and Powell picked it up and signaled that it was for him. Churchill stopped short, chomping on the cigar as Powell spoke into the instrument. He listened a moment, then stumbled a bit as he groped for a chair. Churchill, concerned, was starting to help him when the sound of gunfire, magnified by the Tunnel entrance, came clearly to them in spite of the gale battering off the Channel.

Von Dorn spread the eight men in a skirmish line that curved like a scimitar, the center lagging behind either end, the whole moving toward the arc-lit entrance of the Tunnel. It was daylight beyond, daylight dimmed by overcast and swirling snow.

Inside the Tunnel, a machine gun had been established behind a breastwork of sandbags. The machine gun, a Vickers Maxim, he was certain, faced outward, covering the approaches from the works yards. Three men huddled behind the gun and there were three more at either end of the sandbags that bridged the thirty-foot opening. As he watched, an officer in a greatcoat and steel helmet tramped back and forth to keep warm. Beyond, von Dorn could see a line of military lorries drawn up behind a row of buildings where they would be concealed from the entrance to the yards. He had been right after all. That damned fool Connigham had somehow warned the government—but how in the devil could he? It made no difference now. The sandbag barrier faced outward; at least he had been correct in his assumption that they would be expecting an attack from the outside.

The eight British army-trained Irishmen were all in position. They knew their business anyway, he admitted grudgingly. Now there was no more time to waste. Someone might turn at any moment and see one of them crouching in the shadows. He put two fingers to his mouth, took a last glance at the officer who had stopped beside the machine gun, and blew a sharp blast.

The first volley of rifle fire swept immediately across the intervening thirty yards and cut down the three men at the Vickers gun. Von Dorn brought his own rifle to his shoulder and sighted on the officer who, in spite of the surprise attack, had reacted instantly, pushing away the body of the gunner and swinging the Vickers about, but too fast, and his spray of shots went high. Just as von Dorn caught the officer in his sights, the man fell back against the sandbags, both hands at his face. Without hesitation, von Dorn swung to his right, picked a rifleman who had stretched himself prone and was firing coolly. Behind, he heard screams of pain; he dropped the sights until they rested directly on the soldier's helmet while the man fumbled to insert a new clip into his Lee-Enfield. The rear sight drifted on and he squeezed the trigger and saw a hole appear in the felt helmet. The man's head fell across his rifle and he lay still.

It was over in a moment, and McDougal, with two of his men, was racing forward with the explosive charge to the control panel near the entrance. Von Dorn reached the Vickers just as one of the Fenians tugged the dead officer away, clearing space. Von Dorn swiveled the gun and racked the crank handle back twice, clearing the breech. With his left hand, he squeezed the panels, pulled the half-used cartridge belt out, and flung it behind. He could not chance a jam. The Irishman was ready with a new canvas belt and he thrust the brass end through the block, grabbed it firmly with his left hand, and pulled the crank handle back twice more, tugging sharply on the belt each time.

Von Dorn settled himself behind the gun, feet straddling the tripod leg, and grasped the handles. His fingers tilted the safety catch, and as he pressed the thumb trigger he could see wraithlike figures racing toward them. Rifle fire was beginning to crackle as more soldiers tumbled from the buildings across the way, buckling on helmets and clutching rifles as they ran, greatcoats flapping in the rain and wind. His Irishmen were firing now with disciplined steadiness, but the unexpected number of soldiers rushing toward them was frightening. Von Dorn held the trigger down and swept the muzzle across the ragged line, seeing them melt away. He released the trigger and took a deep breath, then began to squeeze out short bursts, picking his targets through the sight as he had been taught. They fired off one complete belt and had nearly loaded the second when the great doors began to thunder shut. He slammed the bolt back as the Marines made one last effort. The Vickers hammered long bursts as the opening narrowed to ten feet, and he concentrated his fire there before an arc light was swung round to blind him.

As the light swept across the opening, swung past, then returned, he had a glimpse of a lorry lurching into motion and he knew that the driver meant to jam the machine between the closing doors. He ducked his head away as the glare caught him and, by feel, settled the gun's water jacket into the opening in the sandbag wall and held the trigger down, hoping to God that it was hitting the lorry and destroying the engine or killing the driver.

It must have worked because he heard a dull boom as the great doors met and, a moment later, a sharp crack as the explosive charge McDougal had set destroyed the controls and electrical circuitry. They were safe, and he had done what the British military conservatives claimed was inevitable, the military liberals, impossible. He had captured the English end of the Channel Tunnel. The doors could no longer be opened from the outside.

Von Dorn slumped over the gun, exhausted with the release of tension. He had succeeded with the most difficult part of the entire plan. The rest was strictly a matter of perseverance. It would take hours to burn through that dreadnought armor with cutting torches, eighteen hours at a minimum. He himself would open the door, he laughed. When the charges went, the door would open as certain as hell was for the wicked.

* * *

Bannerman flew out of his chair with an astonished expression, as if he could not believe what he was hearing. Churchill jumped to the window, then raced from the room, and Bannerman followed, leaving Powell sitting by the telephone, his face a mask of anguish.

The yard was a flurry of activity as men ran in every direction. Across the way, at the warehouse, soldiers were tumbling from the doorway. Bannerman stopped, trying to make sense of what was happening, but there was only time for impressions—a soldier nearing the mouth of the Tunnel throwing up his hands and falling; flashes of light from the shadowed darkness; the great doors grinding into motion; an officer marshaling his men into a skirmish line. There was an air of unreality about the scene—the sense that he was frozen outside of time and could not will his body to move fast enough even as he realized that the invaders had come from inside the Tunnel, had done the impossible, had come down through the ventilator shafts in spite of the storm. He might stop them yet, Bannerman realized, if he could only move fast enough. The master switch was in the gateman's lodge, a hundred yards away, an impossible distance. He tried anyway.

Bannerman cleared half the distance before he heard the lazy snick of a rifle bullet, saw the gout of mud as it struck the ground near him, but he was moving too fast to offer a significant target to any of the riflemen inside the Tunnel. He vaulted the steps to the lodge, hit the door with his shoulder, smashing it from the hinges. The gatekeeper, who was crouching beneath the desk in terror, shrank away mouthing gibberish as Bannerman burst in. A young soldier firing into the Tunnel mouth from the window swung round, rifle raised to smash down on Bannerman's head, when the porter found his senses and screamed for him to stop. Bannerman was unaware of either man, concentrating only on the gray panel set high on one wall. The door was already open as if the gatekeeper had been preparing to close the Tunnel doors. He flung himself at it, hand closing on the master switch that would shut off the electrical power, when a sharp explosion sounded inside the Tunnel and the doors slammed together with a force that shook the yard.

Bannerman slumped against the wall, head in his hands as

adrenaline drained away, leaving him exhausted and sick to his stomach. He had tried, tried and failed, and that was his second failure that day.

Ventilator Shafts One and Two had been simple enough, if time consuming. The sea bottom lay no more than thirty and fifty-two feet respectively above the Tunnel floor in them. Ten feet above that level, where the great cast-iron flanges had been bolted to the outside of the twenty-foot diameter shafts, four twenty-pound charges of blasting gelatin were placed against the iron plates at equidistant points, and thick wrought-iron covers bolted over each to serve as the tamp. The Imperial Naval Gunnery School at Kiel had developed an explosive specifically for this task, composed of gelatin dynamite and powdered aluminium. The mixture had been tested against similar iron plate at the great Krupp Works in Essen where it was found to be more than twice as effective as a similar amount of blasting gelatin alone.

Von Dorn watched now as, under McDougal's shouted instructions, three men worked their way with ropes away from the spidery line of stairs to the far side of Shaft Number Three to place the third charge.

Von Dorn checked his watch for the seventh time in as many minutes and resisted the urge to shout at McDougal to hurry. They had fallen two hours behind schedule so far and he swore bitterly at the delay, even though it was his own fault. It was the one detail he had overlooked in his haste to put the plan, sketchily drawn for Berlin, into actual practice. If he could bring men down through the shaft, then the English could do so as well. A brief glimpse of the Channel from the top of Ventilator Shaft One—wild waves driven by gale winds against the distant smudge of the Dover cliffs—had only partially reassured him. It would be madness now to attempt to land a storming party on any of the shaft islands—it had been bad enough when they had done so, hours before. But there was every chance that the English would try. The stakes, from their point of view, were high enough. As a consequence, he had been forced to detach two men from his force and send them to weld each shaft entrance shut, and that meant further delay. One man had been killed at the Tunnel entrance and now two more were gone, taking with them the second welding torch.

Von Dorn could restrain himself no longer and shouted up to McDougal to hurry along. But there was little satisfaction to be derived from McDougal's stream of obscenities and no relief from the terrible band of anxiety clamping tighter about his head. His chest ached abominably and he was perspiring with fever in spite of the clammy dankness and the temperature that hovered near forty degress. Von Dorn cursed and continued to curse between the bouts of coughing that were coming at more frequent intervals now.

The gale had strengthened during the long hours of Christmas Eve Day. The snow had stopped, but the wind was blowing Force Nine with the promise of more to come, and the tide was due to peak in an hour. Gale warnings had been sent up all along the east coast and preparations were being made as far inland as London to meet the expected flooding as the great rivers were held back by the combination of tide and wind. Churchill wrapped his naval greatcoat about him, clamped his jaws on a cigar, and cursed the weather. He was also seasick and exerting every bit of willpower he possessed to keep from showing it, obsessed with the idea that the First Lord of the Admiralty must appear above seasickness even while another part of his mind railed at him for his foolishness. Even Admiral Lord Nelson had been subject to great bouts of seasickness.

H.M.S. *Ajax* plunged its bow into a wave and the shock was transmitted to every part of the destroyer. Churchill hung onto the rail watching, unable to tear his eyes away as the bow sank deeper and deeper until water piled against the forward gun turret and he wondered if the ship would ever rise again. But the *Ajax* did, shedding tons of white water as her bow lifted toward the grim horizon and the line of winking beacons marking the ventilator shafts.

Bannerman had raced into the works office without a word, spread a blueprint across the desk, studied it a moment, and slammed a fist down.

"They entered through a ventilator shaft, probably Shaft Number Six. The fans are shut down and they would not have had to waste time disengaging them."

Neither Churchill nor the young Royal Marine captain present had said a word as he tapped the place on the blueprint.

"I estimate that it took them approximately four hours at

minimum to get down the shaft. The Tunnel doors cannot be opened, so they must have destroyed the interior switch panel and cut the circuits to the motors." He paused, his expression grim. "We have two alternate actions. We can cut through the doors with torches, which will take at least eighteen hours. Or we can go in after them."

Churchill could not resist the challenge. "By the same route?"

"By the same route," he repeated, then added, "or nearly so. Somehow they had to lower themselves down the shaft because the walkways were destroyed in the fire and again when the shaft sides collapsed on Wednesday. I think it is safe to assume that they do not wish to perish in this insane attempt and so will leave either through the Tunnel entrance or through one of the remaining ventilator shafts."

In spite of the situation, Churchill found himself troubled by Bannerman's demeanor and Powell's as well. Bannerman's eyes were too bright, his face too flushed, and his voice under such tight control that it was as brittle as glass. Powell, on the other hand, was sitting quietly to one side neither taking part in the conversation, nor, apparently, listening.

". . . will have secured all but one shaft, which will be guarded," Bannerman was saying. "Short of naval gunfire, they are impregnable inside the shaft."

"And if we use gunfire, we destroy our means of entering," the captain interjected in the smooth tones that suggested his East Anglian origins.

"What do you propose then, James?" Churchill asked finally, aware that Bannerman had all but forgotten them as he stared at the blueprint.

After a long moment, when Churchill was about to repeat the question, Bannerman tapped a finger on the print. "We must use Shaft Number Seven. It is the only one left. Eight is in the flooded section."

"But I was under the impression that the rubble from Number Six Shaft had blocked the Tunnel completely?"

Bannerman nodded. "It has. And the Tunnel floor has been smashed in as well. But a way can be found through the pipes beneath. We are still pumping water from the airlock. That means that the main water drain is still intact. Those pipes are three feet in diameter. If we shut down the pump, a small force could make their way through the main, beneath the rubble, and attack from the rear as unexpectedly as they did.'' He stared intently at Churchill. "If we move quickly, we can still take the bastards.''

Churchill contemplated the plan but it was the young officer, Bush, who asked the next question.

"How will we ever find our way through, sir? Surely there will have been a great deal of damage.''

"I'll lead you.''

"I beg your pardon, sir,'' Bush said, "but you are a civilian . . .''

Bannerman turned to him. "This, Captain, is a civilian project. The government, in the person of the Admiralty, has no legal right to be here, as I am certain the First Lord is aware.''

"Be that as it may, James . . .''

"You have no other choice, do you?'' Bannerman asked. "No one else knows the Tunnel as well as I do.''

"Still I—''

"We are wasting time,'' Bannerman interrupted coldly.

Powell nodded agreement, his only contribution since the attack. "James is right, Winston.'' He muttered, "You have no other choice.''

Churchill gave in. "If that is the case then, I want you to go along to represent the civil authority, David. You will make the actual arrests—if possible,'' he added as an afterthought. Then turning to Bannerman, "What would you anticipate they will do?''

Bannerman pointed to the cross section of one of the ventilator shafts shown on a blueprint. "Place explosives here, against the shaft walls, to collapse them and flood the Tunnel. The damage would be incalculable.''

"How long would it take to repair?''

Bannerman shrugged. "A year. Perhaps never. But it won't come to that now, damnit.''

Churchill could now see the party of ten Marines crouched below the lifeboat's gunwales, helmets turned to ward off the spray bursting over the bow as the sailors tugged at the oar looms. Four white blades snatched at the water and flashed to dip again.

Bannerman crouched in the bow, head down and enduring the wild motion of the boat and the bitter wind. He was

seasick, had been since the *Ajax* had cleared Dover Harbour.
He tightened his hold on the thwart to keep from being
thrown forward and hunched his shoulders against the spray
that came sweeping inboard.

"Bail, you bloody bastards," he heard the coxswain roaring at the Marines. A rogue wave dropped away unexpectedly
and the sailors on the starboard side missed stroke simultaneously and sprawled backwards while the port oars bit deep,
slewing the boat broadside to the following wave. They would
have been swamped if the alert coxswain hadn't countered by
throwing his weight onto the rudder. As it was, enough water
came inboard to drench them and refill the boat.

It took twenty minutes to cover the cable's length to the
quay. As the oars came in, Bush roused the men out and up
onto the quay and the coxswain swung the boat about and
began to run down to the ship, incomparably easier now with
the wind behind them.

Bannerman led them up the path at a stumbling trot into the
teeth of the gale. Rain and sleet flew at them like cannon
shot, stinging bare skin and drumming against greatcoats with
the force of rifle bullets. The sudden cessation of the storm's
fury when they clambered into the iron shaft was unworldly,
eerie beyond belief as the thick iron plate muffled the violence of the storm.

They went down endless flights of iron ladders, their torch
beams supplementing the meager emergency lamps. Gaunt
shadows moved against dim recesses, creating black pools,
and far below, a misty patch of lighter darkness grew: the
Tunnel floor six hundred feet below.

They passed the quietly spinning number one fan blade.
Each of the men eyed the whirling edges and pressed close
against the rungs in spite of the three feet of clearance. It took
the equipment-laden party forty-five minutes to complete the
descent into the bowels of the English Channel, and all the
while the faint thrumming of moving air increased in velocity
as they approached the Tunnel proper.

Bush formed them up as they paused beneath the shaft, all
subdued by the empty stillness of the Tunnel. Other than a
few dim lamps still burning to create the illusion of immense
distance, there was no sign of life.

Two Marines were sent forward as scouts, and Bannerman
and Powell were placed at the end of the line, each carrying a

spare Lee-Enfield rifle. Captain Bush marched his men at a steady but easy pace beside the tracks, conscious of the debilitating effect of the two-degree slope and the need to conserve energy.

They had exactly one mile to go and they covered the distance in fifteen minutes of steady marching. When Bush finally called a halt, Powell sank down gratefully, taking no part in the subdued conversation.

Bush and Bannerman went forward to the fall on the off chance that a way through the rubble might be apparent from this side. As they clambered about the broken cement and twisted plate, Bush openly studied Bannerman's noncommittal expression, wondering what it would feel like to know that the greatest achievement of your career might at any moment disintegrate in a violent blast of flame and gas. Bannerman ignored his scrutiny and checked the rubble thoroughly only to find it just as solidly compacted on this side. He shook his head, and without a word they turned back.

Powell was totally absorbed in his own thoughts. He could not rid his mind of the doctor's shouted words over the static of the poor connection from London. "Your wife died this morning! Pneumonia!" Over and over again, the doctor had shouted those same words, forcing understanding past the atmospherics and the fog which seemed to have engulfed his mind. The hours since had been wrapped in haze; there had been a loud argument after the sound of gunfire had stopped. And he recalled being surprised when it occurred to him that there had been shooting. He had heard Churchill and Bannerman arguing and had listened for a while, even taken part in the discussion, though he could not recall now what it was about or what he had said. He seemed to be floating between the real world and the lonely hell of his own existence, and he supposed that his mind was trying to come to grips with the fact of Grace's death. For a moment he was amused that he could stand outside himself and study his reactions with such passivity. And then for some reason, he could recall nothing else until they were in a small boat, pitching in steep seas.

Grace. She would never hear the end of the story. She had died, mercifully in her sleep, before the pain had grown unbearable. She had died as gently as she had lived. But he still had a job to do. He started to raise his head, then slumped back. It really did not matter any longer.

There was a stirring among the party and they got to their feet. Powell followed suit. Bannerman directed a question to him that he did not hear and he merely nodded, not bothering to have it repeated.

They moved back several hundred yards the way they had come to a metal hatch set in the floor between the tracks. Bannerman, with the help of two Marines, got the iron covering plate up. The sound as it struck at metal rail echoed and reechoed into the distance.

Bannerman sat down on the edge and shone his torch past his dangling feet. The light beam flickered across a maze of pipes and wire cable filling either side of a narrow walkway. He eased himself off the edge and down, crouching to miss the festoons of smaller pipes and cables. One by one, the Marines followed him into the conduit and along to where the shattered edge of an iron plate and a jumble of broken cement blocked further progress. The conduit was slightly over five feet high and the area on either side was jammed with pipes of all diameters and heavy, sheathed electrical cables, all painted the same dreary gray.

"This is the one we want." Bannerman tapped the largest pipe. "Give me the cutting torch."

The two Marines detailed to carry the heavy steel gas flasks set them down with obvious relief. One held the torch while Bannerman coupled the meter gauge and hoses to the nozzles, opened the valves, and checked the pressure. He lit the flame with the igniter, then adjusted both the flame and his goggles.

It took twenty minutes to cut into the pipe, cursing cramped legs and back and the pipe, which apparently still contained sufficient water to reduce the effectiveness of the cutting flame, and most of all the time being wasted. Bannerman finally completed the cut, shut off the gas, and staggered up. Bush used a bayonet to pry the glowing metal section loose and it fell outward with a crash, sizzling and spitting in the trickle of water below the walkway. The ragged edges of the pipe were still hot as Bannerman stepped gingerly through the opening. Inside, the water was knee deep, not enough to hinder their progress. He motioned for someone to bring the cutting torch, ducked low, and started forward.

*   *   *

"I tell you, every shaft! Without Shafts Seven and Eight the explosives we have in the remaining shafts will be marginal."

McDougal had sunk onto his haunches in exhaustion, head down and arms dangling over his knees, as he endured von Dorn's harangue. He cursed himself, the Dublin Committee, and the German. There were only a few hours left in this early Christmas morning before the bloody ship came for them. And von Dorn knew as well as he that no captain in his right mind would wait past the exact minute determined beforehand. The dangers were far too great.

McDougal raised his head to stare at von Dorn. Why in the name of the Savior had he not refused to leave Dover? He thought again about the supplementary orders that Finnigan had brought from Boyle and Dublin. Finnigan—the worthless little bastard. The Committee had no interest in destroying the Tunnel merely to aid Germany—which had already double-crossed them anyway by selling weapons to the Ulster Volunteers. Two thousand rifles and £300,000 in credits—which could only be redeemed in Germany on German terms—was a pittance beside what they would gain if it were discovered that Germany, with Fenian help, had engineered the sabotage, successful or not. The damnable Home Rule bill would be dead before introduction, and war with Germany—Ireland's only real hope—brought that much nearer. And the Fenians would once more be the leading force for Irish independence. When war came, as it surely must, recruits would flock to the Movement, and Germany would have no choice but to support them without question. A thousand years of oppression and betrayal, of torture and murder, would be wiped out in a mass rising that would sweep the English from Irish shores.

Wearily he heaved himself up and his men followed suit. They must leave through Shaft Five in any event. If there was time, it would be done. If not, neither he nor the Dublin Committee cared whether von Dorn's foolish scheme worked perfectly. Whatever damage was done would be sufficient for their own purposes.

They left the conduit an hour later and Bannerman wasted not an instant starting them up-Tunnel. They were all tired, wet, and shivering constantly in the forty degree cold. Time was against them and each man knew it. Bush, trotting at the head of the file, was becoming more convinced with each passing minute that they were on a fool's errand. Bannerman's estimate of the time required to enter the Tunnel, to cut into and out of the drain, was badly off. And he was beginning to be concerned about the engineer's estimates of the time it would take the saboteurs to place and wire the explosives in the shafts. He glanced back along the line of shadowy figures trotting behind. They were terribly exposed like this in the vast open cavern of the Tunnel, stretching endlessly before and behind, its red brick walls and cement floor offering little or no cover. He had no idea what the effect of the saboteurs' explosives would be overall, but he knew that if they were detonated, anyone inside the Tunnel would be drowned for certain. Bush prided himself on his inflexible will and the discipline instilled in the men of his command. But he was not a fool, nor did he wish to die making a last heroic gesture.

Powell trotted in their wake, occupied with his own thoughts. The very process of breathing, of fighting the pain of oxygen-starved lungs, would have kept him silent even if he had not been so inclined. Bannerman, in spite of the suffocating gases and the heat that had been thrown off by the torch in the cramped interior of the pipe, pushed himself on, refusing to give in to exhaustion. The thought of stretching out, even on the cold cement floor, of regaining his breath and ridding himself of the pain in his chest and the acid taste in his mouth was overwhelming. But he went on, obsessed with the guilt of his many mistakes. He had misjudged the situation so many times before that he could no more bow out now than he could have resigned that day in November. They had them now, he knew. A few more minutes and it would be over, the threat relieved.

The first rifle shots echoed through the Tunnel, crashing from side to side until it was impossible to judge their distance, or even their direction. Bush's voice shouting orders was lost in the din, but the Marines knew well enough what to do. Before the first volley had ended, they had spread themselves in as extended a skirmish line as the narrow confines of the Tunnel allowed.

chapter════29

*V*on Dorn met the two advance men near the first safety
shelter beyond Ventilator Shaft Five. The Fenians had fallen
back in disciplined order, leapfrogging one another and firing
an occasional shot to keep the intruders at bay.

"Royal Marines, sir," one of them answered his demand.
"Recognized the coat flashes."

Von Dorn suppressed a surge of fear and knelt beside the
man. His companion was on the far side of the Tunnel,
sheltering behind the jut of an iron reinforcing ring.

"How many?"

"Three, near's I can tell. Maybe hit one of the bastards."

Two more of the Irishmen appeared and von Dorn waved
them back.

"Then there are more following," he said, half to himself.

"Aye. Ye can bet on it."

Yes, von Dorn thought. Damned well better keep them
back. He smacked a fist against his knee. One more hour
would have seen them safely away. Already they were near to
finishing. The final wiring and the climb to the surface were
all that remained. Forty minutes of work, no more. He snapped
his watch open. The ship was due in sixty-four minutes—they
could have done it.

His mind worked furiously, trying to plan, to calculate all
the possibilities. With German troops he would merely have
ordered a rearguard to sacrifice themselves. German troops
understood the need for discipline and self-sacrifice. But there
was no chance of doing so with these Irish fools. He glanced
along the Tunnel, which was clear for the moment. McDougal
was the key; if he could be convinced, the English might be
delayed long enough . . .

"Stay here," he snapped. "I am going to find McDougal.
Hold them until I return."

"Aye, mate. We'll do just that," the man beside him growled. "Unless they have a full regiment behind them, ye can count on us."

Von Dorn started back at a trot, knowing that there was not a chance in hell they would do as he ordered unless McDougal backed him. It was time for the confrontation he had sought to avoid, inevitable as it had been from the beginning. Behind, he heard rifle shots and the echoes pursued him with astounding dissonance.

McDougal had reached the bottom of the shaft and with him were two of the three men who should have been working on the installation of the explosives. Containing his anger, von Dorn described the situation briefly.

"That's it, then," McDougal snapped. "We'll be just in time to board the bloody boat if we go now."

Von Dorn was prepared for that. He grasped the Irishman's arm to draw him aside, but McDougal pulled away. "No more now," he shouted. "There's no time to finish. You'll do all the damage with—"

"Damn it," von Dorn roared, no longer able to restrain the fury resulting from weeks of frustration and worry. To have success so close, only minutes away, and to see it thrown away by a cowardly old man threw him into a frenzy that he could not control. Even as von Dorn raged, he knew that everything was lost. "We will finish," he screamed, and his hysteria so astounded McDougal that he laughed. Without thinking, von Dorn yanked the Luger free from his belt. "Twenty minutes more," he shouted, leveling the pistol. "Twenty minutes—"

The roar of the Mauser at close quarters was deafening and for a moment von Dorn did not realize that he had been shot. He was disoriented, dizzy of a sudden, and he looked up at the three men, realizing he had fallen, to see them receding into a fog.

". . . bloody damned Kraut," McDougal snarled. "Here, Willy, run tell the others to fall back. We'll be getting out of here before they catch us up." McDougal glanced up into the shaft. "Aye," he said, half to himself, "once up into there, we can stave off an army."

"What about him?" the man who had shot von Dorn asked.

McDougal laughed at that. "Leave him here and be damned

to him. We wouldn't want the bloody English to mistake the ones responsible for the ruination of their damned Tunnel, now would we?"

Bush stopped Bannerman and Powell and hurried them into the meager shelter offered by the side of the Tunnel. "Stay close to the wall," he ordered. "The ricochets are bad."

"We've found them then?" Bannerman demanded and realized instantly how foolish the question sounded. He swallowed hard and clenched his fists against the sudden tension.

"I would say so," Bush answered drily. "At least two of them. We are unable to develop an effective sweep of fire because of the upward slope. They have the advantage of us and they know what they are doing." He swung around as a disciplined volley of rifle fire slammed back at them—three rounds, no more. The explosions magnified by the hard surfaces were agonizing. "I would say they are trained as soldiers," he shouted.

Bannerman could not keep the surprise from his voice. "German soldiers?" Had Churchill been right after all?

Bush shook his head. "No, I don't think so. I heard them calling to one another in English."

"Irish then." Powell spoke for the first time since entering the Tunnel.

"You may be correct, Mr. Powell," Bush agreed. "A large part of our military force is Irish."

"Never mind that," Bannerman snapped. "How do you intend to get at them?"

"Just as we are doing now, sir. We have superior firepower and we can leapfrog ahead." As he spoke, another burst of rifle fire exploded, the heavy, dull bark of the Lee-Enfield and the sharp crack of the Mauser easily distinguished.

"I have four men up and three supporting. They lay down a barrage of fire up-Tunnel and the two men move forward. If we repeat the process long enough, we can drive them to the ventilator shaft. I brought along a supply of grenade bombs in hopes that we would close with them. They were issued to us a month ago for testing."

"You will only drive them into the shaft," Bannerman protested.

"Yes, possibly. That is a chance we must take."

"You realize, of course," Bannerman snapped, "that if you do so, we have lost the Tunnel. We could not hope to dislodge them and they can set off the explosives at will."

Bush nodded. "I *am* aware of that. But there is little else that I can do. If we press hard enough, they will have no time to climb into the shaft."

Bannerman struck his fist against his thigh. "Damn it, Captain, that is an unreasonable supposition. They know as well as we what will happen if they do not retreat into the shaft. Do you think they will allow themselves to be cut off from their only escape route?"

"Of course not," Bush snarled back, losing his temper. "I'm not a damned fool. But if you have any other suggestions, I would be most happy to hear them. This Tunnel offers absolutely no cover. It would be suicide to try a rush. I would lose every man sent up."

"Damn it to hell," Bannerman cried, the anguish plain in his voice, "We've got to do something. Look here, if—"

The first grenade went off with a shattering roar. Instinctively Bannerman clapped his hands to his ears and opened his mouth, bending forward from the waist. A second blast all but deafened him, and for a moment his eyes fell on Powell, who had neither flinched nor shown any sign that he was aware of the explosions. His expression remained as composed as ever, eyes vacant.

Bannerman followed Bush forward, crouching along the wall until stopped by a Marine rifleman. "Sergeant Rodale 'as taken ta others forrard, sir. Says to cum easy."

Rodale, by bouncing the grenade bombs along the Tunnel floor, had managed to drive back the riflemen opposing them. Two more concussions assaulted them, and Bannerman grimaced with pain. As they approached the safety shelter below Ventilator Shaft Five, one of the Marines spotted traces of blood. Strangely enough, there was no further opposition ahead and they paused to consider their next step.

"I suspect," Bush began, "that they have pulled back to make a stand further along, possibly even to erect a barricade of some sort beneath the ventilator shaft."

Bannerman nodded. "They could do so. There is plenty of material to hand." He drew out the large-scale print of the Tunnel he had stuffed into the pocket of his greatcoat and spread it on the damp floor. "But look here, Captain. The

Tunnel is thirty feet wide. Beneath the ventilator shafts, the Tunnel widens by another eight feet, far too wide to throw an effective barricade across the width.''

"I see your point. You are suggesting that the barricade, if there is one, will be constructed at some remove from the ventilator shaft?''

"Yes. Those inside will need the time the barricade can purchase. But because it cannot close off the entire Tunnel, they know it will certainly be overwhelmed. I have an idea how to speed that process.''

Bush nodded and shifted position to allow his holstered Webley to sit more comfortably. "I'm listening.''

"It makes sense to rig the barricade, but only to delay us while the others withdraw into the shaft. When they do so, they will leave one or two riflemen on the control booth balcony. As they climb higher, they can take advantage of the cover provided by the stair landings. Once into the shaft, we'll never stop them. Therefore, we must go back into the conduit, move up Tunnel and . . .''

He broke off as the sergeant ducked into the safety shelter to confirm that a barricade was indeed being thrown up.

"Can't get close enough to throw the bombs, sir.''

Bush drummed his fingers on the rifle stock. "Damn.'' He shook his head and glared around the shelter, as if seeking enlightenment. "Mr. Bannerman, how long would you estimate it would take them to climb to the top of the shaft?''

Bannerman realized what he was getting at and jumped to his feet. "See here, Captain, you can't go—''

"Forty minutes, Mr. Bannerman?''

"There is another way, Captain. You've got to listen . . .''

"Sergeant. Assemble your men and be quick about it. Leave all packs, take only rifles.''

Bannerman grabbed his arm and swung him about. "Damn it all, Bush, you can't go off and leave them like this. They will certainly destroy the Tunnel.'' He was shouting, on the verge of hysteria, but he could no longer control himself.

Bush's expression was sympathetic. "I realize that, Mr. Bannerman. I also realize that we will be hard pressed to get ourselves out of here in forty minutes. We have two miles to go and six hundred feet to climb. They have only five hundred feet. I do not wish to sacrifice my men uselessly. You said yourself that once they get into that shaft, they are away free.'' He turned and blew a sharp blast on his silver whistle.

"Wait, damnit," Bannerman shouted as the Marines came filtering back in response to the whistle. "There is a way to get behind them. We have only to go down through the conduit again—''

Bush's voice was glacial as he cut him off. "Mr. Bannerman, if your engineering manager is with them as we suspect, he will have already taken steps to guard against that approach. In any event, it is now too late, sir. I do not intend that my command be slaughtered as a foolish gesture. We have a better chance of taking them as they leave the shaft. Sergeant, double time. We have forty minutes to reach the surface.''

None of them had noticed Powell edging away from the group until he was concealed by the shadows. In his hand were two bombs removed from the satchel while the sergeant's attention had been diverted by the dispute between Bush and Bannerman. Satisfied that he was unobserved, he turned and started walking up-Tunnel. His mind was crystal clear now, the depression that had plunged him into despair was under control, and he was completely untroubled.

Powell knew he was about to make that foolish gesture Bush had spoken of, but it might work. If not, no harm would have been done and no loss to anyone. Bannerman was correct. If they did not stop them now, the Tunnel would be destroyed. But Bush was also correct. Once into the shaft, the saboteurs could not be gotten at. The answer was simple enough, he thought. Stop them before they reached the ladders. He twisted the handles from the bombs and clamped the fuse levers down with his fingers.

Powell could see the barricade ahead as a dark blur in the distance. He wished that there had been a chance to say good-by to Churchill. He liked the man, he really did, head-strong and stubborn as he was. He had it in him to become a master politician, but there was too much of his impetuous father in him, unfortunately. Sooner or later, Winston would throw it all away for some grand gesture, as Lord Randolph had done.

Powell stopped some twenty-five yards from the dimly illumined pile of timbers and iron plates and raised his hands. "I am Chief Inspector David Powell, Special Branch," he shouted. "I wish to talk with you."

His voice was even, almost cold, he noted as he waited, conscious that any second he could be shot down.

"Come forrard, slowly, Chief Inspector wotever," a voice answered after a moment.

Powell obeyed, hands still raised. The hard glass casings of the bombs clutched in either hand were cold and distasteful. The barricade, not quite ten feet wide and set squarely across the rails, was just ahead now, and a man was staring at him along a rifle barrel. A second man watched down-Tunnel as if expecting a trick, but darted quick glances toward Powell now and again. The ventilator shaft was still several hundred feet distant.

He stopped a few feet from the barricade. "I want to speak with whoever is leading you," he snapped. "And the German officer, quickly."

The man laughed at that. "Wot the hell do ye want?"

Powell drew a deep breath, knowing that he would get no further with this one. But there were only two men visible. If he showed them the two bombs, he was still far enough from the barrier that they would have no effect, other than to shatter an eardrum or two, and the man on the control booth balcony would probably shoot him before he could throw.

"Your position is hopeless," he said, stalling for time. "If you surrender now, you will be treated as prisoners-of-war and not as rebels or outlaws."

The man laughed at that and his associate also chuckled. "Now, Chief Inspector, I'm no barrister at all. But I know better'n to swallow that. Now you—"

Powell released the levers and threw himself over the barrier. For an instant the two men were frozen motionless. Powell was counting as the force of his landing knocked his breath away. The grenade bombs rolled.

". . . three . . . four . . ." Powell never reached five.

The explosions caused them all to dive for cover. Echoes slammed along the Tunnel, bounding and rebounding again and again from the brick and cement. Bush raised his head as they began to die away, scrabbled to turn himself around, and peered up the Tunnel. "Jesus Christ," he breathed softly.

It was Bannerman who noticed first that Powell was missing. Bush glanced at the engineer, horror and shock contorting his face. "My God . . ." Bannerman managed to choke out. Without thinking, he started running up the Tunnel and the others followed.

McDougal swarmed down the ladder from the control balcony and stared at the torn fragments of the barricade and the three mangled bodies. Shaken, he forced himself to think, but the sight of the bodies mutilated by glass and iron fragments sickened him so that he had to turn away, breathing deeply to contain his nausea. One of his men, a former infantry sergeant, pushed him aside and ran a few yards ahead. He paused, then raced back.

"They're comin'," he shouted and motioned two men to what remained of the barricade.

"One round lads, then up." He grabbed McDougal by the arm, pushing him toward the ladder.

"No," Bush roared at him after the volley had driven them back. "We are going now. Powell did not stop them from getting into the shaft and now they have the advantage of height. They can pick us off one by one."

"Damn you, Bush!" Bannerman screamed. "I'll see you court-martialed for this."

Bush ignored him, picked up his rifle, and followed the Marines trotting down-Tunnel. Bannerman hesitated, then swung around and began to run. Bush roared after him but he went on. The safety shelter was just ahead and he raced toward it, unslinging his rifle. Bush started back, then, recognizing the futility of trying to drag the engineer along against his will, swore bitterly and began to run down-Tunnel.

Bannerman broke the bayonet prying the conduit cover up, but he got one edge raised enough to slide the rifle barrel under. The stock broke as he tried to lever the heavy iron cover. Swearing incoherently, he grabbed the rifle by the receiver, pushed down, and lifted the cover enough to slide it aside.

His electric torch cast only a dim, yellowish light as he climbed down into the conduit and made his way along. The silence was oppressive and the air heavy and dead. Mud and debris filled the narrow walkway between the piping, an indication of how far the flooding had extended. The smell was overpowering, and he wound his handkerchief around his nose and mouth. He forced himself on, trotting where he could while the torch beam dwindled. A measure of sanity began to return, and with it doubts. Bush was a fool if he expected to stop McDougal from leaving the shaft, but then he knew that Bush had no other choice as he would see it. The Tunnel meant nothing to him—in fact, as a military man, he might even consider it a liability. He would never see that the Tunnel represented Britain's . . . McDougal. He realized with surprise that he had not yet come to grips with McDougal's betrayal of their friendship, but there was no time even to wonder . . .

He slipped and fell, cracking his head hard against a pipe. The pain was overwhelming and he rolled in the slime, clutching his head in agony.

Von Dorn had pushed himself into a sitting position. Now he stared at the blood covering his hands. In the dim light of the emergency bulb further along, the sticky coating made them seem black. He began to recall then what had happened, the rifle shot and the crashing echoes of an explosion. He had no idea how long he had been sitting with his back against the cold brick, drifting in and out of consciousness.

When von Dorn pulled his jacket and shirt away and examined the bloody mess below his rib cage, he noted with a detachment that surprised him that the entrance wound was a round hole. Perhaps that had saved his life—for the moment. One neat round hole instead of the huge jagged wound Mauser bullets caused when they tumbled. And he laughed soundlessly at the joke. He was dead. Whether the bullet killed him now or later, he was dead. There were the explosions to come, they would kill him just as surely.

He sat, dreaming, thinking about what might have been if he had succeeded. After a while, another thought intruded— McDougal might very well offer to trade the Tunnel intact for his own miserable life and freedom. It was this that finally goaded him from the dreamlike state that had engulfed him. Faintly, his anger was stirred. He had come too far, spent too much, to see it fail now. If he was going to die, he wanted it to be worthwhile. He would not die a failure.

As von Dorn tried to get to his feet, pain stabbed through his midsection and he collapsed. For a long time he lay groaning with the pain, only half conscious. But gradually, as it began to recede, he tried once more. This time he made it up and leaned against the wall, waiting for his legs to stop trembling. His mind was clear now; he understood what had happened and what he must do. McDougal had never intended to go through with it unless the risks were minimal. Whether the Tunnel was destroyed or not, as the Dublin Committee saw it, they could not lose. He should have seen it sooner, should have guessed when Boyle had agreed so readily to his terms after his previous refusal. Those damned fools. They had destroyed everything and themselves included. There would be no declaration of war by England if the Tunnel was not destroyed, even if it was evident that Germany was responsible. England was not ready for war. The Liberal government's determination to see the Tunnel completed, no matter the cost, would only be increased. They would see the attempt to destroy it for what it was, as an indication of how desperately Germany feared the Tunnel.

Worse yet, he had failed; failed for the first time in his career to carry out the task assigned by no less an authority than the Kaiser. He could not bear the thought of the contempt his name would carry within the inmost circles of the General Staff to which he had so long aspired.

Von Dorn reached the ladder below the shaft without realizing it. His attention was finally caught by a thin wire cord that had slipped from the disguising seam of the cement wall. It required a few moments for him to recall that it was the means of igniting the series of explosives planted in each of the ventilator shafts. It should connect to the timer switch somewhere above through the emergency lighting system which worked independently of the Tunnel's electrical system. The battery-powered emergency system would furnish sufficient current to ignite the explosives in timed sequence throughout the miles of Tunnel. For a moment, he hung onto the ladder, sobbing with the effort that it cost. He was right!—McDougal had no intention of setting off the charges. Instead, he intended to use them to bargain for his safety if need be.

"By God," he muttered. "There might still be a chance."

His hands as he placed them on the rungs were sticky with blood. The pain was growing to unbelievable proportions now that shock had completely worn away. His vision was dimming, and the Tunnel was filled with an eerie silence. Grasping the wire, von Dorn started upward, grunting with the agony each rung cost, determined that all those hours in the London embassy would not be wasted.

In the half-light of dawn the gale had begun to diminish, and the destroyer *Ajax* stood in to the quay to take off the Marines. Churchill stood at the bridge railing, counting the figures slumped in weary dejection, and he knew then that they had failed. Three men were missing.

Bush, filthy and weary beyond belief, saluted, and Churchill helped him down to the mess deck and to a table. The captain shook his head, then forced himself up straight as Churchill handed him a mug of tea.

"We had to turn back, sir." The captain fumbled in his tunic for a cigarette and glanced for permission to Churchill.

"Good God, man, of course!" Churchill found a match and struck it for him.

Bush drew deeply on the cigarette, then continued. "They were waiting for us, sir. Killed one of my men. They had us pinned down, sir. Mr. Bannerman reckoned they had mined all of the shafts but Number Five. I believe we stopped them from doing that. There was no cover, sir. It would have been suicide to go against them and it would have accomplished nothing. They were well armed—Mausers, sir—and they appeared to have military training. They may even have been German soldiers, but I don't think so. In any event, I gave the order to leave. Inspector Powell . . ." He paused and gulped the hot tea, clearly unnerved. "Inspector Powell," he began again, "took two bombs and went forward to the barricade they had thrown up. He must have killed one or two of them. I . . . I think he blew himself up with the bombs as well."

"Good God," Churchill muttered, horrified. He was so badly shaken that he did not hear what Bush said next.

". . . no other choice but to retreat. Mr. Bannerman ran from us, sir. He stayed behind. I think he was going to try and get at them through the conduit."

Churchill took a deep breath and clenched his hands into fists where he had jammed them deep into his pockets.

"They must come out through Number Five, sir. I feel we have a better chance of stopping them there, sir, than we would have had trying to get into the shaft where they had every advantage. If they see us waiting for them, they may think twice before setting off their bombs, sir.''

Churchill nodded. ''Quite right, Captain. Quite right. And you may depend upon me to say so in my report to the cabinet.'' His answer was mechanical; he was wondering if there would still be a cabinet after this debacle. ''About Inspector Powell—his wife died in hospital yesterday morning. I had a wireless message to that effect an hour ago. They were very close. He never told me . . . .'' The First Lord's face was bleak for a moment.

''Thank you sir,'' Bush murmured gratefully as Churchill stood and caught the eye of the executive officer.

''My compliments to the captain. I want the ship underway immediately. Set a course for Ventilator Shaft Number Five.''

The executive officer nodded and hurried out. Churchill started to follow, then hesitated and turned back. ''Inspector Powell,'' he said, hesitating, but Bush knew what he wanted to ask.

''He must have been killed instantly sir.''

Churchill nodded and turned away, rubbing a hand over his face to hide his anguish.

Von Dorn dragged himself over the edge of the balcony, too weak to go further for the moment. He lay huddled on the cold plate, shuddering with agony. His hands pressed against torn flesh in an attempt to ease the pain, and his shirt, jacket, and greatcoat were soaked with blood.

He was alone on the balcony. Only the slowly-turning fan blades above him broke the stillness with a gentle soughing that reminded him of a meadow. For a moment, the scene was as clear to him as it must have been that afternoon so long ago. He saw his mother, her skin tanned to a gentle gold by the summer sun, sitting on the blanket watching as he dashed toward her, showing how fast he could run. She had laughed, her eyes crinkling and her lips kissing him as he collapsed into her arms and pressed his face against the crisp cotton dress. The fragrance of the lilac cologne she always wore came back to him. My God, he thought, I could not have been more than three years old. Had he ever recalled that picnic scene before? And then his mind swooped away as he thought it strange how he could not remember his mother's face clearly, but could feel the cotton of her dress beneath his cheek.

The contrast between that memory of the sun-drenched distant field and the cold interior of the Tunnel was so fierce that he found he was weeping—for what, he wondered? A lost childhood? A wasted life? And he knew he was on the verge of insanity. He was bleeding to death and unless he . . . what? What was it he was supposed to do?

After an indeterminate time, he remembered. The pain had gone now and he was no longer cold. Von Dorn forced himself to his knees. He had to complete the connection to the igniter. When he had done that, then he could rest.

Bannerman had gone down-Tunnel from the ventilator shaft, telling himself that he only wanted to make certain it was clear, but in reality, wanting to know for certain that Powell was dead. There was still time enough. He stared at the horror much as McDougal had done, unable to recognize which mutilated body belonged to David Powell. For a moment, Bannerman wondered why he had done it, but only for a moment. His head ached abominably and he found it hard to concentrate. He was so tired that he was literally falling asleep on his feet, and somewhere above, he was certain, was the detonating device. It had to be. The blow to his head in the conduit had done something to his vision as well—the Tunnel seemed to be darkening. He began to climb then, remembering the last time he had climbed . . . but he lost the thread.

Churchill and the ship's captain stood side by side on the bridge, peering through binoculars across the gray desolation of torn waves under the black overcast. The rain and sleet had eased enough to allow them to see the distant pillar of Shaft Five. The pounding of the destroyer's engines came clearly through the deck plates, signifying the immense effort being made to come up to the shaft. The bow buried itself in a crash of white water that creamed the length of the deck, spilling away through the scuppers in torrents as the ship rose again.

Churchill heard a thin whistle and the duty officer uncapped the speaking tube and listened a moment.

"Masthead reports a distress rocket fired from Ventilator Shaft Five, sir. Also a vessel approaching the ventilator shaft, bearing 397° at five hundred yards. Looks like a merchant vessel. No ensign visible, sir.''

As one, both men turned their glasses in the direction indicated, but the rain chose that moment to close down again. A moment later, the captain grunted. ''May have just caught a glimpse of her, sir,'' he addressed Churchill.

Churchill had not yet mastered the trick of keeping the glasses focused on a distant object in spite of the ship's violent motion and merely murmured an acknowledgment. He lowered the glasses and tapped them on the railing.

''Rescue party, I would wager,'' he said with considerably less satisfaction than he felt. ''They will reach the shaft before we do?''

''Yes, sir. And be away if those people are already in boats waiting for the ship.''

''Then we must stop them.''

The captain grinned and turned to the duty officer. ''Mr. Spaulding, have X battery load and aim. Shoot only on my direct order. Then signal the vessel to identify herself.''

''Very good, sir,'' and the young officer repeated the order for confirmation.

Churchill was aware of the captain's barely contained excitement and with a flash of insight understood the man's satisfaction—years of service, much of it routine and boring in the extreme but all directed toward just such a moment—to culminate in the crash of gunfire. He recalled how during the long empty stretches of his own military career in India he had maneuvered, pulled every string, badgered his mother to use her considerable influence to have him sent to the midst of the action. He knew the excitement that came with imminent conflict and realized for the first time that other men could be affected by it as strongly as he. And if that excitement were not tempered by fear and intellect, disaster could result. Careful attention would have to be paid in the future to the selection of officers for sensitive positions where a single misadventure could reduce the world to war.

Churchill removed the cigar from his teeth and noted that the end had been chewed to rags. ''Captain,'' he said, choosing his words with care, ''I should like to prevent, if possible, that ship approaching any closer. If those aboard the ventilator shaft see their hope of relief disappearing, they may think twice about detonating their bombs.''

"Very good, sir." The captain turned as Spaulding reappeared at his side.

"The vessel ignores our flasher and flag signals, sir. I've ordered the wireless room to try, sir."

"No need, Mr. Spaulding. They see us," the captain replied with assurance. He uncapped the speaking tube marked BATTERY and whistled. "This is the captain. Put a shot across their bow, Mr. Peters. If they do not turn away within twenty seconds, fire again and await further orders."

Just short of the control booth balcony, Bannerman found half-congealed blood on one of the rungs. Powell must have wounded at least one of them, he thought with satisfaction, and pulled himself onto the icy plates.

He lay full length, trying to peer through the gathering darkness as he tugged the Colt revolver from his pocket. The iron plates gleamed dully in the meager light and the iron shaft flowed upward and away. To one side, the glass windows of the control booth were opaque. He would start in there, a quick search to make certain that he had overlooked nothing before going on. They might have left a timing device there.

As he came to his feet, a dull clinking sound stopped him. Half crouching, he turned toward the sound. The balcony was deep in shadow, and as he started to reach for his torch, he remembered that he had lost it in the conduit. He peered into the shadows on the far side, letting his eye run with the circular sweep of the railing. Almost directly opposite he caught a flicker of movement beneath the single bulb still burning. A sudden shock of fear swept him and his fingers worked so convulsively he nearly dropped the revolver. Bannerman forced himself to move, one step at a time, fighting the overwhelming fear that threatened to send him gibbering for the ladder and the nonexistent safety of the Tunnel floor. He pressed against the dripping shaft wall and shuffled on, hoping that the soft whir of fan blades twelve feet above his head would cover the scuffing his boots made against the plate.

A figure was hunched close to the shaft wall. A rattling cough came from it and a clawlike hand grasped and pulled. Von Dorn coughed again and the distant pain caused his hands to shake. He had been right after all. They had never meant to destroy the Tunnel. That blind fool McDougal had left the igniter where it could easily be found, but he would take care of it properly. The spring delay device came away easily, exposing the bright copper contacts. It was so easy now. He was dying quickly, so quickly that he had no use for the delay mechanism. Von Dorn pulled the flex to him and laboriously bent one end into a hook and worked it over the terminal. His awkward fingers could not manage the nut and it slipped away into the darkness. Von Dorn closed his eyes and struggled to contain the cough that was tearing at his chest. He could not allow it, not yet. In his imagination, he could see the bloody mass of lung tissue on the point of bursting. No, he could not cough. Not yet. Please God, not yet.

A noise. Von Dorn looked into the darkness that swam and flashed with bursting lights and shapes. In the midst was a solid blackness, a shadow that should not have been there, and the pale face of it was before him, a face that seemed vaguely familiar. His weakening fingers twisted the second wire on the terminal as he croaked, *"Wer is est?"*

The German words galvanized Bannerman, and he flung himself forward shouting, the revolver forgotten. The white face floated toward von Dorn but it no longer made any difference. Nothing did now, he thought happily. The switch turned easily on its oiled bearing, and Bannerman heard the first roll of thunder begin.

The four-inch gun directly below the bridge bellowed and Churchill jumped, clapping his hands to his ears. He had forgotten about the concussion, so absorbed was he in trying to catch a glimpse of the German vessel through his glasses. He staggered as the ship buried its bow again and fetched up against the rail. He noticed Spaulding's tense expression as the captain sought to restrain a smile.

"Laughing at the First Lord of the Admiralty is no way to look for promotion, boy," he growled, but the wind snatched his words away. He raised his glasses again and this time found the steamer in the wildly tossing field. The gun bellowed again and he swore.

"She's turning away, sir," Spaulding shouted.

"Signal her by wireless that she is under my guns and to

come up under my lee or I will sink her," the captain said, not taking his glasses from his eyes.

Churchill pulled a fresh cigar from beneath the greatcoat, relieved that the vessel had responded so promptly. The claims of England and France to the waters surrounding the ventilator shafts were currently being hotly debated in the Hague Tribunal. Obviously, a claim to three miles of water around each shaft would give both countries complete control of the Channel. Sinking a ship now, especially a German merchant vessel, would cause an international incident more serious even than Agadir this past summer.

He stuck the cigar in his mouth and focused the glass on the ventilator shaft. There came several figures tumbling from the tower, all gesticulating wildly at the steamer which had turned away at less than, he judged, a hundred yards, not certain what the proper nautical terminology was. He heard the captain ordering reduced speed and felt the destroyer alter course to approach the shaft from an angle so as to keep the steamer under her guns.

The speaking tube whistled, and the captain flipped it open and acknowledged.

"Mast here, Flasher from the island. Reads: 'Will surrender in return for amnesty. Germany is—' "

A gout of flame bloomed above the ventilator shaft, and during the next moments, Churchill's mind caught and retained only impressions—a stick figure whirled into the sea on the leading edge of the blast, the shaft itself flaring open to disappear beneath a roiling cloud of smoke and dust shot through with flame, the whitish fog of the concussion sweeping toward them.

Beyond, a flare of light flashed against the dark sky as Shaft Four also blew up, then the sound of the explosion was flung at them in roaring crescendoes that raged and slammed against the ship with the force of a hurricane. The destroyer was thrust violently aside as a breaking wave fully fifteen feet high swept past.

Churchill managed to keep his feet, although he never knew how, and stared at the violent waters closing in one immense whirlpool over the spot where the ventilator shaft had been. The merchant steamer had disappeared as if it had never existed, and dim flares of light against the horizon marked the death of each ventilator shaft in succession. Moments later, a final distant explosion rolled at them across the storm-thrashed waters as the sinister yellow-orange glare on the black horizon died.

They heard it coming as they stood on the crest of Free Down above the valley and the Tunnel yards. Nearly a thousand of the Tunnel workers had come from their homes on this Christmas morning to gather on the crest of the ridge, some to shelter from the gale and the freezing rain in the woods to their backs, others to stand on the crest, ignoring the wind. The rumors had spread from house to house with electrical quickness. Silently, they stood in scattered groups as if seeking comfort from one another's presence waiting for what they feared most, all thought of Christmas Day gone and even the children subdued.

They heard the express-train rumble of the air hammer building inside the Tunnel, not knowing what it was, but knowing instinctively that it meant the end of a way of life, of jobs, of security, good pay and adequate housing and food, and their moan of anger and fear rose and was absorbed.

Beyond the white cliffs, far in the rainy distance, five gouts of flame burst in succession and an instant later the great steel Tunnel doors were blown out in a single stunning concussion, and sailed like monstrous plates half across the valley. The Tunnel disappeared into a boiling caldron of flame pouring from the ruined entrance like a jet of Greek fire. The gathered crowd saw great masses of chalk and soil flung skyward as the cliff above the shaft line erupted. Flame and gas fled from the Tunnel and across the intervening thousand yards to smash against the hillsides above Otty Bottom, destroying everything in its path. The concussion reached them on Free Down, defiantly thrashing trees and flinging sleet and rain in solid sheets.

It was over in an instant and they stood transfixed, two thousand ears ringing from the final blast, staring at the hurricane-swept works and the fires blazing where the timber yard had stood only moments before. After a while, someone pointed out a cut that had appeared in the cliff top. It was little more than twenty feet deep but it marked the line where the great Tunnel shaft had collapsed upon itself.

Epilogue

Winston Churchill folded the **Times** back on itself. *A guard* passed swiftly along checking that the outside compartment doors were all secured and Clementine smiled at him from the seat opposite. Outside the train compartment he could see a worried Eddie Marsh talking quietly with two Scotland Yard detectives. The First Lord touched his pocket to make certain that the speech he was to give in Belfast the following day was safe. What a fuss they were making, he thought. Of course he was baiting Sir Edward Carson in his own territory. And why not? The man was verging on treason. Churchill only wished that he had listened to the Master of Elibank's warning and persuaded Clementine to remain in London.

The *Times* carried a late report of the Kaiser's opening speech to the Reichstag, the subject of which had been increases in both the German Imperial Army and Navy. As Churchill read the report, an uneasy feeling was growing. Just two weeks before his friend Sir Ernest Cassel—who had excellent connections to the Imperial Palace—had given him an advance copy of the new German navy law to be presented to the Reichstag in May. Had it been an attempt to relieve tensions over that ridiculous business in December? Probably so. In any event, he had given Grey, just this past week, his own analysis of the bill, and now here was the Kaiser literally confirming his pessimistic conclusions.

The facts were grim. By 1915—Churchill's own target date for the expected war—the dredging of the Keil Canal was to be completed, thus allowing the largest warships to pass safely and quickly from the Baltic to the North Sea. That would mean that the Germans would be able to bring twenty-five dreadnoughts into action at a moment's notice and require Britain to maintain a fleet of forty dreadnoughts in a state of constant readiness if they were to retain the effective deterrent factor of sixty percent superiority. The economic drain would be extremely heavy.

Churchill laid his paper down on the seat and jotted quick comments in his pocket notebook—*the purpose of British naval power is defensive. Landlocked Germay with no major overseas colonies to defend has a major fleet. Either for offensive reasons, which they deny, or as a luxury fleet they can ill afford.*

He tapped the pencil on the notebook and Clementine glanced up from her novel.

"Just a few notes, dear." Churchill smiled. "The Kaiser has gone off again. This time it is his speech to the Reichstag. He seems to confirm everything I told the Foreign Secretary last week."

"Are you going to speak about it?"

Churchill turned to the window before answering. The crowd bustled about Paddington Station, a sea of hurrying faces, all seemingly imbued with the promise of the New Year. For a moment he wondered if he could ever share their enthusiasm again. Premonition was strong upon him and he wriggled uncomfortably. Perhaps, he thought, it was the coming ordeal in Belfast, where he was to speak tomorrow on Home Rule. He had no illusions about his reception; the presence of the Scotland Yard detectives was proof of that.

"Yes, I think I will," he replied slowly. "Germany's intentions are becoming clearer every day, and I do not see how we can let such a direct challenge pass without comment. Perhaps I'll mention it at Glasgow on Friday."

The First Lord drew a line under the phrase *luxury fleet*. That ought to raise a few hackles in Berlin and let them know that Britain understood what they were up to. As he refolded the paper, a small story near the bottom of the page caught his eye: BOARD OF TRADE ANNOUNCES NO TUNNEL. The article contained a brief description of the cabinet decision not to go forward with the rebuilding of the English Channel Tunnel. The inquiry board had not been able to establish the reason for the explosion that had destroyed the shafts and the works yards, and the government, according to the reporter, was reluctant to go ahead in case a similar incident should occur. The story contained a reference to the collapse of the Anglo-French Submarine Railway Company and the abandonment by the French government of the seven miles of Tunnel completed from Calais, but as usual, far more was left unsaid than otherwise.

Churchill stook his head, recalling the haste with which the issue had been decided. Faint hearts had won again. They were afraid of angering Germany by beginning once more. He had supported the decision only because he knew that the Tunnel would never be finished in time to affect the inevitable war. The money could better be spent for badly needed dreadnoughts.

Churchill tossed the paper onto the seat opposite and leaned back with a sigh. What had the expenditure of so many lives and so much money purchased, he wondered? Close to seventy men dead when the crew of the German merchant ship went down: all those tunnel workers; the German, von Dorn; that stubborn engineer Bannerman; and David Powell. The death of his old friend still hurt deeply. If only he had realized that Grace was so ill, had taken the time, but . . . he had not.

The guard's whistle echoed along the cars as Churchill flipped through his pocket calendar to check the time of his meeting the following week with senior officials from MI.5 and David Powell's successor at Special Branch. They would make a final decision then regarding the German agents named on the list found in the mad Irishman's pocket. What a stroke of luck that had been! Between Connigham's list and the microfilm, they now had a fairly complete list of every German espionage agent and sympathizer in Great Britain. If he could persuade his colleagues to be circumspect; to watch each agent to see who else came to join them, but not to make arrests until war was declared and then very quietly. . . . The majority would prefer to cooperate, he was certain, than to face the hangman. If sufficient false information could be fed back to their masters in Berlin, something positive might just come of this after all.

A bit of irony occurred to him and he chuckled. Would not Michael Connigham be proud of the way he had aided Great Britain after all? Churchill laughed again as the train ran out into the waning afternoon light, causing his wife to look up in surprise.

About the Author

JOE POYER *lives in southern California with his wife, Susan, and two sons, Joe and Geoff. He spends his time writing novels, running an antique shop specializing in the Civil War period and the American frontier, and traveling—which he undertakes at the slightest excuse. Mr. Poyer is the author of seven previous novels including* North Cape, *which Alistair MacLean called "the best adventure story I have read for years," and* The Contract, *which Ernest K. Gann said "hums with excitement."*